Any Sacrifice
but Conscience

Also by Walter C. Utt and Helen Godfrey Pyke

No Peace for a Soldier

Any Sacrifice but Conscience

A Historical Epic of Faith and Courage in the Face of Persecution

Walter C. Utt / Helen G. Pyke

Pacific Press® Publishing Association
Nampa, Idaho
Oshawa, Ontario, Canada
www.pacificpress.com

Cover design by Gerald Monks
Cover art by John Steele
Inside design by Steve Lanto

Copyright © 2008 by
Pacific Press® Publishing Association
Printed in the United States of America
All rights reserved

All Scripture quotations are from the King James Version.

Additional copies of this book may be obtained
by calling toll-free 1-800-765-6955
or online at http://www.adventistbookcenter.com

Library of Congress Cataloging-in-Publication Data

Utt, Walter C.
Any sacrifice but conscience : a historical epic of faith and courage
in the face of persecution / Walter C. Utt and Helen Godfrey Pyke.
    p. cm.
ISBN 13: 978-0-8163-2171-1 (pbk.)
ISBN 10: 0-8163-2171-X
1. Huguenots. 2. Persecution—France—History—17th century.
I. Pyke, Helen Godfrey. II. Title.
PS3571.T77A84 2008
813'.54—dc22
                                        2007026236

08 09 10 11 12 · 5 4 3 2 1

Acknowledgments

In preparing Part II of this book, I had an early draft of work begun by Dr. Walter Utt in the 1970s and left unfinished at the time of his death. The typescript that I received represented his personal engagement with his lifetime of scholarship in the history of France and of the Huguenots in particular. I was compelled to take up the unfinished work not just because I found it interesting but also because Dr. Utt's first book, *The Wrath of the King*, so inspired me that I set about immediately after reading it in 1966 on research that led to my *A Wind to the Flames*. (The young hero in my book was named Walter!) Like Brian Strayer, who completed Utt's scholarly work in *The Bellicose Dove*, my career has been deeply influenced by Dr. Walter Utt's work.

I wish to further acknowledge my debt to

. . . the Utt Endowment and their dedication to sustain this great teacher's passion for history for yet another generation of readers, and especially to Bruce and Audrey Anderson for their encouragement and hospitality.

. . . Brian Strayer, whose scholarly books and articles provided solid background data and whose practical personal interventions prevented many blunders.

. . . to Martha Utt Billington for extending her support and friendship.

. . . my colleague Ben McArthur, chair of the history department of Southern Adventist University, who suggested that this project might be a good fit for me.

. . . Southern Adventist University, for granting me a sabbatical semester in which to accomplish this project.

. . . Rachel Boyd, for transcribing the Utt typescript to a Word file.

. . . my husband, Ted, for taking over many of the homely tasks of our household to allow me *long* hours for concentrated work—and then insisting that I join him for *long* walks to restore blood flow to brain and body.

Helen Godfrey Pyke

Contents

Foreword

A generation of readers who enjoyed earlier books by Walter Utt—
The Wrath of the King (1966) and *Home to Our Valleys* (1977)—may
have wondered about the fate of their Huguenot hero, Armand de Gandon. The publication of this new volume, *Any Sacrifice but Conscience*,
and its companion book, *No Peace for a Soldier*, provides the "rest of the
story" and completes what might be called the "Huguenot Quartet."

These new volumes are the result of serendipity and hard work.
It was long known that at his death, Dr. Utt had left an extensive
manuscript uncompleted that described the further story of Armand
de Gandon. A careful reading of this manuscript led to the realization that it contained the full story of the further adventures and
struggles of conscience of the Huguenot soldier created by Dr. Utt.
However, the manuscript was clearly a work in progress. The seamless and satisfying narrative you will find in *No Peace for a Soldier*
and *Any Sacrifice but Conscience* is the work of the outstanding Christian writer Helen Godfrey Pyke. The story of Armand de Gandon
unfolds clearly and seemingly effortlessly because of her creative gifts
and her love for this story. In its present configuration, *No Peace for
a Soldier* combines the earlier story *The Wrath of the King* with extensive new material from Dr. Utt's unfinished manuscript. Likewise,
Any Sacrifice but Conscience includes the earlier work *Home to Our
Valleys* with the rest of the previously unpublished material to complete the full story.

Dr. Utt was himself a hero to generations of college students who appreciated not only his legendary and apparently limitless knowledge of the past but also his abhorrence of pomp and pretense and his love of students, who so often became his friends and correspondents. After Dr. Utt's death, a group of former students, friends, and colleagues determined not to allow the legacy of this great Christian teacher to be lost. In 1985, this group formed the Walter C. Utt Endowment at Pacific Union College, Angwin, California. Among the results of their work have been an endowed professorship at Pacific Union College in the name of Walter Utt and the completion, with Professor Brian Strayer, of the book *The Bellicose Dove: Claude Brousson and Protestant Resistance to Louis XIV, 1647–1698*. The story of this Huguenot pastor, Claude Brousson, was Dr. Utt's lifetime research interest.

The support of Pacific Union College and members of the Walter C. Utt Endowment Committee plus the generosity of hundreds of former students and friends of Dr. Utt have made the achievements noted above possible. Dr. Richard Osborn, current president of PUC, and former PUC president Malcolm Maxwell have unfailingly supported these efforts. The Walter C. Utt Endowment Committee has been a rock of support. Members of the committee have included Earl Aagaard, Victor Aagaard, Bruce Anderson, Eric Anderson, Charles Bell, Martha Utt-Billington, John Collins, Ileana Douglas, Arleen Downing, Lorne Glaim, Elizabeth Hamlin, Wayne Jacobsen, Grant Mitchell, David Westcott, and Elle Wheeler.

Thanks are due as well to the editors of Pacific Press® for recognizing the importance of completing this story of a soldier and a Christian.

Bruce Anderson, chair
Walter C. Utt Endowment Committee
April 2007

If you haven't read
No Peace for a Soldier...

This book, *Any Sacrifice but Conscience,* concludes the story begun in *No Peace for a Soldier* (Pacific Press®, 2007). The story takes place near the end of the seventeenth century, when King Louis XIV determined that all of France should have one religion. The resulting persecution has torn apart French Protestant—Huguenot—communities and families. Descriptions of the main characters follow.

Isaac Cortot—a well-to-do Huguenot businessman who lived in the town of Saint Martin, France. His children were taken from him and his house broken up by the *dragonnades*—the billeting of French soldiers in the homes of civilians with the intention of forcing their "conversion" to Catholicism. The shock of the experience resulted in the death of his wife. Sometime later, a betrayal has resulted in his being condemned to serve as a galley slave for the rest of his life.

Madeleine Cortot—Isaac Cortot's nineteen-year-old daughter, who nearly four years previously had been helped to escape from a convent to safe exile in Rotterdam, the Netherlands. She is burdened with the realization that her attempt to help her father escape from France has resulted instead in his betrayal. She loves Armand but is too proud to let him know her feelings.

Alexandre Cortot—the lively, blunt fifteen-year-old son of Isaac Cortot. He managed to get himself thrown out of a House for New Catholics—a sort of religious reform school—and to escape to the

11

Netherlands with his siblings. Armand de Gandon found him a position as a drummer boy in the English army.

Louis and Louise Cortot—ten-year-old twins. Armand de Gandon broke up an attempt to kidnap them and helped them escape to Rotterdam with their siblings.

Armand de Gandon—a Huguenot officer formerly in the French army. His heroic stand in battle made him a favorite of the Duc de Lauzières, a well-placed French aristocrat who wishes to promote him to the command of his own regiment and to the highest levels of French society—which would require that he abjure or at least hide his religious convictions. Armand rescued three of the Cortot children and helped all four escape to the Protestant Netherlands. Now he is serving in the army of the Dutch Protestant William of Orange, who has just assumed the throne of England at the invitation of the English. He loves Madeleine but is hesitant to tell her so.

Pastor Merson—the faithful Huguenot minister who served in the Cortots' hometown and is now living in the Netherlands.

Mathieu Bertrand—Pastor Merson's nephew who at one time was a rising star among the Huguenots. He has since ostensibly converted to Catholicism and was instrumental in the betrayal of Isaac Cortot to the authorities. Once engaged to Madeleine, he is extremely jealous of Armand de Gandon.

PART I

1689

CHAPTER 1

Couriers of Conspiracy

A short young man in a frayed red coat a couple of sizes too large for him clambered down from the top of the mail coach. He dropped his haversack on the cobbles and greeted the tall military gentleman, perhaps thirty years of age, who came forward in the post house courtyard to embrace him. In the tumult, others were also meeting passengers. Ordinarily, officers did not embrace privates, but these two were speaking French, and many customs of the Huguenot refugees must have seemed a little strange to their Dutch hosts.

It was a bright spring morning in Rotterdam in 1689. The two Frenchmen walked out into the crowded streets of the busy port city, dodging messenger boys, servant girls out shopping, heavily laden porters, sailors, and businessmen from all over the world who all seemed to be gesticulating, shoving, and shouting at once. The two crossed a square and turned onto a smaller, quieter street along a placid canal.

"I came as soon as I could get permission, Armand," said the new arrival. "What is this all about? Is it worth interrupting my military career? Are we going on another uncomfortable journey?"

Alexandre Cortot, the younger and shorter of the pair, was vivacious, wiry, and dark of complexion and hair. His expression was one of amiable foxiness. The white cross belts on his hand-me-down coat suggested an English soldier, and the empty slots in the cross belts that were meant for sticks indicated that he had been a drummer. A sack was slung over his shoulder, and he wore a short, triangular-bladed bayonet at his belt.

15

"Yes to all of your questions!" the older man laughed. "But did you have a good journey? How did you find your sisters and brother?" Armand de Gandon, onetime major in the armies of His Very Christian Majesty Louis XIV of France, was arrayed in the long blue coat and orange vest and hose of an officer of the Dutch Foot Guards. He was erect and soldierly, with a handsome, thoughtful face, dark eyes, and a rather prominent nose. He wore a shoulder-length, chestnut-colored wig. A straight sword was at his side, and gold lace on his wide cuffs and along his hat brim identified him as an officer and a gentleman.

"We had a good passage," said Alexandre. "I reached Helder two days ago but had to walk most of the way to The Hague. Madeleine and the twins are well and look no different in six months. But where are we going?"

"We go right now to see Pierre Jurieu, the famous pastor, here in Rotterdam, and then we will carry some letters for important people!"

"You sent me money and told me to hurry, so why do we take time to visit a minister?" complained the boy.

"We are truly in haste, Alexandre, but Pastor Jurieu is no ordinary preacher. Surely you know his name! No one writes more continually or furiously against our persecutors."

"My education has been neglected since we escaped," said the younger one with a touch of the impudence that was never far beneath the surface. "Who had time to read when I was pushing bales and boxes about in that fusty warehouse? And since you convinced Colonel Churchill that he needed another drummer—I will be eternally grateful to you for rescuing me—I have been too busy saving the English from the papists to be reading books! Studying is for children anyway."

The officer smiled indulgently. "Grown up at sixteen," he marveled, "and with all the education he will ever need!" He stopped a passing citizen and in his painful Dutch asked directions.

"But what are these letters? Why are they so important?" persisted the boy.

"For now let me say these are troublous times, and not everyone is well-affected by King William, particularly in England. And some of those who joined him so swiftly a few months ago during the Glorious Revolution could just as quickly desert the Good Cause if they calculated King James might come back. You know, copies of the king's dispatches have strange ways of showing up in the hands of French diplomats, and the mails are unsafe too. As I said, great and mysterious things are now afoot. I am less likely to be suspected as a courier, seeming but an ordinary officer posted to a new assignment, so we leave at once for Switzerland. But it is wartime, and the trip through Germany could be hazardous, so I asked to have you as a valet, or, if you prefer, a bodyguard. Does that answer your question?"

"No," said Alexandre mutinously. "What's it all about?"

"It has to do with the affairs of the French refugees in some way, and also with the Protestant cause in Switzerland." Gandon tried to remain patient. "You know, when we sailed for England last fall, I was on the staff of the duke of Schomberg. The king sent him to Ireland against King James and the Catholic rebels. He wished me to come with him, as he had always been kind to me for the sake of my late father, but it seemed to me that fighting the papists in the bogs of Ireland was a long way from our France, and I would rather be where I might more directly help our people still in Babylon. From Switzerland, who knows what might open up? When the duke was convinced I would rather go this way, he recommended me to the British secretary of state, Lord Shrewsbury, who needed an inconspicuous French-speaking courier. There are spies everywhere."

They halted while the officer again asked directions. Then they turned down a narrow alley.

"Whatever these letters contain, I know that if I were robbed, there would be embarrassment all the way from the Alps to the Irish coasts. Of course," he added, his face straight, "the doubts the king and Milord Shrewsbury had of my ability to perform this mission vanished when they learned you would accompany me!"

Alexandre halted and bowed from the waist. "It seems I am in your debt twice over," he said. "You rescued me from that appalling warehouse and away from my dear sister's constant surveillance, and then you took me away from my responsibilities as drummer. In truth, the excitement of that calling was beginning to abate also, and I left my drum in Hounslow without regret. It was a very civilized revolution, after all, and I never heard a shot fired from the time the expedition sailed last fall till now. If I had not been seasick the first time the fleet tried to sail, I'd have nothing to talk about at all—King James running away so fast, you know. Of late, I think the English are growing tired of foreign visitors, and the winter weather was as bad as here in Holland. Well! So when are we going back to France?"

"I didn't say we were, and please don't tell anyone that I said anything like that! There *is* a great war going on now, and it is just possible that, as it spreads, something might occur to the advantage of our poor oppressed brethren."

Armand de Gandon stopped and searched for the pastor's door in the dark little street. The upper stories of the houses on each side of the street appeared almost to meet above it, effectively blocking the sunlight.

Armand spoke with elaborate unconcern and without looking at his companion. "When we met just now, I had wondered if you might be carrying any messages for me. It is six months since I left for England and last saw your sister and the twins. How are things at Rotterdam?"

Alexandre shot him a quizzical glance. "Madeleine and the twins are in good health. It is like your kind heart to ask. I'd say she is snappish as ever, at least when I offer her advice. I offered to carry a message to you from her, and she completely mistook my intention and told me to mind my own business. You'd think working for four years in that House for Huguenot Gentlewomen would have advanced her saintliness. In the kindest and most solicitous manner I merely asked her when she was going to be sensible and find herself a better and more available fiancé than Mathieu. He went back home again, but in four years he has not written or tried to escape from France as far as we know. And I asked did she wish a suggestion, seeing that she is now twenty and maybe already too old to marry. Well, she blew up like a grenade, and what with one thing and another she wrote no messages for me to carry."

The officer bit his lip, and his tone was short. "I'm sure your intentions were good, Alexandre, but I wish I could convince you that I don't consider your sister under any obligation to me whatsoever, nor do I want her harassed on my behalf!"

Alexandre rolled his eyes despairingly but said nothing.

Armand would never forget the wintry journey through the Ardennes four years before, when he took the Cortot children out of France in defiance of the king's edict, and the feelings he then had and still had for Alexandre's older sister, that most appealing and beautiful Huguenot, Madeleine Cortot. Alexandre despised Mathieu, his sister's fiancé, a viewpoint Armand found easy to share, for the absent Mathieu had always seemed an austere and unlikable sort. But Madeleine's sense of loyalty, or perhaps other reasons, kept her faithful to the commitment made long before in happier days in her native French village.

Well, he must not let these memories distract him. He must put those violet eyes and that classic profile out of mind and not dwell on might-have-beens. There was the Good Cause to serve.

Suddenly, Armand realized he was standing in front of the door he sought. Though at the moment he would have liked to give Alexandre a clout across his much-too-busy mouth, it was good to have the cocky upstart as a travel companion again. So, instead, he nodded curtly, and Alexandre stepped up to the door and gave the knocker two vigorous blows.

* * * * *

"I should have liked above all things to be able to be at the coronation of their Majesties," said Pastor Jurieu, his intense, almost feverish gaze on Armand de Gandon. "You have had a privilege to remember all your life, to see how God has visibly taken hold of the affairs of our poor oppressed church and set our Joshua on the three British thrones, and with Her Majesty, too, for Queen Mary has ever been the tender consolation of our necessitous refugees here. I must show you the letter His Majesty has sent me in reply to the little compliment I wrote him after the late glorious and providential expedition to England."

Pierre Jurieu had received Armand in his study and sickroom. He was recovering from a long illness. Clothed in clerical black and wearing a black skullcap, he sat in his armchair with a fur robe over his knees even though the coal fire in the grate made the room almost too stuffy for breathing. The dark little room was piled with books and papers. Even while ill, Jurieu produced polemics and sermons at such a prodigious rate that it was said he could write them faster than his audience could read them. He was a thin, dark man with long black hair and a slim mustache, fidgety and irascible, quick to fire up at a name or expression he disliked—and these were many. One of the most contentious of the Huguenot writers ever since the king had closed the Protestant colleges and he had to leave his professorship at Sedan, he was a power in exile circles, and his pen was feared and respected far beyond Rotterdam. He spared neither Catholics nor his own lukewarm brethren.

His most recent notoriety was from the seeming fulfillment of his predictions about the death and resurrection of the Two Witnesses of the eleventh chapter of the Revelation. In his 1686 book, *The Accomplishment of the Prophecies*, he had identified the Revocation of the Edict of Nantes in 1685, which banned Protestant religion in France, as the low ebb of God's truth—the death of the Two Witnesses. Nearly a million succumbed in an almost total extinction of visible Protestantism. But when the Glorious Revolution of 1688 saved Protestantism in England, put William and Mary on the throne, and added Britain to the list of Louis XIV's enemies in the new war, it seemed that the fortunes of Protestantism had indeed recovered most notably. The time between the Revocation and the crowning of the new British sovereigns on April 21, 1689, was just three-and-a-half years, which, on the year-for-a-day prophetic reckoning, was just the time the Two Witnesses, the two Testaments, were to be dead but not buried in the land of persecution.

Jurieu's father-in-law had written a book of the same title long before, and though their computations differed somewhat, both saw 1689 as a very significant year for God's people. Jurieu wrote that the 1,260-year period of persecution began under Leo the Great, an appropriate "man of sin," in 450 or 455, so he suggested the end of the papacy and the beginning of the millennium to be about 1710 or 1715. The resurrection of the Two Witnesses might mean the conversion of France to the gospel in the meantime, for France was the tenth part of the anti-Christian city that was to fall. The interest in his interpretations was keen, and many writers rushed into print to attack or defend his prediction. Jurieu had hedged somewhat, but the startling events in England, needless to say, aroused the hopes of the Huguenots and the fears of the Catholic authorities in France.

Jurieu had not been waiting idly. He published fortnightly *Pastoral Letters* to his brethren "sighing and crying under the persecution in Babylon." Each number was half doctrinal study and half news notes on the persecutions and martyrdoms inside France. His contacts with the Huguenots stranded inside that unhappy country were obviously good;

and the French authorities, finding his writings wherever allegedly converted Protestants were numerous, were alarmed. The writings, said the Catholic clergy, prevented "good conversions" and incited readers to rebellion and illegal assemblies. The clergy charged that Jurieu's writings encouraged the rash of preaching and prophesying that was sweeping southern France. Was Jurieu the agent of an international Protestant conspiracy?

Jurieu had always been a vigorous champion of the Reformation, but he had remained respectful of Louis XIV personally. Now, however, his tone changed, and in flaming wrath he denounced the king as a tyrant who had broken faith with his Protestant subjects. His assertion that authority in government derives from the people scandalized all Catholics and not a few Huguenots, some of whom still hoped that Louis XIV would realize he had taken bad advice and allow them to return home and to worship freely.

"Milord Shrewsbury presents his compliments, Monsieur. He hopes that your health will soon be fully reestablished to the greater service of God's cause," said Armand when he had an opportunity to speak. "He asked me to give you these letters and with them the thanks of His Majesty for the consolation you have brought the church and the good service you have rendered him. We are all concerned that you spend yourself so prodigally."

The thin lips under the slender mustache curled in a pleased smile, and the sick man looked visibly revived. "The Lord is stretching out His hand in a marvelous way, both in my poor concerns and those greater matters! When it pleased God to reward my diligent searching in the prophecies with some light to guide and comfort His church, the whole crew of Romish scribblers and scorners were quick to deride me, and so did their apes here in our own temples, shame though it be to have to say it. I leave them all to the judgment of God and to their own confusion at the outfalling of events and the notable prodigies that have revived the hopes of the church everywhere. Some here in the exile still yearn for the leeks and the garlic of Egypt, but God overrules. I do hope for some signal event for 1689, but these matters are hidden and only revealed as God ordains. So we may yet have worse tribulations to pass through. Perhaps the death of the Two Witnesses is yet to come. One day soon the Lord will separate out the tares and burn them.

"I will cease to publish the *Pastoral Letters* soon now, but this is not because of my weakness according to the flesh; rather, it is that we are passing from a time of exhortation to a time of deeds. I doubt not that we shall see yet judgments as evident as the overthrow of Pharaoh in the Red Sea and the smiting of Herod with worms. God has raised up William of Orange and the League of Augsburg to abase and humiliate the enemies of His truth and for the encouragement of His people. The bombardment of Genoa; the devastation of Holland and the Palatinate; the treason of Strasbourg; the plottings and conspiracies in England, Scotland, and Ireland; the flow of corrupting gold to every court in Europe; but above all, the destruction of the worship of God in France and the barbarous murders of the poor people who come together in desert places to call upon God—the cup of the wine of the wrath of God is full and running over! The Jesuits will have their portion in the lake of fire, and I doubt not that Madame de Maintenon will suffer the fate of Jezebel!"

Armand, who had seen that prim, black-clad, and matronly *dévote** at Versailles, smiled in spite of himself, but the Prophet of Rotterdam didn't notice it. "I trust, sir," said the officer, "that the journey I am making to Switzerland may advance these events. In that regard, besides the greetings I bear from those well-affected to your person, I am charged by Milord Shrewsbury not only to give you these letters but to carry into Switzerland any you may wish to send."

Jurieu accepted the two letters Gandon offered and broke the seals. He seemed pleased by what he read. Armand, without especially trying, was able to read Shrewsbury's short note upside down from where he sat. It was a letter of credit for two hundred pounds sterling. Putting this together with some of Milord's comments, Armand surmised that as Jurieu did have the best network of Huguenot informers within France, possibly not all the information was directly connected with persecution of the believers. The British and Dutch governments might be interested in news from France too—especially in seaports and fleet movements.

As if reading Armand's mind, Jurieu placed other papers over the letter of credit. "I perceive that you are highly regarded by those who

---

* Feminine of *devotee*—an overly religious person.

sent you and are a man of confidence," he said solemnly. "I will ask you to bear letters for me also to the brethren in Zurich and Lausanne. All is falling into place. I see that besides God's raising up our deliverer, the revival in France itself calls for our moving forward at once. I have the honor to head the Refugee Committee here in Holland, as Pastor Arzeliers does in London and Monsieur Mirmand in Switzerland. Our labors for the restoration of God's church in France have reached a critical time; yet we must be very prudent, for it is a sad truth that we must often have greater caution of our own brethren than of the papists, if all is not to be uselessly unraveled." He frowned as if in pain.

"Our latest advices from France, particularly from Dauphiné and Languedoc, tell of the revival among the people. They have no pastors, but the Spirit is moving upon young men and women, many without letters at all, to rise and lead, praying, exhorting, and rebuking apostasy. This brings on them the fury of the persecutors, and some have already sealed their testimony with their blood."

"Is it possible, sir," asked the soldier, "that this revival of piety may lead to an open resistance? Is it the work of the committee to encourage a revolt against the authorities?"

Pastor Jurieu shot a suspicious glance at Armand, almost as if he would change his mind about the letters. He didn't reply at once.

Armand tried again, very deferentially. "These matters are common rumor in England, sir; and, before God, I am not an agent of the French king. I go to Switzerland to await the arrival of King William's ambassador, who hopes to make a treaty of alliance with the Protestant cantons to furnish hired troops for our cause. Forgive me if I run ahead and speculate if all this may have a bearing on the persecution in France."

"Possibly, quite possibly," said Jurieu at last, apparently mollified. "As I said, it appears that all may very shortly fall in place. The people are being made ready for the time when help may come. When their elders fail, even the children prophesy!" He became excited, the words tumbling out again. "You must read the account I have just now from the printer of Isabeau, the young shepherdess of Crest, who is one of the innumerable children crying out against backsliders and prophesying the imminent restoration of the church. The authorities place them in convents and hospitals, but there are always more. The land is smoking and ready to burst into flame. We of the Refuge must labor to pour oil, not water, on these sparks and to strengthen the hand of princes chosen by God for the restoration of His worship in France. The time is at hand, and the Laodiceans should beware lest they be found opposing the purposes of God."

It was obvious that to Jurieu there was no difference between the purposes of God and those of the committee.

An elderly housemaid appeared at the door. "Monsieur Vivens," she announced. Armand rose to go as the stranger appeared.

"Nay, Monsieur," said the pastor. "Tarry yet a moment and meet this young man."

Vivens, short, dark, and rumpled, limped noticeably as he entered the room. He was clad in brown homespun, and his short black wig fitted poorly. He bowed deeply and awkwardly to the pastor and rather less to Armand. His intense, almost hostile gaze suggested that he might not be pleased to find a uniformed officer in the room. Jurieu sealed the letters Armand was to take, and Armand stood waiting while the monologue continued. The young newcomer fidgeted, obviously ill at ease.

"Monsieur Vivens is one of the new preachers of whom I spoke—a Son of the Prophets, as it were, raised up to console and exhort the people of the Cévennes after the great falling away in 1685. He was so successful in this ministry that Bâville, the intendant of Languedoc, was on his trail day and night to prevent these assemblies. Such was the danger and the suffering of the faithful ones that Brother Vivens finally consented to leave the country if all those who wished to depart peaceably with him might be suffered to do so. The servants of antichrist made him these promises, and in his innocence of heart he gave them the names of those wishing to go. They arrested almost all of them! His desire now is to return to France and rebuke the betrayers. In view of his great services to the cause of God, we have given him an exceptional ordination here, and he now prepares to return to preach 'under the cross.' Perhaps you may meet him there!"

Vivens did not seem thrilled by the prospect, but he agreed vehemently that the time had come to return and console the people, who were as sheep abandoned by their shepherds. Elijah was his ideal, and his eyes blazed as he spoke rabidly in his thick patois of the fate of those who bowed the knee to Baal and of the apostates who had betrayed brethren. He quoted Psalm 58 verses 6, 8, and 10 with feeling: "Break their teeth, O God, in their mouth. . . . As a snail which melteth, let every one of them pass away. . . . The righteous shall rejoice when he seeth the vengeance: he shall wash his feet in the blood of the wicked."

Feeling somehow abashed in the presence of this angry young man, Armand once again made his *adieux,* put the letters of Jurieu safely in an oilskin pouch in his coat pocket, and took his leave. He had to wait a few moments at the street door for Alexandre to be torn from the good eating and the rapt audience provided by the ladies in the kitchen, and then they went on to Armand's inn to prepare for their departure.

* * * * *

Stars twinkled brightly in the clear blue-black sky. Only the dim outline of the peaks surrounding Zurich could be seen to the south. The black waters of the Limmat reflected in yellow ripples the torches borne by lackeys escorting citizens to their evening appointments. A watch-man passed by with lantern and clapper, his boots echoing on the cob-bles.

Armand de Gandon had withdrawn from the reception at the house of the popular Monsieur Fabrice, the envoy of the Dutch States Gen-eral to the Protestant cantons of Switzerland, and was conversing with Gabriel de Convenant, special agent of the same government, respon-sible for the care of the Vaudois* exiles in Switzerland. The eating was good, and Fabrice was generous with "gratifications" of gold and prom-ises to Zurich bourgeois who seemed "well-intentioned" to the Anglo-Dutch cause and who would tickle his ears to that effect.

Armand had become unintentionally a social lion, the objective of the Zurich matrons wishing to try their French on the newly arrived and handsome officer. He had made his escape quite discreetly with Convenant, a quiet diplomat of about fifty, and now they strolled and chatted by the riverbank, talking in low tones as if the dark houses over-hanging the street might be listening.

In these days, this was prudent anyway, for the partisans of the French were everywhere in Switzerland. Convenant had come from the town of Orange in southern France, a possession of the Dutch royal house, and from which they had taken their name. The French army

---

* The Vaudois are perhaps better known as the Waldenses.

had "converted" the district four years before, and Convenant, like Armand, had left the country for freedom elsewhere. His post was now Bern, but he was a frequent visitor to Zurich.

"Besides the letters I brought you today," said the officer, "I have others from London and Rotterdam for the Committee of Refugees at Lausanne and some for Geneva. I am here principally to be of use to Monsieur Coxe when he arrives to negotiate the treaty with the Swiss. I now learn he will not be here before October, so I am free until then to be of service to any of His Majesty's agents who wish to call upon me."

"I am grateful to have you here," said Convenant. "I have word to send to Geneva also, but I am so well-known to the French resident there that it could be an embarrassment or even a danger to those I would see. You are not known in those parts, and it would serve the Good Cause well if you could go."

"Gladly," agreed Armand. Then he asked, "Sir, you represent the interests of the poor Vaudois. How do their affairs connect with those of the Huguenot exiles here—or, for that matter, why are they of concern to King William?"

Convenant lowered his voice. All Armand could see of him in the dark was the white lace of the jabot at his throat.

"It is an intricate matter, captain. As you know, these simple evangelical folk were almost destroyed in 1686 when their duke had to permit the French army to 'cleanse' the Piedmont valleys of the Reformed Faith. Those who survived are mostly in exile here in Switzerland.

"But Switzerland is overcharged with refugees, and these unhappy people are a burden on this poor country, so the churches in England and Holland collect offerings for their support. Her Majesty Queen Mary has the most tender concern for these unfortunates, and I disburse these 'collects' for their food and shelter as she intends. But not all the money I handle [and his voice dropped almost to a whisper] goes thus.

"Twice now this pitiful handful of Vaudois have tried to go home to their valleys to regain their patrimony, but the Bernese authorities have been embarrassed in their relations with France and Savoy, for these attempts were made, of course, from the territory of Bern. So, for both financial and diplomatic reasons, the Swiss Protestant cantons wish to settle the exiles far off in safe, permanent homes in the German states or even Holland or Ireland. The Vaudois have had to agree to go, but the exodus has been delayed because of the incommodity of the weather in winter. Now spring is here, and the Swiss press for the departure." He stopped and glanced suspiciously behind him, but the sound he had heard was only a mongrel trotting by on his lawful occasions.

"Last year we settled some hundreds of the poor Vaudois in Württemberg and the Palatinate, and even a few went to Brandenburg. But now, with the outbreak of war, those in the Rhineland have had to flee and are back in Switzerland again. Most are now in Schaffhausen, and were it not for the collects, that little canton couldn't bear the expense. In truth, the Swiss have been both patient and charitable.

"We sense that His Majesty and the Estates of Holland are, may I say, favorable to having the Vaudois remain all together in a body. Yet we are committed to moving them hence, and the agreed deadline has already passed. If we could but move for appearances' sake some of the very old and very young and the females! It is a delicate matter, for many Swiss, not all necessarily Catholics, ask questions, and the spies of the duke of Savoy are also vigilant. I hope to convince the Swiss authorities that very important personages are concerned with the fate of these poor folk and that no great haste be used to solve the difficulty."

"Do I suspect that a third attempt will be made by the Vaudois to return to their valleys, perhaps with the charitable assistance of these good Samaritans?" asked Armand quite innocently.

"Odd you should think so! One does hear so many rumors." Convenant smiled. "But speaking of rumors, it is whispered that the young duke of Savoy is sick to death of the heavy hand of his kinsman Louis XIV and the tutelage of his French mother. He is so discreet, or as some would say, devious, that one does not know if he would really oppose the Vaudois if they should try to return to their valleys. Some have said that if we waited till he breaks with the French, he might then call his Vaudois subjects back home again, for it was Louis XIV who made him expel them. But then this may never happen, and the Vaudois are becoming impatient. The war is somewhat of a religious war, and as they are the original, primitive Protestants, their return might commend itself to the Protestant princes. You and I, as Huguenots, should wish to help this pious project along, Brother Gandon."

They stopped in the shadows. Armand scuffed his shoe on the cobbles thoughtfully.

"Hard by the Vaudois valleys lies Dauphiné." Armand seemed to be speaking to himself. "Next to Dauphiné lies Vivarais, next to Vivarais lies Languedoc, and in all of these are thousands of irritated and repentant Protestants who might be inspired by a successful return of the Vaudois or by the appearance of a rescuing army coming from the Vaudois valleys into France." He ended his summary with a direct question: "Do I read you aright, Monsieur?"

"You are very astute, Monsieur Gandon," Convenant whispered. "Does it seem too fantastic?"

"I am not a prophet nor a seer," replied Armand. "I did have a long conversation with Pastor Jurieu the day I left Rotterdam, however. What troubles me is the somewhat chimerical nature of such projects—and even Pastor Jurieu is not immune—the nonchalance with which it is assumed that one has but to call these poor folk of the Religion to arms some fine day and the success is assured. Am I doubting God when I wince at this easy assurance that the people, angry as they are and sorely mistreated since the Revocation, can hold their own against the king's army? Oh, I grant you the king would be embarrassed if he were fighting a war elsewhere, but these folks are neither armed nor led. The same lovely emotions that would bring them out suddenly could send them home again just as suddenly, and utterly discouraged. As I see it, there must be a real invasion by regular troops and with proper leaders, and then the support of these folk would be very helpful. Pray correct me if I view matters too darkly."

Convenant thought for a moment. "You are acquainted with the wild country over the Rhône? The valleys, the abysses and gorges, the wilderness around the headwaters of the Tarn, the Ardéche? Determined people, supplied with arms and chiefs, could embarrass large armies, which could hardly fight them in the usual fashion." He paused for a while as the significance of his words took effect.

"When Monsieur Coxe arrives," continued the diplomat, "I hope the Swiss Protestant cantons will agree to join the allies, but if they will not furnish the Grand Alliance with soldiers, at least they should recall their men from the armies of the great persecutor.

"True, Switzerland has no other considerable business or commodity to sell than the blood of their young men, so they may not wish to break their perpetual covenant with France—their best customer. At the very least, they ought to allow us to recruit French and Vaudois exiles here and to concert measures for the restoration of our faith in France!"

"Well and good, Monsieur," said Armand after a silence. They were leaning on the balustrade of a bridge, looking down at the water, which they could hear but not see. "There is another point that troubles me. You well know there is contention among us Huguenots whether our duty to the king of France requires us to suffer patiently until God softens his heart or whether we are released from allegiance to him because he violated the solemn edict his grandfather made for our liberty of worship. I gave up my rank and prospects in France rather than my religion, but I am not certain that I could in conscience serve against the king, even in the name of our religion. Fear God and honor the king says the Scripture. Is my conscience an enlightened one?"

"I understand your scruples," replied Convenant, "but does not God come first? Our fathers resisted persecuting kings once even to the point of civil war. I don't see that to serve a Protestant prince and force Louis XIV to restore the liberties he has violated would be more reprehensible than that. You know, this question is debated in a great battle of books in Holland and England since the late happy revolution. Was it legitimate to rebel against King James when he violated the law, or is a king above the law? May the people resist a faithless tyrant? Some of tender conscience say this is republicanism, but it seems to me that there are times in the history of the church when resistance to tyrants is obedience to God."

"Pastor Jurieu, in his sixteenth *Pastoral Letter*, affirms that sovereignty belongs to the people. At Lausanne, Pastor Merlat argues such absolute submission to authority that he says Bathsheba didn't sin but that on the contrary she was virtuous, for she obeyed her king." Armand shrugged.

"Because the early Christians did not use arms, does it follow that no Christian can?" Convenant asked. "To restore liberty to one's fatherland is to render an inestimable service to Catholic and Protestant alike!"

The older man paused when Armand didn't reply. "Well, would you see any difficulty in being of service to the poor Vaudois?"

"Not at all," said Armand. "I would help them with very good will."

"You may have the opportunity, Monsieur. Soon I hope you may meet the very remarkable leader of the Vaudois, Pastor Henri Arnaud—like us, born a Frenchman—who is the heart and soul of their enterprise. He must depend upon us to supply the needs of his people and the wherewithal for any return to their valleys. But as we must answer to our governments, we have to be careful not to let him run ahead of us. That is not easy to prevent; for, as I say, he is a most remarkable man, and his ways are mysterious.

"Spies and assassins from the French and Savoy embassies dog his footsteps, though by the particular favor of God he has thus far escaped them. I can't, any more than they, tell you where he is—closeted with William of Orange at The Hague or secretly parleying with the Spanish in Milan, perhaps even in Turin—who knows? His family lives in Neuchâtel, and I will get word to him about you as soon as I can. When you have an opportunity to talk to him, you will understand the Vaudois better and perhaps gain enlightenment on one's duty to one's prince and to the Good Cause."

The gathering at the Fabrice house was breaking up. Sedan chairs gathered at the door for the ladies, and other guests walked in cheerful groups down the street, their way lighted by torches held by their servants. Convenant laid his hand on Armand's sleeve. "In the meantime, say little of your doings to Monsieur Fabrice. He is a loyal colleague and well-intentioned but a little indiscreet. When in pleasant company he finds it hard to remember that Zurich is one big whispering gallery and that some very amiable people here are sold to the French. My business here is to dispense *relief* to the poor Vaudois—you understand me? We do *not* speak of expeditions."

He patted Armand's sleeve, bowed, and disappeared in the darkness. Not feeling sleepy, Armand strolled down to the lakeside. For a long time he stood looking out over the dark waters.

* * * * *

The next morning Armand and Alexandre lounged in the common room of the inn where Gabriel de Convenant lodged, awaiting his instructions. Soon the latter entered the room accompanied by a stocky, florid gentleman of forty-five or fifty with a thin mustache, shoulder-length chestnut hair, and lively black eyes. Under his red riding cloak he wore a suit of excellent blue material with lace at neck and cuffs. The broad-brimmed hat he carried had a white plume.

"It is my pleasure, pastor, to introduce to you Captain Armand de Gandon of His Majesty's Dutch Guards, on special duty here. He has long served the Good Cause, as has his companion, Alexandre Cortot, lately of His Majesty's troops in England. This is Pastor Henri Arnaud, leader of the Vaudois!"

Everyone bowed, but the newcomer caught the look of surprise on their faces.

"Ah, gentlemen, you feel I ought to be wearing a black clergyman's suit and a white collar." The pastor laughed heartily. "Where I go and for what I do, it is not prudent to look like a parson!"

"It is a great honor to meet you, Monsieur," said Armand. "I have already given Monsieur Convenant a letter for you from Monsieur Clignet, the postmaster at Leiden. I didn't know that I would be meeting you in person."

"My thanks, Monsieur. Truly without Monsieur Clignet and his sister, all our purposes would come to naught. May God reward him according to his works! Brother Convenant has already passed this letter on to me. Once again, thanks to this good brother in the Lowlands, the bill of exchange is most providentially at hand just as we need it!"

"I trust, Monsieur Gandon," said Convenant, "that you have been thinking of the matters we discussed last evening. I had not expected to see Pastor Arnaud this soon, but he tells me he has just had word that the difficulty at Schaffhausen is serious."

"Yes," agreed the pastor. "The Swiss must be dissuaded from carrying out their threat, for God most visibly intends that His poor peoples of the valleys not be scattered but held together in one place. I leave the matter in the capable hands of Monsieur Convenant. Unfortunately, I must journey elsewhere.

"Brother Convenant tells me of your serviceable qualities, Monsieur, and of your disposition to forward the work of the Lord for His poor people of the valleys. We work to restore the light of the gospel in the Wilderness from which the servants of the Red Dragon have driven us these three years. I leave at once for the Grisons and perhaps farther. Could I have your company for the journey?"

"I should like it above all things," said Armand with a bow, "but tomorrow I must go to Lausanne and Geneva to deliver messages I brought from England and Holland. I hope I may be of service later. However, if you wish, I can recommend my friend Alexandre Cortot as a trusty travel companion. We have seen some rude journeys together, and we were in King William's expedition last fall. He is a young man of prudence and steadiness and would be honored if you would have him."

Alexandre hung his head modestly. Pastor Arnaud looked him over quickly, noting his slight but wiry build and his alert, slightly vulpine expression. The pastor smiled broadly and clapped Alexandre on the shoulder. " 'Tis done, then," he cried. "Monsieur Convenant and I have matters to discuss about this affair of Schaffhausen, but I must be on my way within the hour. Meet me here, if you please," he said to Alexandre.

The two older men disappeared into the parlor, and the double doors were shut behind them. The two soldiers looked at each other.

"That was smoothly done," said Alexandre a little sourly, buttoning his ragged red coat. "Only my dear sister was faster at volunteering my services for some foul *corvée*."*

"You were always one to dramatize." Armand grinned. "I thought I did you a favor. We have done nothing for Monsieur Convenant that a stable boy could not have done, and I have had an impression that Zurich was boring you already."

Alexandre didn't trouble to deny it. "It's true I have many good qualities," he said as they climbed to the garret where they had been staying, "but that doesn't include money or good looks, and you need both to make much sensation in this town. I think they are weary of foreigners, too—especially those who speak French."

"Pastor Arnaud seems an unusual man," mused Armand. "Were I not carrying these messages—and some are oral—it would be a privilege to travel with him. I can see that he would be an extremely interesting person." They entered their little cubbyhole and began their few preparations for travel.

"They are all overblown talkers," said Alexandre ungraciously as he pulled on a heavy boot, "but it will be better than sitting around here day after day."

---

* Unpaid labor.

* * * * *

"I worry about him. I hope you'll forgive my saying anything to you, but we know that they have tried at least twice to kidnap him, and there is a price on his head." Marguerite Bastia Arnaud, a plump, gray-haired little lady with a careworn face, sat in her parlor attempting to sew, but she was too distracted to accomplish much. She dropped the work in her lap and looked most pathetically at Alexandre Cortot, who stood uneasily before her while the pastor finished preparations upstairs. "We are safe enough here among our friends. There are thirty of our Vaudois families here in Neuchâtel. We receive free lodgings and a pension, but to have my husband traveling all the time, and often in Catholic lands . . ." Her voice faltered as a tear escaped down her cheek.

Only four days had passed since Alexandre joined the pastor, and already he was almost wilted by the pace. They had rushed from Zurich to Neuchâtel—less, it appeared, to visit the family than to consult mysteriously with certain armorers and retired soldiers. This morning the town council, learning that the pastor was in town, held him for hours in close examination. They wished to know about reports of orders for muskets and powder and about rumors that Arnaud was undercutting efforts to move Vaudois to Brandenburg, where they could, indeed, have peace and freedom of worship. Why were the Vaudois not yet on the road to the Germanies?

Arnaud had talked his way out, not for the first time, but hadn't vouchsafed many details to his young companion, who had cooled his heels for those hours on a bench in the town square. Alexandre felt sorry for the distressed lady. She might not have known all that was going on, but she knew enough to be worried.

"You know," she was saying, "city officers and even complete strangers come here and want to know where he is. My heart stops beating when they do that. The duke and the king of France have their spies everywhere, and here in Neuchâtel, after all, we do have a Catholic governor, though he has not yet done us any unkindness."

"We will do our best, Madame," said Alexandre with more assurance than he really felt. "The pastor knows what he is doing. It is God's work, and surely the Lord will protect us."

"Yes," she said, sighing. "Henri's work is important, and God has spared him most wonderfully in the past." She made a halfhearted stab at resuming the sewing. "He doesn't tell me where he is going, and, for his safety, this is right, of course. But if you should go as far as the valleys—" She paused and lowered her voice. "My sister and her husband are at Torre Pellice. They abjured," she said apologetically, "and he is a magistrate. The name is Gautier. It was weak of them, surely, but I know their hearts are still with us. They must feel dreadful, knowing that they have sinned exceedingly; and yet they are still suspected by the priests and the duke's people on the one hand, and they know what we think too. If you should see my sister, tell her we pray for her and her family always. My husband is a kind man, but he is God's minister and cannot excuse apostasy. If you could, see how they do, if they are well, and give them my love—"

She broke off as her husband's footsteps sounded on the stair.

"I have everything now, Madame," he said heartily. "I must be going. I pray God be with you and the children."

He kissed her. She dabbed at her eyes and rose to her feet.

"How long will you be gone, Henri?"

"There is no need for worry, wife. The matter is the Lord's. I could hardly say whether it will be two weeks or two months, but I have this excellent young man with me and our own Baptiste—and our guardian angels."

His tone was cheerful and patient, as if he had been through this before. He handed the saddlebags to Alexandre, patted his wife's cheek kindly, and headed out the door. Alexandre, sympathetic but stricken momentarily dumb, could only bow deeply to the unhappy lady and follow the pastor.

CHAPTER 2

Assassins

Two men sat around a smoldering fire in a peasant hutment on a steep hillside in northern Italy. Through the doorless opening they could dimly see the mists settled in over Lake Como. The breeze blew cold, but not strong enough to scatter the clouds that obscured the night sky. Alexandre Cortot and Baptiste Besson, wrapped in cloaks, felt cold, but this was not the chief reason for their discomfort. They were in the mountains bordering Spanish Milan. Though Spain was an ally now against France and her satellite state of Savoy, this was not a healthy place for Protestants, particularly Vaudois, to be seen. Pastor Arnaud was down the hill in some village below them meeting someone, presumably arranging alternate routes by which Vaudois might return from Switzerland to their Piedmontese homeland. If it was dangerous for the two huddled by the fire, it was many times more so for the pastor, but he would not permit them to accompany him. It seemed to them he had been gone for hours and was much overdue.

Besson, usually a silent and morose man, was a stocky Vaudois twice Alexandre's age. He had traveled much with the pastor and didn't really seem to approve of having Alexandre tag along. Each sat silent with his thoughts but jumped sporadically at the crackles from the embers glowing in front of them and at any strange noise outside. There was much futile stirring of the coals. Finally Besson got up, looked into the blackness, and then stood glowering down at the seated boy.

"You know," he said, apropos of nothing in particular, "the troubles we Vaudois have now are the fault of you Huguenots when all is said and done." He was edgy and seemed to want an argument.

"How do you see that?" Alexandre replied carefully.

"It's plain enough. All the time the world was worshiping the beast, we were preserving the light of truth in our valleys. And we have endured thirty-three wars and persecutions—did you know that? However, we were getting along all right as such things go, but then in 1685, when it got a little warm, you all caved in. That's when the trouble started again for us."

Alexandre forbore to challenge Besson, but he remembered the ruin in his own hometown in southern France when the dragoons came to convert the Protestants. His mother had died, and his father was still missing, probably in a dungeon or on a galley somewhere these past four years. He himself had been locked in a school for Protestant boys for a time, and he remembered the escape through the snow to Holland with his sisters, brother, and Armand de Gandon. "A little warm" was hardly accurate. Besson paced back and forth.

"There were a lot of you—a million? Two million? Yet you let your king bully you. You were a lukewarm church, and the love of the truth was not in you. When the king sent his priests and dragoons and they cuffed you around a bit, you fell on your cowardly faces and abjured. The king saw that all that was needed was a little push, and you would give in or get out."

Alexandre stirred angrily but Besson cut him off. "If it hadn't been so easy to run over *you*, then your king—whom may God smite!— wouldn't have thought to force our duke to try to convert us and send in General Catinat and his fiends when our poor duke hesitated!"

Alexandre was, for once, speechless.

"Time and again," Besson continued passionately, "the Inquisition and the pope and the whole hellish crew tried by tricks and massacre to ruin us, but always God preserved us in the hour of danger. And this time it was obvious that the duke had no wish to bother us—we were only twelve thousand or so, and loyal and no threat to him—and we could have stood off him and the militia and the priests till they gave up again; we've done it often enough before. But it was the

French army and the treachery. Hardly one in four of us is alive today after what they did to us." He stopped and glared fiercely down at Alexandre.

"Well," said Alexandre wearily, moving back just a little, "if my people were punished because they were Laodicean, what was God trying to tell your Vaudois?"

It was Besson's turn to be speechless. He stood for a long moment, still glaring, and then with something like a sigh sat down. When he did finally speak, his tone was quieter, almost discouraged.

"You know, you could be right. I think if we had been firm as we should have been, more of us would still be alive. 'Who gave Jacob for a spoil, and Israel to the robbers? Did not the LORD, he against whom we have sinned?' "

"I didn't really mean what I said," responded Alexandre quickly. "This world is the devil's, and the good particularly have to suffer, don't they?"

"When the decree came that we must abjure," said Besson, not heeding Alexandre's disclaimer, "we protested that it was a violation of the duke's solemn pledge and that he had no justification. And we asked the Reformed brethren abroad for help. But Cromwell was dead, and the king of England was a papist, and all the Swiss would do was send emissaries to beg the duke to let us leave the country, because, they said, we were too far away to be helped.

"The French 'converted' the Pragelas Valley fast enough and said their dragoons would do the same to us if we didn't bow the knee to Baal by the appointed day. We should have fought, and we started out to; but we were lied to, and the duke made promises, and the Swiss envoys pleaded with our timid ones to be reasonable, and so they divided us in our simplicity. Even so, those who did try to stand firm made a good start!

"It was in April 1686—the twenty-third—to be exact, when the French came in at St. Germain. We handled them roughly enough that they went back across the river so fast they didn't even bother to use the bridge! We had Vielleville cut off and cooped up in the convent, and if it hadn't got dark too quick, we would have had the slates off the roof and burned him out or run water in through the ditches we were digging and drowned him out, but he was relieved. But when some of us put down our arms, others were being massacred. The pastor escaped, disguised as a monk.

"In spite of all the promises, they rounded up everyone they could catch or persuade and threw us all—men, women, and children—into their filthy dungeons. Do you know how many crawled out of there a few months later? Three thousand out of twelve thousand! Three thousand skeletons!" His voice broke, and he was silent for a moment. "Bad air, bad food, bad jailers. They took our children away to raise as papists, and we've never seen them again. Some few dozen held out in the hills, and to get them to quit, the duke had to let us all leave for Geneva. The miracle is that any of us lived through that journey. It was winter, and many did not.

"It's not over yet, I tell you! Our lands have been given to others, but they're not going to live long to enjoy them. Those valleys have been ours since long before there were any dukes in Savoy. In fact, we've tried twice to go back, but it scares the Swiss. They're afraid of Louis XIV and his puppy, our duke, and so twice they have broken up our little expeditions. Well, maybe it was well that they did, for we were too hasty and the thing wasn't well planned. The second time, the pastor was leading us, and we hoped to go by Valais over Grand-Saint-Bernard Pass, but the word got out. In Geneva they caught on when sixty of our fellows in their garrison deserted the same day to join us. Then the bailiff at Aigle, Monsieur Thormann, came and talked us out of it. He told us that over in Savoy the signals were lighted and the bridge at Saint-Maurice was guarded. We should have our opportunity later, he said, infallibly so, in God's providence, but it couldn't work that time.

"Pastor Arnaud was convinced, and so he preached to us in the church there on Luke chapter twelve, 'Fear not, little flock.' Thormann gave us food and lent us two hundred *écus**** to travel back to our homes again. Some of the Swiss, like him, felt truly sorry for us, but others think only of money and hate truth. At Vevey the council forbade anyone to feed us or give us shelter when we passed through. And when a poor widow did, they were going to pull down her house. Right after that, the whole town burned down, but her house wasn't touched! It was the finger of God, without doubt.

---

* Coins, usually silver—perhaps forty dollars in present purchasing power.

"Well, that was a year ago, but we have been busy since! The pastor and I were in Holland this spring, and we had a private audience with the Prince of Orange. He told us to keep our people together and not to let anyone scatter us over Europe. Some of the princes are very kind and want to help, but if we spread out in tiny groups in Brandenburg and the Palatinate or wherever, we wouldn't be ready to go home again. Sure, the Swiss feel that we are a burden and that we haven't moved away as we said we would, but it is God's providence that we are still in Switzerland and that we haven't had to scatter. Monsieur Convenant disburses the money that comes for us from Holland and England, and we spied out the routes through Savoy last year. Now the duke has taken his guard boats off the lake and no longer garrisons his mountain forts. It is providential that he is poor, too, and has many troubles.

"God sent all this trouble on us, I think, to show us how dependent we are upon Him. But we are His people, and He will save us very soon now."

"Do you think the Swiss will try again to stop you?"

Besson shrugged. "They may, but we won't stop for anyone this time. We'll try to be more careful and not reveal our secrets aforetime. Some of our friends will, we know, look the other way until the matter becomes notorious."

"Do you think it is known that we're here?"

"Possibly. The pastor's whereabouts are of great interest to many. That's why we never go twice the same way and he doesn't dress like a minister. God willing, when they learn we've been in a place, we're already gone."

"Who do you think he meets tonight?"

"If he didn't tell you, why should I?" replied Besson a little sharply. "What you don't know, no one can wring out of you. You have little idea what they might do to make you talk. Your dragonnades were a picnic compared to what has happened to us. We've had both the Inquisition *and* your French army!"

Besson continued to talk—a somber monologue—of the surpassing horrors of the 1686 atrocities—butcheries, mutilations, dismemberments, barbarities scarcely endurable to talk about. A seventeenth-century army given free rein to deal with enemy civilians in its usual savage way but with the added incentive of knowing that the victims were heretics too!

Alexandre, a little sick, thought he'd had some reason to feel bitter about the cruelties his loved ones had suffered in 1685, but he had to concede that the Vaudois had suffered more than he could have imagined. Besson, who had seen his own wife and father murdered, and whose children had been taken away and were still missing, would have no reason to withhold his hand should he ever have a chance to smite the persecutors again. " 'The wicked shall be turned into hell, and all the nations that forget God,' " concluded Besson.

The two stepped outside the hut to see if there was any sign of the pastor. The moon was coming through the cloud cover, and the white mist at the lower elevation now made a gleaming floor to the valley. Nothing moved in the cold stillness. They could only wait.

* * * * *

As Alexandre had frequently done during the past month, he stood guard as inconspicuously as possible outside the door of a narrow house in a redolent alley. It was almost dusk. Alexandre, Pastor Arnaud, and Baptiste Besson had come in that afternoon on their journey from Milan, on foot most of the way. Avoiding the mail trails, they had crossed over spectacular heights, forded mountain streams, slept in stone shelters in the passes, and lived mostly on dried meat and ice water. They had come once again to the little town of Coire, the chief center of the thirteen little republics making up the Grisons, the Gray League. It was a buffer zone, long in contention between France and Spain—a troubled area of mixed sympathies.

Standing in the shadow in a smelly street that a few feet farther on opened into a small square with a fountain surrounded with arcades, Alexandre noted that two of the passersby didn't pass but loitered at the corner. He couldn't see their faces, but their manner troubled him. They were muffled to the eyes in cloaks. He couldn't see if they were armed, but having been followed often enough before, he felt uneasy. Whether it was the French resident in Geneva or the Savoy envoy at Lucerne, someone was very much concerned with their movements. Was a false brother keeping the pastor's enemies informed?

Alexandre felt it prudent to investigate the other end of the alley. He found that it went around the corner of the building and ended in a stone wall. It wouldn't do to get penned up in such a trap. When the pastor came out, they would have to pass the two loiterers. There might be more of them in the surrounding alleys. It would be dark soon.

At this point the door opened, and Besson started to come out. Alexandre threw himself into the doorway, shoving Besson roughly backward. Startled and alarmed, the Vaudois reached for his knife but then realized it was Alexandre.

"Is there any other way out of here?" Alexandre whispered urgently.

Besson and the pastor looked at their host, a local sympathizer, who shook his head.

"The alley is a cul-de-sac," said Alexandre, "and there seem to be two bravos waiting at the corner that we must pass. Pastor, you and Baptiste should change hats and cloaks."

The pastor had his red cloak and Besson a dull brown. The two were of similar size and build. The exchange done, the three emerged from the doorway and walked rapidly toward the square. Twilight still lingered as they came up to the waiting men. Across the square they saw two more also waiting in one of the arcades. The four started forward, and the nearer pair made a grab for Besson. There was an instant of scuffle, and Besson's borrowed hat fell off just as one of the assassins slashed him lightly in the face with his dagger.

"Mother of God!" exclaimed the other one. "He's not the one! Let's get out of here!"

He bolted, and the two coming from across the square took fright also, turning and fleeing. The thug who had grappled with Besson also tried to run, but Alexandre tripped him, and he and Besson flung themselves on him, pinioning him on the ground.

"Not too much," Pastor Arnaud cautioned his two companions. Then, turning to the groaning prisoner, he demanded, "Who sent you?" The answer came in Italian. Arnaud switched to Italian. "You had best tell what you know—who hired you—and tell me quickly, for the gentleman you injured may not be as forgiving as he should be."

Besson, blood dripping from the slash on his cheek, put the point of his dagger on the helpless man's throat and smiled unpleasantly. The result was miraculous. Though a bit incoherent from fright, the man

confessed that he was Cavuzi, of a band of *cappellatti** brought up from
Venice to do the *colpa*† professionally, local talent being incompetent or
unavailable. He and his friends had been given an exact description of
Arnaud, what he was wearing, and where he could likely be found in
Coire. They had been promised three hundred *doppie*§ for Arnaud dead
and six hundred if delivered alive to Solaro di Govone, the envoy of the
duke of Savoy at Lucerne. He wanted the gentlemen to know he had no
personal grudge at all; it was purely business. His face was gray with
fright, and he began to say prayers rapidly under his breath.

Arnaud laughed aloud, which upset Besson and Alexandre. "Let the
rascal go," the pastor said.

"But, pastor," expostulated Alexandre, "shouldn't we at least turn
him over to the watch?" Besson, wiping his cheek with his kerchief,
didn't get off the man's chest right away. Possibly he had another idea
of how to dispose of an assassin.

"No," said the pastor, "I don't want to advertise our presence here.
For everyone who wishes us well in this town, there is another who
doesn't. The bailiff here is sold to our enemies and perhaps set this ambush for us. Send him away!"

Besson grunted, rose unwillingly, and gave the prostrate criminal a
sharp kick. The man stared wildly at them and then leaped up and ran
at top speed across the deserted square and down another street.

"What a pity!" growled Besson, still dabbing at his cheek. "No one
in Venice would have missed the scum! But why do you laugh, pastor? You could have been killed if Alexandre had not seen them first.
For six hundred *doppie*—twenty-four thousand *livres***—they'll keep
trying."

"Poor Govone!" said the pastor, and he laughed again. "We have
been such a perplexity to him. How he worries whenever I stir out of
my house or he hears that three Vaudois chat together in one place!
How surprised he would be if he knew of some of the people I have

---

* Bandits, thugs.

† Deed, murder, etc.

§ Gold coins with a present purchasing power of perhaps four hundred twenty-
five dollars.

**Standard French coin, later the franc, with a present purchasing power of
perhaps ten dollars. Three *livres* made a silver *écu*.

been talking with these past weeks and how suddenly his instructions may yet be changed! But it is obvious that they don't bother to keep the poor fellow informed."

* * * * *

Entering the apothecary shop next to the city hall of Geneva, Armand could at first make out little in the dimness. Then he saw a lone thin gentleman sitting very straight at a table against the wall. This was the place, and this was the description of the man he sought.

"Have I the honor of addressing Monsieur Valmont?" he asked, removing his hat and bowing. The other put down his cup of chocolate and graciously acknowledged his identity. Armand gave the man a little packet of letters.

"From Monsieur Convenant and from the committee at Lausanne," he murmured. The cadaverous gentleman broke the seal and read. Then he looked up sharply, searching Armand's face. "Excuse me, sir," he said, rising stiffly to his feet and steadying himself with a hand on the wall. "Do I not know you? Were you not in the service in the Regiment of Maine?"

"I was," replied the soldier, searching the face of the Swiss in his turn. "There is something very familiar about you also, but I cannot at the moment—"

The other took Armand's arm in one hand and his cane in the other. Then he glanced around the room carefully. Besides several chocolate drinkers, he saw a young man with a blond wig who was splendidly dressed in lavender. The proprietor was shaking his head at some question the man had asked.

"Let us go for a walk on the ramparts, major. I know you now. I don't blame you for not knowing me. I am David Valmont, captain in the Erlach regiment of the Swiss. We were stationed together one winter in Flanders about ten years ago. In the service, I used the name of Thierry."

"Of course!" Armand apologized. "I remember now, but have you not changed? You are unwell?"

"Yes for both questions," said Valmont with a rueful little laugh. "In my twenty years of service for His Very Christian Majesty, I have lost my digestion and gained rheumatism, so I have retired to a little place my parents left me near Coppet. But tell me of yourself. I heard that you had refused the preferment of the duke and had emigrated after the Revocation."

Armand briefly sketched his adventures of the past four years and said that he was now carrying messages from Jurieu and others while awaiting the arrival of the British envoy to the Swiss cantons. "But if you are Swiss and retired," Armand asked, "what have you to do with all this?"

They had crossed the square and entered the rampart area. The Swiss walked with some difficulty, but this was not why he halted twice and looked around. The young man in lavender followed some distance behind them. Now he also stopped and looked away, apparently interested in the arches of the city hall arcade.

"I am after all, a Protestant," replied the Swiss finally in a lowered voice, "and my heart is still with God's people who suffer over there in France. The poor wretches who reach Geneva with scarce a *sou** in their pockets are the fortunate ones. In my last two years I served in the *Midi*,† and though the Swiss troops were not actually used to hunt the Huguenot worshipers in the wilderness, I saw too much to forget it soon.

"These are not only very difficult times for the believers but also for Geneva," Valmont said. Then, pointing his stick over the edge of the rampart toward the meadows and the river, he continued. "Yonder is the Arve, and there it joins the Rhône. Across the river is Savoy; and on that side, France. There are only fifteen thousand souls in this little republic, and while one is ashamed when our council abases itself to placate our vigilant French resident, the Sieur d'Iberville, one can understand why they feel they must conciliate him and the Great King. The French threaten from time to time to put an end to Geneva as one abates a nuisance, for to them it is a nest of heresy and a magnet for hundreds of Huguenots who flee here every year in spite of all the prohibitions. I think that if the French didn't wish to keep their good supply of Protestant Swiss soldiers, Geneva would have been lost long ere this.

---

* A twentieth of a *livre;* colloquially, a penny.
† Southern France.

"Of course, if our mob had its way, they would throw d'Iberville into the lake this afternoon, but some prominent bourgeois, on the other hand, sell themselves, their religion, and their city to the French interest. The resident listens there in his big house on the Grande Rue." Valmont turned and pointed with his cane. "And sooner or later his creatures tell him who spoke to what point in the council or what preacher in a Sunday sermon alluded to the persecutions in France, and which of the refugees are discouraged and homesick and would be willing to be corrupted with offers of the return of their property if they go back to France."

"This would seem a very difficult place in which to keep any secrets," said Armand.

"True, but much the same kind of espionage goes on also in Bern and Zurich. Protestant convictions there clash with special relations to Louis XIV and the profitable business of supplying him with Swiss soldiers. But I wouldn't have you too disappointed in us. Geneva is a city of great heart and has been a most generous refuge for Huguenots and Vaudois. The city can't afford to keep them all, so they're passed on to other places of refuge in Switzerland or the Protestant countries as soon as they are restored enough to travel."

Valmont looked down again at the river.

"We do all we can, but the tragedies under our very eyes break one's heart. That bridge down there over the Arve is as far as some get. They are seized as we watch from the walls. That village on the other side—Carrouge—is in Savoy. That inn you can see there, the Golden Lion, is where the French soldiers take captives to 'question' them. The resident is in touch with these proceedings and even goes over there at times to handle the interrogation himself."

"Before the Revocation," said Armand, "one sometimes heard it said that if a strong stand would be taken and perhaps even a few of the brethren were martyred, the king would be convinced of our sincerity and would draw back from the risk of civil war and ease the persecution. What do you think of that idea?"

Valmont shook his head gloomily. They slowly descended from the wall down a long stone ramp.

"If it had ever been so, it is no longer. Flight is all God's people can look to now. They are leaderless sheep at the mercy of the butchers. The

45

young prédicants who rise up to admonish the people do not live long. Assemblies are held in the wildest thickets, but infallibly, they are soon known. The troops come, and there are killings, heavy fines, and the pulling down of houses. I saw some of this in my last year in the service. Not only is it death for a pastor to return to France according to the edict of 1686, but I have seen orders from the war minister not to take too many prisoners when dispersing these assemblies and not to distinguish between the sexes.

"True, there is much exasperation, and the people now repent the haste in which they abandoned the truth during the dragonnades; but they lack leaders and arms; and, while I don't wish to limit the overrulings of God, I fear the zealots will provoke reprisals so that the last state of the people will be worse than the first." He shook his head sadly. "I help those trying to escape, but I don't think God can bless utter folly. I greatly fear the land will be put in a blaze prematurely."

Valmont stopped in the shadow of the city wall. Armand paused also, and they looked about. The young man in lavender, seeing that he was observed, approached them. He bowed very deeply, sweeping the grass with his plumed hat in hand, and greeted Valmont by name.

"This is Monsieur Barbin," said Valmont without enthusiasm. "He is a refugee from Picardy and resides here this past year. He is well-known to the distinguished people in this city." This last was in a curiously cold, almost ironic tone.

Barbin babbled heedlessly on, practically pushing himself between the two men. He prattled of his joy at Armand's arrival in town. Where was he from? How long would he be staying? What did he here? He, Barbin, knew everyone worth knowing and would make it his particular pleasure to introduce Armand around to the *peuple du bien** and would show him everything in the town worth seeing. As they finally parted, Barbin assured Armand that he couldn't rest until he had performed for the newcomer all the services and made his better acquaintance. Armand, noting Valmont's attitude, wasn't certain that his happiness required that much of the young man's company, but he produced the appropriate exaggerated politeness necessary to terminate the encounter.

---

* Substantial citizens.

* * * * *

"I'm not made of money, you know," said the young diplomat irritably. "You think because His Majesty is kind enough to let some of you penitents show your gratitude by bringing information useful to his service that you can badger me for money at any hour."

It was two in the morning in the French residence, and d'Iberville was meeting his caller in dressing gown and nightcap. A single candle struggled with the shadows in the little room. His visitor was Monsieur Barbin, his gaudy plumage now covered by a long black cloak. "I don't give you these gratifications just to support your idle way of life," d'Iberville continued. "His Majesty's pardon and the return of your estates depend—and don't forget it—on your serviceability, and I don't consider your chocolate-house tittle-tattle as 'serviceable.' "

The French resident glowered at his crestfallen visitor. He didn't believe in having his agents think too well of themselves. It really wasn't unusual for him to receive callers at this time of night, though; for those on his payroll or those who came secretly to abjure in his chapel didn't wish to be seen entering the premises.

"A thousand pardons, your lordship, but it is hard to get much information about Monsieur Valmont. He seems so cold and unfriendly. I am almost certain that his visitor today brought him letters, but there is no way I could see them, and while they spoke of refugees and the new converts in France, they stopped when I came near. The new man is a French officer, Armand de Gandon, a major at one time in the King's service. I think he is in the service of the Prince of Orange and must have come lately from England or Holland. When he asked a question about the Vaudois, Valmont changed the subject. I'll do my best to please your lordship. I know now where this officer lodges, and I'll cultivate his acquaintance assiduously."

Barbin looked so pleadingly and humbly at his master that d'Iberville was reminded of the beseeching eyes of a spaniel. Also like a spaniel, the informer seemed to wiggle in his anxiety to please. It occurred to d'Iberville that it would be perfectly natural for Barbin to lick his hand. He shivered slightly with distaste.

"And what of the son of the bailiff at Nyon? You were going to get him to reveal to you the secrets of his father."

"Ah, yes, my lord!" cried Barbin with more of his sickening, moist-eyed sincerity. "He will presently prove to be *very* useful to His Majesty's service. He will get me proofs that his father turns a blind eye to the French refugees in the area. The young man says that the refugee ministers and also the Vaudois are scurrying about very busily of late—particularly out of Lausanne."

"There is a connection?"

"I shouldn't wonder, my lord. All the known troublemakers and firebrands among the refugees are on the *qui vive.** Something is brewing."

"Well, find out quickly if this be so and attach yourself to that officer you met today. If there are any plans for sedition in France, I must know at once. If there is some plot afoot, insinuate yourself into it. If you do well, I may be able to overlook some other stupid things—"

"I can hardly entertain these gentlemen, my lord, without money, though I blush to even mention such a matter to you." Barbin was all humble meekness.

"You should blush, God knows!" snapped d'Iberville. From a leather bag he took from his escritoire, he counted out twenty silver *écus* of France and pushed the pile across the desk to Barbin. "That makes two hundred forty *livres* I have advanced you this past month. Use good judgment, but I cannot hand out His Majesty's money indefinitely without results."

"You can count on me, my lord," Barbin simpered. "I would give my life for His Majesty!"

"It would be more useful to him if you stayed alive and under cover and fetched me quickly the news of what these traitorous rascals are up to! After this, rather than coming in person, see if you can send me messages."

He called his servant. "Show Monsieur Barbin out. Use the back gate into the alley. There may be watchers in the Grande Rue even at this hour."

"Your servant, sir," Barbin gushed, and with two more deep bows he followed the servant.

D'Iberville blew out the candle and, pulling the window drape aside, he looked out over the cobbled courtyard. But he could see nothing of

---

* Alert.

the Grande Rue through the gateway. Were there spies in the black alleys? He could almost feel the hostility of Geneva, Calvin's city.

Pale moonlight silvered the roofs, and the St. Pierre Cathedral stood out boldly. D'Iberville was proud of his work in this difficult post; he rather enjoyed this situation, touchy and delicate though it was. He hoped his superiors at Versailles were aware what a good man they had in Geneva. If they weren't, it wasn't for lack of frequent reports from him.

He was, however, a little worried. It was obvious that something was going on, and he wished he had a better instrument at hand than Barbin. One of his agents had been fished out of Lake Geneva recently, and though nothing was ever said publicly about any French connection, it *was* odd for the man to go for a swim with feet and hands bound.

There were at least two hundred French refugees in town, and many gathered at the post house to read each other tidbits from their letters. Barbin picked up a lot there. Besides the pernicious principles they derived from their religion, the refugees absorbed a republican, independent spirit living in a place like Geneva. They would do anything to humiliate France. But serious plotters like Valmont and the newly arrived officer wouldn't be babbling in post houses!

"These turncoats are either fools or knaves," he sighed to himself, drawing the curtain again. "Barbin is probably both. He is surely greedy enough, but is he clever? If I could penetrate some great conspiracy of these accused heretics, I wouldn't be stuck in this joyless town forever. Why would that officer have come here from Holland? I must get a good description of him for my next letter to the king."

*   *   *   *   *

"That Christ's poor sheep bleat in desolation, devoured by wild beasts and exposed to the rage of the demon touches my heart." The host, the distinguished lawyer Claude Brousson, was speaking to a score of members of the Lausanne Refugee Committee and their guests at his home. It was an evening in mid-July. On the morrow, two recently ordained young prédicants, one of them François Vivens, planned to leave the safety of exile and return to Languedoc. Armand de Gandon, still the courier, had brought letters for Mirmand, head of the local

Refugee Committee, and Monsieur Brousson had most cordially invited him to stay for the evening.

"I have discussed this much with my guest, Brother Vivens, since he has been in my home. I feel the leading of the Spirit and am fully resolved, brethren, to accompany him and the others when they return to France tomorrow to preach under the cross." Brousson was a slight man of dark eyes and complexion, a serene manner, and an excellent speaking voice with a touch of a southern accent.

"But brother," objected one of the ministers, "in your state of health is this wise? You have rendered many services to the church in France and now in Switzerland, and have pleaded our needs most ably before princes and diets. For a man of your legal training, is it the best use of your talents to go in this fashion? And you are a layman, not even ordained!"

"Thank you for your concern, but I am decided. I see the leading of God in this, for as soon as I was resolved to go and console our brethren, God has given me a most remarkable remission of the distresses in my chest and the slow fever that has plagued me these many months. It is a direct sign! God will raise up preachers and give even the most *idiote** words to say. If the regular pastors do not do their duty, the very stones will cry out!"

"Are you returning to your views that the pastorate is remiss when it does not return to France to seek martyrdom?" There was just a suggestion of an edge in the voice of the speaker.

"No, sir!" said Brousson very humbly. "I regret that my writings a year ago offended so many of our pastors, and I didn't urge martyrdom on anyone. But I repeat what I said then, that even should a pastor be put to death, he may yet witness more effectively from his grave than he does from a pulpit in a land of safety. I was no doubt too forward in my manner of speaking, but where *are* the shepherds? We have young men such as Brother Vivens and the other prédicants, and even child prophets arise. But is every one of our ordained ministers so old or so poor in health that he doesn't feel he can defy the king's edict and return to serve his flock? That I am going should gratify those whose sensibilities I wounded." He smiled a sly little smile.

---

* Simple.

50

Except for some disagreement over the wisdom of Brousson's intentions, the atmosphere was one of a holy joy, for the departure of the prédicants and Brousson, their expenses paid by the Dutch government, their plans perfected by the exile leaders in Holland and Switzerland, represented a first step toward the recovery of Protestantism in southern France. François Vivens was the hero of the evening. He was the homely, ill-constructed young man Armand had met briefly at Jurieu's home in Rotterdam. His manner was quieter than some of the more ebullient older men. His intense, almost brooding gaze seemed to see beyond the crowded parlor on to the mountains of the Cévennes and the standard to be raised there against the beast and the Scarlet Woman. The duplicity practiced on him by the agents of the intendant of Languedoc had transformed him from a well-intentioned young schoolmaster and amateur preacher into a fanatical prophet with a holy hatred of the Roman Church and all its minions. It had, indeed, been a costly trick the authorities in Languedoc had played when they violated the trust of the earnest young preacher. Now, thanks to Jurieu, he had been officially ordained and was the advance agent of the Huguenot counteroffensive.

Perhaps he had not been fully at ease at first in this assemblage—mostly experienced pastors of education and social standing—but in spite of his pot belly, his limp, his ill-fitting wig, and his thick patois, when he began to speak, he awed them by his passion, his zeal. The words simply poured out. He was convinced and convincing that the time for the restoration of the church in France was at hand. Zeal was reborn. The dreams, portents, and prophecies gave promise of supernatural aid. Private worship alone was not sufficient witness. God was moving on hearts in France. Deliverance was nigh. God does nothing in vain. He, Vivens, would execute the judgments of Jehovah, and, like Elijah, would take the priests of Baal and the apostates who worshiped him down to the brook Kishon and there smite them. The time was at hand to give the trumpet a certain sound. The armies of the League of Augsburg, the Grand Alliance, were even now beginning to move. His little party would prepare the way. The Vaudois would soon be in motion also. France, the tenth part of the Great City, would fall, and the worship of God in the manner He commanded would be restored in His land of France. God had punished His people for their slackness, but He would also deliver them. The temples broken down and desolate would be repaired, and God's wrath would fall upon those who had so cruelly slain his servants or confined them to galley, dungeon, or convent. The "powers" in France knew of the 1,260-day prophecy. They knew it might end in 1689. They knew exiles were beginning to come back.

Vivens's hearers, mostly middle-aged or elderly, were swept along by his tirade. Some expressed regret that their years and ill health prevented them from joining. Others, obviously delighted to see things moving, evidently seeing Vivens more as an instrument than a leader, expressed concern about timing and procedures. Some raised these points with the young man, but he seemed almost scornful of such considerations, as though this would be limiting the Lord with "counsels of flesh."

Fascinated, Armand listened and watched. *They may have started more than they can finish,* he thought. *What control will they have over this firebrand once he is out of their reach and coursing the hills? There must be thousands of simple folk in those southern provinces repenting of their weakness under persecution, goaded to desperation by the cruelties and stupidities of Bâville and his agents, spied on, taxed, deprived of their own children by the priests, slaughtered by the Catholic militia or the king's soldiers when they meet to pray in the woods. If Vivens stirs them up, will allied armies be ready and able to help? Will aiding the return of the Vaudois to their valleys help open the way to rescue the brethren in France?* His thoughts were interrupted by a new voice.

"The last letter I have had from Lyon says that if we can throw three thousand men into the Dauphiné or Franche-Comté, one hundred thousand men will join us in two weeks!" The speaker was a stout white-haired pastor. "The discontent is so great that even the Catholics will join us!" he predicted.

Armand demurred. "Who will command all these folk? Are we ready to arm them? Do they rebel barehanded? Is an allied army ready to support them?"

The older man turned on Armand, red color rising in his face. He glared at him as if he were a Catholic spy. "We will leave that in the hands of the Lord! Take heed, sir, that you do not suffer the fate of the doorkeeper who beheld the deliverance of Israel but didn't share therein."

Armand noted that several others watched him with some amusement. He realized that there was no use in argument. He didn't, therefore, cite Ahab's reluctance to hear unfavorable prophecies but merely shrugged.

Seizing an opportunity to speak to Monsieur Mirmand privately a bit later when delivering the letters, he mentioned his concern. "I see we have in mind a very grand design indeed," he complained, "but do these people have *any* idea how slowly an army moves? The Imperial forces have not even entered Italy yet. We don't know what the duke of Savoy will do. The Vaudois may indeed start soon, but the British envoy has not even reached Switzerland to discuss a treaty with the cantons. It seems to me that neither a rising of the people nor an invasion from outside of France could prevail without the other. Would it not be wise to persuade this young zealot to wait a little until all parts of the grand design can move together?"

"Perhaps so, captain," said the older man somberly, "but you forget the great appeal of the prophetic date of 1689. As the Catholics fear, the prophecy could encourage its own fulfillment. If something begins, the momentum may carry it further than our caution suggests. A success for the Vaudois—who are not inclined to wait either—would also be a mighty encouragement. Brother Vivens is indeed a furious and hasty person, but it would be useless to try to detain him, and who is to say that the Lord cannot use such an instrument?"

Mirmand paused, but Armand made no reply.

"As you know," continued Mirmand, "I have been working for the resettlement of our refugees in the Protestant lands. I also hope against hope that either our king will be impressed to change his mind and let us return to worship God in the way He desires or that indeed some great revolution may be in the making inside France. But if I may be indiscreetly frank, captain, since I perceive we have some of the same concerns, I wouldn't see drenching the land in blood as an advantage to the cause of truth. No accusation is more perpetually leveled against us than that the Reformation caused civil war and slaughter. Rather, if the right may not prevail in France, I feel we must accept God's purposes for us and indeed flee to another city—be it in the Germanies or possibly in the British Isles.

"For example, King William will have much land to populate in Ireland with the flight of some of the rebels and confiscations from others, and I have already begun discussions with the English authorities on a Huguenot settlement there. I must, sir, keep these plans afoot, for we cannot know how this great war will turn out. But come, let us rejoin the company."

They returned to the sitting room to find the conversation still on the hoped-for revolutions. Madame Brousson was serving refreshment—agreeable cool drinks for a warm evening in a crowded room. She was Brousson's second wife and thus had acquired two stepsons. Standing in a corner, Armand sipped his drink and noted her rather sad face. He surmised that she was not as enthusiastic about Brousson's ventures as were the refugee pastors. She doubtless still remembered quite vividly how her husband was outlawed following the failure of the peaceful protests in 1683, a protest planned in the Brousson home in Toulouse when he practiced law before the regional court there. Shortly afterward, her husband had barely escaped betrayal and crawled out of Nîmes to safety in the middle of the night through an open sewer. She and her little stepson had escaped later.

This boy, a solemn youngster of nine, was helping his mother. When he approached Armand to refill his lemonade glass, Armand asked, "Master Brousson, would you like to go back to Nîmes too?"

"Yes, Monsieur," he replied doubtfully. "It was very frightening to come out, and I would be frightened to go back, but not so much if I was with my father. I would like to see my little brother again. He is with Grandma Brousson in Nîmes, but he is too sickly to travel. I wish we could go and bring him and Grandma out."

Pastor Clarion, one of the directors of the Lausanne committee, overheard this exchange. A look of pain came over his face, and he patted young Barthelemy on the shoulder. "At least your little brother is with his godly grandmother," he said, "and you must thank God every day for that. *My* little boy is in the school of the Jesuits at Pezenas. I know he is a good boy and grounded in the truth, but three years is a long time, and I would do anything to get him out. He is my Daniel in the lions' den, for his name *is* Daniel. But,"—and he smiled wryly at Armand—"it is rather Daniel in a nest of vipers!"

The rest of the evening, as excited and optimistic talk continued and Vivens and Brousson basked in the attention and approval of the company, Armand kept thinking of the silent pair, the mother and son, who would be facing their own kind of terrors, those of the imagination when the husband and father vanished into a silent, dark void, not to be heard from for weeks or months, hunted, and with a price on his head.

"The matter of the Vaudois must be advanced. The snows will close the passes in a couple of months."

"It is very likely we will all meet soon again—this time in France!"

* * * * *

When early in August, Pastor Sagnol de la Croix asked to have a word with Armand, he was nearly certain what would be on his mind. The pastor was one of the most active of the Lausanne Refugee Committee in recruiting for the Vaudois expedition, and though in a general way it was known that the Vaudois were stirring, a seemingly infinite number of conflicting rumors circulated. Experienced French officers would be needed as captains, and Armand had long since indicated—both to Pastor Arnaud and to the Refugee Committee—his willingness to serve. Armand and Alexandre had been waiting in Lausanne now for nearly a month for matters to move.

Sagnol de la Croix was in a hurry, as always, but seemed embarrassed. "I can only take a moment, Monsieur," he said, drawing Armand into a corner of the common room of the Inn of the Three Crowns. "I am afraid some unexpected changes—"

"Don't trouble yourself, pastor," said Armand pleasantly. "I told you that I would be happy to serve the Good Cause in any capacity."

"I know this, Monsieur, and the committee is grateful, for every experienced officer we can get will be needed, but some with whom we have to work have been more—ah, difficult, shall I say? I am desolated to say that at the moment no company is available."

"It makes no difference, pastor. If I can help the poor Vaudois and perhaps prepare the way for the restoration of the church in France, I would be willing to serve as a private soldier!"

The pastor was visibly relieved but still apologetic. "We have had troubles in these matters," he said with a shake of the head. "It seemed appropriate that a Swiss should command. Monsieur Guy of Bern has refused the offer, and now Captain Bourgeois of Neuchâtel has agreed to take command. In the captaincies of the foreign volunteers, it was the feeling of the refugees from Dauphiné, who are the largest number among us, that for second, we should choose Captain Turrel, but unless we are able to raise more volunteer companies than we could at the moment equip, the best we can do is to offer you and Francois Huc lieutenancies."

"I will support with all my heart anyone the brethren choose," said Armand. "After all, the important consideration is that the companies be well led."

"You have a good spirit, Brother Gandon." Sagnol sighed. "So often in the work of the Lord we find these considerations of vanity and rivalry. It is wonderful that the Lord can find any use for us at all!" He brightened. "Well, then we agree! There is much to do, and I must be off. We may have to advance our departure before all our men or supplies can reach us, for the Bernese authorities cannot ignore our preparations much longer. Hold yourself in readiness, brother. Do you need money for subsistence?"

"No, thank you, pastor," replied Armand as he accompanied Sagnol to the door. "What is the role of Pastor Arnaud in all this? I should have thought he would be the natural leader of his people."

"The pastor feels that a man of war should hold the command. He prefers to be the chaplain, or, as he says, the patriarch of the expedition. The expedition is preparing in a foreign country, and he felt it appropriate that a Swiss or Frenchman should lead."

Somehow, I doubt he will have any difficulty making his wishes known, thought Armand as he regained his lodgings. He found Alexandre lying on the pallet they slept on and reading Jurieu's seventeenth *Pastoral Letter*, given Armand by Gabriel de Convenant.

"Did you know, Armand, that the people ultimately make kings, that the people are naturally free, and that they are not obliged to share their goods or their authority with anyone? Kings came in only to preserve order after the entrance of sin. By this natural law and rights of people, what we helped King William do to King James last year was perfectly legal and approved by God. Violence must be 'just' if we have to rebuke kings; they cannot claim to control our consciences."

"It is reassuring that what we are hoping to do for the Vaudois meets with Pastor Jurieu's approval," replied Armand solemnly. "Somehow, I had the impression that the fearsome pastor felt it the duty of magistrates to suppress false doctrine."

"Indeed he does," said Alexandre happily, "but magistrates may not suppress *true* doctrine! Surely, you see the distinction! And, anyway, out of humanity, he objects to *killing* heretics, but they may be silenced rightfully in the name of public order so as not to spread their false ideas."

"Thank you so much for this clarification," said Armand, smiling. "I shall feel so much better now if on our march we run into troops of the Great King."

"What did Sagnol want?" asked Alexandre, realizing that Armand was indulging in irony.

"Behold, a lieutenant of volunteers in the forthcoming expedition!"

"Lieutenant!" exclaimed Alexandre sitting upright with manifest displeasure. "It's time you retired—can't you see that you're losing ground? Your rank goes down every time you change armies. And the armies are each time of less account! You're going backward! You were major in the armies of the king. You were captain for the Prince of Orange. Now for this little gaggle of *bandoliers** you are a lieutenant! I think there is an injustice somewhere. Pastor Jurieu ought to look into it."

---

* Bandits, irregulars.

CHAPTER 3

The "Army" Sets Out

"This is a marvelously public kind of secret!" Baptiste Besson complained to Alexandre one balmy evening in August. Hundreds of Vaudois, French Huguenots, and Swiss sightseers, male and female, were milling about in the little woods of Prangins a few miles east of Nyon on the shore of Lake Geneva. Wood smoke drifted through the trees from many bonfires, and men carrying torches traipsed back and forth. The flickering light created ever-new shapes of shadows and dancing reflections on the dark waters of the lake. Alexandre and the other volunteers were unloading muskets from farm carts and arranging them in orderly stands in the little clearings.

"It seems a shame that there might be *anyone* in Switzerland who couldn't be here at our 'secret' rendezvous," Alexandre said. "I hope they remembered to send invitations to Their Excellencies of Bern—and the French resident in Geneva!" Alexandre and Besson had gotten along well since the matter at Coire. Alexandre would have had trouble keeping quiet anyway.

"Captain," objected a young Vaudois, rolling a small barrel of powder over the foot of a Swiss onlooker who didn't step back in time, "I'm as anxious to get home as you are, but do we leave tonight? Our friends from Brandenburg can't possibly get here in time, or even those coming from the other end of Switzerland. Don't we need every man we can get?"

"I don't make the decisions," Besson snapped. "Just keep working, will you!"

Then, turning to the curious onlookers, he said, "Pardon, messieurs and mesdames. I beg you to give us some room, for time presses. Would you give us a hand?" Two or three of the Swiss men stepped forward silently and began to unload one of the carts.

Besson decided then to comment on his compatriot's question. "This isn't much of a secret," he said. "Some of us may not have known exactly where we were going when we left home, but we all knew why we were going, and a lot of the Swiss do too. How could they help it? It's a small country, and every Vaudois male disappeared from towns and villages almost at the same moment. Do you think the bailiffs couldn't guess who all these fellows are, tramping the back roads of Bern? Messieurs of Bern can hardly pretend blindness much longer, and they'll be forced to stop us again, as they've done twice before, if we aren't out of here in a hurry. It's a shame, and I'm sick about it—but even the timing is the Lord's doing. This war gives us many things: our opportunity, the Huguenots who are going with us, and these muskets and supplies from our friends in England and Holland."

He stopped and mopped his brow. "Keep at it, all of you! It *is* the Lord's doing," he added fiercely, "so a few more or less makes Him no difference."

Alexandre and the others continued to unload the guns and powder as Besson turned away for a moment.

"Do you think there'll be enough to arm all of us? Does anyone know how many we will be? We haven't even been assigned companies yet, have we?" a French volunteer asked Alexandre.

"How could anyone know?" replied Alexandre. "I hear our commander-in-chief himself hasn't showed up yet and that Govone, the Savoy man in Zurich, has wind of this and has tipped off the Catholic cantons. They'll be arresting anybody on the road now, whatever his business, so I think we're going when we get this stuff unloaded and hope the others can come later. It does seem confused; it would be nice if each of us could at least have a gun. Hey, what are these? Aren't they pretty!"

He was admiring a collection of small metal spheroids, each with a touchhole. He hefted one of them speculatively. They were hand grenades. The grenadier carried a piece of slow-burning match.* The idea

---

* Essentially similar to punk.

was to insert a fuse in the grenade, light it, and hurl the grenade soon enough and accurately enough to avoid its exploding amid friendly ranks.

"I wouldn't mind being a grenadier!" said Alexandre, more and more smitten with the idea.

"Not while I'm around!" objected an older comrade emphatically. "You infants make me nervous enough when you want to carry muskets. I'd feel safer if you were a drummer. Too bad we aren't taking any drums along. But God preserve us from runts who want to be grenadiers, who haven't the height or the arm to throw the nasty things far enough away! Nothing personal, of course, but I want a rookie to be in front of me, just in case he gets rattled and his musket goes off too soon."

Alexandre glared. "Who made thee a ruler and a judge?" he asked maliciously. "If you know so much, why are you just a private like the rest of us?"

"Hurry up there!" shouted Besson, his arms full of hard loaves of the perdurable Vaudois bread. "I keep telling you—we haven't all night!"

Armand de Gandon emerged from the shadows at this point to query Besson on his progress. At his heels were two young men in rather incongruous finery, the fabrics of their pastel suits shimmering in the firelight, the feathers and the lace in sharp contrast to the coarse and sober clothing of the expeditionaries. One was Monsieur Barbin, and the other a very blond young man trying to raise a mustache. He was the son of the bailiff of Nyon and was one of Barbin's confidants and information sources. The two had showed up suddenly at the beginning of the evening and had not let Armand get more than ten feet away from them for the last three hours. They stood now just behind Armand, taking in the scene—Barbin's glance darting brightly about, his friend staring more vacantly at the ordered confusion.

"What in the world do you have there?" asked Alexandre rudely. Armand glanced wearily at the precious pair as the Vaudois stared in amazement at their plumage and the Swiss visitors did likewise.

"I would really like to know," he replied with a shrug and turned back to Besson. Armand had given up on Barbin. His presence did suggest something sinister, but the young fellows seemed almost too stupid to be dangerous. A half dozen times during the evening Armand had tried to pin Barbin down. Each time the gorgeous young visitor expressed his interest and sympathy for these simply marvelous poor Vaudois and those so heroically volunteering to go with them. He said he was almost impressed to join the expedition! Armand, each time, urged him to do so and offered to make room for him in his company. But there were always quick, voluble, and vague excuses. The last time, Armand had remarked sarcastically, "I have married a wife and cannot come!" but the allusion seemed to escape Barbin entirely.

Through the eerie scene Pastor Arnaud circulated with a group of officers. For reasons of security, he wished to be addressed as "Monsieur de la Tour," but certainly no one—French Huguenot, Vaudois, or even Swiss sightseers—could fail to identify him. He professed satisfaction with the progress of the night's work. He and his colleagues visited the various campfires, giving orders and suggestions, answering questions, and making encouraging predictions. He was untroubled by the nonappearance of Captain Bourgeois, their chosen leader.

"There is nothing to worry about!" he kept saying. "If he does not arrive in time, we will appoint another. We must sail tonight, and those still on the road can sail the next time. Pastor Sagnol is already making plans for a second expedition."

Several French Huguenot volunteer officers came up to the fire. "Pastor," said Armand, "only four of the boats that were hired have come. What shall we do?"

"That is perplexing," said the pastor, momentarily taken aback. "I have already paid for twenty. They will doubtless be coming."

The officers looked at each other, and the soldiers and sightseers listened as well. It was the presence of the latter that gave an idea to François Huc, a Huguenot lieutenant, a tall, extraordinarily handsome soldier from Le Vigan in southern France. He had an open and instantly likeable face. "This craze to come and see the spectacle has brought many by boat," he said. "We could perform a military 'execution' and simply commandeer these craft. Isn't it a providence that it is a fast day and so many are free to come and gawk at our assembly here?"

Pastor Arnaud brightened. "An excellent idea," he said. "Assure them that we pay in coin for all services but take no refusal!"

Huc and Armand, already good friends, rounded up a squad of nearby soldiers and set off for the shore at a run, most of them laughing at the prospect of the surprise for the boatmen and of the spectators, who would likely be walking home.

The boatmen were scattered through the crowd but heard quickly enough what was up and came running to the shore also, highly indignant. "The bailiff of Nyon warned us you Italian riffraff were up to something," bawled one of them. "He said that if we took anyone across the lake to Savoy, it is to be the death penalty."

"But you didn't mind floating in here with a bunch of sightseers to get in our way, now did you?" said Huc sweetly. "He can hardly cut off your heads unless he catches you, can he? We are all Protestants here, and surely you wish to help the Good Cause. If you don't—well, we have guns and we have your boats and we say you are going to take us across the lake and we will pay you well. So what do you say?"

In the circumstances there was not much that could be said, but after grumblings for effect, the boatmen agreed.

The next hour was devoted to loading the boats. The expeditionaries and many of the spectators formed human chains and passed the arms and supplies to the little flotilla. By one in the morning of Saturday, August 27, the fires in much of the woods, deserted, had died down, and the throng was on the narrow strand, where other fires were kept up. The job was done presently, and the time to embark was at hand. Standing in the prow of one of the boats, aground in the shallows, Pastor Arnaud offered a prayer for divine protection for the great enterprise. All—prospective participants and spectators, men and women—knelt on the ground for the lengthy appeal. The pastor quoted extensively from the seventy-ninth Psalm:

> "O GOD, the heathen are come into thine inheritance; thy holy temple have they defiled; . . .
>
> "The dead bodies of thy servants have they given to be meat unto the fowls of the heaven, the flesh of thy saints unto the beasts of the earth.
>
> "Their blood have they shed like water round about Jerusalem; and there was none to bury them. . . .
>
> "Pour out thy wrath . . . upon the kingdoms that have not called upon thy name. . . .

"Wherefore should the heathen say, Where is their God? let him be known among the heathen in our sight by the revenging of the blood of thy servants which is shed.

"Let the sighing of the prisoner come before thee; . . .

"We thy people and sheep of thy pasture will give thee thanks for ever."

When they rose, Armand was at once aware that his faithful shadows had disappeared. He asked Alexandre and the others around him if they had seen where Monsieur Barbin and his blond puppy had gone. Some of the soldiers began asking in the crowd of spectators, "Did you see where the gentleman in the yellow suit went?"

"If you find him, bring him back!" said Armand to Alexandre and several other French volunteers. "The more I think of his prying questions and wonder how he knew something would be going on here tonight, the more I think we ought to keep him with us."

The searchers were gone a quarter of an hour. Alexandre returned winded. "Your precious fops gave us the slip," he puffed. "We are told that he and that pimply friend of his from Nyon ran out of the woods after the prayer and rode off in a cloud of dust toward Geneva."

"Well," said Armand sourly, "if they are bringing the word to d'Iberville, they'll have the rest of the night on horseback, but it's all the more important that we get out of here."

The boats were shallow-draft affairs with low freeboard and a sail or two. Between seven and eight hundred men and a few horses were packed in eventually, leaving perhaps two hundred behind for a return trip. Those who could not be fully armed also had to remain. A breeze had sprung up, and with poling and sails, it would be possible to cross the lake quickly to the invisible south shore. Boat after boat pushed out into the darkness accompanied by the good wishes of those on shore. The lights of the bonfires grew dimmer as the boatmen poled into the overcast, starless night. Sprinkles of rain fell occasionally.

The boats carried no lights and soon drifted apart in the darkness. At first, the boatmen kept together by calling to each other, but after a time the officers forbade it and everyone stared intently through the Stygian black, wondering what reception waited on the Savoy beaches.

* * * * *

It was still very dark when the boats began to ground on the strand near Yvoire. The shore was deserted—no signal flares, no warning shots. Taking courage, the expeditionaires lighted torches so that other boats could find the rendezvous. The boatmen pushed off again for the Swiss side, paid in advance for a second trip, but only three of them honored their commitment. At the last moment a small boat came in from Geneva with eighteen more volunteers.

No time could be taken in mourning these mishaps, though the Savoyards gave no sign of life as the first streak of dawn appeared in the east. The little force was arrayed on the beach. Sentinels were posted, and the men divided up into fourteen Vaudois companies and six companies of foreign volunteers. The Vaudois were territorial, each from a particular town or district in the valleys—Torre Pellice, Saint Martin, Angrogna, and so on, and each with a local captain. Turrel, a French veteran from Dauphiné, was named military commander in the absence of Bourgeois. Most of the foreigners were French Huguenots, but some were Swiss. Most were ex-soldiers.

Two Brandenburg grenadiers, Huguenots who had served the Great Elector, put the little army in array, and three corps were formed for the march: an advance guard, the main body, and a rear guard. A flag was unfurled, said by some to be King William's banner but it was actually that of Duke William of Württemberg. Armand and the other former French officers carried a commission from King William that they were in fact his officers and not French traitors, which they would depend on if captured by their erstwhile comrades. It remained to be seen whether such legal distinctions would interest the servants of Louis XIV should any of the little force unhappily fall into their hands.

After prayer, Arnaud made a short appeal. If any were more concerned for their safety or feared gallows or wheel over their soul's welfare, he advised, they had best quit now. They gave cheers for their august sponsors in England, Holland, and Germany, formed in column, and just as the dawn came on from behind the Alpine peaks to the east, the long march began.

The little force marched through a silent countryside. Only a few remarks from the earliest birds could be heard besides the tread of marching feet and the clop-clop of the hooves of the half-dozen horses on which rode the three pastors of the expedition, Captain Turrel, and a couple of the senior captains. The force seemed formidable perhaps, but an introspective marcher might already be getting over the excitement of the beginning of the Great Adventure and be thinking: Here are eight hundred lunatics proposing to cross one hundred forty miles of the roughest country in Europe, through land 100 percent Catholic, proposing to seize back from their enigmatic prince their ancestral lands now given to others. Thus they would infallibly stir up the wrath of the king of France, the most dangerous and inflexible human enemy of all.

Not that an observer wouldn't have been impressed. Individual officers wore their uniforms representing various Swiss, Dutch, or German regiments and sported gold or silver *galons** and trim with orange ribbons. The other men looked more alike. The Vaudois, in particular, were a sturdy lot: short, powerfully built, and marching under fifty-pound loads, including a musket weighing about fifteen pounds, with a sword or dagger at their belts, sacks slung across their shoulders, and pouches for powder and ball. Most wore long leather jackets over flannel shirts, short mountaineers' trousers, leggings, and heavy sandals. Everyone wore broad-brimmed hats, often turned up on one or two sides for a tricorn effect. The foreign volunteers were usually less heavily loaded. Some of the men and most of the officers wore heavy waterproofs of hide or heavy woolen capes. To the extent that Monsieur Convenant had been able to provide uniform coats, they were gray. It was an infantry army. They had no cannon. Later on, perhaps, there would be pack animals to lighten the loads for the marchers, but they would have to be requisitioned first.

Orders were that they should march in ranks through any town for the effect on morale, that no needless violence be offered any inhabitants of the country as they passed, and that anything requisitioned should be paid for in cash. Then one might hope the local population would see no point in trying to oppose their peaceful passage.

In a few minutes the advance guard approached the first hamlet, and they realized that they had been observed after all. As the most disarming procedure, Pastor Chyon went forward to request peaceful passage.

---

* Lace stripes indicating rank.

As the pastor rode up to a knot of horsemen, the local seigneur and his retainers, he was seized and hustled off at such a speed that Arnaud and Turrel dashing forward could not catch up with them. As it turned out, Pastor Chyon was not seen again for nine months.

Chagrined by this inauspicious start, the column moved on the little village of Yvoire, but so as not to repeat the previous mistake, the advance party consisted this time of officers and musketeers. The light was still dim enough for the signal beacon that suddenly burst into flame to be quite visible to surrounding villages. There was no time to waste.

The dozen in the advance party went into the village on the double and encountered the city fathers, who suspected that an imprudence had been committed. They were most conciliatory, blaming the lighting of the signal beacon on local juveniles and offering passage and provisions. After a brief discussion, the Vaudois officer agreed not to burn the town down as it deserved but took the local chatelaine and a government collector of the salt tax as hostages. Then they signaled the column to come on.

In step and in their companies, the expedition marched through Yvoire, bayonets fixed, providing a most impressive spectacle to the Catholic inhabitants. Some even were heard to cry, "God be with you!" It seemed a good start, and the leaders hoped that other Savoy community leaders would be equally prudent.

However, the alarm had been given, and the question was what His Royal Highness Duke Victor Amadeus II of Savoy could do about it. His poor but extensive and rugged realm stretched from Nice to Geneva. Three of his best infantry regiments had been virtually kidnapped by Louis XIV and were in Flanders, apparently nonreturnable. He had six feeble ones left, each under five hundred men, and, with other units, hardly five thousand trained soldiers, none of whom were in Savoy. The defense would have to rely on the militia, a turnout of all able-bodied villagers and peasants. They would be led by local gentlemen and were armed very indifferently—some with scythes and pitchforks—and certainly disinclined to run great risks. It wouldn't be difficult to sweep them aside in a battle, but in a country as rugged as Savoy, with so many impregnable positions that could be held easily against large numbers of invaders, even these reluctant warriors could check far greater invasions than that of the Vaudois if inspired by determined priests or gentlemen.

Above all, the Vaudois couldn't afford delay, for then their small numbers would be known and there would be time for regular soldiers, Savoyard or even French, to hurry in to stop them. To avoid battle would be to avoid delay, and to do that, local hostages would be helpful—that and the realization that the Vaudois would harm no one if not opposed.

Emerging on the far side of Yvoire, the advance guard was challenged by four mounted gentlemen in the road. They evidently assumed the advance party was the whole body of intruders, for they haughtily ordered them to throw down their arms and explain by what right they were trespassing on the lands of His Royal Highness. A moment too late, they discovered their error and turned to flee, but they were seized and forced to dismount. The swarm of militia watching a couple hundred yards up the road prudently melted into the trees and made no effort to rescue their chiefs. The crestfallen quartet then had to lead the column on foot.

Soon the road ascended a hill with thicket and trees on both sides, so the advance guard, for the first time, fanned out and plunged into the woods to flush out the lurking peasantry. The latter fled without resistance, dropping muskets and drums to make better speed. A few slower ones were captured and brought back to join the hostages, and the discarded arms and drums were broken. The captives, whether of high or low degree were assured that they were to be guides and intermediaries for their captors, and if there was any attempt whatever at cleverness, they would all be hanged on the nearest trees. One of the captives, now very contrite, invited his captors to stop at his chateau nearby to refresh themselves; but Pastor Arnaud declined, as time was pressing.

The senior captive was prevailed upon to write a little note to send on to avoid misunderstanding in the next villages. It said: "These gentlemen have come here to the number of two thousand. They have asked us to accompany them that we might render account of their behavior, and we are able to assure you that they are very reasonable. They pay for whatever they take and ask only to be allowed free passage. Therefore, we beg you not to ring the tocsin or beat the drums, and please withdraw your people in case you already have them under arms."

It didn't seem necessary to correct the slight arithmetical inaccuracy, and the note secured untroubled passage through the next two villages.

Food, drink, pack animals, and even wagons were forthcoming. However, along the route, occasional shots were fired from the trees, and
several skulkers were chased and caught. One, a Dominican friar, was
carrying a concealed knife. After some expressed their disposition to
hang him, he offered to be useful. He lived up to his promise, and his
tongue proved well hung. On several occasions he persuaded his com-
patriots to let the expedition pass without resistance. At nightfall, the
four gentlemen hostages were released, and the march resumed under
bright moonlight.

About midnight, they paused for refreshment at the village of Saint-
Joyre. The magistrates were waiting for them and had rolled a barrel of
wine into the road. Some of the marchers drank with gratitude. Some
refused, fearing poison. More hostages were selected, and they marched
on a little farther. As they made camp in open fields, clouds came in
over the moon and a light drizzle began. So ended their first day.

* * * * *

Sunday the twenty-eighth turned out to be a gray day with frequent
rain squalls. They were approaching Cluse, the largest town on their
route, and there was enough tension to keep their minds off the weather. Because the valley of the Arve was fairly narrow, the expedition could
not avoid the town. The marchers tramped down the pleasant valley
and past villages hastily deserted at their approach. The men helped
themselves to ripening fruit from the trees by the roadsides. The bridge
at Marni had not been tampered with, and they crossed it unopposed.

About ten in the morning, they arrived before Cluse, an attractive
little town astride the river, protected by earthworks and a ditch. On
the ramparts waited nervous townsfolk and peasants from the vicinity,
all under arms. Orders were given to the Vaudois to close up, and they
continued their march in formation to about a musket shot from the
defenses, where they halted and waited for the order to attack. Depend-
ing on the determination of the defense, this could be a costly matter,
both in time and in wounded to care for—bad business for so early in
their march.

A dozen hostages huddled dispiritedly together in the drizzle, the
plumes of the gentlemen's finery drooping in the wet. On either side of
them stood a Vaudois company, arms grounded but in rank and alert.

A Vaudois captain, his eye on the hostages, walked over to the next company. At the right and a little in front stood Armand de Gandon, a fine martial figure, resting his sword point lightly in the ground.

"Monsieur," said the Vaudois in a voice sufficiently loud to be heard by the hostages, "I think we shall be very busy if this rabble forces us to assault their walls, and it might be prudent to execute these hostages at once."

Armand replied in the same spirit, loudly and clearly. "Very good, sir! I will detail a firing party, and we will shoot them at the first sign of resistance."

There was visible emotion among the wretched captives and some urgent whispered discussion. In a moment, the oldest of the hostages approached the officers very humbly, bowed, and in a most respectful manner suggested that he knew the leading citizens of the town well, was able to affirm that the Vaudois wished injury to no one, and could write a note to the town council to that effect, to reassure them that they would have no reason for complaint if the Protestants were given free passage through the town. His proposal was accepted and writing material brought to him.

Just then, four mounted gentlemen emerged from the opening in the ramparts. A parley followed, and two of the men were detained. The other two were sent back to town with a Vaudois officer. He not only carried Monsieur de Fora's note but also made it plain to the councilmen that they trifled with the safety of their town in their hesitations and that his authorization for demanding free passage was the point of the sword. In a very short time it was agreed the Vaudois could pass provided they touched nothing and that provisions would be supplied after they had gone through. The civic militia lined the streets, arms in hand, as the Vaudois marched through in a smart and soldierly array.

Halting outside the town, they waited for the promised food. Eventually, they sent a peremptory note, which brought results in another half hour. Disturbing as was the delay, more so was the realization that the boys of the town, who had run along beside them, had kept going up the road toward Sallanches, presumably to carry a warning. The Vaudois had them pursued and brought back. Then they discovered that a local citizen who had claimed that he wished to join them had insinuated himself into the ranks. Upon being searched, he proved to be carrying a note from the Cluse commandant. Apparently, he was to dash on ahead at a propitious moment and urge the people at Sallanches to bar passage to the Vaudois while the Cluse forces closed in on their rear. In view of these tokens of bad faith, it was decided to release none of the hostages here. But Arnaud did pay five *louis d' or** for the supplies, which was overgenerous. So the parting was amicable enough, considering.

The rain continued, and the valley became narrower. The little force passed places where enemies could have rolled stones down on them. The road became a rocky track. Armed peasants watched them from beyond musket range but made no effort to interfere. Across the rain-swollen river, a horseman also was watching, so the order was given to break ranks so as to make counting the force more difficult.

To reach Sallanches, the troop had to cross a covered wooden bridge a quarter of a league† from town. The bridge was a substantial structure with houses on it. This time, without delay, the hostages, now grown to twenty gentlemen and priests, were told they would be shot if there was resistance. Firing squads formed in full view of the defenders. As they came to the bridge, six mounted men who had been observing them turned to retire. But the Vaudois, though on foot, ran up and caught one of them, whereupon the others turned around and came back to talk. They were the chiefs of the local levies, and their spokesman was Monsieur Cartan, first syndic of the town. He argued that permission to pass was too great a matter for them to decide; the town council would have to discuss the matter.

"They make us waste time for a council of war ten times a day!" sputtered Captain Turrel to the other officers. "They must be expecting more militia to be coming in from the countryside."

"True, but if we have to force the bridge, there will be loss of life and perhaps even more delay. Let us for now be good Christians and avoid shedding of blood," countered the pastor. "Give them half an hour with the understanding that we then will force our way."

Despite some grumbling, the officers agreed. The gentlemen then rode back across the bridge to town. When the time expired, two riders

---

* French gold coins; present purchasing power of perhaps two hundred dollars.
† A little less than half a mile.

ambled out again to the waiting Protestants. They explained that the time had been too short and further discussion was required.

The Vaudois officers then presented pistols to the heads of the duo and in politest terms besought them to dismount and become part of the collection of hostages. The two protested and then in desperation suggested that one of them, two Vaudois officers, and one of the other hostages be sent back to explain more clearly the danger that everyone was in. Again, some of the officers objected to this waste of valuable time, but to save the lives of their own men it seemed worthwhile enough if this time it worked. They demanded a definite answer—either Yes or No—without more equivocating.

In a few minutes the quartet disappeared inside the gates, but instead of their reappearance, the tocsin sounded and a swarm of perhaps six hundred ragtag militia streamed up to the bridge. The Vaudois who had gone into the town were evidently captives, and the answer must be taken as No.

The companies were deployed, weapons checked, and the Vaudois prepared to strike at the bridge. Two groups of the best men marched rapidly forward, the officers in front with swords drawn. Before anyone had to learn how firm the defense would be, four Capuchin monks emerged from the bridge, making peaceful gestures. The order to halt rang out. Arms were grounded, and hundreds of very suspicious eyes followed the approach of the reverend fathers.

Pastor Arnaud, in his capacity as chaplain to the forces, advanced with the officers to consult with the new arrivals. They were most conciliatory, full of flowery phrases, wishing to avoid bloodshed, *bien sûr.** If, they said, the Vaudois would release the hostages and their mounts and ground their arms, they would give them two local hostages, syndics of the town, and allow free passage. Again there was a good deal of wrangling. What purpose would be served? Was it a trap? But Arnaud carried the argument, once again talking down the military men, and the proposal was accepted. At least they would have two hostages for the good behavior of the Sallanchois.

What was Arnaud's indignation when he saw the two "syndics" being led out? They looked rather as if they had been selected from the

---

* "Most certainly."

denizens of the town jail or charity hospital. The priests, reading the faces of the Vaudois, thought it time to get out, and they ran for it. Two were caught, but the other two hitched up their robes so dexterously that they made it, sprinting, to the protection of the militia array.

The two being held, a little roughly perhaps, protested loudly about the violation of laws of nations and the arrest of mediators. They were reminded that they were a disgrace to their robes, condign liars and deceivers. Once convinced that they were indeed hostages and all was up with them if the townspeople were unwise enough to start hostilities, they became very helpful indeed. Then, and for several days after, their expostulations and assurances were most useful in getting the expedition past bridges, villages, and blockades where resistance and delay would have been most unfortunate. They had remarkable persuasive powers and evidently did not feel that martyrdom was their proper vocation. Far from wishing to be translated out of a grim and damp life in Savoy into heavenly bliss, they took good care that their spiritual charges did nothing imprudent to annoy the Vaudois.

The Vaudois formations resumed their march and crossed the bridge without resistance. Their ranks halted again at twenty paces from the defense line; no firing yet. One of the Vaudois captains told the defenders with assurance that the attack would begin in five minutes and the town would be burned if the capitulation were not rendered forthwith and without further frivolity. This worked. The two Vaudois were released, and the force marched through town at last, without any hostile gesture visible.

By nightfall they were encamped in a deserted village, soaked by the rain and without fires. However, they were not too displeased with the heavy rain as it probably dampened the ardor of any possible pursuers too.

* * * * *

The third day, all pieces were discharged and reloaded as a precaution against dampness. Then the real ascent began. Under the continuing light rain, they seemed to climb more than they marched. Except for Megéve, all the villages they passed were deserted, but the Vaudois disturbed nothing, much to the amazement of their hostages, who had never heard of any soldiers conducting themselves with such restraint.

By afternoon, however, this rigid discipline began to break down somewhat. The men found empty cabins in the high pastures where the owners had been turning milk into cheese. The marchers were hungry. They helped themselves then and thereafter to milk, cheese, or other food they found. "We would have paid," they assured each other, "if there was anyone to take the money."

They wandered some in mountain paths in an extraordinary fog, the guides ready to believe when they told them it was a cloud sent by the Lord to hide them from their enemies. They passed through gorges and under cliffs where a resolute twenty in ambush could have embarrassed twenty thousand. One of their guides, however, led them astray, and Pastor Arnaud had to counsel with him very seriously to mend his ways or they would infallibly hang him. If the hostage had been intending to lose them time until their enemies could close in on them, he failed.

Going down the slopes was harder than going up, with the sitting and sliding downhill that it required. The men were nearing exhaustion when they reached another deserted village of shepherds' cabins in a dark ravine. The rain continued all night, and they decided that their need for fire was greater than for roofs, and there being nothing else to burn, the roofs of the huts were stripped and fed into bonfires. All in all, it was a most miserable night.

Before daylight, as the men were stirring around, a rumor circulated that hundreds of Savoyards had infiltrated in the night. In the nervousness of phantasms and shadows, two men were shot, one seriously, by panicky discharges in the dark. One of the French captains disappeared before daylight with one of the few horses, obviously feeling enough was enough and this project was more than he had bargained for.

The next morning, when scrambling over the rocks in intermittent snow and rain by the light of early dawn, the men saw the rocky escarpments of fortifications built the previous year when the return of the Vaudois had been feared. To their vast relief, these sturdy little forts, with embrasures and cleared fields of fire, were not garrisoned. The duke had withdrawn his garrisons some months before, but if the militia had been hurried into them this time, the prospects of the Vaudois could have been very bad indeed had they been forced to assault these works uphill and in the open. On the spot, they knelt and gave thanks to God, who had so marvelously spared them.

Passing Mount Bonhomme and straggling down into the Isère Valley, the rear guard fell behind and caused an alarm when they signaled the main body by firing several shots in the air. Assuming that it must be an ambush, the main body rushed back to help them.

Progress through the narrow valley was impeded by the river Isère, rushing along its serpentine way, overflowing its banks and gouging out the poor little road at intervals. The little army was strung out vulnerably, singly and by twos, when they became aware that on the hillside, virtually over their heads, numerous peasants had taken positions well provided with rocks. Another moment of sheer disaster seemed to face the Vaudois, but to their great relief the watchers above did not seem disposed to bother them.

The watchers, however, continued to follow along above them. When the advance guard of the expedition reached the bridge a short distance from the village, they found it barricaded with logs, and peasants with guns and scythes guarding it. Once more, the tired band fell in and prepared to force the bridge, but the lord of the place came out very peaceably and offered them passage to avoid damage to either side. He and the local curé had the peasants remove the obstacles, and the little army passed over. They could hear the alarm bells ringing up the valley, but not a shot was fired. The gentleman withdrew hurriedly, however, not wishing to become one of the "birds in Arnaud's cage," as the hostages called themselves. The lord shut himself up in his chateau, and the Vaudois camped for the night nearby, once again buying provisions from the villagers. Arnaud paid three *sols* to the pound for bread though the usual rate was two, which made for goodwill all around.

On Wednesday, the fifth day, matters began well. At Sainte-Foy, the villagers had stayed home and were peaceable, even complimenting the marchers on their purpose. The rear guard was very civilly solicited to tarry for a while and rest. Food and fresh meat were offered. After a time Arnaud noticed that the rear guard had not kept up, and he hurried back. When he found out what was going on, he forcefully reminded his men that even the most cordial folk in these parts were not trustworthy and might well be planning to delay them to betray them later. He then added the "flatterers" to the group of hostages.

The rest of the day was spent negotiating narrow gorges and clambering over rocks. The loads were becoming heavy, and it was not only hostages whose shoes were starting to deteriorate and whose feet developed stone bruises. That night the little army camped in a meadow near Laval and built a huge fire. The altitude was now considerable, and it was very cold. Pastors Montoux and Arnaud accepted an invitation to stay with the village head and enjoyed three hours in a real bed. No one really begrudged the leaders the comfort, but some Frenchmen, like Alexandre, wondered out loud how Arnaud was sure of the good faith of their host, seeing how he had excoriated them just that morning.

Arriving in Tigne the next morning, they released most of the hostages who had not already escaped. Pastor Arnaud had some more advice for his chastened flock that morning, for the escapes displeased him, and he darkly surmised that the hostages were "corrupting" their guards. They still kept a lawyer and two priests with them as they began the ascent of the nine-thousand-foot pass over the Iseran.

Once in a while they encountered herdsmen in high pastures who prudently offered them milk and cheese along with warnings that many soldiers awaited them at Mount Cenis. This didn't unduly alarm them, for they had passed so many obstacles successfully by then that they had little doubt of God's care. Surely He had not brought them this far to destroy them. So far, the only shots had been fired at an occasional fugitive or an escaping peasant porter.

In the tiny village of Besas, unlike most they had seen thus far, the residents had stayed by but were exceedingly arrogant and defiant, perhaps assuming that the Vaudois would soon be coming to grief. Irritated by this insolence, the Vaudois made hostages of the principal men of the place, the priest, and six peasants, tying them together in a human mule train. Nearby they spent an uncomfortable night under unremitting rain.

Friday, September 2, the little army slipped and slid down steep slopes to Lanslevillard, a miserable collection of hillside huts with rocks on the roofs to keep them from blowing away. As usual, the local curé was invited to join the rest of Arnaud's "birds," but after crossing the river and starting up the grade toward the highlands of Mount Cenis Pass, it became evident that the priest was too old and too fat to make it, so he was permitted to return home.

There was a post station on the high plateau. Realizing that a place that kept horses could very swiftly spread word about their progress,

Arnaud sent a flying party on ahead to seize the animals. On their way back to the main body, they encountered a mule train and captured it too. Yielding to curiosity, they investigated the cargo and found that some of the mules were carrying the effects and papers of Cardinal Ranuzzi, the papal nuncio in France. The muleteers complained to the officers, and after some argument among the disappointed Vaudois, it was decided to let the whole train go, including the baggage—first, because they wished to avoid the impression that the Vaudois were common bandits, and second, most of the loot was the property of Genevese merchants. Some of the party grumbled that this scrupulousness was being carried much too far.

The rest of the day brought increasing trouble. When they left the highland flats with their frozen ponds, the "road" virtually ceased, and the trail was exceedingly rocky and ill-marked. To add to their troubles, a heavy fog descended. Not only did the men get separated from each other in the gloom, but there were terrifying drop-offs into bottomless chasms. The pace was telling on many of the marchers by now, and some simply sank from exhaustion, or, sitting down to rest, could not make themselves get up in time to keep up with the main body. By nightfall, scores of men were crouching miserably under rocks, waiting for their friends. There was snow on the ground too, which made things no better. Most eventually stumbled down to the lower elevation and found the campfires lit in a relatively dry patch of woods. All night long stragglers came in and dried themselves around the fires. Once again, there had been dozens of places where tiny numbers of determined defenders could have checked the expedition with heavy loss or ruined the whole enterprise.

On the next day, they would experience the dangers they had escaped thus far.

CHAPTER 4

The Very Memorable Day

Before dawn on September 3, long remembered as the "very memorable" day, with many of the stragglers of the previous day now back in the ranks, the leaders decided to attempt the descent on the side of Chaumont, avoiding Susa, the strongest Piedmont border fortress, where the Count of Verrua had at least two hundred fifty dragoons out looking for them. A small patrol preceded the advance guard and soon found that they were expected. On a height overlooking their path were numerous peasants—and, apparently, French soldiers. The latter might be from the garrison of the little fortress of Exilles, for the Vaudois now were going to have to cross a finger of French territory that stuck forty miles into Piedmont to connect France with the fortress town of Pignerol. This finger was the valley of the Pragelas and the Cluson, formerly a stronghold of the Vaudois but in the past few years "converted" to Catholicism. And now, it was not a matter of just bluffing the ill-armed militia of Savoy but of confronting the French army. By turning up the Jaillon and cutting across west of Exilles, it had been their hope that they could avoid this.

Their opponents, whether French or Savoyard, had innumerable rocks to roll down on them, and the little valley was very narrow—sometimes with room for only a footpath—and the Jaillon Brook rushed down its rocky bed. The place could become a death trap if the expedition let itself be caught in those confines. However, thus far, boldness had paid.

The advance guard, a hundred strong, marched firmly forward to within fifty paces of the watching enemy and then halted. Captain Paul Pelenc led a little party forward—several soldiers and two of their priestly hostages—to negotiate for passage as they had often done before. Something went wrong this time. The two priests suddenly bolted into the enemy line, crying for the French to seize Pelenc and his men. Before the helpless gaze of the waiting advance guard, the Vaudois were seized, thrown to the ground, and tied. Their comrades couldn't fire without risking hitting the prisoners, so the tables were abruptly turned.

Then, with incredible strength born of desperation, one of the captives broke his bonds, leaped the rocks that served the enemy as their natural parapet, and flung himself down the slope to the advance guard. The enemy instantly opened fire and began to hurl rocks and a few grenades on the Vaudois down the slope. There was nothing to do but run for it, dodging rolling rocks and ricocheting bullets. By the edge of the creek were many huge outcroppings of rock, and the Vaudois hid behind them until they could decide what to do next.

Fortunately, the enemy fusillade was more impressive in volume than accuracy, and, after a few moments, Armand and the other officers spotted a growth of chestnut trees farther along the streambed and enough rocks sticking out of the boiling torrent to offer at least a little protection from the enemy above while they crossed to the other side. By hand signals, the officers directed their men to crawl up to the trees and then wade or skip on the rocks across the rushing stream. One Vaudois officer was missing. It turned out that he had been shot by mistake by one of his own men because he was wearing the coat of an enemy dragoon. There was no doubt that by now he had been captured, since his men couldn't bring him off over the creek.

After making certain they weren't followed, what remained of the advance guard made their way back to the main body crestfallen and with the very strong opinion that the route up the streambed wasn't for them. So, there was no help for it but to bypass the opposing force by scaling the mountainside, clinging to the rock face, crawling along ledges with long drops to the rocks below that so frightened the remaining hostages that some begged to be shot rather than be forced to scramble around such hazards. It was impossible to stay together and, once again, whole companies strayed in the mist and fog. Some individual soldiers, Huguenot and Vaudois, realizing they were utterly lost, crouched, terrified, waiting to be found. Some were lucky and eventually were found by friends; others less fortunate wound up in Savoy or French prisons or were killed trying to get away. It was a costly morning for the little army. Both the surgeons of the expedition were lost this way, and so were two of the Vaudois captains. (They didn't see their friends again until released from prison nine months later.) About two hundred men disappeared, half of them for good, and, of course, the entire supply train and its animals were lost, as well as several hostages.

Coming to a sort of plateau on the top, the leaders held an anxious consultation and, though delay was dangerous, called a two-hour halt to enable as many as possible to straggle in. Visibility was extremely poor in the swirling mists, so the trumpeters blew their calls several times to give their wandering comrades direction.

At last, the order had to be given to resume the climb. It was a heart-breaking moment, as many were hoping against hope their comrades would yet appear. One Vaudois of the village of Rodoret, wounded and almost insensible, obviously couldn't be moved. His friends, with tears rolling down their cheeks, left him some rations and water and had to turn away to go with the army. Two of the hostages broke and ran in the confusion, and it was thought that one, a priest, was killed by the shots fired after him.

Hardly had the main body reached the top of the mountain, which was relatively level, when they heard the sound of marching feet and the beating of a drum. They hastily formed a battle line, and in a few moments they perceived figures dimly through the mist. It was the force that had given them the unpleasant reception previously in the ravine. The enemy sensed their waiting presence or saw them and stopped out of musket range. In a few minutes a soldier was seen with a white flag, picking his way over the rocks toward them.

The enemy commander, the governor of the fort at Exilles, wrote that he had no intention of barring the passage of the Vaudois as long as they would kindly keep above and beyond his fort. He would even sell them supplies. If, however, it was their intention to force passage on the highroad and go by his post, he requested eight hours in which to consider the matter.

While no one put great faith in the word of this French officer, still it sounded as though he didn't feel obliged to resist their transit through the territory of Louis XIV as long as they didn't beard him directly and would pass on speedily into Savoy territory again. His proposition was accepted, and the Vaudois continued on the heights until they were well past Exilles and then began to descend down out of the mist toward the valley floor. It was getting dark now, and they suspected that they were followed by these same troops. Were they making certain the Vaudois continued in the direction they had been going, or were they hoping to surprise them at a disadvantage if they ran into enemies up ahead? Word was sent back asking with some asperity what they were up to, and the officer apologized and precipitately fell back. Not overly confident, the Vaudois pushed on.

They were now descending the slopes down into the valley of the Doire. It flowed rapidly through meadows. The flat land was in some places fairly narrow; in others, several miles wide. The southern slopes led up to the valleys toward which the march was directed. The only practical crossing of the river for miles in either direction was a wooden bridge at the village of Sallebertrand. The question was, would this bridge be defended, and if so, how firmly?

Soon it was dusk, and the column descended with frequent halts to be certain that all kept together. About a league* from the village, they encountered a peasant and asked if they could buy food at Sallebertrand. "Go ahead," he replied with a visible sneer. "They'll give you all you want and are preparing a fine supper for you!"

At a nearby hamlet neighbors did provide some food on demand, but a few moments later, just as the advance guard came over an outcropping and saw in the valley below them the lights of no less than thirty-six campfires, they stumbled into an ambush. Several volleys were exchanged, and the foe fell back downhill toward the village, now a half league away. None of the advance guard was seriously hurt, but as they picked their cautious way forward, they discovered five enemy bodies.

---

* About three miles.

* * * * *

In little clumps, the groups of the Vaudois force lay or sat among the rocks on the northern slope of the Doire Valley. It was dark—the stars didn't give much light, and the moon hadn't risen yet. The range opposite could just be discerned as a black mass in contrast to a not quite so black sky. They couldn't see the river rushing through the valley flatland nor the scruffy little village of Sallebertrand immediately beneath them. It's only importance was the bridge, and the tired men on the slope couldn't see that either. What they could see were the enemy campfires, presumably on the far side of the stream. Various guesses of how many men to a campfire led to estimates of the number of the waiting enemy at anywhere between a thousand and three thousand. The Vaudois knew they were being followed and that only by cutting their way through the forces below could they progress farther toward their goal—the valleys of home.

The captains came together around a tiny fire beside a huge rock. They were studying maps and arguing. It hadn't been a good day. Many men were still missing. No one suggested going back, but some did strongly feel that they should try nothing further until daylight. All were tired, and some tempers were a little short.

"Even trained troops have difficulty in night attacks, and our men are not trained," said Captain Turrel. "There must be at least two thousand men down there, and we know we're being followed. We'll be taken front and rear and cut to pieces in the dark."

It was true that the Vaudois, while brave, hardy, and strongly motivated, were indeed not seasoned troops.

The group of captains was a little smaller than before. Two of the Vaudois were missing and one captured. One of the French captains had deserted; Gandon and Huc were filling in for him. In general, the Vaudois captains were for boldness, and Huc and Gandon agreed with them. The pastor allowed the soldiers to argue for a time.

"According to the peasants we've talked to, the French are mostly militia and that means they are no more experienced than we are and probably a lot less courageous. Remember that so far, they're all infantry, like us. We simply can't wait until dragoons join them. And if we try to fight them in daylight, they'll see how few we really are. I say we must try it tonight," insisted Armand.

The argument became general. There were Savoy dragoons known to be in the neighborhood of Susa, and they must be hurrying up the valley to aid the French. Armand pressed on. "The French know as well as we do that if we don't cross the river, come daylight the troops following us will flush us down into the lowlands, and we'll be cut to pieces. We can't wait no matter if it is dark. The Savoy troops have acted peculiarly ever since this expedition started; maybe they have orders not to actually attack us outright. Indeed, if we wait, whether the Savoy dragoons show up or not, the French will have some here from either Briançon or Pignerol within a day."

Pastor Arnaud said that he trusted that the Lord would darken the understanding of both the general at Susa and whoever was commanding in the camp down below them. This encouraged the bolder spirits, and they finally talked down the timid ones. Armand and François Huc supported the Vaudois majority. This annoyed the other French captains, friends of Turrel. Armand de Gandon finally said, "Brethren, we would never have attempted this march had we not known that French troops in the Alps were few and the resolution of the Savoyards uncertain. We'll never have fewer French troops to face than tonight, and while I agree that night battles are difficult and unpredictable, let us remember the cause for which we fight. Our men have loved ones to avenge and homes to regain; our opponents are militia who are not happy to be here and would rather be home for the harvest. Even if they have good officers and some are regulars, the advantage is ours if we act now!"

Pastor Arnaud forthwith overruled Turrel and proceeded as if he didn't notice the captain's exasperation. Victory was theirs if they would move in faith. He spoke briefly of Gideon and of Jonathan and his armor bearer and quoted Psalm 33:16: "There is no king saved by the multitude of an host." The meeting of the captains broke up, and they went to rouse their men.

Except for the pickets, the little army gathered around the pastor, and he offered prayer and made a short exhortation. Then the companies began to pick their way down the rough slopes, keeping in touch by calling back and forth in low voices.

As the ground began to level off, several reliable companies were sent in loose order on either side of the village, and the bulk of the force massed in tighter formation in the center for the main attack should Sallebertrand be defended. It was too dark to tell if it really was deserted.

The skirmishers soon found the French outposts and rousted them out of the fields on either side of Sallebertrand with much firing and yelling in the gloom. The main force proceeded at a quick step on the village. Armand, at the head of his company, noted with satisfaction that the men were taking all this calmly, and, as far as he could tell from the occasional flashes, were coming on behind him in fair order, considering the roughness of the ground. He drew his sword and, for a few moments at least, was leading a regular attack in a proper fashion. The French in the village, shaken by the din on either side, pulled back hastily in some disorder. The Vaudois, their lines breaking as they reached the dark and deserted houses, poured through the village and joined up with their skirmishers, finally coming to a halt as they reached the bank of the river Doire.

There was some confusion as the French retreated across the bridge. Some were hit by bullets from their own side fired at random in the dark. The French camp was fully roused, and the men were running to the stream bank on their side.

The guards at the bridgehead, not certain whether all their comrades were across yet, kept shouting "Who goes there?" at the unseen noise-makers. The Vaudois promptly shouted, "Friends!"—meaning that they intended no one any harm if they were not opposed—and during a momentary lull, it was possible to hear the rushing stream below, the pounding feet, and the clanking, slapping equipment on running men.

The pause was brief, but the Vaudois leaders had time to make some swift decisions. No one in his right mind would attempt to ford the stream in the dark, icy from Alpine melt and lined with enemy troops on the opposing bank. The problem was purely and simply the bridge. Why had the French not broken it down? Had they not expected the Vaudois to be so bold? Or had they expected the Savoyards to keep the intruders better entertained? Men would have to mass for a sufficient shock effect to dislodge the defenders, and before they could get across it, they would be under French fire. The Vaudois facing them could be firing in their turn, trying to minimize the French defense, but everyone would be in the dark firing at point-blank range. The darkness would probably be a help to the Vaudois, whose meager numbers wouldn't be detected and who had the advantage of the initiative, but there was the danger that in the darkness and confusion the attackers would lose control of their men, and either side could be stampeded by some unexpected turn of events. In any case, if brave and self-sacrificing assault troops cleared the bridge, would enough of them still be on their feet if the enemy launched a counterattack?

Hastily assembling the assault force near the bridge, the rest of the little army stood by the stream. Occasional flashes of musketry showed the French likewise along the stream facing them. By almost instinctive reaction, the Vaudois officers yelled to the men to lie down. The tension was almost unendurable. As the Vaudois flung themselves to the hard ground, they could hear voices across the stream screaming, "Kill! Kill!" Either spontaneously or on someone's order, the French line cut loose with a tremendous fusillade, somewhere around two thousand men loading and firing as fast and frantically as they could in the dark. Afterwards, experienced soldiers on the Protestant side said they had never seen the like and with so little effect—undisciplined men out of any control simply blazing away, the men on the opposite bank lying on their faces, unhurt by the leaden storm flying overhead. After a quarter of an hour of this waste of powder and ball, the fusillade slackened, and the officers began to regain control.

It was the right psychological moment.

"Up and at them!" bellowed the Vaudois officers, scrambling to their feet. Those near the bridge rushed forward. Only then did they begin to take casualties.

"Come on! The bridge is ours!" yelled someone prematurely, and the Vaudois poured across the structure, furiously assailing the defenders with bayonet and saber. The impetus of the rush, the feeling that they were being overrun by hordes of savages out of the night, shook the defenders. The *"fureur inconceivable"* of the Vaudois was widely feared by both French and Piedmontese soldiery. Resistance at the far end of the bridge was stubborn for only a few minutes; then it broke. By the hundreds the French militia began to think with their feet. They ran in what the French call a "terror panic." The remaining defenders at the bridge then broke too. In spite of anything their frantic officers could do, the defending forces dissolved into a frightened mob. In another fifteen minutes the Vaudois had poured across the bridge, spread out, and were shooting and stabbing anything that moved. The entire French camp was overrun.

A counterattack at this moment still would have been ruinous for the Vaudois, completely disorganized in victory and pursuit, but this was never a real possibility. The enemy survivors were in full flight or captured. Some would hardly stop until they had climbed the pass of Mont Genévre and were behind the walls of Briançon. The enemy commander, the Count de Larrey, was carried there badly wounded. The Vaudois heard later that Larrey, a ferocious persecutor of the Protestants, later blamed the Savoy commander at Susa for misleading information about the numbers of the "heretics" and thus subjected him to his unspeakable humiliation.

While all this was going on, Pastor Arnaud, Captain Mondon, and two Huguenot volunteers held off two companies of the troops following in the rear of the Vaudois and effectively discouraging them from interfering in the proceedings. One of their hostages was killed by a stray bullet, thirty-three fled into the night, and they found only six remaining when the battle was over.

The moon rose on the victors sorting through the impedimenta of the French camp. They took all the food, arms, and ammunition they could, but it would have to travel on their backs, so this wasn't much. They piled the remainder—baggage, tents, ammunition chests—in huge mounds and set them afire. The gunpowder ignited, and there was a spectacular explosion, a thunderous reverberating roar rolling down the valley, followed by numerous lesser explosions. It was a most satisfying moment. "They'll hear that all the way to France!" the Vaudois told each other gleefully.

Trumpets were blown. The soldiers threw their hats in the air and cried together, "Glory to the Lord of hosts, who has given us the victory over our enemies!"

They buried their fifteen dead, cared for the ten or twelve seriously wounded, and disposed of about two hundred enemy prisoners with the nonchalance of the seventeenth century, not common again until the twentieth. Then began the climb up the eastern slope of the valley.

The moon was now shining with exceptional brightness, and the whole valley and the scene of their stupendous triumph was clearly visible.

Then reaction began to set in. They were desperately tired, almost climbing in their sleep. Some had not slept during forty-eight hours of tremendous exertions and very little food. Dozens of exhausted men simply sat down or lay down for a rest and could hardly be roused. The officers tried to search the hillside and find the sleepers, rousing them by ungentle kicks and shakes. Even with the bright moonlight, however, not everyone was found, and some simply sank back again to the earth when the officer passed on.

Reaching the crest of the ridge and comparative safety, they dropped where they stood. Some of the tired and the wounded who didn't keep up in the final climb that night eventually rejoined their comrades. About eighty were not so fortunate. Enemy patrols hurrying up from three directions in the next two days found some of these fugitives in the foothills, and some were being held by villagers, who turned them in. Even so, the toll was smaller than the six hundred dead suffered by the French at Sallebertrand.

* * * * *

At dawn on the slopes of Mount Sci, the expeditionaries roused themselves for a thanksgiving sermon and prayer led by Pastor Arnaud. Through the morning mists they could now see the final mountain barrier between them and their home valleys. Once again they shouldered their packs, heavy with new booty, and descended into the French valley of the Pragelas. Once across the Cluson, which flowed down toward the enemy fortress of Pignerol, they would climb again up the other side, back into the lands of the duke of Savoy and, surely by the following day, would reach the first of their home valleys.

Exhilarated by these hopes, they were surprised and hurt by the coldness of the villagers living along the Cluson—those who stayed to see them pass. These were their own people, normally very hospitable. Just four years earlier, before the French army briskly and brutally converted them, they had shared the same faith. No mass was said in the Pragelas Valley that Sunday morning; all the priests had fled down the valley to the garrison towns. But they had left most convincing and horrible threats—if their sullen new converts gave any aid and comfort to the heretic "Barbets," their houses would be burned over their heads. And the villagers, having seen for themselves the peculiar efficiency of the altar-and-sword combination in their recent conversion experience, were taking no chances. About a dozen young men sneaked off to join the Vaudois as they passed, but everyone else watched with apparent fear or loathing as the little army trooped past village after village. This was the force's first intimation that everything was not necessarily going to be as happy as they had anticipated.

At dawn the next morning, across from Sestrière, they encountered their first Savoy regular troops. The Vaudois formed up quickly in two bodies and advanced at the double, a third formation in reserve. But the enemy Savoyards only rolled a few ineffectual rocks toward them and scattered without a fight, leaving baggage and supplies. Soon afterward came rain, which never seemed to stop completely. Time was crucial, for the militia was undoubtedly out by now, and the Vaudois had to get into their valleys fast, before the enemy could establish themselves in the strong points of the valleys.

That night they crossed by the Col du Pis into the valley of Saint-Martin by the light of guttering torches over a villainous excuse for a trail so rugged that if the militia had got there before them, it would have been difficult to force a passage. They had the usual problems of trying to keep the remaining hostages secure. Tuesday morning they came down into the first of their own valleys and found the village of Balsille deserted.* They camped there to get a little rest and dry out. Dining on bread and mutton, they were interrupted by the arrival of forty-six militiamen from the Catholic village of Cavour, who, mistaking them for levies of the duke, walked into the camp waving friendly handkerchiefs. These were the ones who were to have defended the Col du Pis. Before they realized their mistake, they were Vaudois prisoners.

At the beginning of the expedition Arnaud had been anxious to avoid violence to anyone, not only to save time and danger for the

---

* The mileage of the march from Yvoire to Balsille day by day was: first day, 23.5 miles; second day, 10.0 miles; third day, 17.0 miles; fourth day, 12.0 miles; fifth day, 12.5 miles; sixth day, 14.0 miles; seventh day, 15.0 miles; eighth day, 11.5 miles; ninth day, 6.0 miles; tenth and eleventh days, 7.0 miles; total, 128.5 miles.

expedition but also to avoid the shedding of unnecessary blood. The arrival of these unfortunates forced the Vaudois to have a council of war then and there in the meadow to consider their policy for the future. Offsetting the natural repugnance of Christian men at taking the lives of their fellows were some very real considerations—"politics" as the pastor called them. First, the Vaudois were few now, scarcely seven hundred, and it was important to keep the enemy guessing as to their actual numbers. Second, they didn't have the manpower to guard captives, nor would the kind of war of movement their numbers forced them into permit establishing camps for prisoners. True, the Piedmontese militia was not much of a fighting force, but the surrounding villages were hostile, the new settlers on the Vaudois lands, whether Piedmontese or Irish, were hostile also, and it would be expecting angelic behavior in the extreme if some of the Vaudois didn't remember the cruel and enthusiastic cooperation of these neighboring villagers in the ghastly campaign of extermination of 1686. After long debate it was finally agreed that there was no help for it, and so the miserable and frightened captives were invited to say their prayers and then taken two by two to the Balsille bridge, killed, and their bodies thrown into the Germanasque River.

The exodus of interlopers from the lands that had been confiscated from the exiled Vaudois began even before word of these proceedings was noised abroad. Any whose greed or imprudence led them to tarry till the arrival of the returning owners paid for it with their lives, regardless of sex. Pastor Arnaud urged his men to be careful when dealing with the valley inhabitants that they not unwittingly harm their own backslidden brethren or secret sympathizers, but in the swift and violent kind of guerilla warfare that now developed in the Vaudois valleys, it wasn't always possible to take precautions, and for a time at least, whether interloper or old inhabitant, most fled to the towns or tried to keep out of sight in the woods until it would be clear what was happening. Wednesday saw the Vaudois at last in their home valley of the Lucerna. They burned a Catholic chapel and at Prals were delighted to find one of their own still standing. All the Roman images and decorations were stripped from it, thrown out the windows, and consigned to a bonfire. It was then rededicated to the Lord's service—Pastor Arnaud standing on a bench in the doorway and preaching to the assembly on Psalm 124:8: "Our help is in the name of the LORD." Then they sang Psalm 129 as thanksgiving for the salvation of Israel from their enemies.

Arnaud was having problems now in keeping his little army together. Now that they were home, some simple souls whose one great purpose in life had been to return there, wished to go and take possession. Arnaud and the captains had to argue vigorously that if they scattered to their villages, they would be destroyed by the ever-increasing swarms of militia being brought in. That same day an officer of the ducal guards was captured, and, with some persuasion, he informed them that two hundred men of his unit were camped in Col de Julien, having just arrived from Nîce. For the time being, there was nothing the Vaudois could do but stay together and keep up the fight until it was clear that their enemies would leave them alone. The nearness of this detachment of what were supposed to be Victor Amadeus's best troops won the day for the pastor and his supporters, and still grumbling and not all entirely convinced, they moved hastily to meet this new threat.

Forming their usual three divisions, the Vaudois hastily scaled the heights. The fog was descending, as so often happened in the late afternoon, and a drizzle began. Hearing their approach, the enemy drew back, unnerved because they couldn't see them but knew they must be out there somewhere. Possibly more to encourage themselves than to terrify the heretics, the Savoyards kept up shouts and threats: "Come on, come on, Barbet devils! We have all the strong points, and there are three thousand of us!" and much more. The Vaudois attack force crept forward to within a few yards of the enemy outposts and then lay down on the ground to prevent any premature contact. Selected scouts sneaked forward in the deepening gloom until they had located an unsuspecting sentry. Then on a signal, an advance man killed the sentry, and, without a word, the Vaudois force fired, leaped to its feet, and threw itself on the enemy. It was over in less than a half hour. The guardsmen panicked and ran in the confused melee, leaving all their equipment behind. In the pursuit, about a dozen were captured and dispatched. One of the victors, Josue Mandan, was shot in the stomach. He died the next morning and was buried under a rock.

The next day they attacked Bobi, the second-largest town, which was full of fugitives, and the whole aggregation of fugitives, soldiers, and civilians fled over the bridge out of town. Because some were insubordinate and disgruntled, no pursuit was launched, and many of the Vaudois amused themselves by pillaging the town. Some firm measures were obviously needed or the little army could well disintegrate before its task was done. Those who wished to pursue the foe were irritated at the looters, and the looters had their justifications and took the criticism unkindly. At this juncture, to their general surprise, about twenty of the Huguenot refugees deserted, discouraged at what seemed an endless prospect ahead.

The next morning was Sunday, September 11, and as the enemy apparently had taken enough for the moment, it seemed an opportune time to draw aside and straighten matters out. A saintly and respected Vaudois, Monsieur Montoux, stood on a door laid on two large stones in a meadow near Bobi and preached an eloquent appeal to the army. He took his text from Luke 16, that the kingdom of God should be preached.

Pastor Arnaud then stood up and read to the assembly a comprehensive pledge he had prepared:

> God who by His divine grace has led us back to the inheritance of our fathers, to reestablish the pure worship of our holy religion, in continuing and achieving the great enterprise that our great Lord of hosts has thus far so divinely led in our favor: we, pastors, captains, and other officers, swear and promise in the presence of the living God and on the damnation of our souls to observe among us union and order and not to separate or disunite so long as God shall preserve our lives, and, even if we should be so unfortunate as to be reduced to three or four, never to parlay or negotiate with the enemy, be it France or Piedmont, without the participation of the whole Council of War, and to turn in all the booty we have taken and will take to serve the needs of our people and for extraordinary expenses. And we, soldiers, promise and swear today before God to be obedient to the orders of all our officers and to swear to them with all our heart fidelity to the last drop of our blood to remit prisoners and booty to them to dispose of as they find appropriate.

Further, it is forbidden under the severe penalties for officers and soldiers to search any dead, wounded, or prisoners during and after combats except those who are commissioned to do so. It is enjoined on the officers to take care that all the soldiers keep up their arms and munitions, and above all, to chastise severely those who swear and blaspheme the holy name of God, and finally, that union, which is the soul of our enterprise, remain always unshakable, the officers swearing fidelity to the soldiers and the soldiers to the officers, promising above all to our Lord and Savior Jesus Christ, to tear, as far as possible, the rest of our brethren from cruel Babylon, to establish and maintain His kingdom until death and to observe this present regulation in good faith all our lives.

All then raised their hands and solemnly swore to keep the oath read to them.

In the vexatious matter of booty and to prevent unbrotherly contention in the future, a list was made of the previous day's loot. Four treasurers and secretaries were appointed to keep matters straight and distribution fair. A major and an aide-major were elected, and it was agreed that men could, with good reason, change companies.

Most everyone seemed to be in better humor after these proceedings, though a little sheepish. The force rested that night with renewed determination to accomplish their purpose—in witness whereof a party went over to Bobi and took down the bell from the tower and hid it under some rocks. The internal danger had passed, and they were an army once more.

CHAPTER 5

The Long, Hard Winter

The next day dawned unusually clear and bright. The little army came down the slopes into the Lucerne Valley along the banks of the Subiasque. At Pianta, after prayer in a meadow, the force split. The main body marched along the high road, while a smaller group moved off over a spur toward Rospard Creek with the wounded and the mule train. This group blundered into some enemy forces and only with the greatest difficulty reached safety in the hills.

Hearing the distant firing, the main body of several hundred Vaudois increased their pace and soon encountered the Piedmontese drawn up along the road in front of Villar. Once again the direct approach paid. The Vaudois broke into a run and went yelling for the enemy outposts. The opposition, hardly more than their own number, abandoned the bridge and bolted. Some headed to the safety of the highlands of Val Guichard across the river, while several score others ran back into Villar, taking refuge in the convent, the strongest stone structure. From its windows and tower they fired continuously but wildly at the oncoming heretics.

While their men returned the enemy fire as best they could, a short but heated exchange took place between Turrel and several other officers. Turrel didn't fancy being tied down in one place long enough for the enemy to find them, and he also felt that to try to storm the convent would be too costly. Pastor Arnaud, more the chieftan and less the chaplain all the time, accepted the last point but resisted the first. Backed as usual by the Vaudois captains, he announced that they would stay in the village and besiege the defenders of the convent. It would be, he insisted, a great and exemplary success. Turrel stalked off in a fury, but Arnaud seemed not to notice and ordered his men to proceed with the attack.

Part of the Vaudois force was stationed at the edge of town to cover the bridge and oppose any efforts to relieve the defenders. Others set some of the houses ablaze to clear a field of fire. But in order to surround the defenders completely, the army had to get closer to the convent. "They wouldn't dare to try a sortie," said Arnaud, "if we could get a few men—just a half dozen—in those houses next to the convent."

The musket balls whistling down the narrow streets made this seem a suicidal proposition. The sight of wine barrels stacked outside the inn suggested a solution, and orders were given to bring every barrel or keg that could be found in the cellars nearby. "Keep close to the barrels. We'll cover you—just keep moving!"

Slinging his musket on his back, Alexandre grasped an empty keg and began to roll it along the rutted dirt street as close to the wall as he could. Musket balls ricocheted off the stone walls, and one struck the barrel with a convincing thump. Alexandre prayed rather incoherently, but it was worse to stand still than to keep moving. Behind him two other barrels began to move too, and he caught a glimpse of a grizzled Vaudois and one of the Swiss volunteers, Monsieur Turin, coming along at his pace. After a few moments, his heart began to settle back where it belonged as he realized the enemy couldn't see him well in all the smoke from the musketry and burning houses, and that aimed fire was hardly possible over fifty yards anyway.

Now the enemy spotted the moving barrels. No doubt there were others working down the other street toward the convent, but there seemed an awful lot of balls flying on Alexandre's side of this alley. He heard a cry behind him, and a quick glance showed Turin lying full length in the dust, his head bloody. He hadn't kept close enough to his barrel. Another Vaudois streaked down the alley and threw himself behind Turin's barrel, sliding in a cloud of dust, and the barrel began to move again past Turin's body.

After what seemed a very long time but was probably only a minute, Alexandre reached the house nearest the convent across the little piazza.

He jumped into the doorway, which wasn't visible from the enemy side, and stood there listening to his heart pound. In a moment, the two Vaudois joined him. They kicked the door open and entered the house, cautiously giving it a rapid search. The inhabitants had gone, and the three had it to themselves. Finding a pick and an iron bar, they began chipping at the wall facing the convent to make loopholes. After an hour's hard work, the three had small, irregular loopholes overlooking the square and the convent. Using these was much healthier than trying to shoot from the large windows. Now, the older of the two Vaudois took charge.

"One of us must keep watch at all times," he said. "And no shooting unless you have a real target—we haven't all the ammunition in the world, you know." He peered through a hole. "They're making loopholes too," he said after a moment. "Unless one of them stands in front of a window, don't waste powder."

For several hours there was nothing to do but watch. Firing ceased for long stretches, but then some real or imaginary target would present itself and there would be a flurry of shots. The enemy was now very circumspect too, and there was less activity at the convent windows. The Vaudois ate their scanty provisions. In midafternoon they were visited by a messenger who told them prisoners said the besieged had neither food nor water and so it was hoped that they would soon have to surrender. As they were not too far from the bridge and the vineyards on the other side of the creek, it was important to stop any attempt to break out. So far, one enemy attempt to bring supplies in had been stopped half a mile down the road, and the mules with provisions had been captured.

Late in the afternoon the besieged, evidently feeling they couldn't hold out any longer, burst from the front doors of the convent and began running wildly across the square. Firing as fast as they could, the waiting Vaudois blazed into the exposed group from the neighboring houses. Perhaps their victims had not realized how many musketeers were in position all about them, and, wavering visibly under the shock of the discharge, they turned and ran back for the door. Not all made it. Their commander was down, riddled at the first volley. Two of his men grabbed his body by the heels and dragged him inside, but his plumed hat, sword, and wig lay in the dirt along with half a dozen bodies. The whole business hadn't taken two minutes, and, except for the cries of some wounded inside the convent, all was quiet again.

Just before dawn, shots from the outposts above the highway signaled the approach of another enemy relief column. As if this was what they were waiting for, the defenders of the convent burst forth again and this time didn't let the bullets of the Vaudois stop them. The light was bad, and it was hard to hit fleeing, indistinct figures scattering in several directions. Some ran into the waiting Vaudois at the end of the street, but most made it into the nearby vineyards and patches of woods beyond. The Vaudois didn't have long to regret the escape. A considerable battle developed at the bridge over the Rospard, and then, shortly afterward, it became unpleasantly obvious that a second enemy force was entering the town from the south. The Vaudois at the bridge, having given a good account of themselves, then retreated down the road to Bobi, the way they had come the day before, but in the village itself, posted in the various houses, eighty or so found themselves cut off from the main body by the soldiers of the Marquis de Parelle.

Alexandre and his two companions suddenly realized that it was they who were now going to be besieged. It was time to get out. Pausing at the door, they glimpsed mounted men, Piedmontese regular troops, pouring into the settlement.

Alexandre and the older Vaudois together broke from the door and ran at top speed down the street and out into the vineyards, but this time northward. The third man hesitated in fright and then began to run. He was too late, was seen, and was shot down. The other two dared not stop until they reached trees and gullies and started to climb out of the valley floor. Then they stopped to get their breath.

The Vaudois puffed and blew. "I don't know where the enemy may be, but we ought to get up high to be safer. Then we can work our way back toward Bobi, maybe tonight." From the cries and shots, it appeared that the new arrivals were hunting for Vaudois stragglers. Taking a line from the newly risen sun, Alexandre and his friend began a rapid but furtive climb up the rocky slopes, trying to keep bushes or outcroppings between them and anyone who might be behind them.

In a few minutes they came on a trail. Seeing no one around, they used it to make more rapid progress. As they jogged up toward a narrowing of the ravine, they realized that a party of a dozen men was ahead of them. Their miscellaneous equipment and general aspect suggested that they were probably peasant militia from the Catholic villages brought along to back up the regular troops. Alexandre and his companion turned to flee back the way they had come, but then they saw three men of more soldierly attire coming out from between the olive trees, muskets leveled at them. Trapped, they prudently stood still.

"Who are you?" demanded the sergeant, mopping his florid face with his sleeve. "Where are you from?" He spoke in Italian.

"I am from Torre," replied the Vaudois sullenly, but Alexandre obviously didn't understand. The sergeant noted this. "You're a Huguenot," he said in bad French. Alexandre's start of comprehension didn't escape him. "So," he said triumphantly to his companions in Italian, "we have here a subject of the king!"

"What difference? They're both heretics!" exclaimed several of the peasants angrily. "They were trying to get away. Let's hang them right now!" Hatred fairly radiated from them.

"Just one moment—I'm in command here!" bellowed the sergeant. "If the young one is a deserter, the French may pay us for delivering him so they can hang him. Are you a deserter, you loathsome lump?" he asked, turning to Alexandre and switching back to French.

Alexandre didn't answer, and several of the peasants started to kick and strike him. Others clustered around the seated sergeant and argued shrilly with him: "It's too much trouble. Hang him *now!*" Only a gray-haired farmer with a pitchfork and a soldier leaning on his musket were very close to the prisoners. The Vaudois muttered out of the side of his mouth without looking at Alexandre, "When I say 'Now!' run downhill and I'll go up. Meet me at the creek."

The sergeant was having the better of the argument until one peasant asked furiously who would get the reward for the French prisoner—the sergeant? What about their share? Suddenly, the Vaudois yelled "Now!" and made a sweeping grab at the musket the soldier was leaning upon, whisking it out of his grasp. As Alexandre leaped away, the grizzled peasant stabbed wildly at the Vaudois but missed and sank the tines of his pitchfork into the calf of another peasant instead. A couple shots were fired. The injured peasant was screaming. The would-be captors collided with each other, yelling and cursing. Meanwhile Alexandre bounded over several rocks and ran as he had never run before. He presumed that his companion was doing likewise but didn't try to see. Finally, the sergeant and his force started out after their prisoners, but the two fugitives had vanished among the underbrush and rocks. Disheartened, the pursuers soon quit and straggled back for more recriminations.

After a while Alexandre heard no more sounds of pursuit. He slowed down and threw himself under some bushes to get his breath. An hour or so later, picking his way carefully from tree to tree along the stream and avoiding the open, he glimpsed a furtive figure—his friend.

The two moved warily uphill toward the heights of Vendellin and about noon encountered Pastor Arnaud himself with six other fugitives. They told of similar hair-raising experiences, and Arnaud said they had halted three times for urgent prayer. Arnaud, optimistic as ever, dismissed the unfortunate outcome of the Villar affair quite casually. By nightfall, about seventy-five of their group had turned up on the heights. It seemed likely that all but a half dozen of those cut off in Villar had made their escape. Under cover of night, tired as they were and with several lightly wounded, they marched toward Angrogna, where they could shelter more securely until they could determine how to link up with the main body.

* * * * *

The next two months were hectic. If the Vaudois couldn't possess their lands in peace, they made certain no one else could either, and with their flying camps and foraging parties always on the lookout for food, they gave the enemy little rest night or day. While most of the action was in their own valleys, they at times ranged over into the French valley of the Guil. This was a legitimate response to the arrival of French troops, who poured into the valleys in mid-September to exterminate the group of returnees nicknamed the "Barbets."

The desolation increased daily. Every village was burned and reburned, and crops and livestock were carried off—reciprocal courtesies at first. The Vaudois kept to the heights, falling on enemy convoys, surprising outposts. They carried on such a thorough search for food that it was said that if the peasants baked bread, it would be carried off that same day by the Barbets. The local peasants, Catholic or ex-Protestant, who tried to carry on, suffered from both sides, for the French destroyed anything they thought might be of use to the Barbets, and the Vaudois were very short with the peasants whose knowledge of the land was helpful to the enemy or who incurred scores that needed settling. Neither Piedmontese militia nor Vaudois wore uniforms. The Barbets put straw in their hatbrims as insignia, but sometimes they removed it and hostile peasants mistook them for friendly forces, usually the last mistake they would make. The Vaudois nursed special bitterness for *revoltés*, or apostates, who had actively assisted the enemy in 1686. When caught, their fate was summary.

Women with many children were sometimes spared, as were prisoners whose skills were needed. Both Vaudois surgeons had been lost the day before Sallebertrand, and the sick and wounded desperately needed skilled attention. A surgeon was captured on the road near Villar early in September and promised to serve faithfully if granted his life. He did so very loyally until he was killed in action later in the winter.

There were fewer companies now. Armand was still a lieutenant, but he was acting captain for a Vaudois company that had lost its native captain on that costly eighth day of the march. The original six companies of foreign volunteers had been decimated by death and desertion and the men distributed through the Vaudois companies. Alexandre found himself in the band of Captain Martinat, one of the most active of the "flying companies." There were occasional frictions between the Vaudois and the French and Swiss, but most foreigners continued to give their special skills unstintingly. Eventually, both Armand de Gandon and François Huc were rewarded by formal promotion to captain-lieutenant.

Almost everyone was perpetually hungry. The enemy tried untiringly to locate caches of food and the flocks of sheep the Barbets controlled occasionally, and matters fluctuated between feast and famine. Somehow, however, the Vaudois never ran out of arms and ammunition.

As the Martinat company loped off into the twilight one evening, Armand, sitting by a fire near the crude huts of piled rock and tree branches that passed for the base camp that week, was glad Alexandre's sister couldn't see him now. Alexandre's appearance was a far cry from the decorous and sober dress style he had maintained in the Dutch capital. Now, as a toughened guerrilla fighter, he was swarthy and unkempt beyond belief, with hair like Nebuchadnezzar in his sixth year of grass eating, clad in rags and a shapeless wide-brimmed hat, stained and filthy, his feet in sandals and his legs in leggings of cloth strips tied by crosshatched cords. He looked like a bandit or an escaped demoniac, but so did almost everyone else.

Alexandre carried a musket and two sacks slung over his shoulders—an empty one for food (if any should turn up) and a smaller one for his precious grenades. A few officers somehow kept a dress uniform coat in their knapsacks for some future special occasion; but most, like Armand, were nearly indistinguishable from their men, and the gold or silver stripes on torn and discolored coats were hardly noticeable. Armand still carried his straight sword, but most of his *confreres** preferred the more handy sabre or just bayonets or long knives.

That night the Martinat company performed one of its more notable exploits—the storming of the enemy at the stockade at Sibaud. So fearful were their enemies because of the almost supernatural ability of the Vaudois to materialize at will that many of them carried charms and amulets against the demons they thought were collaborating with the Barbets, and they went to great trouble to fortify themselves at night. At Sibaud, wooden palisades enclosed a camp for several hundred enemy foot soldiers and horsemen.

Captain Martinat personally located and dispatched the sentry. Then, on a signal, his forty Vaudois, moving as one, scaled the six-foot fence—rushing at it and swinging over and down among their sleeping enemies. In utter confusion, trying to locate their weapons and to light their torches in the midst of screaming men and neighing horses, the enemy fled out into the darkness in panic. Thirty-four of them never made it. The Vaudois suffered only one casualty—a man who landed in a tree as he jumped over the fence in the dark and was hung up in the branches until his friends cut him down. He suffered nothing worse

---

* Colleagues.

than scratches and loss of dignity. There were some remarks about Absalom, for both the Vaudois and the Huguenots were saturated in the Old Testament.

Less happy for them a few nights later was a seven-hour firefight along the highway in a deepening fog. Three of their comrades were killed. After it became plain that nothing was going to be accomplished that night, the captain drew off the survivors so quietly that the enemy kept up a heavy fire in the dark long after the Vaudois had gone elsewhere. That long dreary night all they could find to eat were cabbages right off the ground and eaten raw, as they couldn't risk a fire.

After the first snowfall, a dozen Vaudois realized they were being trailed by one hundred and twenty-five militia. They turned around, set an ambush, and killed thirteen of their pursuers without the loss of a man. Even more remarkable was the occasion at Mount Vachére when outposts signaled the approach of a Piedmontese column. In haste, cutting short a prayer Pastor Arnaud was offering at the time, every available man raced desperately for the top of the ridge, getting there as the Piedmontese were barely fifty paces away. Secure among the rocks at the crest, they mowed the enemy down with such dreadful efficiency that a hundred enemy bodies lay on the slope while not a Vaudois was scratched. No wonder the enemy developed a superstitious respect for them!

More dangerous than enemy forces was illness. Food was often short. Some of the weaker men became ill, and frequently there were no medicines or even broth to give them. The day of the Mount Vachére exploit, the ration of the victors was a piece of bread the size of a nut. Some detachments of foragers would go two days, perhaps, finding nothing. When in luck, they feasted on cabbages and radishes without salt or seasoning. They were delighted to get anything. For a time they had a flock of sheep, but when a lamb wandered over the side of a trail, the mother followed, then another, and another, and in a few minutes the whole flock had "deserted"—to the surprise and joy of the enemy patrol following close by. They had few other victories over the Barbets to brag about!

There were a number of accidental shootings due to poor discipline and taut nerves, and battlefield deaths were few, but they did occur. At the village of Essart, Martinat's company was finally trapped in the ruins of a stone farmhouse. They held their own all day and escaped under cover of darkness. However, their gallant captain was wounded in the withdrawl and overwhelmed by his pursuers. He died fighting to the last. In that tiny band, such a loss was a major tragedy.

Yet there were grimly humorous moments too. One market day a Vaudois band made a sweep down the south bank of the Cluson in French territory, boldly appearing right across the river from Perouse in full sight of hundreds of merchants and their customers. Having caught two particularly detestable *revoltés*, in the pleasant fashion of the day, the Vaudois made one of their prisoners hang the other in full sight of the crowd, and then they hanged the first man. The crowd applauded happily, thinking it was the governor's men hanging Barbets. Then they realized the truth, and the ensuing panic emptied the community in a few moments, to the vast amusement of the Vaudois.

Less mortal was the fate of some hostile Piedmontese village women who were having social drinks when the Vaudois came through. They were forced to drink a series of toasts to the health and prosperity of the Prince of Orange (the chief devil figure of the Catholic world, especially after he became king of England); the duke of Schomberg, the prince's chief commander; His Electoral Highness of Brandenburg; and Their High Mightinesses, the States General of the Netherlands. The only suffering the ladies had to endure was presumably severe hangovers.

* * * * *

After Captain Martinat's death, the company was scouting a little valley near Saint-Germain when they came suddenly upon a farmstead with several half-burned-out buildings. Equally surprised were two men working in the farmyard. They dropped their implements and fled for the thicket at top speed, shirttails flying. The leading Vaudois snapped a shot after them but missed. The raiders searched the building but found nothing of interest except for a little food, so they moved on.

Later that afternoon, coming back that way, they saw a woman on the path at some distance, walking slowly as if expecting someone. There had been a number of unpleasant affairs involving peasants—men or women—either being decoys for ambushers or simply spying on the paths taken by the Vaudois to discover their hidden food supplies or where they might be gathering chestnuts or fruit. The woman saw them and came toward them very slowly. The Vaudois sergeant waved his men to cover, muskets at the ready, and signaled to Alexandre to go see what the woman wanted.

Not especially pleased at the honor, Alexandre walked slowly toward her, his musket leveled, his eyes searching the trees and bushes for signs of danger.

When they were within speaking distance, both stopped. "Who goes there?" Alexandre challenged as ominously as he could manage. He stared at her suspiciously. She was a young woman of a little over twenty, well-built, a kerchief on the back of her head, and a shawl wrapped around her shoulders. Her black hair was braided around her head, her legs bare, and her feet in sandals.

"Friend, Monsieur," she said, holding her calloused hands, palms outward, to reassure him. "I am alone. There is no trick!"

"Then what do you want coming out here this way?" It occurred to him she was answering him in French, but many of the peasants, especially in the Pragelas Valley, spoke some French.

"I would like to make a proposition to messieurs les Vaudois," she said urgently. "I am Guiseppina Venturi," she said, "and I used to be one of you. I had to abjure in the troubles of '86, but I was helpful to our people. Have you anyone there from Pramol? Monsieur Robert would remember me as Josephine Peirot."

"We'll see," said Alexandre. "What is it you want?"

"Listen," she said, her brown eyes staring unwaveringly at Alexandre, "I since have married a Piedmontese, but my heart is still with God's people. My husband is a good man, and I love him. He was one of those who ran away this morning when you came on him working with a neighbor on this farm. I know you do not spare Piedmontese papists, but I would ask you as a favor not to harm him. I would be willing to give you twenty-four five-pound loaves of bread tomorrow and as much as I can every week thereafter as long as I have flour. Will you speak to your commander?"

"Walk in front of me and slowly," said Alexandre, "and we shall see what he makes of this."

Drawing her out of sight of the path into the thicket, the sergeant and the others surrounded her. Two of them agreed that they had heard of her and of her usefulness in helping fugitives to escape during the mop-up of 1686. While not very trustful of one who had not only abjured but had also married a papist, the men thought her proposition was still an attractive one.

"But," said the sergeant, "don't you know that the French governor has the death penalty for those who supply us with anything at all?"

"I certainly do," she answered with a level gaze. "Last week they hanged a woman in Saint-Germain for just that. Her nine-year-old son, who was arrested with her, may have been hanged too, for all I know. That doesn't frighten me. God is on your side. Even the papists know it. I know I haven't been as strong as I should have been, but I will help the Good Cause any time I can. You have promised to spare my husband," she added earnestly. "You are still men of your word." A place to leave the bread was agreed on, and the bargain was concluded.

As the little band returned to the camp that night and another skimpy supper, they could only wish there were more like her. "I've never met her husband," Alexandre commented to Armand as he fished for more cabbage leaves in the watery liquid of the pot. "He didn't wait to be introduced this morning, but he must have some good in him for a girl to risk her neck for him like that."

* * * * *

Captain Turrel became gloomier and gloomier as the prospect of an endless winter of guerilla warfare and hardship stretched before them. The French officers frequently argued these prospects. The Vaudois, at least, were in their home valleys again, even though the enemy was still there too. But many of the chilled and hungry French and Swiss volunteers were terribly disillusioned.

"We did as we promised," said Captain Turrel, not for the first time, as a group of the French refugees chewed the topic over once more. (There was little else to chew.) "We got them back to their valleys. It's not our fault that we've had no reinforcements. What are we accomplishing now?"

"Help is gathering in the Milanais, at least for spring," countered another.

"And where will we be by then?" growled the captain. "Frozen or starved, I shouldn't wonder. I'm sick to death of chestnuts, and even they are getting scarce. Nothing is happening in Switzerland either. You have to admit that."

Turrel's brother and neighbors from Dauphiné had joined the expedition with him and usually sided with him in these arguments. "Remember," interjected one of these, "that we joined this expedition to open the door to France and restore the worship of God in Dauphiné. When was the last time you heard anyone say anything about France? We'll leave our bones in this wilderness. We'll never see France." His voice rose shrilly.

"It's still the Good Cause," Armand replied patiently. "It's going to take longer for the Allied army to reach these valleys than we had hoped, but I wouldn't want to have that day come and the task be harder because I failed in my duty. Do you think you would really advance the cause more by fighting in those interminable sieges along the Rhine? I think not!"

"You are mad," was the usual answer. "We could all die here, and nothing would be changed at all."

Daily, Turrel grumbled to the other French officers about his anomalous position. He was the commander in chief—so it had been announced the first morning when they landed in Savoy. Yet the pastor repeatedly overruled him or countermanded his orders, and the native Vaudois paid him little attention. He was increasingly frustrated and bitter. While his complaints were true, what could one say to the formidable pastor?

Every so often, one or several of the foreign volunteers would disappear, unable to stand the situation any longer. Unkind remarks from some of the Vaudois didn't improve the morale of the remaining French or Swiss. To the Vaudois, anyone who left was purely and simply a deserter.

*　*　*　*　*

As autumn advanced, raiding parties were sent as far as the Queyras Valley in Dauphiné, raising contributions for the needs of the Vaudois. Besides tying down French troops, the little band managed to keep the whole vast, rugged, almost undefensible frontier in an uproar. Fighting in October at a mile high in elevation was almost like fighting in winter, with snow and sleet flurries instead of rain. Armand's company went out in mid-October and was gone ten days.

Speed and surprise were the essentials. They would burst out of the underbrush or from behind rocks at the edge of a village, yelling and shooting. Usually the villagers would offer no resistance. A conference would be held with the trembling village syndics. The attackers would requisition supplies or money. The villagers could keep their animals, and their homes would be unburned. But woe to those who tried to be clever or resisted. Woe also to any soldiers who put up a defense. Defenders usually threw themselves into the church, which was often the sturdiest building. Sometimes they slept there in fear of a Vaudois attack. On such occasions the Vaudois would have to decide whether to besiege them. This would irritate the Vaudois, who had no time to waste, for a relief column might be on its way. Sometimes they ambushed such a column and harassed it all the way back to its base. While French commanders raged, they could do little to prevent these attacks.

The Gandon company had a very satisfying action at the last village they struck. The church was garrisoned with Dauphinois militia when battle erupted. It was pandemonium. The rattle of musketry mingled with the crackle of the flames of burning houses, the bellowing of cattle, and the shrieks of villagers caught in crossfire around the church. The Vaudois fanned out, pounding down the alleys and racing musket balls past fresh corpses in the freezing slush.

Alexandre was vindicated that day, but it was almost his last. Dashing by the side of the church, he saw shutters open and musket barrels protruding through the grilled windows. He couldn't throw accurately while running, so he paused and lit and flung a grenade at the window. But he did so too hastily, and he saw the missile hit the wall and roll on the ground. The fuse hadn't stayed lighted though and he managed to pick up the little black ball, relight it, and lob it at the window grill again, hoping those in the church were too excited to aim at him carefully. He saw it go in trailing its tiny plume of black smoke. As he was running away, a two-ounce slug slammed into the musket slung on his back and sent him sprawling in the frozen dirt. Then, with a roar, the church window belched smoke.

Panicked, not knowing what had exploded among them, most of the defenders in the church fled the smoky confusion out into the street, right into disaster. Meanwhile, Alexandre picked himself up and staggered on, surprised that he was still alive. The stock of his musket was split, and as a souvenir, he soon had a huge bruise on his side. He dropped his weapon and picked up one from the street that the original owner would no longer be needing. As his head was clearing, he felt tremendous satisfaction that he wouldn't be hearing any more snide remarks about puny children pretending to be grenadiers.

The villagers, once the tumult had ended, appeared grateful the destruction had been no greater than it was, and the Vaudois party marched home with bulging haversacks of salt, simple medicaments, dried meat, a little money, and four horses for their wounded to ride.

Trotting down the trail into camp two days later, still very pleased with themselves, they found somber faces. Captain Turrel, his brother, and four other of their Dauphinois comrades had decamped, pretending they were going down to pick up the bread. The captains had already met and elected Pierre Odin, former notary and secretary to Arnaud and second in command, to replace Turrel.

The abashed Frenchmen drew to one side to discuss the affair.

"Courage!" said François Huc. "We've made a promise before God, and we shall keep it. We shall have to work even more efficiently to make amends where our unfortunate brethren have failed."

Armand sadly agreed. "We know that the Woman in the Wilderness beset by the Red Dragon* is a type of the Vaudois church, and not all the persecutions of these last years avail the devil anything. The battle is hard, but we have the honor to be defending the Woman in her extremity." The dwindling band of Huguenots murmured agreement and went back silently to their posts.

Arnaud had attributed Turrel's defection to spiritual deficiencies. When word reached the camp weeks later that Turrel and his party had been arrested wandering in the mountains and had died horribly on the wheel at Grenoble as traitors, it seemed to the simple Vaudois a clear

---

* Symbols from the prophecy of Revelation 12.

case of God's justice at work. To the refugee officers, it wasn't very cheering to note how little protection carrying a commission from the king of England afforded.

* * * * *

Few as the Vaudois were, their progress was followed with the keenest interest in far places. They were much on the mind of Charles de la Bonde d'Iberville as he sealed his final letter of the week to Pontchartrain, the secretary of state at Versailles. The energetic young resident felt that, in all modesty, he had served the king well from his critical post in Geneva, keeping a vigilant eye on the doings of the heretics in all directions—Switzerland, the Vaudois valleys, and the disaffected parts of southern France. If all the servants of Louis XIV did their work as efficiently as he, there would have been far fewer Vaudois holed up in their hills and hardly any Huguenot preachers in the wilds to trouble His Very Christian Majesty.

He would admit his extreme distress in mid-August when he had learned that agitators had slipped back into France to stir up sedition among the new converts and, even more unforgivable, at about the same time nearly a thousand Vaudois and other riffraff had left Bernese territory from under the very noses of the authorities and invaded Savoy.

To counter the agitators, he had secured the names and descriptions of Vivens and Brousson and sent them to Bâville, the formidable intendant of Languedoc, and it would surely be only a matter of time before the agents of that relentless administrator would lay these "perturbators of the public repose" by the heels. The danger, if real, seemed to have evaporated in October with an abortive tumult at Florac in the Cévennes. With his network of priests, spies, and turncoats, Bâville was in full control. Certainly, if these foolish people persisted in their fanaticism, running about at night in the wilderness, they could have no complaint if the king's servants applied the law against heretic assemblies rigorously. D'Iberville regularly sent along further newsnotes on the doings of the refugee pastors in Switzerland.

Far more vexatious at the moment was this matter of the return of the Vaudois. Now d'Iberville saw the connection between the two affairs. He shared at least one opinion with the Protestant man in the street—that the Swiss authorities had connived in the business. It was inconceivable, he felt, that in so small a country the expedition could have gathered supplies and assembled their rendezvous without it being known. The buying of arms and powder and of fifteen hundred quintals of bread at a time? Bern was incredibly lax, and, if anything, Neuchâtel was more so! Nor was he so sure that the duke of Savoy wasn't implicated as well. How else could these wretches have crossed the lake in puny barks to a conveniently denuded shore and marched through fifty leagues of Savoy unhindered—even through passages where ten could hold off a thousand?

D'Iberville knew a return was planned but had been surprised that it happened so soon. He had instantly sent notification to the duke's commander in Savoy when Barbin and his friend galloped in the morning of the departure with the news. And what had the Savoyard done? He had sent the news by *foot messenger* to Turin to save expenses! D'Iberville made no secret of his opinion that the Savoy militia was the worst military body in the world and the gentry commanding them the most pitiable poltroons. It had been a bad week.

He and Amelot, the French ambassador to the Catholic cantons, stationed at Soleure, had leaped into action. They protested the violations of neutrality, threatened French reprisals, and, referring to the Huguenots going with the Vaudois, expressed their astonishment that the Swiss would permit "a mob of His Majesty's armed subjects out of Switzerland to carry their fury and their rebellion through his provinces." The Swiss had, indeed, reacted then. His spies had collected details for them on the subordinate officials who had been helpful to the Vaudois, and Bern began to investigate. Catholic cantons, tipped off, arrested late-arriving Vaudois who were passing through, and the Catholic Swiss were encouraged to add to the expostulation and pressure on the guilty Protestant cantons. A Swiss postmaster in d'Iberville's pay had also let him see some incriminating letters Savoy agents in Switzerland had written to each other about the business.

It was almost unbelievable, then, that after all that, on September 20, the second expedition had sailed under Captain Jean Bourgeois, incredibly repeating the same violations—with the same local officials unable or unwilling to intervene! D'Iberville had taken the precaution of sending three of his creatures to enlist in the expedition, to keep him informed and also to spread divisive rumors among the volunteers. This second and larger expedition sailed in broad daylight from Morges just a few hours before the commissioner specially sent from Bern could arrive—knowing full well he would arrive too late. The Huguenot refugees had been so ecstatic over all of this that their insolence in the streets of Geneva could hardly be believed.

D'Iberville couldn't take full credit for what happened then, but the Bourgeois expedition had only a couple of hundred true Vaudois, and the rest were mostly Swiss and other foreigners—who joined more for adventure than to strike a blow for the Good Cause. Bourgeois turned out to be pitiably indecisive and couldn't control his men. Unlike the first expedition, his rascals stole everything not nailed down, and there was arson and outrage. The officers quarreled with their chief; and when the Savoy militia at last made a stand, the invaders stumbled around ineffectually and finally broke up without even getting as far as Cluse. The backwash flowed into Geneva, where they were disarmed and relieved of their loot. The plunder was returned to the Savoy churches from which much of it came. Then the prisoners were ferried back to Bernese territory.

Bern had exploded angrily. Indictments and judgments rained down on the promoters of this sorry business. Most fled, and their property, if any, was confiscated. Sagnol blamed Convenant and Bourgeois, saying he had only helped at their request, and it was a surprise to him that Bern objected to the enterprise. Convenant, forced hastily to move to Zurich, claimed unconvincingly that he found out only at the last minute what Arnaud had been up to and had then tried to stop him. The money he handled, he maintained, was for resettlement and relief, and no one was more surprised than he to learn that it had been used to buy guns and ammunition.

The only one arrested (others were condemned *in absentia*) was Bourgeois, and he indignantly denied the charges of cowardice and treachery and said that the whole affair was the fault of Sagnol, who ran it from start to finish—including the decision when to sail—from his command post at the Bear Inn in Vevey. Bourgeois said he had originally been persuaded by Arnaud to join up to help the Protestant cause. After a long trial and many pathetic appeals, Bourgeois was charged with levying war on Bernese soil against a friendly state and condemned to be beheaded at Nyon. He was a scapegoat offered by Bern to appease the wrath of the king of France.

D'Iberville had been enjoying the confusion and embarrassment of the refugees in Switzerland ever since. Huguenots were still trying to enlist volunteers to help in the Vaudois valleys, but it was more than the early snows closing the Alpine passes that chilled their enthusiasm.

Everything seemed to be under control now. Since the Catholic cantons in Switzerland forwarded their prisoners to Turin, there might by now be nearly as many Vaudois in Piedmontese jails as in the mountains. These were the lucky ones, for Louis XIV had ordered that when Vaudois or foreign volunteers were captured, they were to draw lots, and one-third was to be executed, one-third sent to the galleys for life, and one-third drafted into the French army. In addition, foreign officers, or those holding foreign commissions, were to be executed at once—this to forestall tedious protests and correspondence with foreign countries.

D'Iberville now had twenty Savoyards and Swiss on his secret payroll. Barbin had managed to get a job as secretary to the newly arrived British envoy in Zurich, Thomas Coxe—evidently a trusting sort who believed Barbin's "pathetical story." Thus, much that went on in Allied circles in Switzerland was soon known to d'Iberville, who hoped the young idiot Barbin wouldn't betray himself too soon. No doubt the allies played the same game, but so far d'Iberville had caught none among his servants in enemy pay.

All this cost money, but d'Iberville felt that his expenditures had been useful even if there had been some complaint from Versailles at the size of his intelligence expenses. He knew what Coxe was spending, but there was no harm in letting Versailles think the Britisher spent more than he really did. He knew that Coxe was telling *his* government the same kind of story: "Wagonloads of money coming for the use of French diplomats!"

As d'Iberville read Barbin's secret copies of Monsieur Coxe's letters to London, it amused him to note the Englishman's scandalized amazement at the expense of living in Switzerland—"more than any place he had ever lived by half." Coxe was irritated to find that the members of the Swiss diet had bid up the price of making a favorable speech—at the last diet, he'd had to pay one member a full twenty pounds for a pro-British discourse to counter a French offer in *louis d'or*.* In addition, he'd had to provide gold coronation medals to councilors' wives and to maintain a well-patronized table set for twelve places for the ten days of banquets and continual "refreshments" for all and sundry at the latest diet. It had cost the Englishman two hundred pounds sterling! Yet the Swiss seemed unable to advance matters at all; they delayed decisions on a British alliance indefinitely—dragging out the negotiations and playing hard-to-get with both France and the allies, and bathing all the while in this golden flood of "gratifications."

It was difficult, of course, for d'Iberville to understand why Catinat seemed to have so much trouble rounding up the remnants of the Vaudois in their mountains. Probably it had something to do with the two-faced duke of Savoy. With thousands of men at their disposal, the French and Savoyard forces should have been able to end the business promptly. Surely no more than a handful remained, and those in the direst extremity. At least, few in Versailles would think he wasn't doing his job. It was really rather scandalous that the soldiers couldn't seem to wipe out the Vaudois. The longer they lasted, the more legendary they became, and the more these miserable heretics inspired Protestants everywhere to make trouble. Until the Barbets were destroyed, the religious problem in France would never be settled.

---

* An English pound was a little less than a *louis d'or*.

Captured Dispatches

Six tattered figures rested warily on the rocks at streamside. With gaunt, leathery faces under shapeless hats and unkempt hair, they certainly looked the bandits the soldiers of Louis XIV considered them to be. The two Frenchmen among them, Alexandre Cortot and Armand de Gandon, appeared indistinguishable from the four Vaudois. All were in rags, but their bandoliers, muskets, and knives were in good order. In a moment they would climb back up the slope again, for in height was safety.

They had come down to drink the icy water of the Cluson, to find food, and to keep an eye on the French, or as Pastor Arnaud put it, "the enemies of God in garrison at Pignerol." They were in the Perouse Valley at the moment, on the main road from Briançon to Pignerol. Activity kept them from freezing. The November weather was cold, and patches of snow lay on the ground. The landscape was perpetually wet from what seemed to be endless rain and snow. Most of the villages were deserted, the stone houses roofless and open to the dreary sky. Forested mountains and snowcapped peaks might normally seem inspiring, but now they comprised a depressing vista of rain, mist, rocks, and ruins—wet and debilitating to the stoutest heart.

It was poor consolation that the French were suffering too. The Piedmontese plain had been nearly stripped of provisions by endless requisitions, and there was illness among the French garrisons. Rumor said that wagonloads of French corpses were taken out of Pignerol every night for burial. Supply trains coming from France often arrived—if at all—significantly diminished thanks to the harassment of the Vaudois bands. Fortresses like Pignerol were in no danger, for the Vaudois had no heavier weapon than a musket. But anything that moved beyond cannon range from the walls was subject to surprise. It was the age-old story of a professional, disciplined army baited by unseen irregulars who knew the landscape intimately and who had no strong point whose loss would make any difference. French desperation showed through in talk of cutting the trees and brush along the roads—but the chore was too vast, and had it been done, darkness and rocks would still have protected the guerillas.

Eons ago, this would have been unsettling to Armand. As a trained officer, he was used to proper butcheries in set-piece battles between disciplined armies officered by gentlemen. But as a boy, he had served with his father in the Pyrenees and was thus not completely unfamiliar with mountain warfare, and he was used to it now again. He also had long known that nameless skirmishes, ambushes, brutal requisitions, and starving were more often the soldier's lot than was a famous victory.

As the squad rested, Armand looked at Alexandre. He was certain the boy had a slow fever. All this damp and privation—could it lead to consumption? This life must be more depressing to the recruit than to the experienced campaigner, but one would never get an admission of discouragement from Alexandre. Armand wished he could devise some plausible way to send the boy back to Switzerland—or better yet, to his sister in Holland. Useless idea! Alexandre was too acute to be taken in that way!

Armand became aware that one of the mountaineers was listening intently. He respected their abilities and waited patiently. In a few moments the Vaudois signaled for them to find cover. They ran lightly up the slope and settled behind rocks well above the path. Then they saw a party of mounted men coming at a fast trot down the grade from Fenestrelle and France. They were too few to be a cavalry unit, which probably meant they were carrying dispatches.

The picket signaled with his fingers: five and five and four—fourteen men. Too many for six to attack without planning. If their quarry kept their heads, they might pick off some of the attackers, whose presence would be advertised by clouds of smoke when they fired. And even if the Vaudois got several of the guards, the courier might well escape by the simple expedient of galloping off too rapidly for the Vaudois to get in more than a shot or so apiece with their muzzle loaders.

"Alexandre, I want them stampeded by here," Armand said urgently, pointing. Alexandre took off, and one of the musketeers went streaking lightly among the rocks at his heels. Turning to the remaining Vaudois, Armand continued, "All of you aim for the officer. If the rest get away, no matter. We want the dispatches." Then he and his three marksmen lay down, cheeks to their pieces, and waited.

With the noise of the river brawling over the rocks, the horsemen heard nothing. And even if they had looked, there wouldn't have been much to see, for no musketeer need expose himself to begin these proceedings.

Alexandre carefully blew on his burning punk, which he usually carried on patrol. He inserted a fuse in the little metal sphere he took from his sack and touched it with the glowing end of the punk. As soon as he was certain the fuse was burning, he flung it without wasted motion high in the air. Hissing faintly, the grenade described a smooth arc, trailing a wisp of smoke, and it exploded among the horsemen just before it hit the rocky path.

The blast probably did no serious damage, but it was totally unexpected. Horses reared, whinnied, and plunged this way and that, making it difficult for their riders to see clearly. At a musket shot from the rocks to the front, the seven or eight cavalrymen who could still control their horses turned and fled as one back the way they had come. As they passed, the three Vaudois fired together. The officer fell from his saddle, but his foot caught in the stirrup and he was dragged a few feet before the frightened horse broke free and fled after the others. The first marksman had reloaded, and Alexandre, unslinging his musket, joined him in firing at the riders who were trying to turn their plunging mounts around. Another dragoon fell from his horse and a gray went down, pinning its rider. The three men with Armand dispatched them. The rest of the party was gone, leaving one horse dead and three men killed, one the officer.

Covered by two of their comrades, the other Vaudois ran down to inspect their handiwork. Armand, not as fleet of foot, joined them a moment later. They were methodically stripping the bodies of everything useful—cloaks, pistols, sabers, powder flasks, blankets, food, tobacco, and a few coins. Ordinarily, saddlery and cavalry boots were valuable prizes, but not to those who in the mountains could operate only on foot.

The dead officer, a red-haired youth of the Second Languedoc Dragoons, occupied one of the Vaudois. He straightened up. "Here you are, captain!" he said and offered Armand an oilskin pouch that had been inside the officer's coat.

Still breathing hard, the five gathered around to see what they had. What had cost the officer his life were four sheets of heavy paper of foolscap size folded several times, and two small, flimsy sheets written in tiny lines on both sides.

Armand glanced over the heavy sheets. They were from the minister of war at Versailles to General Catinat and had evidently come down from Briançon to Fenestrelle, whose commander had sent this party on to Pignerol with them.

As Armand read, he smiled. Louvois was forcibly criticizing Catinat for an inexplicable lack of energy in destroying what everyone said was a mere handful of starving Barbets in the mountains. It appeared that some subordinate of Catinat had been making helpful criticisms behind the general's back—in the interest, of course, of the better service of His Majesty.

Another letter, three sheets from the same correspondent, dealt with the unsatisfactory attitude of the duke of Savoy and his curious lack of cooperation against the Barbets. But even more, it mentioned the persistent rumors that he was conspiring with the allies behind the back of the French king. Much of this particularly sensitive letter was in code.

Armand told his little audience the gist of the two letters, and they grinned appreciatively. Nice to know the enemy had problems.

"The rest is cipher," said Armand regretfully. "Perhaps Captain Huc is better at this than I, but if not, we ought to send these letters quickly to Switzerland. They do look important." The code was groups of three numerals for each word. Vaudois encipherment Armand knew, and it was simplicity itself. Letters Pastor Arnaud sent by their secret contact in Pignerol to Convenant in Zurich were in the clear, except for referring to the campaign as "manufacturing," arms as "bolts of cloth" and "yards of braid," and officers as "foremen"—ostensibly in a dry-goods store. The signatures were the names reversed, "Duanra" for Arnaud and "Nido" for Odin. It seemed unlikely that the French would have much difficulty breaking such a code.

Armand glanced at the small, closely written sheet and the accompanying letter and tried to repress a start. The Vaudois were loading themselves up with the booty and didn't notice, but Alexandre saw Armand's face. "Well," he said, in a low voice, "that must be the best of the lot." He waited expectantly.

"Curiosity in children is a very bad habit!" murmured Armand with a glance at the Vaudois, chattering happily and obliviously. Alexandre's face fell, and he looked annoyed. "Later," said Armand, hastily stuffing the papers back into the pouch.

* * * * *

That evening Armand called Odin, Arnaud, and Huc aside and showed them the documents. It was a stunning surprise. The small sheet listed Vaudois caches of food and other supplies in the various valleys and the names of their secret sympathizers. Someone would have to know the little army's business exceedingly well to have that much detail at his disposal. The covering note identified this person as one Jean Gras, a backsliding Vaudois in 1686 who had presented himself to Arnaud soon after the Return. On the testimony of old friends who had been pleased to see his change of heart, he had been received back in the "peace of the church."

In the six weeks he had been with his brethren in the hills, he had not only collected this information for his French masters, but it appeared that he was the one who had betrayed a secret mill of the Vaudois at Macel. That affair had cost the lives of three French refugees, two killed on the spot and revoltingly mutilated, and the third dragged back to Pignerol and publicly hanged, though he had died with heroic steadfastness. Just a week ago, Gras had been "captured." It now appeared to have been by arrangement, and at the cost of the life of Gras's nephew, who was not in on his uncle's secret. Resisting, he had been mortally wounded by his uncle's friends.

"They won't know for sure whether or not we have these papers because we threw the body of the officer in the river," said Armand. "Why don't we try exchanging for this villain as if he were a valued comrade? Sometimes they will, and sometimes they won't. We had best not make this known, or Gras may get wind of it."

After several days of parleying, Gras was indeed returned to them in exchange for a young ensign, who probably (and rightly) felt this was the luckiest day of his life. Not so for Jean Gras.

Suspecting nothing, Gras dismounted on arrival at the Vaudois camp and emotionally greeted his waiting comrades. Indicating his escort, who were not in on the secret, he cried in his resonant baritone, "How beautiful on the mountain are the feet of them who bring good tidings." It was as if he were the host at a reception, smiling graciously. He was quite overcome and wept with virtuosity over this demonstration of love among brethren and also for his lamented nephew, a young man of such promise! His remaining days, he said with the most affecting piety, would be devoted to the service of the Lord, whose providence had been so touchingly manifest in his behalf this day.

Gras was a powerfully built man in his forties, with iron-gray locks and a profile, as he was aware, not unlike that of a Roman emperor. He embraced his way through the throng nearest him, but when he reached the half dozen senior officers, he was visibly startled at their grim and silent mien.

"What is this, brethren?" he began.

"Tie him," said Arnaud sternly. Four men as burly as himself left him no opportunity to struggle as they grasped and bound him. His face went ashen gray, and his eyes bulged dangerously as Arnaud turned to the assemblage and in crisp emphatic words told of the discovery made in the French officer's dispatch pouch. Gras's thunderstruck friends, utterly mortified, were invited to identify the handwriting of the list. Arnaud kindly assured them that they shouldn't blame themselves—everyone had been taken in by the traitor.

The council of war sat briefly but formally, and Captain Odin pronounced the sentence of hanging. The prisoner, invited to speak, could not. Within half an hour, the solemn spectacle was finished.

"I have the idea that Monsieur Lombraille, our redoubtable commandant at Pignerol, is not a very nice person," said Alexandre as he walked away from the execution with Armand and others of their friends.

"None would consider him tenderhearted even as French general officers go," agreed Armand. "Why say you this?"

"Lombraille couldn't know for certain that we didn't have those letters. If we did, Gras was as good as dead; if we didn't, Gras would be discovering more of our secrets presently. In any case, he was of no use to Lombraille in safety at Pignerol."

"This *is* the devil's world," said Huc soberly. "I hope that all of us here may soon be out of it and with our Lord in His kingdom."

* * * * *

Even if the enemy paid thirty lives for one, there was really no future for the little band if it remained in the "flying camps." It was exhausting, especially as winter worsened. The expected reinforcements hadn't come, and while there were rumors of an Allied army preparing in the Milanais, the invasion never went beyond rumor. After September 12, French troops had been operating in the Piedmontese valleys as if the land belonged to Louis XIV instead of Victor Amadeus II. Even the chestnuts were failing. The Vaudois needed rest and time for outside help to materialize. Altogether, after battle deaths, illness, and desertion, about two-thirds of the original expedition now remained—slightly more than five hundred men.

The leaders therefore selected a base for the winter with these considerations in mind. In the valley of Saint-Martin, a natural fortress of a mountain, the Quatre-dents—named from the four-toothed silhouette of the top—loomed over the village of Balsille. Difficult of access on one side, it was virtually unscalable from the other three, with precipices behind and sticking out as a rocky promontory separated from Mount Guinevert and the Col du Pis by deep ravines with icy torrents flowing in each. The Balsille, as it was also known, ascended steeply with three stages of comparatively level ground and was admirably adaptable for bastions and defense works. On one of the higher levels was the chateau, which they could turn into their home fortress. In November, the bands were directed on the Balsille and reached it safely after a harrowing night march over the peaks from the Lucerne Valley.

To the natural defenses, the Vaudois added on the approachable side no less than seventeen lines of entrenchments, protected by palisades and dry stone walls. Whole trees, with their branches toward the enemy, roots toward the Vaudois, were laid in the stonework and loaded with great rocks to keep them in place. The trench lines were connected and receded up the steeps to the barracks and huts where they planned to rest for the winter in comparative warmth and comfort. The French Huguenot officers contributed their engineering knowledge, and everyone was kept busy constructing and improving this formidable system.

In two weeks, eighty huts or cabins had been constructed, insulated with hay, straw, and boards. Drainage conduits were dug, for there was heavy rain and snowfall. The greatest problem since arriving in the valleys had been a regular supply of food, but a pair of providences eased their burdens considerably and greatly encouraged the beleaguered little army. Deep snows made some of the mountain tracks nearly impassable and limited the forays they could make, but they discovered in nearby high fields that, due to the troubles of the times, grain had not been harvested, and it lay on the ground, where it had been covered with snow. Irregular thaws exposed the grain and provided time to gather it. If it had been harvested at the proper time, it would have been carried off during the fighting or burned in barns.

To grind their grain, they had a mill nearby on the Germanasque, but it lacked the millstone. The owners, the Tron-Poulet brothers, were members of the band. In the troubles of 1686, they had taken the millstone and put it in the river and covered it with sand. Now they located it, ran a pole into the hole, levered it off the creek bed, and with a dozen helpers, carried it back to the mill. Livestock was accumulated and penned on the mountain, too, and with better and more regular diet, the sick recovered and everyone felt better. The fainthearted who had left them would have been amazed to see how much better provided for they were compared to just a few weeks before. To keep in practice and to be informed, parties still went out occasionally, levying contributions on the countryside or ambushing a French supply column.

Twice on Sundays and once on Thursdays work stopped and Arnaud held a preaching service and psalms were sung. In the barracks, prayer was offered thrice daily, and a chapter of Scripture was read in the morning in some huts. No detachment went out on a mission without asking

God's blessing on the enterprise—all kneeling, but some with face to the earth.

Even in these idyllic circumstances, or perhaps because the men were no longer in such a state of desperate emergency, a problem of covetousness cropped up. Arnaud made this the subject of more sermons than any other, with Achan, quite naturally as an example. The regulations on booty going into the common pool were still in force unless a small group had special permission otherwise, but a number of the men were not turning in money they "found." Sometimes this became known, and several deserted rather than give up the filthy lucre. Regrettably, these deserters were not French or Swiss but native Vaudois. This provoked gloomy commentaries on the corruptible nature of man even in their wintry communal Eden.

In due course, the enemy learned where Arnaud and his band had gone. At first the French nourished the delusion that if the Vaudois were at last standing still, they could be wiped out. In spite of the December weather, Lombraille led a column into the little valley and attacked Balsille village. At the cost of sixty casualties, the enemy managed to get across the stream on the second try and burned the houses on the far side. Then, floundering and freezing in the snow, literally dying of exposure and completely unable to force their way up that formidable slope, they capitulated to the weather and the topography and after three days pulled out, shouting threats that they would be back at Easter.

With the enemy in winter quarters, too, the valley had a couple months of unusual quiet. The snow blanket, continually renewed in large healing flakes, covered the burned-out shells of the village houses and hid the scattered French corpses. The only sounds were the muted echoes of picks and shovels on the mountain as the Vaudois improved their fortifications. The scene was as peaceful and as beautiful as though it were some time other than 1690.

* * * * *

With the lessening of the winter storms, and the possibility of the hardy getting out a bit, the Vaudois were subjected to a new kind of harassment—war by correspondence. The moving spirit seemed to be the Chevalier de Vercellis, the duke's governor at Torre Pellice, who promoted the humane idea that having had their fun and with dim prospects for the future, the Vaudois might be willing to accept safe-conduct out of the country again. And might they not even come to some understanding with the government?

As emissaries, Vercellis used some of the Vaudois who had changed their religion. In the six months since the Glorious Return began, it had become reasonably well known who had relatives on the two sides. At first it was a request from a prisoner in Turin for a Vaudois relative on the Balsille to pay a visit, with safe-conduct of course. However, in spite of his persistence and even his offer to accompany personally the visitor on this consolatory mission, Vercellis couldn't overcome the distrust of the Vaudois for any proposal coming from Catholics. For centuries they'd been victims of broken faith and shabby tricks, so they were suspicious. A more convincing show of faith would have been high-quality hostages for the Vaudois to hold at the Balsille against the return of their *confrere*. Courteous letters traveled both ways several times—always without result. And now some of the garrison on the Balsille were complaining that too many apostate relatives had been allowed too free access to their refuge.

One morning in late February, a lone horseman carrying a white cloth on a stick appeared riding along the stream bank into the ruins of Balsille village. He was surely conscious of Vaudois sentinels watching him with extreme suspicion. The men grinding at the mill quit and picked up their weapons. Stopped at the footbridge, the horseman identified himself as Jacques Richard. He wasn't a new visitor. He said he bore letters for Pastor Arnaud personally. He was allowed to dismount and cross the bridge up to the first line of breastworks but was told to wait until the pastor should come down to see him. He sat stolidly on a rock for an hour or more before Arnaud and a half dozen of his captains appeared.

As the grim party approached, Monsieur Richard scrambled to his feet and bowed obsequiously, sweeping the ground with his broad-brimmed hat. He was a chunky little man with three days growth of beard and so bundled against the cold that he seemed fatter than he really was.

"I had thought, Monsieur," began Pastor Arnaud with a distinct chill in his tone, "that there would be no advantage to further discussing the matter of Monsieur Puy. I regret that Monsieur Vercellis has put you to the further trouble of journeying hither."

"Oh, Monsieur! It is not Monsieur Vercellis, but your own brother-in-law, the worthy Jacques Gautier, lately magistrate of Torre Pellice. Your own dear nephew, Henri, a delicate child, was to accompany me, but the incommodity of the weather and roughness of the mountain paths made it seem wise that he tarry at Bobi, so I have come on without him, I am desolated to say."

Richard's manner was one of such extreme sincerity and desire to please that it seemed possible he might break into tears. His listeners remained unmoved. They knew the man to be a talented actor.

The officers had looked at Arnaud at the mention of Gautier's name. His face remained expressionless. Aware of their scrutiny, the pastor made a decision. "It is gracious of Monsieur Gautier to write, Monsieur," he said. "At least he has done nothing hasty. We have been in the valleys for only six months. Anything Monsieur Gautier has to say can be said here." He took the letter and read aloud:

Monsieur and Brother-in-law:

I have word about you from the wife of Jacques Oger, sister of Jean Frasche, who tells me you are in good health. I am delighted, but I cannot say the same for myself. I have been very sick and am not yet recovered. [He then spoke of the efforts to get Jean Puy to go visit his relative in prison and how trustworthy Vercellis really was and how kind to him and to his wife.]

Your coming in these parts has caused me heavy loss, but there is yet a remedy if you inform me of your sentiments by way of my son, Henri—your nephew—whom I send you specially, sickly and feeble as he is, overlooking no means to discover if there is some way in which one may establish peace. For peace causes everything to blossom; but on the contrary, war ruins everything. Oh! How beautiful are the feet of him who brings peace. Where peace is, God will be. Monsieur le Chevalier Vercellis will work for that as well as for you personally. Have the goodness to take care of my son and to send him back to me by the man who has accompanied him. I await this favor of your goodness and am not able to say more for the present. I am completely ruined in body and goods. The family is well and wishes to be remembered to you. I am—Jacques Gautier.

Arnaud finished and looked up at his officers, raising his eyebrows. "You know him better than some of us, pastor," said an officer from the valley of Saint-Martin. "Are these his words, or is he being used?"

"They are his, all right," interjected a Vaudois from Torre angrily. "He's a sniveling coward and has been for years. Begging your pardon, pastor," he concluded gruffly.

Arnaud showed no offense. "We all know pitiable souls such as he," he replied, and turned to the messenger. "Monsieur, you must be anxious to be on the road, and I shall not take long to write a reply to carry back to Monsieur Gautier. It has not seemed apropos of late to invite visitors up our hill, so you will wait in the village and something will be brought you to eat. Your servant, sir!" and he bowed slightly and turned to go. The others mumbled courtesies, and then a suspicious Vaudois private walked the intruder downhill to the village.

An hour later, Arnaud summoned the officers again and read them his reply. He mentioned that Henri had not been able to make the full journey and then said,

> I am very happy to learn that you are still alive, but I would wish that you were in sufficiently good health to be able to work usefully for the public good; that would be the finest occupation for a man of substance and honor. You note that peace makes everything blossom but that war destroys everything, and you wish to know my sentiments on that. Here they are, without reserve, in fidelity and sincerity.
>
> You know that our fathers have possessed these valleys from time immemorial, that they have very faithfully served Their Royal Highnesses, paid the taxes as ordered, and obeyed all that was commanded them. However, they have been driven from their houses for some years now, to wander with their families in foreign lands. It must not therefore be considered strange if this poor and obedient people are so strong of heart that they return to the place of their birth, to live in and possess the heritage their ancestors left to them from all time.

Our intention was not, and is not, to make war on His Royal Highness, our natural prince. . . . You should see that we ask but to render to God that which is His, and to Caesar that which is his due, and that we do no evil to anyone unless they do it to us. We hope that you will have the kindness to make some careful reflections on everything in these evil times, where almost all people have drawn the sword one against the other and one sees streams of innocent blood flow on land and sea. May God's wrath toward us be appeased, for His anger is strongly kindled against humankind, and grant some repose to those who wish it. I salute you with all the family and pray the Lord may bless you and restore you to health.

Monsieur and Brother-in-law,

Your very humble and very obedient servant,

HENRI ARNAUD, pastor.

Several days later a new letter from Gautier arrived that accused Arnaud of "writing that which is not appropriate for the times in which we live nor for the place where you are" and that he should "profit from this warning without losing a moment of the time remaining. It is your brother and sister who give it to you and give it with all their heart. The bearer will discuss it further."

Arnaud sent by the indefatigable Richard his *baisemains** to his relatives but said he couldn't write a letter in reply because he had "lost his writing desk."

Others on the hill also received urgent warning of imminent doom unless they asked for passports to leave the country while there was yet time. They replied in terms even sharper than Arnaud's and referred to the lamentable weakness of these relatives who had apostatized and were now trying to get them to commit the same sin against God and His truth. The pastor's blunt reply to those being used by "seducing spirits" set the mode.

The last effort in this propaganda war was supposedly from two French Huguenot deserters who had been "integrated" into the king's

---

* Formal greetings—literally, "kissing hands."

army. Placards appeared outside the Vaudois perimeter addressed by name to some of the French who might still be in the Balsille. For example, "Our dear friend Alexandre Cortot: You should know that the king has accorded an amnesty to all his subjects who will put down their arms as we did. We are in the Regiment du Plessis. His Royal Highness the duke of Savoy is doing the same thing. Jacques Causse, Retournat."

This recruiting poster attracted no takers at all. It was easy to verify that Louis XIV had never forgiven any of his insubordinate Protestant subjects and likely never would. But it was flattering to know that one was remembered!

Monsieur Richard was back the last time on April 2 with an invitation from the Marquis of Parelle, the duke's chief minister, whose soldiery rarely bothered the Vaudois anymore. The Council of War edited a reply, signed by Arnaud and Odin, restating their loyalty to the duke and his dynasty, asserting their ancient claim to their lands, reminding him of their previous services, and assuring him that they would harm no one not trying to harm them. Monsieur Richard responded that the French would be coming back soon to try other means to resolve the question, and this concluded the public statements.

Armand and Huc did note that some couriers came to Arnaud who didn't receive public receptions, and even more interestingly, that the pastor himself would be gone on errands of several days at a time. He was not away long enough to travel as far as Switzerland, but what about Torre Pellice or Turin? The Frenchmen knew better than to question the comings and goings of the pastor, for the confidence in which his flock held him was absolute, and if he was doing something secret, they would be certain it was appropriate. When his friends discussed these matters, Arnaud would shrug his shoulders and quote Convenant: "What the Good Cause needs, in this order, is secrecy, diligence, and money."

"And," Huc would add, "the favor of the Lord of hosts."

Huc and Gandon were also certain that Arnaud was not playing them false, but they speculated that his activities might have more to do with the government of Piedmont than with that of the French. One might imagine the duke making almost any shift if persuaded it was to his advantage, but not so the implacable king of France!

* * * * *

General Catinat took the button from the cadaverous-looking man standing before him. It was large and covered with coarse red cloth, the edges drawn together on the flat underside and sewn together, the whole being a flattened sphere. The visitor had broken the thread so that the general slipped the wooden button out of the circle of cloth. As he did so, a small piece of flimsy paper dropped to the table. He picked it up and unfolded it. It was a letter signed by "Henri Arnaud, pastor," and it urged unnamed persons in Switzerland to hasten supplies and reinforcements in view of the impending French attack.

Catinat was one of the generation of professional soldiers who ornamented the first half of the reign of Louis XIV. A commoner, undistinguished in appearance, quiet and efficient, he could be trusted to defend a long frontier with inadequate forces, husbanding the lives of his men, making few mistakes, and content to leave more ambitious commanders to seek glory on better-publicized battlefronts.

While His Majesty and Louvois trusted Catinat, the devout clique at court did not. To such as Père La Chaise, the royal confessor, and Madame de Maintenon, the king's secret second wife, Catinat was insufficiently fired with zeal in the cause of the Roman Catholic Church. This point of view would have astounded the Vaudois, for Catinat was the monster who had so cruelly ruined them in 1686. By the standards of the day, however, he passed as a humane commander, doing dirty jobs quickly and efficiently, neither bloodthirsty nor fanatical.

The general finished reading and stared at the haggard specimen in front of him. Two officers of Catinat's staff stood silently behind the visitor in the little office in Fort Sainte-Brigitte, suspicion and distaste plain on their faces.

"If, Monsieur, you are the brother-in-law of this Arnaud, as you claim, why do you bring this to me?"

The other did not raise his eyes. "It was my duty, sir," he said in a low voice. "It grieves me that my own kin has followed courses so prejudicial to the service of His Royal Highness, my master, and of His Very Christian Majesty, your master. And while I hope that Monsieur Arnaud will see the error of his ways one day, I felt compelled to inform you of what transpires—for the good of the service, as I said, and of our Holy Catholic Faith."

"Which faith you have not always embraced, is it not so?"

"True, my lord. I abjured the errors of Calvin about ten years ago."

"So now you are such a loyal son of our Holy Mother Church that when you were asked to carry messages for the Barbets in and out of Switzerland in this somewhat bizarre fashion, your conscience compels you to stop off in Pignerol and come to me!"

"Indeed, sir. It is just as you have said." Gautier licked his lips and dropped his head even further. Catinat and his two aides stared fixedly at the visitor.

"Your dutifulness does you great credit," said the general after a long moment. "Most of the Barbet correspondence goes by way of an agent they have, perhaps here in Pignerol. Do you know who this may be? And why did they not use him instead of you—a magistrate and surely a sincere convert to the True Church?"

Gautier licked his lips again and darted a look at the general's face. "I suppose the person you refer to is Monsieur Grousset. I don't know why I was asked. Perhaps they no longer feel safe to use this other channel and thought I wouldn't be under suspicion. They were very pressing, my lord, and for the sake of the safety of my family, I felt I must agree. I hope you understand my position."

"Well, perhaps I do," replied Catinat, handing the button, the cloth, and the letter to Gautier, with just a touch of a smile. "I will ask only that as you pass through Geneva on this journey of yours, you will stop and see His Majesty's resident there, Monsieur d'Iberville. If you do, it will speak to your good faith, and perhaps we may have further conversations. The sergeant at the door will see you safely outside the fort."

"Thank you, my lord," said Gautier, bowing humbly. Catinat responded with a curt nod. The visitor backed, still bowing, from his presence and turned to follow the soldier.

"Well, what do you make of that?" asked Catinat, still smiling to himself. His orderly at the sideboard filled a wineglass and handed it to his master. Catinat nodded at the other two officers, and the soldier filled glasses for them too. The younger of the two aides, a pudgy, smartly attired young man with a beautiful wig and carefully trimmed mustache, wiped his lips with a scented handkerchief.

"Is there anything in that letter, sir, that we do not already know about their situation? Do they think we know already so they send such a 'secret' to prepare the way for a later dispatch that will be intended to mislead us?"

"Or would this sad creature be playing a game of his own," suggested the other officer, a sallow, slender man of middle age, "that he builds credit with us by betraying his precious brother-in-law but salves his conscience—if he has one—because he assumes nothing in this letter does any real harm to the Barbets? Maybe later, after we have accepted him, he would be in position to turn an important matter to his profit." He choked over his glass and had to cough.

"You both may be right," said the general thoughtfully. "He might be avoiding the vengeance of the Barbets—you know how they treat their 'apostates'—and at the same time be gaining our favor as a well-intentioned and serviceable spy. I wonder if he plans to stop by Turin and see Monsieur de Parelle, or perhaps the duke himself? A loathsome object he is, but not stupid. That he was a Barbet but is now a ducal magistrate gives proof of a certain cunning." He leaned back and contemplated the dishes on the sideboard without really seeing them. "Keep a closer watch on Grousset," he said. "This may not be his intrigue at all, and, in any case, as long as it is possible to learn anything useful, it would be a wasteful satisfaction to arrest him.

"I am more concerned if this Gautier or Arnaud are working with the duke and Parelle. Will the duke yet join the allies after all these months of teetering on the knife edge and finally become the Prince of Orange's cat's-paw in the Alps? I have *never* seen such a slippery prince as this Savoyard. Is he merely amusing us while he bargains with the allies?

"One thing is certain, gentlemen," concluded the general, rising wearily from his chair. "We *must* finish off these Barbets on the Balsille at once. If Savoy changes sides, we will have to fight the duke as well as the allies—and that would be profoundly inconvenient, particularly with Barbets still in their valleys, reinforced and encouraged and harassing our supply lines into Italy."

CHAPTER 7

Deliverance

Late in April, the French appeared again in the valley of Saint-Martin. Spring was late, and snow was still piled deep wherever direct sun didn't shine. With the soldiers were fourteen hundred peasants from the Perouse, Pragelas, and Queyras valleys to carry supplies over the Col de Clapier and to build roads. The French advance parties were forbidden to make fires in hopes of coming on their quarry unobtrusively, but the excellent Vaudois outpost system made this precaution useless. However, the advance parties suffered two freezing days in the snow before the main body caught up with them.

Closing in cautiously, the siege forces encircled the mountain—first at a distance—in a closing noose. But the steep cliffs on most of the circumference of the Balsille meant that no one could ascend or descend except on one side. Only a little distance from the fortress mount were the facing sides of the adjacent masses, Col de Pis and Mount Guinevert. But to reach them, one would have to scramble down difficult ravines that in places had almost sheer rock walls, cross rushing streams, and then ascend similar topography. To cover a distance of a few hundred yards as the crow flies would require hours of dangerous descent and ascent.

On the village side, it was somewhat easier. The ascent was irregular and steep in spots but relieved by several little plateaus. It was here that the Vaudois had carefully constructed their defense lines. The enemy began to take up positions along the streams in fringes of woods, much of it within musket range of the Vaudois outposts farthest down the hill. Vaudois sharpshooters harassed the troops in the woods by the stream bank; their food could be delivered only under cover of darkness. Sometimes the Vaudois ambushed these supply parties. The only answer was for the French to scale the facing cliffs and thus command the lower reaches of the Vaudois positions from across the chasm. Doing so occupied hundreds of miserable climbers for several days of danger, freezing cold, and blinding mists.

While the Vaudois outposts had to pull in when the French attained these positions, it didn't end their activity at night. On one occasion a party slipped through behind the still-loose enemy ring and took position on a crest with many loose rocks that overlooked the dragoons camped in the woods. Sighting their target by their campfires, at a signal the Vaudois rolled rocks down the slopes in the dark, with frightening and fatal results for many of the enemy around the fires.

The struggles of the French and Savoy infantry with obstinate nature offers strong evidence for the suggestion that nothing spurs human beings to greater effort and more self-sacrifice than the determination to kill their fellows. Wet and freezing, the men made exhausting climbs to the tops of Mount Guinevert on one side of the Balsille and the Col de Pis on the other. The regiments of Vexin and du Plessis ascended the latter and Cambresis and the Savoy detachment the former. The Savoyards, caught in one of the frequent mists, had to crouch overnight in the swirling white nothingness without water, wood, or tents, unable to move for fear of falling into an unseen void. This cost them an extra day. From these heights they could fire on some Vaudois positions, but an actual attack would require hours of descending to cross the stream and then still make the ascent up the Balsille.

With the siege forces as close in as they could get, General Catinat arrived to size up the situation. After studying the mountain and the Vaudois lines, he and his staff decided the right side of the scalable slope offered the best approach. Orders were given to make the attack on the morning of May 2.

In front were about twenty-three hundred men from the regiments of Bourbon, Artois, La Sarre, and the Second Languedoc Dragoons, dismounted of course. On the left, four hundred men from Cambresis and the Savoyards, who were expected to come down the cliffs and cross the stream, found themselves delayed by ten-foot snowdrifts and all manner of rocky obstacles. After descending from the heights, the Savoyards spent three hours trying to locate a crossing over the treacherous stream and then hopping from one snow-covered rock to another amidst the torrent. They weren't in position to fight by ten o'clock, as Catinat had hoped.

Then it began to snow. The Savoyards and their French fellow sufferers must have felt that Heaven was visibly interested in the fate of the Vaudois, for the tiny group of defenders seemed to have the elements warring for them. These troops could do little except to watch for Vaudois fugitives if the main attack succeeded.

The Vaudois, in their positions, checked their rock barriers with the whole trees wedged in, branches outward and the roots planted into the stone barricades by the weight of loose rocks. As the enemy preparations were visibly nearing completion, Pastor Arnaud led them in singing Psalm 68. Then all they could do was wait.

* * * * *

"They're coming!" shouted a sentry crouched among the rocks down the slope. He'd been looking over the edge of the drop from the little plateau above which the first Vaudois entrenchments stood. The outposts now ran back to the shelter of the entrenchments and palisades. The defenders of this "approachable" side of the Balsille watched the enemy assault get under way.

"They must be crazy!" exclaimed Armand. "There aren't more than a thousand of them in this attack, and it's uphill against strong defenses!"

"They haven't learned the right lesson since last September," said Captain Odin. "We've always met them in hit-and-run guerilla actions; they still assume we're undisciplined riffraff who will inevitably run away when we see a line of bayonets approach."

"Better for them this day that they be the 'undisciplined riffraff,'" said Armand. "Their steadiness and discipline will mean many more of them will be killed trying to reach us."

Captain Odin turned away and called to the other officers standing behind their men at the stone and log breastworks. "Remember—no one fires till I give the command!" He knew his independent and relatively undisciplined force and how they would be affected by tension as the enemy came nearer and nearer. The word was passed down the line.

Meanwhile, the attackers had formed in lines as regular as the unevenness of the ground permitted and advanced as well as they could over rocks, tree stumps, and other irregularities. From above, it seemed that they moved very slowly. They came up over the drop-off onto the narrow plateau, and it was a temptation to open fire at once. But they were still two hundred yards away, and at that distance, hitting a target would be largely luck. The French officers and sergeants walked ahead, calling to the men and dressing the lines. In front was a cluster of officers, drummers, and color-bearers. Their voices carried clearly to the silent and waiting Vaudois.

A Vaudois captain pointed. "Look to their right!" he cried. "They're having trouble getting over the creek. They aren't all going to get here together."

The detachment on the French right was indeed delayed. They'd found the stream more of a problem than expected. With snow covering the ice, men had broken through to flounder in freezing water. And the steep rocky bank lay hidden under snow. Once on solid ground, they put on a very creditable burst of speed and had climbed almost within fifty paces of the steeper ascent to the log-and-stone barrier. On the French left, beyond the stream, the Savoy contingent remained motionless. One could guess that they too were watching with interest, quite content to let the French have the glory.

As the opposition came on, still pretty much in a line, Armand felt his breathing catch a little. He saw the familiar flags under which he had once fought, and the uniforms of regiments beside which he had once battled. Now they were coming straight at him. There were not many French refugees left now in the Vaudois camp, but he wondered what the others might be thinking. Coming right at Armand was Bourbon, with La Sarre on his right and Artois behind, struggling to catch up.

Features of the approaching soldiers became discernible. Those who had the breath to spare began to yell insults and threats, perhaps mostly to encourage themselves. The first attackers, knots of sappers and grenadiers, reached the barrier and found the trees weighed down with immovable rocks. They couldn't be pulled out of the way to gain access to the trenches. The main line was about fifty paces away when Captain Odin gave the command to fire. The other captains repeated the order, and there was a long rolling volley from the Vaudois trenches.

The fire continued without further command. After each musketeer fired, he handed his piece to a younger soldier, who gave him a loaded weapon and recharged the first. At the fourth or fifth such exchange, Odin ordered them to cease fire. As the billows of smoke drifted away, the Vaudois could see the havoc they had wrought. Many gray-clad figures either lay on the ground or were struggling to rise. The French line was no longer visible. Under the deadly hail, the attack had fragmented.

But the French were veterans. The surviving officers began to reform the semblance of a battle line. After a brief hesitation they came on again. The men in the rear were urged forward to fill in the decimated front.

At Odin's signal, a score of Vaudois clambered up from the protection of the trench and levered stones loose from their lodging places among the tree trunks and branches. They sent trimmed logs rolling down the slope too, which gathered speed, and occasionally bounced end over end. There was no way for the French to dodge the torrent of rocks and logs. They broke and ran.

The scattered fire from above wasn't necessary to complete the rout. In a few moments, the slope was cleared of standing figures, and almost every enemy who remained was dead or sorely injured. French casualties were over four hundred, but not a single Vaudois had even been hit—another miracle for the little band.

Groups of Vaudois ventured down the slope to examine the damage and retrieve the leavings of the vanquished. A few wounded prisoners were brought in. The most notable was the lieutenant-colonel who had led the detachment from the regiment of Artois. He was found lying close to the Vaudois defense line with a smashed hip. His two sergeants were taken with him, as they refused to leave their wounded chief.

" 'The conies are but a feeble folk, yet make they their houses in the rocks!' " quoted the Vaudois Captain Fraische triumphantly to the captive sergeants as they carried the unconscious colonel into the Vaudois first line. Though the captain had spoken to them in French, the sergeants looked blank.

"I doubt there has been much study of the Scriptures in the French camp," said Armand de Gandon. "You'll have to excuse them. At least this poor officer will now know that the Balsille conies have teeth!"

Behind them came Alexandre Cortot dragging several muskets by the barrel.

"I wouldn't want to be the one who has to write a report of this day's work for the king," observed Armand, shaking his head sadly as he joined his young friend.

"There's no need to feel sorry for anyone," replied Alexandre. "The best thing about being the general in chief is that he's the one who gets to write the reports. He can blame someone else."

"You show real promise," said Armand fondly. "You already have one of the necessary qualities to be a great general."

* * * * *

The Vaudois celebrated their stunning victory with a thanksgiving service. Pastor Arnaud's sermon so touched his audience that most of them and he himself wept. Their victory was to them renewed evidence of Divine interest in their affairs. They were as encouraged as they knew the enemy would be discouraged and humiliated when the waiting world heard the details. It was reported that the French had to bring back to Pignerol the ropes with which they had planned to hang the entire Vaudois army. Such items of booty as clothing, linen, and money the defenders divided among themselves. Though they knew their trials were far from over, their courage was high and their spirits joyous.

After prayer the next morning, to signal to their enemy their defiance and determination, heads removed from the fallen Frenchmen were stuck on posts in front of their lines. This rather barbaric gesture was nothing unusual in that day, and certainly not original with the Vaudois. It was an indication, perhaps, of the brutalizing consequences of their long persecution. In the desperate battle to survive, eventually and unconsciously the Vaudois had suffered distortion of their own humane standards. In an age of horrific penalties for commonplace crimes, when loaded gallows could be found at country crossroads and in the market squares of the cities, no one was likely to be especially shocked at this deed. It was, at least, language the enemy understood.

In the days that followed, Armand de Gandon and François Huc became acquainted with the most distinguished prisoner yet taken by the Vaudois, Lieutenant-Colonel Parat. The captive asked for his regimental surgeon, and, under a flag of truce, his request was forwarded. Doubtless in some trepidation, the surgeon and a servant presented themselves at the defense line. They were blindfolded and conducted to the hut in the so-called chateau, high on the mountainside. The surgeon was amazed to be greeted by courteous, French-speaking officers, some of whom, for the occasion, were wearing Dutch or Brandenburg uniforms with galons of gold or silver.

The smashed hip was set as carefully as possible, and drugs eased the pain. The besiegers had permitted the surgeon to go on the condition that he was *not* to assist ill or wounded Vaudois. But these stipulations were blithely ignored, and the surgeon was kept in the camp as a prisoner. His services were effective and much appreciated, for the previous captive medical man had been killed just a few days before. It was soon evident that the colonel would survive, but he would be a long time in walking again, if ever.

As his fever waned and he was able to converse with his visitors, he expressed his amazement at finding officers like Huc and Gandon in such company. "Barbets I can understand, but to find gentlemen like yourselves here—"

Armand laughed and said, "Your surgeon was surprised to find that Vaudois didn't have two heads or forked tails! You must remember, Monsieur, that we Huguenots also take our beliefs very seriously, and when one does that, he may find himself in strange and unpleasant places indeed. God is our Refuge, but He doesn't promise that His confessors will necessarily enjoy a life of ease here on earth."

Parat said nothing for a time. "Well," he remarked at last, "my duty has put me in an awkward place, too, though I'm glad to find that it includes such congenial company."

Because it was customary for captured officers to finance their own release, special efforts were made to keep such captives alive. Parat made it clear that his family had wealth and that a good ransom could be expected for his release. The Vaudois Council of War considered the matter and then went as a body to discuss the question with the colonel. Money, they assured him, was not the important consideration with them, but they did have brethren, four in particular, languishing in the dungeons of Turin, and they would be most gratified and willing to effect the exchange of his person for these comrades.

To their surprise and to the consternation of their prisoner, Feuquières, the new commander of the siege forces around Balsille, flatly refused to discuss any exchange. Parat had been happy to learn that this man, a friend of the Parat family, had been placed in command. But the ambitious and relentless Feuquières didn't wish to sully the reputation he hoped to build as the foe of heretics and the destroyer of Barbets by accommodating them, even to save the life of a family friend. He made no secret of his intention to succeed where Catinat had failed, and it became increasingly obvious that he hoped to leapfrog his rival to higher and more glorious commands elsewhere on the strength of destroying the Barbet nuisance. Feuquières rudely rebuffed every attempt by Parat's worried fellow officers to discuss an exchange.

One evening late in mid-May, Parat's Barbet visitors seemed unusually somber. He asked why.

"I fear, my friend," said Armand reluctantly, "that matters go badly for you. The guns have now arrived down below, and when they are emplaced, the bombardment of our works will begin. You are probably safe enough from the cannon balls up here, but in time the guns may open the way for another assault. If it is successful, I much doubt that your friends will find you alive no matter what happens to us. Surely Feuquières understands this quite clearly also."

Parat calmly considered his situation. "I have already thought how this may have to end. I'm not responsible for this situation, and neither are you. I want you to know that I forgive you my death. What will be, will be."

* * * * *

By the light of a single candle on the table in his sparsely furnished quarters in Fort Sainte-Brigitte, the main defense of Pignerol, General

Catinat paced back and forth with hands clasped behind his back, pausing occasionally while he dictated to his secretary. A staff officer sat astride a chair, his chin on his folded arms. Catinat was not a man who spoke much of his private feelings. But he must have thought without great sorrow of his disloyal and ambitious subordinate, Feuquières, in his chilly command post on the Balsille, the winds howling off the snow-covered slopes. It was a morose enough affair to be chasing the Barbets at any time of year.

Catinat well knew there was no certainty that anyone could conquer these mountain people. No one had come closer than he had four years earlier, when perhaps only twenty or twenty-five of them remained in the hills out of twenty-five hundred fighters. Yet here they were, seemingly a problem and a frustration that could go on forever. With these thoughts in mind, the general was very carefully dictating a letter to Louvois, the hot-tempered minister of war, who would very likely share it with the king himself, for Louis XIV had a passion for detail. It needed saying, but knowing the king's obsession with matters of religion and his enormous self-esteem, Catinat had to dictate the letter as if to the war minister without suggesting that the king's policy was a failure. He said,

> It is probable that we are near the end of this cursed affair of the Barbets. We have almost all of them at bay in this mountain, but as they know these hills so well, one must not be surprised if some elude us. The unseasonably heavy snows have so diminished the ability of these people to live off the country that it appears we have the opportunity to force them to stand and fight, but these same snows do, of course, add immeasurably to the difficulties of our attack, and were the chief reason for the unhappy outcome of the assault earlier this month.

The secretary, being both loyal and competent, didn't object to this considerable tampering with the truth.

> In view of the increasingly equivocal behavior of the Piedmontese, of which you have been long aware, I am not relying on them for any important part in this final attack. We shall, of

course, keep you fully informed as the Comte de Feuquières continues his preparations for the attack.

As you are aware, Monseigneur, the good execution of His Majesty's intentions has been complicated not only by heavy drafts on our forces for service in Flanders and the deliberate mystification of his intentions that His Royal Highness the duke of Savoy has maintained now for some months but also by the nature of the campaign against the Barbets. I would be surprised if at any time during this campaign the *true* Vaudois, as the Barbets call themselves, have exceeded four or five hundred. We have reason to believe that they are weary of the war and wish but to be left in peace on their ancestral lands. Until they are either destroyed or granted peace, they provide a haven for foreign adventurers, deserters, and brigands, some of whom are His Majesty's subjects of the allegedly Reformed Religion.

We are therefore occupied in a war of ambushes and sudden affrays. I would guess that in the past six months we have suffered two thousand dead and wounded, and I would be gratified if I thought we had killed or hanged as many as two hundred of them. In any case, less than a thousand of them in their various bands tie down ten thousand of my men uselessly and prevent good preparation for the troubles we expect at any moment with His Royal Highness, the duke.

How can one get the better of folk so little concerned with comfort that when one captures one of their camps, all one finds is a pound of rhubarb and handwritten quotations from the Maccabees? I have used a little cruelty in an effort to discourage the people of the valleys from giving supplies to them, but we cannot guard every farm or hamlet in this province, and the Barbets take what is not freely given.

If His Majesty deems it apropos, I would be willing, without use of your name nor any commitment in the name of His Majesty, to explore with the leaders of the true Vaudois through contacts that I have the possibility of an arrangement whereby they might withdraw from their allegiance to the duke of Savoy, whose protection by now they must realize is worthless, and accept the protection of His Majesty for their valleys. It would be preferable, Monseigneur, to have a neutral little Barbet republic under our eye, thus releasing thousands of my men for His Majesty's service elsewhere, than to perpetuate the present situation, should any considerable number of the Barbets escape our forthcoming attack.

The staff officer had been listening with growing uneasiness. "Pardon, my general," he said at last. "Your proposal is sound, and it would be of inconceivable utility to end this wretched campaign. But surely, sir, you must realize the calamitous effect your words would have on your own reputation. Can you not hear what the fanatics at Versailles will make of this proposal—and that you *have* made it will infallibly leak from the council even if His Majesty never replies to your proposition. They will say that General Catinat wishes to reestablish within His Majesty's dominions a nest of heretics! The devout will rend you limb from limb, and if you are answered at all, it will be with an order to retire to your estate. The only joy in this would be for Monsieur de Feuquières and the duke of Savoy—and, of course, the more fanatical of the Barbets."

"That is well said, colonel," Catinat replied, smiling thinly, "and I appreciate your concern. But if His Majesty's servants fear to offer suggestions, will not his service suffer? In any case, I will carry out my orders as best I can and as I have always done. At least, I shall not have to regret that I feared to set before him unpleasant truths. I've thought of waiting until we see the outcome of this next attack, but if it is partially successful, we shall then have tiny bands to hunt down for an interminable period, scattering through these mountains. If there is any possibility of making an agreement with their leaders now, it would prove advantageous in the long run."

The officer lowered his head and shrugged.

"Whether or not we succeed in dispersing this rabble," continued the general, "we will have to force the duke to decide which side he's on—and to give us the citadel of Turin as an earnest of his loyalty. Some activity by his forces now before the Balsille would be an evidence of good faith. One would like to know for certain just who one's enemies are! At least the Barbets have never left anyone in doubt on that score!"

* * * * *

The command he had yearned for was at last his. The Comte de Feuquières determined that no premature effort would endanger his ambitions. It took nearly three weeks for two eight-pounder cannons to be dragged from Pignerol by ox teams, with swarms of peasants to widen and smooth the dreadful roads. The blockade continued in the meantime, but as long as the enemy lines remained at the base of the mountain, Vaudois could still slip out.

Serious operations resumed on the tenth of May. The approach to the defense line took twelve days of continual pressure. On the "approachable" side, the enemy infantry, regardless of cold and bullets, inched up the slopes from the stream banks. Once established, they moved slowly and inexorably uphill, using bags of wool or fascines made of bundles of wood as shields. If a Vaudois stuck his head up, enemy musketeers below and across on the opposing slopes poured in such a hail of bullets that there simply was not much the Vaudois could do to halt the advance.

The besieged force watched with apprehension as the guns arrived and, with incredible effort, were dragged and hoisted almost an inch at a time to positions prepared on the slopes facing the Balsille and on a level about even with the chateau. The muzzles of the guns looked at them no great distance away across the steep chasm; inevitably, the Vaudois stoneworks and palisades wouldn't be standing long. The defenders could continue to back up hill, but with their defense lines knocked over and the palisades splintered, the enemy could break through and pursue them until they were trapped at the top.

At intervals the French addressed the Vaudois with speaking trumpets, demanding their surrender and promising incredible payments—such as nine hundred *louis d'or* apiece plus a passport—if they would capitulate and leave the country. No one believed, and there were no takers. Firing and rolling stones when they could, the defenders withdrew, suffering some wounded but none killed. The final warning shouted across the battlefield was that no terms would be given after the flags went up for the guns to commence firing. This was positively the last chance to save themselves.

As they had before, the Vaudois replied firmly that they weren't subjects of the king of France, nor were they under any obligation to pay attention to him. They assured Feuquières that they didn't fear his cannon—the thunders of their mountain storms were louder. As long as ten men remained, there would be no capitulation, for they counted on the help of the Lord of hosts.

On the morning of May 23, a white flag went up, followed by a red one. Then the sound of the first shot echoed off sheer cliff faces. Eight-pound cannon balls began to fall on the unmortared stone barricades and on the wooden palisades, and wood and stone splinters flew. And though there were no human victims, the rhythmic cadence of the discharges of the two guns continued. One of the Vaudois with nothing better to do while waiting above the destruction counted 114 shots by noon.

To keep away from the cannon fire, the defenders had to pull back so far that the French infantry was out of musket range, and they moved up and over the first smashed-and-tumbled defense lines without much trouble. The beleaguered little band drew back up the hill to the last redoubt, the Cheval la Bauxe. Previously, their great advantage had been in forcing the enemy to make a steep climb under fire against strong entrenchments. Now, hemmed in on the narrow space near the top of the peak, they could no longer effectively stop assaults. Night fell, and by the last daylight they could see that several thousand French soldiers had bivouacked in the lower entrenchments. The campfires they had started lit up all the areas where there was footing, blocking any hope of escape. The steeps on the other sides of the mountain were sheer drop-offs and offered no way out.

At about six o'clock that evening, Feuquières sent a smugly triumphant dispatch to Catinat. "We have lost almost no one, their stones being without effect. As of now, unless a hippogriff* carries them off, I see no way they can escape. They are surrounded on all sides at pistol range with good entrenchments." It was a dutiful report to the general, no doubt, but also some salt in his wounds from the disaster of May 2.

Some sixty of the Vaudois were away on a foraging expedition. About three hundred thirty remained in the Balsille. They also held a few prisoners—notably Lieutenant-Colonel Parat, still bedridden. That evening there was little sleep and much prayer among this group. If every man

---

* A mythological winged monster.

struck out for himself, some could no doubt slip through the enemy lines, but most would not be able to—the enemy was too close now, and the firelight too bright. Those who got through would no longer be even a band. Such an action would extinguish the last organized resistance. And if no Vaudois army was left, their families would be permanently resettled in scattered refuges throughout Europe, and the Glorious Return would have ended in complete catastrophe for God's people.

As the night wore on, less and less was said. Each defender was inclined to be alone with his thoughts. From below, they could hear the hilarity of the French as they celebrated their victory a little prematurely.

It was always cold and damp, but by midnight, at first scarcely perceived or seen, a slight change began to take place. The fog was settling in again. The sentries noticed after a time that the French campfires were blurry glows of red or had disappeared entirely. As so often happened, a wet, cold blanket of dense fog was covering the mountaintop. There was perhaps a little comfort in not being visible to the enemy, but surrounded and with no possibility of escape, it changed nothing really. They were still cut off in an impenetrable white void.

One man, however, was watching the weather change with growing excitement. About midnight, certainty took hold of Captain Tron-Poulenc. He rose from his resting place on the wet ground and sought out the little knot of officers lying or sitting around a fire. The discussion was short and to the point. "God has heard us!" Tron-Poulenc exclaimed. "We have a chance yet. If we can get through the French lines in this fog, I think we can escape. A goat trail runs up the side of Mount Guinevert. I know it; I used to climb it as a boy. We'd have to go on hands and knees much of the way, but by the time the fog lifts, we could have a fair start over the summit if we go now."

There was little argument, for the situation was so patently hopeless that no one could suggest an alternative. No one could remember seeing any way to climb that rock face. However, it might be better to try it in the dark than to be paralyzed by fright in the light. But first they would have to go down the Balsille through the French lines.

The officers roused their men quietly and urgently. Instructions were given: Equipment that might rattle or bump about was to be left behind. Unfortunately, the seriously wounded would have to be left also. Short but fervent prayers were offered, fires were built up to give an appearance of normalcy, and the little companies assembled for a final roll call.

At a murmured order from Captain Odin, several men slipped away to the huts where Captain Parat and the other French prisoners lay. With every moment counting, the Vaudois couldn't risk the prisoners speeding the pursuit by giving any information when the French arrived in camp at dawn. Parat's surgeon, however, was compelled to accompany the expedition.

Silently, the little army slipped over the makeshift breastworks and in single file crept down the slope toward the French lines. Then, scarcely daring to breathe, the line of Vaudois crept past sentry after sentry. To the French, there was obviously no place the Vaudois could go and nothing they could do other than to make some insane gesture like a suicide attack. So certain were they, that their guards, while numerous, were somewhat relaxed. But how long a confident or even a slightly inebriated sentry would fail to pick up rustling and scuffing in the dark repeated three hundred times was the question. One sneeze, one stumble, one loose rock dislodged, and everything could end for the Vaudois in a brief and violent struggle in the dark and the fog. One pebble *did* roll down to a sentry, but as it didn't respond when he shouted, "Who goes?" he must have assumed that he had imagined it.

The Vaudois crept on, each man holding the coattail of the man in front. If anyone let go, the whole line had to stop to reestablish contact. The captain had removed his shoes for sake of quietness regardless of ice and snow, and some others did so too. After what seemed an eternity, the last man left the last French sentry out of earshot. Creeping and slipping, grasping shrubs to steady themselves, they reached the foot of the Balsille. Soon they were approaching the base of Mount Guinevert. How Tron-Poulenc could tell where he was going—unless guided by his guardian angel—no one could even guess, and most were so intent on keeping up and not falling that they didn't speculate on such things.

Tron-Poulenc searched for and found his trail, though at times it wasn't even that. The dawn was coming, and as the light suffused through the fog blanket, the men began climbing. Frequently, steps had to be chopped in the hard-packed snow. Mercifully, they couldn't see how far down they would fall if they slipped. The procession wound along the cliff face, bunching up for a few moments but never stopping for long—each man urging on the one in front. It was a slow business, as no one could go faster than the most fearful or the weakest, yet a wonderful concentration of the faculties affected everyone, from Pastor Arnaud to the dullest private soldier.

As the day brightened, the French lines hummed with activity. Bugles blew. Drums beat the assembly. Flags were broken out. In spite of the cold and wet, the men moved smartly, convinced that the end of their term in this freezing hell was at last in sight.

As the lines formed, advance parties moved up the slope to feel out the defenses. They moved warily into the thinning fog, anticipating the crash of musketry from behind the rocks, which so often was the last thing many a French soldier ever heard.

But nothing happened.

Emboldened, the pioneers scrambled over the tumbled rocks and litter of the abandoned defense line.

No defenders were in sight.

The French pushed forward a little faster, and in a few moments overran the camp—only to find the Vaudois gone.

But how? Demons that they were, could they fly? Some had thought all along that the famous Arnaud was a magician.

The rest of the assault force was now hurrying up behind them, puzzled by the shouting. Rushing into the huts, they found the wounded Vaudois—a dozen or so—whom, of course, they killed. They also discovered, hiding behind a rock, one able-bodied Vaudois; they shot him dead as he tried to run. Then they found Colonel Parat and the other prisoners dead in their huts. It was obvious that they hadn't been dead long—so where *had* the Vaudois gone? Were they indeed witches? Feuquières, cheated out of his great moment, toiled uphill carrying on like a madman. Arguments, imprecations, and general confusion reigned.

Silently, the fog lifted, and suddenly someone shouted and pointed. Seeing him but not really hearing him amid the brouhaha, others turned to look where he pointed. There, perhaps half a mile away but incredibly high up, a string of dots like ants in single file was winding up the sheer rock face of Mount Guinevert, the front of the line disappearing into the fog that hid the mountaintop. Once again, their prey had eluded them!

Feuquières screamed orders that the soldiers follow the Vaudois. It seemed for a moment he might have a mutiny on his hands—his subordinates didn't think they could do it. To the French, the Vaudois could perform such feats of mountaineering only through the particular help of their father the devil. Very unwillingly, and prophesying their own doom, the pursuers began. But they couldn't climb as fast as the pursued. Every so often, a Frenchman's foot slipped on the wet and icy rock, and he fell with a scream into the abyss below. But armies perform because the men fear their own sergeants more than any other danger, so they pushed on. However, the gap between the two forces only became wider and wider.

Eventually, the Vaudois reached a relatively level place among the crags on the way to Rodoret, and they paused for a rest. They were exhausted from their exertions and famished. They ate a little from the scanty supply of food they carried in their packs. How much more of this deprivation human beings could take one might wonder, but they were still a Vaudois army, and once again they had been miraculously saved. Especially grateful were the lightly wounded who somehow had managed to make the journey. And, no doubt, the French surgeon, who had been forced to come along, was dazed but grateful to find himself still breathing. A thanksgiving prayer was offered as they knelt in the sleet.

As they rose to resume their march, Armand counted his company twice. One man was missing. "Where is Perrin?" he demanded suddenly of his bedraggled little group. "What happened to him?"

"Pardon, captain," said his sergeant, flinching from Armand's anger. "When they went to kill Colonel Parat, he told me that the colonel had such marvelous damask shirts that he was going to slip in afterward and take some of them. He told me not to say anything to you because he could get out all right by himself and catch up later."

Armand was speechless and could only shake his head. To lose one's life for a damask shirt! Alexandre smiled grimly with frozen lips as he chewed his last hazelnut. "There has to be one in every army!"

* * * * *

Tired, hungry, and chilled, the bands struggled down to a little hollow in the hills beyond Angrogna on May 29. Now far behind, their pursuers posed little danger. Weary as the Vaudois were, they felt a sense of expectation. Rumors of changes at Turin were continual. The day before, Piedmontese prisoners taken in an attack on Pramol told them the French had given the duke an ultimatum—give them the citadel at Turin as surety by the thirtieth or be considered an enemy of France.

They found a little party waiting for them in the vale. In notable contrast to the rags and wrappings of the weary Vaudois, the new arrivals were smartly attired—as became Monsieur de Vercellis just arrived on an urgent errand from His Royal Highness the duke to his loyal subjects of the Vaudois persuasion.

The rumors were true! The duke had broken with Louis XIV at last! He had finally rejected the connection that had brought such unspeakable calamity on the mountain folk these past four years. Not only that, but he had formally joined the Grand Alliance against France. As Pastor Arnaud said later, "The almighty hand of the Lord of hosts has checked the progress of that terrible crown."

Vercellis brought a letter to the pastor that was read to the little army. The duke invited his subjects of the Reformed Faith to return to their valleys once more, confiding in his protection, and he besought them to continue their fight against the common enemy. In return, he promised money, supplies, and the liberation of all the Vaudois prisoners in his dungeons. He also said that inquiries would be made about their missing children. If the two or three hundred Vaudois released from prison so chose, they would be armed, outfitted, and on their way to join the others at once.

When Pastor Arnaud finished reading the duke's promises, he added words of his own: "I shall write at once to Switzerland and invite all who wish to reestablish God's Holy Zion to throw themselves into the hills with us. We already have six months of marvels to tell of. To God be the glory! It is the Lord's doing, and it is marvelous in our eyes!"

Armand, Alexandre, and the remaining Huguenots stood apart and watched in some wonder at the readiness of the joyous Vaudois to accept these fair promises from a sovereign whose weakness and faithlessness had cost them so dearly. Their gratitude was touching. They wept for joy and kissed the hands of the ducal officer.

Alexandre, a symphony of rags and tatters, his shapeless and discolored hat obscuring half his face, leaned on his musket. "How can they believe all this so easily?" he whispered disconsolately.

"They needs must," sighed Armand. His once beautiful blue coat was so faded and discolored that it was difficult to tell what the original color might have been. His legs were wrapped in strips of cloth like those of the others, and he also carried a musket, a haversack, and bandoliers. Except for his sword, which he had stubbornly kept through all their recent trials, he was indistinguishable from his men.

Armand continued, "This brings their long odyssey to a happy conclusion. They are simple folk, and God has wrought wonderfully for them, overruling kings so they might return to their homeland. Thus they don't see anything unbelievable about their duke changing his mind, and they don't worry that he might change it again a year hence."

The French Protestants drooped with fatigue, silent and sad, as the Vaudois celebrated. Their eyes strayed to the peaks to the west. Beyond lay France and their own oppressed Huguenot brethren—five hundred times more numerous than the Vaudois. Was no deliverance coming for them? Was the cup of their persecution not yet full? What of the Grand Design? Were the allies even interested in using the Alpine door that the duke of Savoy was opening? Or was this the forgotten front in a great war? Were the Allied leaders fighting on this front on the cheap, using these tattered handfuls of Vaudois and Huguenot exiles to keep the French occupied while they prosecuted their real concerns elsewhere?

"They don't need us anymore," said Alexandre dispiritedly after watching for a time. "Do you remember the verse from Jeremiah chapter twenty-two? I keep thinking of it: 'Weep ye not for the dead, neither bemoan him: but weep sore for him that goeth away: for he shall return no more, nor see his native country.' I know it was said to the unfaithful of Israel, but perhaps it is meant for us too after all."

"It isn't over yet, Alexandre, and with Savoy on our side, help may come the sooner. We've been fighting a small skirmish in a long, long war. Should God will, it could go on long after our time. We did ourselves a disservice to build too high hopes for 1689, but in God's time, not man's, the redemption of Israel will come.

"This isn't the end for the Vaudois either," he added soberly. "It's more the beginning of a new chapter."

Armand straightened himself and patted Alexandre's slumped shoulder. "You know, Alexandre," he said, "it matters little where we're found in this world as long as it is on the Lord's side. Think on the eighteenth psalm, where David says that God will save His afflicted people: 'For by thee I have run through a troop; and by my God have I leaped over a wall. As for God, his way is perfect: . . . he is a buckler to all those that trust in him.' Let's rejoice for our Vaudois comrades, but we mustn't lose heart."

A scout slipped in, and, seeing the Vaudois officers occupied, came over and reported to Armand. The latter then spoke to Huc, and the two went to Captain Odin, who listened, and, in turn, addressed the Savoy officer. "My lord," he said with a low bow. "How widely known is this new alliance of His Royal Highness the duke? Do the French know of it yet?"

"Not all of them, surely," replied the Piedmontese. "It was known at the court only last night and is announced in Turin today. Of course, there are many French spies in the city, and it is possible that Catinat has heard of it in Pignerol."

Captain Odin said, "Our scout reports that the French have called off the pursuit, and their main body is returning toward Pignerol. But he says that three hundred men under Clairambault are crossing the mountain to Torre Pellice. He's been under way some hours, so it's quite possible he's had no opportunity to learn that Savoy is at war with France. May we have some of your uniformed soldiers? We'll cut across the hills by our own paths and be there to welcome him. He'll assume that your Piedmontese are allies, so it will be easy for us to break the news to him in a way that will surprise him!"

The ducal officer quickly agreed and told a dozen of his escort to march with their former enemies. "This should be an auspicious start for our collaboration in arms," he said grandly.

The Piedmontese collaborators regarded their unkempt new allies with some uncertainty. Alexandre Cortot had been eyeing the tallest of them, who wore a long blue coat with a dozen tiny buttons down the front in a single row. It was, however, the tall man's bulging haversack that interested Alexandre.

"Comrade," the young Frenchman said with a sort of salute, "I left my grenades back there due to the circumstances at the time. I wonder if you would be so kind as to lend me a half dozen of yours?"

The Piedmontese looked surprised.

"I still have my fuses and my match," Alexandre added winsomely.

"*You* are a grenadier?" blurted the tall man. He looked a mute question at the Savoy officer, as if to say, "We knew these people were strange, but this—?"

Alexandre stiffened, but before he could comment, the officer made an imperious gesture, and the soldier reluctantly reached into his heavy sack and gave six of the black metal globes to Alexandre one at a time. The little grenadier tenderly stowed them in his sack. "Thank you, comrade," he said. "I'm sure there'll be more for both of us after we're done at Torre Pellice!"

In a few moments the little force of new and uneasy allies—mountaineers and Piedmontese regulars—began the climb back up the rocky slopes and into the trees, toward the misty crests to the south to break the news to Clairambault.

PART II

1691

CHAPTER 8

Another Grief

" 'We are persuaded that if God had intended to remove His candlestick out of this kingdom, He would have opened the door and facilitated the egress of an infinite number of good souls who have remained. Do not believe, therefore, dear fathers, that we shall take the advice that you have given us to follow you in your flight. Our churches have been torn down, our pastors have abandoned us, and our property has been taken away, so grottos and caverns serve us for churches.' "

Pastor Merson was reading from an anonymous pamphlet. He sat in the parlor of the House for Huguenot Gentlewomen in Rotterdam, and listening was Madeleine Cortot. The pastor was a small dark man with a gravely humorous eye and a low, pleasant voice. The sun streamed in the windows on the spotless, wide-planked floor and gave the china in the cabinets an iridescent glow. A grave Madeleine, sitting with hands folded in her lap, followed him attentively but with a small frown clouding her brow. The pastor was the uncle of her onetime fiancé, Mathieu Bertrand, but more than that, he had been a family friend for many years, and his visit, Madeleine felt certain, had something to do with the long silent Mathieu. Madeleine was now the chief housekeeper of the home for gentlewomen. In this spring of 1691, she was a little more careworn but more composed than she had been in the wrenching crises of 1688—and more beautiful, the pastor thought with almost paternal pride.

"I know," continued the pastor, "that some suspect this pamphlet to be a provocation by our enemies and not the cry of our own people, but whether it be or not, I cannot but feel that it speaks to our ministers here in the safety of our exile. Where *are* the shepherds? The wolves tear at the flock of Israel, and the shepherds from their refuge write pastoral letters of good advice. Does this acquit us of our responsibility?"

"Why should you blame yourself?" asked Madeleine, her deep-blue eyes flashing. "I know Madame your wife and many of the pastors must have debated this with you many times, but it was required that you leave France if you would not accept Romanism, and it is death to return. Did not the Lord make an ark of refuge for us here in Holland? And such generosity to those of us who had lost our means—free citizenship, taxes exempted, special collections in the churches. It seems like a leading indeed."

She paused as if she were herself in the pulpit, waiting while the truth of her argument took hold of her audience. Then she continued, "I wonder if it is you pastors who deserted the flocks? One writer claims that the flocks deserted the shepherd, and, in fact, I remember how our neighbors in Saint-Martin grew most uneasy to have you about, attracting unwelcome attention. You had no choice but to leave." Her face was flushed, more obviously so because of the white cap that covered her dark hair.

Pastor Merson had not expected such a heated response to his proposed visit to the south of France.

"If that were ever so, Mademoiselle—" he said, "and I do not deny some truth in that argument, for I have heard it many times these past six years—if that were ever so, it is not always so, for the few pastors who have dared to go back have been welcomed. The eagerness for the spread of the Word is so great that scores of untutored *prédicants* have been called by the Spirit to nourish their famishing brethren, who now repent with groanings and tears. That the sheep were ungrateful in no way excuses a pastor, but how much less does it excuse him when they cry for him in their need? The reports that come out of the Wilderness show that nothing is impossible for God and that He can protect those who do His will."

He took a deep, slow breath but didn't give the young woman time to speak. "I know some of my fellows are old and infirm," he said, "but surely of the hundreds of pastors expelled in October 1685, a few at least might have dared to return under the Cross. I should have dared!

Perhaps some have been chafed by the criticism of Claude Brousson, but if he expressed himself bluntly, still, what he said was true. Though criticism from a lay person was bitter medicine to some pastors, one sees that Brousson himself went back and is now ordained and living up to his own challenge. How much more should we do so who have been pastors all along!"

Madeleine's face was a picture of agitation.

"I really didn't mean to chide you again on this matter," she said with a despairing gesture. "I am sure Madame Merson has said all these things, and no doubt you have quoted Scripture to her as you needed to."

Merson smiled. "Yes," he agreed quietly. "It has all been said, but even when we have said it all, there is still a residue of the house of Israel, and Ezekiel still warns, 'Woe be to the shepherds of Israel that do feed themselves! should not the shepherds feed the flocks? . . . They were scattered, because there is no shepherd: and they became meat to all the beasts of the field when they were scattered.' "

Madeleine studied her fingers. "If you are determined to go," she said after some hesitation, "I'm wondering whether you are going to visit our old home in Saint-Martin and whether you might hear further of Father, or if you should see Armand de Gandon and my brother Alexandre?" She paused, embarrassed that the soldier's name had slipped unbidden from her lips.

"Yes, Mademoiselle, I hope, God willing, to visit my friends at Saint-Martin, and of course, I can seek these gentlemen out, for I, too, have heard they intend to enter France. Is there a message—a special message—that I should give them if I am that fortunate?"

Madeleine hesitated. She *had* composed such a message but could not now speak it.

He read her heart, for he had known her since childhood, and he and his wife had been like second parents to her. Her back stiffened and her chin jutted—just as her mother's had—with a most formal solemnity.

"To be sure," he said, "at one time I had some expectation that notable events would occur in 1689, as Pastor Jurieu's prediction seemed to indicate. Perhaps he—and we—misunderstood the way in which the Lord works with His church and the way in which last-day events will conform to the prophecies concerning antichrist."

Pastor Merson's grave face twitched with amusement in spite of the pain that he knew she felt.

"Yet, even if the end is not as near as we then believed," he continued, "the care of the sheep is still the responsibility of the shepherd. The sheep feed badly or not at all, and is it not the fault of the shepherd? I must go, whether the end of the antichrist kingdom comes next year or in the next century. God is testing His people to see whether they will uphold His truth and honor His holy name. It is a shame that I and my brethren in the clergy tarry here taking our ease."

She nodded as if she had accepted that argument.

"I've had much time to think since Alexandre and Monsieur de Gandon left for Switzerland and Piedmont. My brother is not a writer of letters, but Armand—Monsieur de Gandon—has written twice to tell me that Alexandre was well and that the Lord had protected them in the affair of the return of the Vaudois to their valleys and that they would be going into France this spring. I don't know how to reach them but thought that perhaps in the Wilderness, where believers pass word, one would know how to trace them."

"*Certainment,*" agreed Merson, nodding with a faint smile.

"Before they left, the duke, who had so loved Monsieur de Gandon, wrote him to ask him to come back to France and make his peace with the king and the church—with his tongue in his cheek, to be sure—and resume his life there and enjoy the protection of the duke. In some secret way he knew of Armand and of his friends—even of me, for that matter. A few months ago he wrote again, but this time to me, for he assumes Monsieur de Gandon would have returned to France ere this had it not been for me, and now he wishes me to second his propositions and likewise conform outwardly and return with Armand—to be a great lady, I suppose. Armand must have refused him before, but the duke is old and unwell and I fear in some disfavor, for he is on his estates in Dauphiné. The duke can, however, arrange to have Armand pardoned if he will pretend to abjure, and we would be under his protection."

The pastor was surprised, even a little alarmed.

Madeleine shook her head vigorously. "Don't worry, Monsieur. I am not tempted. We didn't leave our *patrie* just to be bribed to return! But I can't be conscience for another. I am certain that over the years

Armand has been too proud to seek my hand when he had no prospects, and now he sees his duty to serve the Good Cause, but it is only honest to let him know the situation and let him decide for himself. Oh, I did wonder if perhaps we could in some way help my poor father in the galleys if we had the favor of a duke, but my father would spurn help at that kind of price. It was just a moment of weakness, and I really can't see Armand bowing the knee to Baal after all he has endured for us and for the Lord. But would you be so kind as to inform him of the duke's offer?"

She had made her speech, and her resolve collapsed.

Merson was no longer amused. "If I am to carry the duke's message, is there none from you? It might be germane, you know."

Tears glistened on her lashes. "As I said, I have thought much about him. I was proud and foolish even while I blamed him. I don't wish him to be concerned for us, nor do I wish any obligation he might feel to stand in the way of the preferment the duke offers. I would like to tell him now what I should have told him long ago and to say how sorry I am that I was too young and silly to understand how he felt. I suppose he thought me cold and ungrateful or perhaps still fond of Mathieu when really he was the one I esteemed. After all this time, however, would he still be able to forgive me? There was a time when I thought he . . ."

Her voice trailed off. The pastor could think of nothing to say.

"Once, you know, I thought we would go to America—Father, the twins, Alexandre and I, and . . ."

"Ah, yes, that bitter experience with Monsieur de Tillieres making off with your money and then betraying your father into the hands of his enemies. We were all heartbroken!"

"I've been able to replace the money I lost by my folly trusting that wretch Tillieres, and we could still go. However, though Louis is only ten, he is content to be a printer here, and Alexandre is the soldier, and I too have work. I should be content and return the money to my very kind and patient cousin in America whose loan I lost."

"I think I understand," said the pastor. "I also think I should tell Monsieur de Gandon that his duty requires him to repair, with all convenient speed, to Holland and that the two of you should make up for the time lost. My guess is that if both of you will set aside your pride, the enticements of the duke won't matter greatly!"

Madeleine sniffled a bit and blew her nose and wiped her eyes. "What I fear is that he has felt rebuffed and that it's too late. I know my brother tried to play cupid, but we wouldn't let him. I think I see matters in a different light now." Her eyes were filled with anxiety. "Do you think I presume too much? If he really no longer cared, would he still feel obligated to come when in his heart he might wish to return to France after all his disappointments?"

Merson felt trapped in a web of confidences, well remembering conversations with both Madeleine and Armand over the past two years. "You must trust him more, Mademoiselle. I don't see the gentleman as easily bribed. I think he will follow his heart, and I think it will be the same direction as his duty. In any case, let's find out. The Lord's arm isn't shortened—He can speak to the heart as easily in France as here in Rotterdam. You've waited, and possibly you both have been too proud and have misunderstood each the other, but it may be that Armand was needed where he's been and it has worked out best for the Cause and, I hope, for you. Our friend has been serviceable in the Good Cause—in England, in Piedmont, and now, I'm sure, in France. The prophet never would have said of him, 'Curse ye Meroz. . . . Curse ye bitterly the inhabitants thereof; because they came not to the help of the LORD, to the help of the LORD against the mighty.' "

The pastor rose and took Madeleine's hand and kissed it. She also stood up, and he was surprised that she was taller than he. No, Madeleine Cortot was no longer a girl. She was a woman of integrity and purpose, torn very much as his wife was torn between her willingness to sacrifice anything to the cause of God and her longing to be with the man to whom she had given her heart.

* * * * *

"I have appreciated your capable services," said Charles, duke of Schomberg, to the tall, deeply tanned officer standing before him.

They were in a bare room in a shabby chateau in the western end of Piedmont. The building had been burned and bombarded several times, and the repairs had been inadequate. Nevertheless, in the early spring of 1691, it served as headquarters for the forlorn aggregation that was His Britannic Majesty William III's force in Italy. It would have been very difficult to find an Englishman in the entire army—certainly, neither of the two men facing each other was English. The duke, a quiet man in his fifties, was expensively and tastefully attired in blue coat, lace cravat and cuffs, and full wig. The younger man's shabby, much-stained coat had been at one time part of the uniform of a soldier of William III, though its current wearer was a French Huguenot exile. The army was made up of such exiles in addition to Vaudois soldiers and mercenaries from Germany and Switzerland. The duke of Schomberg had held his title only since the previous July, when his father had, at the age of seventy-five, been killed fighting Irish Catholic supporters of James. That battle, at the Boyne, had been decisive. Unfortunately, none of the engagements here in Piedmont had been remarkably favorable.

The previous June, the somewhat slippery Duke Victor Amadeus II of Savoy had changed sides and made his strategic realm available to the allies fighting the troops of Louis XIV, the preeminent persecutor of Protestants. The British and Dutch now paid the Savoyard ruler a monthly subsidy of thirty thousand crowns to use Piedmont as the base for an invasion of France, in hopes that disgruntled new converts might rise in rebellion across the south of that country. Schomberg was a career soldier like his father. The old duke had served Louis XIV for many years until forced to leave at the time of the Revocation. The present Schomberg and his polyglot army waited in growing frustration for the cumbersome coalition against France to start moving.

The young officer was proud of his performance and almost as proud of his own shabbiness in the presence of his leader, this distinguished son of the great Marshal Schomberg, who had been his father's commanding officer thirty years before.

"I realize," continued Schomberg, "that it is unpleasant for our officers to see the hatred of the local Catholics for our refugee soldiers and the refusal of the Dutch commissioner to disburse funds with which to pay them—not to mention the squabbles of certain Swiss and French officers among us. I truly am grateful for one who is reliable in holding things together. It is a sorry place, and I am reluctant to send you off on this mission."

"Your Grace is very kind," responded Armand de Gandon. "My apparent imperturbability stems from my longer experience here than most of my colleagues, for I have been here in Piedmont with the Vaudois since their 'Glorious Return' began a year and a half ago, and one gets accustomed to the way things are done—or not done. But I would say a word in behalf of our poor discouraged Huguenot brethren who hastened here last June when the duke of Savoy joined the allies. They assumed that the notable providences that preserved the Vaudois would continue and the liberation of our oppressed people in France would shortly follow. Not only has little happened, but these refugees are often hungry and penniless, and no man can say what the duke of Savoy does with the subsidy King William pays him, nor can one say whether a Hapsburg force will ever enter Italy. Only the Vaudois, with their simple, tireless devotion, keep hounding the French. I don't marvel that our refugees are discouraged, Marshal; I marvel that they haven't all deserted."

"You speak the truth," said Schomberg, and he sighed. "I have written again and again to The Hague and to Whitehall, but nothing happens. The English are trying to be English even as they welcome William of Orange as their new king. The Dutch are pleased that their prince is now enthroned in England but are uncertain whether he still keeps Holland at heart. It appears the campaign in Italy is by no means the principal interest of our masters. That is why I wish to send you to sound out the situation in the Cévennes and Languedoc and to see what is possible if we should someday—soon, I hope—be in a position to move. I haven't heard from Captain Huc these two months, which isn't surprising considering the difficulties we have in getting messages to and fro. But even so, I would value your judgment on the realities of the case."

Schomberg turned toward a table at his elbow and pointed toward a map of the alpine area of France. "I want to make use of any opportunities that may arise, but I'm aware that the *prédicants* in the Church of the Wilderness are not always *au courant* with military reality and that their hopes color their estimates of the situation. Since Vivens's effort played out at Florac two years ago, I have seen little indication of coherence and leadership among these brethren. Devout they are, and earnest, but in terms of men and equipment . . . ?" He raised his hands in despair and then slammed them both flat on the table top.

Armand glanced at the stack of documents, the unfinished letter, and the bottle of ink beside the map. He cleared his throat. "I am honored by your confidence in me, my lord, and will do my best. Might I ask permission to take, instead of a half dozen soldiers, a single companion on the journey—a young man who also has served in these mountains since the late Vaudois expedition? He is a grenadier in the company of Captain Julien, but I am much attached to him and, in fact, would like to keep an eye on him if he can be spared."

Schomberg's smile was almost patronizing. "Certainly, captain. I will write Captain Julien. What is the lad's name?"

"Alexandre Cortot. He is a sturdy, reliable, and battle-seasoned young soldier; and we two, traveling on foot, will attract little attention."

"Of course. I wish all the requests that come here were as easy to grant."

Schomberg scrawled a few words on a piece of paper and handed it to Armand de Gandon.

"You are now a commissioned British officer, captain, and no longer in the Dutch service."

"In that case, my lord," said Armand, bowing and turning to go, "should you be able to persuade Monsieur Vandermeer to release enough of the subsidy so that we can be paid our arrears, I shall make it a point to procure a red coat."

"Your point I comprehend all too well, captain," said the duke with a wan smile. "But I hope that you can make your present raiment do for a long time yet." He thought to himself as Armand reached the door, *With a Swiss treaty of alliance that seems less likely every day, a slippery Savoyard ally who is probably already negotiating to change sides again, a pigheaded Dutch commissioner who won't pay the troops without further orders, and mutinous troops of four nationalities, I think it would be more pleasant to go where Captain de Gandon is going than to sit here watching opportunities dissipate and the skies darken.*

Although Armand was satisfied with his new commission and eager to be on his way, he also needed to be briefed, to study the maps, to memorize names and connections. And, of course, it would be several days before he could expect Alexandre to arrive.

In the officers' mess, Armand sat at a table with a crusty lieutenant just back from a minor defeat on the Savoy border. "Did you know," the officer asked, "that your old commander in the Regiment of Maine, the Duc de Lauzières, is so ill that he has left Versailles? Some speculated at first that he might be banished from court—the next thing to a secret royal arrest warrant for a man of his rank."

Armand set down his mess knife and stared at his companion. "Has there been a public charge?"

"*Mais non!* For you—for me, that would be the case, if he had indeed offended the king—which, as it turns out, he did not. But for a man of the blood, a nobleman of his standing, just a tap on the wrist, a reminder that all he enjoys at court is due to the king's grace. However, the duke is truly sick but is making some recovery. The king asks for Duc de Lauzières' health almost daily to be certain other courtiers don't mistake his present status. The duke is a charming old man. He knows how to oil the machinery at Versailles. And the king needs him there."

Armand took up his knife as if it had been a sword and cut the tough mutton on his plate. He chewed slowly while his mind scrambled through mixed emotions and fragments of information that had been swept aside during the past two years.

The Duc de Lauzières was indeed in poor health, with gout his most debilitating ailment, but this was no new malady. Yet the duke was at least seventy-five years of age, a man for whom every day was an uncertainty. Armand's first instinct was to ask leave of Schomberg in order to rush to his former patron's bedside. But that could not be. A visit from a soldier commissioned in the British army, whether wearing a red coat or not, would have been an unacceptable breach of conduct that would doubtless be reported at court and do the old man harm. *I'll write a letter expressing my sympathy,* Armand thought, *an apology, for most certainly the king's favor is tenuous, and that change is in some way related to his long devotion to me.*

When he had a quiet moment, he took up his quill pen.

When Your Grace gave me leave from my duties in your regiment, it still lingered in my mind, as perhaps you knew, that it might be possible to return to that duty and to the protection offered by Your Grace after carrying out certain personal responsibilities that I feared were not consonant with my commission in His Majesty's service. I have been honored more than I can say by the confidence and interest that Your Grace has displayed in so many ways, and it has been my reluctance to seem ungrateful for these numerous favors that has delayed my final decision this past year. The high favor you have had in mind for me would have been beyond any dream of glory, and I would have gratefully accepted your benefactions save that I would have had to carry water on both shoulders. I had not been faithful to that heritage of faith left me by my fathers, but I have decided that I can deny the Lord no longer. I have seen now how little earthly glory may amount to and that my former ambitions were ill-directed.

If I may presume to offer Your Grace the words of John Calvin, which are more aptly phrased than my own: "Time is nothing, and eternity is all, and we ought chiefly to aspire to the eternal and glorious liberty of the sons of God. We shall be free enough in the midst of our slavery when we are loosed from the bonds of the sin that so easily besets us and know how to rule ourselves and our own passions."

Pray do not blame the young lady whose influence you have suspected. It is my own doing. Again, my lord, my heartfelt thanks for your many kindnesses. I trust you will find another who will be more able than I to meet your expectations and who will not prejudice your reputation by association with persons or beliefs abhorrent to those who surround His Majesty.

Sealing the letter with wax, Armand placed it in the breast pocket of his vest. It would be a minor diversion when Alexandre arrived for the two of them to pass near enough to his former patron's chateau to send the young man on a swift detour to deliver the message.

There was also word from Madeleine, a missive that left Armand confused. She mentioned no actual names but referred to individuals well known to them both—though she made not so much as even an inference to Mathieu. She wrote that she had seen Pastor Merson and sought his counsel on several matters of importance. She said her brother Louis, now ten years old, was doing well as a printer's devil and wished to learn the trade and someday become a printer himself. She prayed for the safety and success of Armand and Alexandre. And she said that Madame Merson had resigned herself to her husband's return to the fields of his lifelong labor. With her blessing he would do what he could to encourage the disheartened, to lift up the fallen, and to bind up the wounded.

No mention of a projected journey to America. No plea for him to convince Alexandre to join her in such an enterprise. Indeed, she seemed to cast herself in a role parallel to the one to which Madame Merson had surrendered—and the only logical conclusion Armand could draw from Madeleine's resignation was that she cared for him.

Did she? If she did, how could he place on her the burden that rested on the heart of her beloved pastor's wife?

* * * * *

All was ready for departure when Alexandre arrived at the Allied headquarters, and so it was that Armand de Gandon and Alexandre Cortot once more set off to travel—this time to return to their native land, to travel by footpaths worn into hillsides across western Piedmont, through snow-choked passes in the Cottian Alps into the deep gorges and along the rushing streams in Provence and Dauphiné by way of the chateau of the Duc de Lauzières.

When they were encamped near the duke's chateau, Armand sent Alexandre with his message to the man who wished to make him his heir. Before an hour passed, Alexandre returned with two lieutenants. Armand could not pass by without appearing in person before the aged duke.

After brief greetings, the duke launched into a passionate plea for his cause. "*Mon fils*, it is more than just my desire to have you near me during my final years, and you understand how much pleasure it would give me to see you established in the career for which your military genius qualifies you." His raspy voice dropped to a whisper as if he feared servants across the room might hear and repeat what he was about to say. The words sputtered on his ample lips. "One would like for once to outmaneuver Madame de Maintenon. You may not realize the fact that it is she more than anyone else—more than Pere de la Chaise with his sly piety, more than Louvois with his visions of military grandeur—it is *she*, Maintenon, who holds the king's heart in her hands, who inspires his passionate need to control the consciences of all his subjects."

The old man's face, seamed with a thousand wrinkles, sagged at the jowls, but his eyes burned. "You know, Armand, I am at best a skeptic myself. I am uncertain whether God is to be feared or to be brushed aside as a joke, but I cannot see how spoiling the human and material resources of the nation for the sake of bringing all Frenchmen into Catholic uniformity makes sense. *Ce n'est pas possible!"*

With both hands, he moved his swollen left leg from its stool to the floor and leaned forward as if he meant to rise. "The king's army is the only thing he loves more than Maintenon. And the army suffers badly because he can't find leaders or even common soldiers of the quality previously supplied by the Huguenot communities. Your record, *mon fils*. Your *record*. That day on the battlefield in the Palatinate will hold the imagination of the nation forever. You were but a boy not yet twenty, but in every way your father's son. You saved your entire regiment by your swift action. Alas, I lost my only son that day, but I vowed that thereafter you would fill his place."

Armand was about to speak, but the duke renewed his plea.

"Indulge the sentiments of an old man, Armand. What matters is France. One must be a patriot first, and when like me he is no longer able to defend France in the field. . . ." The duke's customary cynicism was gone, and his eyes misted. "I can but attend the king at court. It is my only hope of helping my country.

"Is the king my friend? Who has friends? In the end, one has only one's family." The duke held out his hand, palm up, as if he asked for some small, tangible gift that he might clasp.

Armand strove twice to speak before the words finally came. "I love my country. I love France, my lord. I love my king, and I love you."

"Then, Armand, convert. At least appear to. Survival, I have found, requires a certain suppleness of conscience. You wouldn't be expected to dally at court. You would always be the man of action in the field, always excused from even the intrusion of the chaplains, whom you know hover like butterflies over a dunghill. All would be overlooked. More than likely, all would be forgiven."

"I can't." Armand reached to take the duke's withered hand, and his own trembled. He couldn't bring himself to explain again what he thought he had made clear in the letter that still lay upon the aged duke's lap. "I am en route to Languedoc."

"*Mais oui!* I forget in my enthusiasm that you, too, have affairs that require your attention. *Eh bien.* There is time. I will be here for six months at the least 'to recover' sufficiently to bear up under the demands of life at Versailles. Come back by this route, Armand."

The usual undertone of sarcasm was missing from the duke's voice, replaced now by such hopeful accents that Armand felt his heart would break.

The duke smiled. "At least there is the solace of good food—better here than at Versailles, you'll agree!" he said. "Come, Armand. There is time to eat together before you go."

* * * * *

Madeleine had not yet grown used to awakening alone in her cot. Though keeping her fragile young sister Louise with her here had been most difficult, there had been comfort in holding her close at night, kissing her cool cheek as she slept, taking her little hand when she reached out in troubled dreams for reassurance. And now Louise was dead. Madeleine wept without a sound. Each of her companions in this attic room suffered her own griefs. All had lost what was most dear: parents, brothers, sisters, friends, and homes.

It is almost summer, she thought, *and at home in Saintonge the sun will shine today on bright fields of new grass, chestnut trees in bloom, the brilliant white stucco and red roofs in Saint-Martin.* Through each window here the gray sky grew lighter. But today, like yesterday, would begin with fog and end with fog, and her own lungs would ache with the dampness—the chill—that had taken Louise from her.

Well, she thought resolutely, pushing her grief aside, *Louise is dead, and her soul's salvation is sealed. Of that I am most certain. But I am not dead, and Louis lives. Pray God Alexandre and Armand live. One must bear up and go on.*

"If the help had come sooner . . . If you could have all gone to America two years ago, poor Louise might have . . ." a member of the laundry staff had offered the night before as they lay on adjoining cots in their attic.

Madeleine had caught the sob that threatened. "*Mais oui*, Elaine. It was an affection of the lungs brought on by the miserable cold and gloom of these damp North Sea shores. Louise had been brought up in the warm south."

CHAPTER 9

The Prison Break

After enjoying the duke's sumptuous hospitality, Armand and Alexandre set out again, crossing the Rhône and heading toward the Cévennes. Armand did, of course, visit his own inheritance, a stony estate on the *garrigue*, the second such step-up from the plains. Here a jungle of low-growing shrubs and trees competed with flowering grasses. Among dwarfed live-oaks, wild olives, and stone pine, a few fields were still customarily planted to wheat and barley. Vineyards struggled in the thin soil, and a feeble, aged orchard of apple and plum trees tottered into crumbling stone walls and buildings—all that remained of the larger estate once managed and even enlarged by Armand's great-grandfather when Protestants dominated this region.

Armand apologized to Alexandre Cortot as they approached the ancient chateau. "It was shabby in Father's day, for he always cared more about providing home and shelter for displaced brethren than for bringing a profit. You can see it has only grown shabbier under my regime."

"Such is the fate when the landlord is absent," Alexandre commented. "I can't imagine what has become of my father's lands in the countryside, although five years ago the farms were productive and the houses trim and secure."

"We've been like the Swiss, I fear," Armand said. "When the land cannot support a gentleman, he hires himself as a soldier to whichever duke or king offers the best wages. Father had no stomach for life at Versailles, and when he was faced with choosing between the army and the court, he took up his sword. I was as young as you are, Alexandre, when my mother died and I joined Father."

After a simple meal of bread, cheese, and dried fruit, Armand spent an hour discussing matters with his manager, a spare man with one shoulder awry, broken long ago in a fall from a wheat rick. "You've done well to be self-sustaining," Armand said, praising this second-generation steward.

"We're almost like free owners," the man said, his leathery face stretched with a smile. "You've asked for little, and we've made do. It's best not to prosper sufficiently to draw notice. We're remote. The king's dragoons don't care much for the fresh winds blowing over wild lavender and thyme."

"And rosemary," Armand added, crushing a sprig of new growth between his thumb and forefinger."

"The cobbler can fit the two of you with some new boots, but I'm sorry we've nothing to offer to replace your uniform."

Armand shrugged. "It's better for you if you see little of me here. And it's better for me if I look as little of the gentleman as I can."

"I understand," the steward replied. "I know who I am and who you are, but when the tax men come, I'm the proprietor—a poor man staggering under adversity with more peasants than the land can support. That is best."

"*Vraiment,*" Armand said, "If I should fail to return, that will truly be your station. *Continuez, mon ami.*"

Their haversacks refilled, Armand and Alexandre took their leave after just one night's stay.

Skirting the towns and villages, they ascended the limestone slopes, ever steeper, of the Cévennes. From the ridges they could see rows of blue granite peaks receding into the distance. In the valleys between those ridges lay the harsh uplands, the refuge of Huguenots since the Reformation began one hundred and fifty years before. It was a land of tiny hamlets and sheepfolds, a land of fogs, mists, strong winds, and always rocks and more rocks.

On these slopes, thorny brush and herbs occasionally gave way to clumps of chestnut trees or scattered trees standing alone. Walking was easier on the ancient footpaths, poor as they were, but the pair didn't wish chance encounters with the Catholic militia prowling the foothills, and it was better that few eyes, even friendly ones, should see them. Today, a hot spring breeze swept the wasteland, and Armand chose whenever possible to follow wild animal trails among the trees, for it was a trifle cooler in the shade than scrambling across shimmering rock faces.

Alexandre, walking in front, suddenly held out his hand, palm backward. He'd seen someone up ahead sitting on a rock under a large tree, facing away from them. Armand stepped forward silently, one hand inside his jacket on his pistol. Then he grinned at his companion as he realized the person was a young girl, who, taken completely by surprise, stared up at them with wide brown eyes and open mouth. If she had thought to run, she was at a disadvantage because she was holding one of her shoes in her hand. Those shoes were in sad condition, and she had been attempting repairs.

Armand guessed the girl to be in her early teens. She was sandy-haired, and her thin face was streaked with sweat and grime. Her clothes—not the crude garb of a mountain peasant, but the dark street attire of the respectable classes—were covered with dust.

The girl dropped the shoe she'd been holding and sat up very straight, hands braced upon the rock as if ready to jump. Her eyes were wary.

These are strange times, marveled Armand mentally. From what he could see of the girl's scrawny neck and chest, she wore no cross or amulet. She was obviously not a peasant, so what was she doing out here dressed for town? She was almost certainly a Protestant runaway.

Armand bowed slightly and removed his hat. "My apologies, Mademoiselle, for startling you. We hadn't expected to come upon a young lady out here."

Though his tone was gentle, the girl continued to stare with pursed lips.

"We are soldiers, Mademoiselle, visiting the homeland between campaigns. Would you care to tell us who you are and what brings you to this desolate place? Can we be of service?"

Finally, eyes still set on a distant mountain, she whispered, "I go to visit friends."

Alexandre snickered.

She turned to scrutinize him coldly from head to foot. "Is this child also a soldier, Monsieur?" she asked Armand.

Amused at her spirit, Armand spoke hastily before Alexandre had time to digest the insult. "Yes, Mademoiselle. We have both been in the campaigns in Ireland and Savoy. Believe me, we mean you no harm. I perceive, however, that you are not dressed for the country, and may I further guess, Mademoiselle, that you are of the Reform and have left town a little suddenly. We are Reformed also, and we won't turn you in."

She nodded, her lips pressed tightly together.

"Where are you from?" Armand probed gently.

She opened her mouth and shut it twice before she spoke. "Nîmes. I have left the House of New Catholics."

"Nîmes!" exclaimed Armand. "That's rather a long walk from here! When did you leave?"

"Yesterday morning."

"You must not have tarried to get this far."

"Well, I left during the early Mass."

"What have you had to eat?" Armand inquired.

"There were some berries—and this and that," she concluded vaguely.

"Would you like something now?" he asked, unslinging his pack.

Suspicious though she was, she couldn't conceal her eagerness. Armand offered her a strip of dried meat and was touched by the way this proud and hostile child grabbed it in spite of herself. He gave her a second strip and then the heel of a piece of heavy black bread, rather dried out and unappetizing. It disappeared rapidly. Only when it was gone did she look up and offer a rather guarded, "Thank you, Monsieur."

"We should be on our way," said the officer, feeling awkward. "If your journey takes you in our direction, we would be happy to have you walk with us."

She didn't move.

Armand felt the courtesies still incomplete. "I regret, Mademoiselle, that our business makes the giving of names somewhat indiscreet, but I hope you will forgive us." He extended his hand and helped her to her feet. When she stood up, she was a little shorter than Alexandre, but not much.

"It's all the same to me," she commented shortly, wiggling her battered shoe onto her foot. They began to walk.

The girl cast an occasional wary glance sidewise at her escorts. Armand looked at Alexandre and raised an eyebrow. Alexandre made a whole series of faces and shrugs behind the girl's back, as if to ask, "What have we gotten ourselves into?"

After walking for a time, Armand tried again. "You know, Mademoiselle, you can talk to us and tell us how we can serve you. My friend here also escaped from a House of New Catholics when he was younger, and I myself had a hand in rescuing a young lady from a convent. We are your brothers in the Faith."

"That's all very well, Monsieur, I'm sure. One will see!" Her tone was bitter. They trudged on.

After a while, she broke the silence. "I'm sorry, Monsieur. I shouldn't have been rude, but this is the third time I've run away from that house of idol worship, and I won't go back to that place again. No matter what anyone says!" she added emphatically.

Once she overcame her reluctance to speak, there was no stopping her. Her father, a wealthy merchant, had gone abroad before the Revocation and left her with an aunt in Nîmes. She didn't know what had become of him. Her aunt had taken her to the night assemblies back when Monsieur Rey had first begun to preach contrary to the king's command. They'd been reported, so she was taken from her aunt and placed in a convent, a House for New Catholics, with about a hundred other girls, to be drilled in the catechism as well as the usual subjects. The first time she ran away, she went to her aunt, and they had tried to escape from the country. But the guide was a thief. He had taken their money, and they were lucky not to have been arrested before they could get back to Nîmes. There, the girl had been beaten, and the aunt was fined.

"Then this House for New Catholics is not in Nîmes?" Armand was beginning to get the picture. She hadn't come from Nîmes but was hoping to return there.

She arched one eyebrow to acknowledge his question but went on without answering. "The second time I got to a village near Nîmes, to the house of one of our church elders who was also a friend of our family. What a Judas! He turned me in. 'You must understand,' he said"—and she mimicked a prissy, righteous tone—" 'that I can't have any trouble with the authorities!' So, who can I trust?" she cried despairingly. "Can I trust *anyone?* He kept saying 'You understand, my dear, don't you, that one cannot do what one wishes these days!' So I was taken back to that place again, and they told my aunt that if it happened again, she might be jailed too, and she told them they could do as they liked with her as long as I was able to get away before they destroyed my soul!

"This time I'm not going near anyone I know. I don't want them to be able to accuse my aunt. When I get to the Refuge, I'll write her, and then maybe she can get out sometime too."

The path grew steeper, yet the girl kept up her steady recital. Armand didn't know to which refuge she referred, but he decided not to ask.

Again he readjusted his thinking. Her home was in Nîmes. The house from which she had escaped was in some other unnamed town. She sought refuge in still another place, which she obviously didn't wish to disclose. Yet, still secretive and omitting most specific information, she plunged on with her story.

"This time another girl and I lagged behind when they took us to church. We sort of dawdled among the pillars, and when none of the sisters could see us, we ran out the door and down the street. We got separated in the market, and I don't know what happened to her. They might not have missed us right away—maybe not until they were back at the convent. They didn't trust me one bit! I hope old 'Rednose' gets blamed for letting me out of her sight. Sister Marie-Joseph, the old vulture," she added vindictively. "All her teeth are black."

"Do you realize, Mademoiselle," said Alexandre when she paused for breath, "that you have been walking west. Or did you plan to seek refuge in Catholic Spain?"

Armand realized that the girl was far from certain where she planned to go. Though she fell silent, she struggled to maintain her dignity as she slogged stubbornly onward.

Alexandre wouldn't let the matter rest. "You know," he said, just a bit too sympathetically to ring true, "the first person who sees you will be suspicious. You can't help but attract attention wandering about dressed like a person of quality."

"I *am* a person of quality!" she snapped.

Alexandre snorted with laughter.

Her only response was a withering glare.

The heat was getting worse, the rock faces glowing like live coals, yet the girl carried her sad shoes. Armand realized they must have hurt her feet worse than this stony path did. He sympathized, remembering long travels with similarly inappropriate footwear.

They reached the top of a rise where a strong wind cooled the air. They leaned against the coarse grass of the bank while the crickets sang. Armand studied his two companions covertly. He and Alexandre could pass as vagabonds, recruits, deserters, or *colporteurs* with their backpacks. With prudence, they could circulate in almost any village without arousing much suspicion. To be accompanied by a girl, however, was something else. They were on serious business and couldn't afford to delay or to raise questions. What would the *prédicants* or Captain Huc say if they turned up with a girl in tow? But they couldn't just turn her adrift. Alexandre looked at her out of the corner of his eye. She was staring stonily ahead, still angry at Alexandre and perhaps more tired than she cared to admit.

"You know, Mademoiselle," began the officer, "we are on a mission that requires haste, and I'm afraid we won't be able to travel long with you."

In words that were strong and pithy, she replied that she cared not a whit.

Alexandre affected shock. "Where did you learn that? In the convent or at your aunt's knee?"

She ignored him, leaning against the bank and shifting her weight from one bruised foot to the other. Without question, she had no idea where she was or where the trail led.

The sweat ran in little rivulets down her dust-streaked face and neck. Her once white blouse and cap were streaked gray. She avoided eye contact. Armand couldn't judge whether she was trying to seem unconcerned or she was afraid of losing control if her glance met sympathetic eyes. *Will we have tears?* he wondered, dismayed.

"It is sad that she can't come with us," persisted the insensitive Alexandre. "She could have cooked and washed for us and added to our stock of informal expressions."

She cast a hateful look at the boy.

"Enough, Alexandre," Armand said sharply, though he did wonder if the baiting might have a happy effect. Now she would probably drop dead before she would exhibit any weakness in front of this tormentor.

Trying to be matter-of-fact, even cajoling, Armand said, "No, Mademoiselle, don't mistake me. We wouldn't think of abandoning you here, but when we reach one of our villages we'll have to make some kind of arrangement for you. We have a long and difficult journey yet, and you aren't safe out here by yourself."

"I was doing all right before you two came along." She shrugged indifferently. "But while we travel together, I won't slow you down."

Armand sent a warning glance at the boy before he could respond to such a ludicrous untruth. Then he rose to his feet.

"We have far to go before sundown," he said quietly, "so let's keep on."

They walked without speaking, and Armand several times slowed the pace. Alexandre caught his eye but at least made no audible comment.

It was already dark when they reached a herder's hamlet, its crumbling stone buildings hardly discernable from the stony rubble of a recent avalanche. A whispered password, and they were spirited into the loft over a lambing shed and provided with bowls of cooled pottage of mutton and barley and a jug of water surprisingly cold enough to turn the mutton tallow to candle wax in their mouths.

"There's the matter of clothing for the child," Armand suggested when the shepherd's wife came to collect the bowls. The girl was too far gone to say much while Armand persuaded the woman to give the demoiselle clothes of her own—a blouse and skirt—in return for the much better garments the traveler had been wearing.

Cupidity may have helped the clothing exchange along, but the peasant couple were adamant when the soldiers tried to talk them into keeping the girl until some arrangement could be made to get her out of the area. "It would be her life for ours, and we'd all of us hang," the man said with some heat. He remembered then that he had a message left by an earlier courier, and he retrieved it from under a feeding trough. "You'd best be out of my pastures before a man can see another in the morning mist," he said as he handed the message over. Armand was uncertain whether the comment was advice or a threat.

With the last flickers of the guttering candle, Armand read the message. Huguenot preachers Vivens and Brousson had moved ahead of them upcountry. The soldier realized that now their route would be more dangerous than before, with the authorities having been alerted to possible resistance among the mountain people.

Early the next morning, Armand stood at the door of the ancient farmhouse where they had spent the night and whispered, "What do we do now, Alexandre?" It would be dawn soon and time to be going. "What do we do with the girl?" he repeated. "I can't see leaving her with these wretched folk."

Alexandre seemed tongue-tied. He shrugged. They had slept in piles of barley straw so that the proprietor could claim, if his house was raided, that he didn't know there were strangers in his outbuilding. The object of their concern was still sleeping, exhausted; a shapeless mass in her straw pile. In these times of suspicious priests, false brethren, and unannounced searches by the militia, the herders couldn't risk having a stranger on their premises—even if the fugitive agreed to stay.

The subject of the debate, who had thus far refused to give her name, had fallen sound asleep the night before, and Armand had carried her like a stray kitten to a nest in the barn. He didn't have the heart to abandon her, though, like a kitten, this stray could obviously spit.

"We'll have to try to locate the *prédicants* as soon as we can. Surely they must know some safe people she can stay with. But for now, we'll be conspicuous with a girl along, and we'll have to travel at her speed. So what do we do?" Armand was speaking half to himself, half to Alexandre. He was startled by Alexandre's sudden outburst. "I'm sure she can do it," he said.

Armand gave him a curious look and stepped into the barn to see if the sleeping demoiselle could be roused.

* * * * *

Their next contact, as they dropped into lower elevations, was with an old friend and comrade-in-arms of Armand's in the Regiment of Maine who had kept his thriving vineyard by appearing to convert. It was here that Armand expected to meet the *prédicants*—local leaders of the "Church in the Wilderness." In a wine cellar without a window, they sat on long-empty barrels, studying one another by dim candlelight.

The Chevalier de Paynole and his wife were not happy people. Their position was delicate in the extreme, for he was responsible for the tranquility of the parish. He explained that if the intransigent presumed on his forbearance as a former brother in the Faith and held assemblies on his land, he had to take action or run the risk of losing his position, his property, and perhaps his liberty besides. Yet Madame de Paynole, with a softening expression, agreed to take Judith, who had finally given her name, as a kitchen maid.

Later, when the men had left the manor house for an outbuilding, one of the *prédicants* remarked, "Our 'noble' hosts—they want to keep what they have in the world, but they want their salvation too. So, they hope to earn their salvation by being serviceable to the people of God— if it isn't too dangerous!"

As the travelers prepared for departure the third morning, Armand stepped into the kitchen to bid Judith farewell. The spirited girl, used to bourgeois comforts, was less pleased than Armand and Alexandre to be out of the hills and in the kitchen. Though she understood that their journey was harsh and dangerous and that she was too young to be a courier, she stood with tears in her eyes. Soot-smudged, bare-legged, and in wooden shoes, she was indistinguishable from the rest of the servants in the huge kitchen of the chateau, where she would now spend long days plucking fowl and scrubbing pots.

"I've talked with all the brothers we met here," Armand told her. "I had hoped *prédicants* and couriers would know a way to send you to safety immediately. But with the famous preachers in the territory, matters are much more dangerous for all of us. I promise to do everything in my power to find a way to get you out of France, but my main concern just now is estimating the true situation of the Cévennes and its restless inhabitants and passing that information back to the leaders on the outside."

Judith rubbed a chapped hand on her skirt, her eyes on her wooden clogs. "I suppose I'll have to make the best of what is," she muttered, wiping a tear from first one eye and then the other. Armand noticed the way Alexandre and Judith avoided eye contact but watched each other almost constantly, as if loath to part. A budding romance, if he wasn't mistaken. His smile reflected his own bittersweet memories. What chance was there in all this upheaval for their young love to mature?

"You'll be treated well at my estate if I can get you there," he promised. "My steward has never been of the Reform, though he has always been congenial during my father's life and in the several years since. Alexandre and I will come for you as soon as we find safe passage for you out of France. But until then, Madame de Paynole's kitchen is the best we can do."

He entrusted a letter for his steward to a single courier on his way to Toulouse. Then he set about finishing his reconnaissance for the British crown.

*　*　*　*　*

Armand and Alexandre moved about Languedoc rapidly during the following weeks, aware that hesitation in any location presented the greatest risk to them. The Church in the Wilderness, comatose for nearly four years, was being revived by the presence of French lawyer-become-preacher Claude Brousson and his sometime companion, the zealot François Vivens. Like a physician with his fingers on the pulse of the movement, Armand tried to judge which local noblemen, which merchants, and which villages filled with uneducated peasants could be counted on to back organized leadership in a rebellion against His Magnificence, Louis XIV.

The duke of Schomberg, he knew, doubted the figure of fifty thousand men capable of bearing arms that Brousson and Vivens had claimed were ready to follow real leaders. His own estimate was that ten thousand seemed more reasonable.

Twice Armand sent reports of his impressions by courier to Schomberg at his headquarters in the Italian Piedmont. The third courier returned soon after his departure from Armand's temporary hideout in a cave overlooking the Tarn River Gorge. Schomberg's most recent reply had been intercepted, he said. Schomberg had been forced to abandon his center of operations in the chateau. The British were pulling out of Italy, and Armand must no longer try to contact them.

"That means, of course, that we are again unemployed and will receive no pay for this expedition either," Armand commented as he and Alexandre crouched before a small fire at the mouth of their cave.

"Except for shoes, I'm not suffering," Alexandre said with his usual acceptance of whatever ill wind blew. "The more worn we look, the easier it is to disappear among the villagers."

"You sound each day more like a seasoned soldier, *mon ami*. I do believe you are beginning to support a beard," commented Armand with more humor than he felt. "With a mustache, you would be nearly as handsome as if you had all your teeth."

Alexandre feigned anger. "What? Cover evidence of my valor?" Then he laughed aloud. "You mistake, Captain. This is a mark of honor, for in losing them, I made my first escape from the dragon's den."

Armand thrust another dry olive root into the fire and sat down with the last chunk of hard bread from his supply. "Let us then resort to Gandon. There we can eat well and be shod again while we decide where we travel next."

"What about Mademoiselle Judith?"

The boy's voice broke on the question. He turned away from the firelight for a few minutes and then returned, his shoulders squared. "We can't leave her at Paynole."

* * * * *

Any assumptions Armand de Gandon had about Judith's safety or her ability to remain incognito didn't prove true. The spies of the *Intendant* Lamoignon de Bâville had been busy, and the authorities were aware that foreign officers were circulating through the upcountry. Such reports were much more alarming to Bâville than was sporadic misbehavior of the Cêvennois. Coupled with reports that assemblies were becoming more numerous, the talk of foreign agents suggested something big was afoot. Therefore, the intendant decided to make one of his periodic sweeps through the district, encouraging the priests and the militia and putting subversives on notice that the authorities were watchful and close at hand. His retinue included clerks, soldiers, and an executioner. The local justice accompanied them—an official "more Catholic than the pope" and anxious to impress the intendant by his severity with any unfortunate heretics who fell into his hands.

When the party arrived at Paynole, they installed themselves in the chateau, and the master and mistress had no choice but to provide hospitality and stand by nervously while the intendant and the judge threw out their nets, interrogating, arresting, and sending back to trial at Arles or Montpellier a mixed bag of suspects. The local Catholic militia, galvanized by the presence of such luminaries in their midst, struck out almost nightly to track down the meetings reported by the parish clergy and their spies.

The fourth night, a young *prédicant* named Romans was surprised in a loft in a nearby village, positively identified, and hauled back to the chateau in triumph. The catch was not as good as a foreign officer but good enough for a trial and interrogation that might lead to more arrests and then a satisfying public execution when the prisoner was sentenced. Because it was expected that he could be persuaded to provide valuable leads to his colleagues, the prisoner was not hanged on the spot but locked in a makeshift cell improvised in an empty storeroom on the upper floor of the chateau. The room was considered secure because it was next to the one the intendant was using. The room's two small windows—which looked out on the center courtyard—each had iron bars to keep out thieves, its heavy door was secured with an enormous lock, and a sentry was posted at the door. In the morning, an escort was to convey the prisoner to his unpleasant fate at Montpellier.

Though no instructions had been given, Madame de Paynole thought of the prisoner after night fell and sent Judith with bread for him. There was a considerable gap between the bottom of the door and the uneven stone floor. Hearing a girl's voice, Romans asked who his benefactor was and if she was alone. When she said she was, he asked, "Would you do something for me?"

"If I can, but I'm certain I can't get the key."

"No doubt, but could you slip me a good-sized knife—one with a strong blade?"

Judith started to demur, misunderstanding his intention.

"I'm not going to harm myself or anyone else," he said quickly. "The mortar around these windows is old and in bad condition, and I think I can pry a bar loose. Be sure the knife has a strong blade."

"You know the intendant sleeps in the next room to you, and there's supposed to be a sentry, though I don't know where he is just now."

"The old ram is deaf, you know," said Romans disrespectfully. "That's why I want to work now, while there's lots of noise in the courtyard and the stables; when everyone is asleep, it would make too much noise. Look, I know I'm asking you to do something that could get you in a lot of trouble, but remember, they'll torture me to make me betray the others. They wouldn't go that far with you. Please?"

Judith had no trouble making up her mind. She had to invent a story to take the knife from the kitchen. The guard was still gone when she slipped back twenty minutes later and pushed the knife under the door. She then decided it would be prudent to go to bed early.

Romans chipped away at the crumbling mortar. By the time the noisy courtyard began to quiet down about midnight, he could pull one of the bars far enough inward that he could squeeze through the window. He dropped unobserved into the shadows of the courtyard; ambled quietly through the soldiers, grooms, and servants who were still moving about; and slipped out the main gate.

In the morning, a score of mounted men were assembled to escort the captive. While they sat in the courtyard, horses stamping their feet and tossing their heads, their breath steaming in the chill morning air, the prisoner was sent for. His room was empty. A knife with a broken blade lay on the stone floor, and an iron bar swung loose in the crumbling mortar. It was as if all the demons in hell had been let loose in the chateau. There was blame enough for all. The sentry, who had heard nothing after resuming his post, was threatened with hanging and thrown into the cell himself. The intendant ordered a squad of his soldiers to pursue the fugitive. Then, in cold fury, he informed Monsieur de Paynole that he deserved to be sent to the galleys and have his chateau razed. After reducing his wretched host to bonelessness with his threats, he silently watched his subordinates carry on.

The story of the broken knife traveled rapidly, and soon a kitchen helper volunteered that it had been Judith who took the bread to the prisoner and who had later removed a knife from the kitchen. Things then began to move rapidly. Judith was located in the kitchen and dragged by her colaborers, most of them new converts, to the courtyard, where a noisy discussion was under way. Pushed forward, Judith found herself confronted by a very angry judge—a bald, red-faced little man who had forgotten his wig in the excitement. Others fell silent as Judith became the center of attention, but the judge continued to scream. He seemed to feel this mischance would damage his standing in the eyes of the intendant—that his efficient service to his king and his God had been derogated, and someone must pay.

The majordomo of the chateau wrested Judith's arm from the scullery knave who held it. Then, gripping both her arms, he propelled her forward in front of the judge and tried to bow. "We found her, Your Worship," he bayed excitedly. "She's the one who gave the knife to the preacher!"

Speechless with terror, Judith wasn't allowed to confront her judges with any dignity, as the majordomo had her arms twisted so tightly behind her that she couldn't stand upright. The little judge wheeled on her in rage. He screamed at her, calling her a "dirty little slattern," and shook his fists in her face. "You did it! *You did it!*" the judge roared. And then "Why did you?"—as if she might have been more considerate.

As the judge was losing his self-possession, Judith recovered hers. "He was God's minister. I had to," she answered faintly as he paused to get his breath.

He gave a strangled yelp and struck at her with his fist. She saw the blow coming and tried to turn away, but she was held too tightly. The blow caught her on the side of her head instead of her mouth, and though she couldn't fall, she was knocked senseless.

"She should be hanged!" the judge said, her unconscious state having calmed him somewhat. "These rebels have to be taught their duty. Take this filthy slut away."

She was dragged to the stable wall and dropped limply on the ground in a sitting position. Three resplendent dragoons, formidable in heavy boots, muskets, and sabers, stood over her drooping form. Someone drenched her with a bucket of water, and soon she began to come around, sneezing a bit.

Inside the makeshift courtroom, the judge returned to a chair. The intendant, with just a hint of sarcasm in his voice, suggested that the rest of the proceedings might move more quietly. After a short discussion, he and the judge decided the guilty servant girl should receive fifty lashes.

"But she's only a child!" cried Madame de Paynole.

"Madame," retorted the judge, "if she were not, she would hang!"

Monsieur de Paynole grasped his wife's arm, alarmed at the possible consequences of her outburst. He propelled her roughly into her private sitting room, where he exhausted himself reminding her of their dangerous situation—that he might well be sent to the galleys for the rest of his life and that she might herself become the scullery maid in a convent. Then Paynole scurried about the chateau, trying to learn just how matters stood.

It took an hour or so to make Judith's sentence formal and to locate the executioner. When he was ready, everyone assembled again, and the prisoner was brought in and made to stand in the courtyard embracing a post, her wrists tied together. The heavyset executioner, with an appropriately brutal mien, ambled over to the prisoner, flicking his whip nonchalantly to limber up. The whole community gathered around the pair, not only because this was public entertainment but because law officers expected everyone, regardless of age or sex, to be present and well-edified.

Approaching his scrawny victim, the executioner thrust his scarred face toward her frightened eyes and whispered, "Look, *enfant*, and listen well. Madame has paid me fifty *livres* not to hurt you, so you yell and carry on and make it good, you hear, because if it doesn't look right, I'll have to really lay into you. There has to be some blood, so I've got to hit you sometimes, but you yell for all of them, you understand?"

After what had looked like a professional inspection of the target, he ambled back again, and the dual performance got under way. His artistry with the wicked-looking lash fascinated the audience, and Judith's cries lacked nothing in sincerity. The judge complained to the intendant that the executioner had not removed the girl's blouse, but the sadism of the intendant was perhaps less developed, and he made no comment. Probably many realized that the flogging was not all it was supposed to be, for Judith should have been dead or nearly so. But the executioner carefully positioned himself between the officials and the girl, and the judge, at least, was fooled. As it was, when the soldiers pitched her into the cellar and she hit every step on the way down, she was hurt badly enough to cry with real sincerity.

The next morning she was brought out again. The intendant was in a vicious mood. The search for Romans had thus far turned up nothing. The judge glared when he saw Judith. "Send the little reprobate down to Arles right now. There'll be room for her at Sommieres." That place had the reputation of being the worst prison for Protestant women.

"We're shorthanded, sir, what with the search going on and all."

"What's the matter with you louts," snapped the judge. "How many of you would it take to keep the little tart from running away?"

Flushing and humiliated before the onlookers, the sergeant angrily detailed two men to ride down the trail to town with Judith behind one of them, her wrists tied and the rider holding the end of the cord.

After about a half hour on the rough trail with her sulky escorts, she became more worried about a present danger than the more distant prospect of Sommieres. She feared that if the horse stumbled, she wouldn't be able to save herself with her hands tied.

Ambling along the bank of a rushing stream, the little party had just entered a grove of chestnut trees when suddenly a dozen masked and armed men appeared and surrounded them. The two soldiers prudently obeyed instructions, and to their relief, they were only tied to trees and relieved of their horses, arms, and captive. Once out of sight, the masks came off, and Judith saw that she had been rescued by the "Sons of the Prophets"—young men who served as bodyguards to some of the *prédicants*. But the most welcome face was that of Alexandre, who held her horse's bridle as they climbed toward the camp of the *prédicants*.

Alexandre glanced up at her with a touch of his old malice, but he couldn't repress his concern. "We go to all that trouble to put you out of harm's way, and look what you do! But it was the right thing," he admitted. And then he asked, "How do you feel?"

"Oh, just a little sore here and there," she replied with a quavering jauntiness.

"Your face is certainly bruised."

"I don't suppose it looked like much before anyway."

"You said it; I didn't," Alexandre snapped.

Painful as her swollen face was, she screwed it up and stuck her tongue out at him. He seemed visibly relieved. "I'm glad to see you're all right," he said with a grin.

The Sons of the Prophets escorted them a little ways. Then, after discussing with Alexandre the route he and the girl should take, they took their leave. Following their directions, the young couple crossed a stream and found a trail so low and tangled that they had to drop to their hands and knees as they followed it up a steep and narrow defile. Coming out near the top of the ridge, Alexandre sighted a landmark he recognized. Already, however, the sun had sunk into a cloudbank on the western horizon.

Scratched and bruised, with gashed shins and torn skirt, her arm almost pulled out of its socket, Judith fell on the ground when Alexandre decided they should stop to rest. Then, in the growing darkness, they set off into the next valley, still miles from the cave in which he and Armand had made their headquarters until they might return to the de Gandon estate.

When Alexandre and Judith had walked another half hour, they heard distant shouting and an occasional gunshot. But in the deepening darkness, they couldn't see the troop of soldiers that they could hear. "I hope you don't mind stopping," Alexandre said after halting to listen, his head cocked and his lips drawn tight against the gap between his teeth.

Judith could still feel the grip of the guards throwing her down the cellar stairs and the sting of sweat in raw wounds. She trembled in terror at the thought of recapture, but she was too tired to quibble. Easing herself down to the rocky path, she sat with her elbows resting on her knees. Then the noisy party on the slopes below them began to move away, and she dared to breathe.

"They're after me?" she asked.

"Who else?" Alexandre said, sounding amused. "Now they'll have a reward out for you, dead or alive!"

Judith shivered and tucked her skirt around her ankles.

"You're too tired to go on." Alexandre said. "We'd just get lost in the dark and blunder into the soldiers."

Judith watched him search for a place to spend the night. He found a tree with overhanging branches, raked last year's leaves into a pile to soften the ground under it, and said that would be her bed. Then, gathering a few leaves for himself, he stretched out too, and there they slept.

With the first streaks of dawn, Alexandre got up.

"We'd best get out of here," he said, looking around. "They'll be beating the bushes on this mountain for the next couple of days. We must get back toward Mount Lozere."

They began to head east, toward the gradually increasing daylight, slipping cautiously from bush and tree to tree and bush. As they passed one open place, they saw a man's hat and a shoe in the trampled grass. Some kind of scuffle had happened there. Judith noticed an object in the grass.

"Look!" she said, "It's a pistol—a really big one!" It was a long-barreled horse pistol, like those that dragoons carried. She started toward it.

"Don't!" commanded Alexandre, pushing her aside and striding toward it himself. "It's cocked. You could hurt yourself. In the dark, someone—"

But Alexandre didn't finish his sentence, for, a split second too late, he saw a horseman break out of some nearby trees and gallop toward him, obviously intending to ride him down. Alexandre was knocked sprawling as the horse thundered past him. The dragoon slashed at him with his saber, but having to duck his own head at that instant to avoid an overhanging branch, he missed the boy.

The dragoon wheeled his horse around to try again. Alexandre, on his hands and knees, couldn't seem to move. Judith grabbed the huge pistol from the grass with both hands, raised it—the heavy barrel wobbling—and pointed it at the dragoon, who was now nearly upon Alexandre. Then she squinted both eyes and pulled the trigger.

At the explosion, the horse screamed, reared, and fell over backwards, smashing the dragoon to the rocky ground. Alexandre leaped to his feet, grabbed the still-smoking pistol, and ran toward the downed man. But it was obvious that he wouldn't ever again threaten them—or anyone else, for that matter. Safe for the moment, the two ran rubber-legged from that place and hid under some bushes till they could recover.

Later that afternoon they found the pastor, Armand, and most of the pastor's party near a disused sheepfold, their base for that part of the country. All were sobered and tired but grateful for their narrow escape. Armand embraced Alexandre and Judith, and Alexandre recited their adventure. He gave credit where credit was due. "Once she figured out which end the bullet would come out, she could hardly miss the horse," he explained.

"This can't go on," said Armand firmly. "It would be a pity if because of some mischance like this you two didn't have fifty or sixty years yet to exchange these compliments!"

Alexandre glanced at Judith with a sheepish grin, and she felt herself blushing.

* * * * *

"You understand, of course, that Madeleine, Alexandre's sister, can't afford to keep you on the small pay she receives at the House for Huguenot Gentlewomen. Like her, you'll have to work for a living," Armand said as he examined the rope that secured several crates of crockery in a cart hitched to a single, aged horse. They were in the courtyard of his chateau, cleanly clad in coarse peasant garments and finally recovered from the perpetual hunger of the past two weeks.

Judith shrugged. "It can't be as bad as being a scullery maid at Paynole. I just hope this guide is more trustworthy than some."

"I'm glad you've learned that there are indeed a few people you can trust," Armand said. Then he gave the girl a thin packet of letters, charging her to give them to Madeleine in person. "I have named no one, but she will understand. And any French official who got hold of them would understand enough to convict you of subversive activity."

Judith grinned. "I can do what I have to. But this is a rather large amount of paper to chew and swallow if I'm discovered." She turned to Alexandre, and suddenly she threw her arms around his neck and buried her face in his shabby jacket.

"Just in case something happens and I never see you again," she said. "You have to know."

At first Alexandre stood totally stiff. Then his arms went around her waist. "I know," he muttered into her hair.

Judith drew a shallow breath. "I'm sorry. You've been so good. I—"

"We'll get back together. We have to get back together. It's been a leading."

His peculiar lisp was suddenly more endearing than something to ridicule. Judith pushed back and kissed him soundly. "That's a promise," she said.

Alexandre grinned. "I take it for one."

She climbed into the potter's cart and settled herself among the wares. She was off for the Atlantic coast at Bordeaux.

"That, Captain, is how one does it," Alexandre said to Armand. They watched as the wind stirred up golden dust behind the cart as it disappeared around a rocky outcrop.

Armand might have chided his young companion on letting the girl make the first move, but his throat tightened as he thought of the other girl who would receive his letter in perhaps a month if all went well. Unlike Alexandre, he was of an age at which he should understand something of wooing. Unfortunately, he berated himself, wooing had not been part of his education, Frenchman though he was.

In Bordeaux, Judith changed her identity, becoming the personal maid of the wife of an English banker on her way back to Cardiff. At Cardiff, she became the nursemaid for three small Welshmen going to join their maternal grandparents in Amsterdam after the death of their parents in an epidemic. In their gratitude, the Dutch grandparents provided Judith with money for two changes of clothing, including undergarments and shoes. When they left her at the House for Huguenot Gentlewomen in Rotterdam, she looked and felt respectable, like the merchant's daughter she had once been.

Madeleine Cortot recognized Armand de Gandon's handwritten address on the envelope the girl handed her, and before so much as opening the letter, she accepted Judith in full faith. After reading Armand's request and his explanation that here was the young woman who would become her sister, her heart was ready to give her the sisterly affection that she had previously lavished upon the frail Louise.

"Once, you know, I thought I would go to America." Madeleine shook her head thinking of the bitter experience, remembering her high hopes, how certain she had been that it would be only a matter of weeks before her father was safely out of France. Her own scruples now compelled her to begin at the arrival of Armand de Gandon at her old home in Saint-Martin six years past, relating in most brutally self-effacing honesty all that had transpired.

She recounted her short, despairing stay in the House for New Catholics, and Judith seconded her reactions, interrupting to tell of her own escapes. Madeleine portrayed Armand's heroic rescue, and Judith told how Alexandre with the Sons of the Prophets had snatched her from the soldiers of the Intendant de Bâville. Finally, Judith gripped her hand and listened to the remainder of the story.

Madeleine had paid Tillieres most of the money Cousin Daniel had sent for their passage to America. It had seemed possible then that between her and Alexandre, they could work and save enough for all of them to cross the Atlantic to begin their new life. Anything seemed possible once Father was safe. But Tillieres had betrayed them, and Father had gone to the galleys, a slave for the remainder of his life. He was probably dead by now, considering the terrible hardships and rampant diseases in Mediterranean harbors.

"I have almost given in to despair concerning Father," she said, "but your coming has given me new hope." She watched as Judith drew a smooth white stocking up the calf of her heavily muscled leg and then stretched to reach the serviceable brown shoe.

"I came to you as a stranger," Judith said with a grin. "I truly am grateful for the clothing and a place where I can earn my own way."

Madeleine watched as the girl from Nîmes put on her other stocking and shoe and then rose and smoothed her new but also serviceable linen skirt. "You look very nice, *mon chere*," she said.

"Have you read all the letters?"

Madeleine thought she understood the girl's anxiety. She certainly understood Alexandre's intentions. Judith was past her sixteenth birthday, just the age she had been herself during the fateful flight from Saint-Martin four years before. It was hard to realize that Alexandre himself was now seventeen and that he fancied himself in love with this very plain but self-assured refugee. Yet his letter, pure Alexandre, had left nothing in doubt.

Very well, Madeleine thought, *I'll do my part. She can stay with me, work with me, and in the meantime gain a little education. And then, if my daring brother survives to return, she'll be my sister.*

"You've read the letters?" Judith persisted. Her face showed a mixture of embarrassment and uncertainty.

Madeleine nodded. "I understand. Once I had thought to go to America, but I think now that such a plan would be a mistake. Our younger brother Louis is content learning to be a printer here in Rotterdam, and Alexandre will be a soldier in spite of anything I might do to change his vocation. I have saved enough money now that we could make the journey, but I don't wish to make it alone."

"One does not enjoy being alone," said Judith.

"Well, I'm not alone now with you here to be my companion." Madeleine rose and embraced the girl. Judith stood straight and her speech was firm, yet at this moment it was obvious that she was fearful of her future. Madeleine gripped the girl's shoulders and held her at arm's length, smiling. "We will manage however best we can, for we have work to do that makes life better for others, and we may be quite certain that Alexandre will come back whole. He has a history of getting through, and even with his headstrong ways, he is God's man, and God will take care of him."

The look in Judith's eyes told her that such a statement presumed what God had never promised. God's men died on galleys and fleeing over mist-shrouded mountains and in battles. Godly women were raped, tortured, and sent to convents, their children torn from them.

Madeleine kissed the sun-browned cheek and held the girl close. "We are God's sons and daughters, all well-beloved," she affirmed. "Whatever befalls us, we are beloved, and our souls will be saved."

The muscular young body relaxed in her arms, and then the girl began to cry. And she seemed so embarrassed by this development that Madeleine wondered how long it had been since Judith had indulged the luxury of tears.

* * * * *

Alexandre Cortot, almost eighteen years old when he figured his age himself, was not in the least abashed by the difficulties he expected to confront finding his way back to Rotterdam. Two weeks with Armand de Gandon at the "captain's" estate in Languedoc had been a stomachful. The steward was old, and most of the peasants went about their work as if their brains were as stiff as their aging knees. There probably hadn't been an innovation in their methods of farming since their ancestors arrived here in 1209. He'd heard the housekeeper remind Armand of this when he offered a suggestion about renovations that might make the ancient building more livable for the fifty-some people from the surrounding countryside who had settled there when their own property was confiscated.

"I don't think the word has gotten around to the regional authorities that Henri Armand, le Sieur de Gandon, major of the Regiment of

Maine, is the same Captain de Gandon lately of the British Army," his friend mused. "Or else everything here is so pitiful they don't want to bother with it."

"Or so quiet that no one takes notice," Alexandre scoffed. "If there's a Calvinist among them, there's none that makes a peep."

"They go back three hundred years before Calvin," Armand explained. "Though Father himself became a Huguenot, these folk rather shrugged off something so 'new and untried.' "

Armand had invited Alexandre to stay to enjoy a bit of the rural bounty—to rest a while. "I'll stay just long enough for your cobbler to make me another pair of boots," Alexandre asserted.

Tiens, he had his boots. Plain. No, crude. But they fit, and they had thick soles. They were boots to inspire a wearer to walk, and he set out less than a week after Judith's departure, suddenly concerned over his sister's welfare. Twice he hired on as a deckhand on river boats, first on the Allier and then on the Loire. He'd cut across country to the Seine on foot, hired on for the most menial work on a coal barge, and then trekked to the Rhine and onto another barge. Each time, he agreed to work for a wage little more than the abundant plain food and felt no pangs of remorse jumping ship when he'd given more in labor than he'd cost the shippers.

"I never needed a guide," Alexandre boasted when answering to his sister's belated worries about losing his way or being apprehended. "There's no one looking for a shabby boy who needs his hair cut—one with his front teeth missing and smelling like he's run away from home to avoid a bath."

"You're safe, at least," Madeleine conceded. But he could see by the look in her eye that he would spend an hour in the washhouse before she allowed him into the House for Huguenot Gentlewomen.

"Judith won't care," he shrugged. "Tell her I'm here."

"Aha!" said Madeleine.

The instant the door opened, Judith flew to the shabby Alexandre as naturally as a bird to its mate. They showed no false restraint, only ecstatic joy at being reunited—mixed with childlike fretting, complaints, and open expressions of devotion.

Impatient to be earning enough to replace his homespuns with something resembling military garb, Alexandre found work unloading cargo at the docks, talking each evening over his supper of the arrival of his friend Captain de Gandon.

"But I thought you wanted to be with Judith," Madeleine objected when he talked of another military foray. "I had hoped that with you safely back we could arrange passage to America?" It was more a question than a statement. "You might convince Louis there'll be work for printers in New York," she said. "And Judith is favorable to travel. You might both stand a chance of reaching twenty with a little more distance between you and the king's men."

Alexandre grinned. "Judith's game for anything." He thrust out a foot sporting a boot hardly two months off the cobbler's bench but now scuffed and worn down at toe and heel. "Give her stout boots like these, and she'll keep pace with a marching army."

Madeleine threw up her hands in horror. "You wouldn't take her to such a life, would you?"

"I was thinking about your American proposal," Alexandre said. "It's the wilderness there that interests me. I could—"

He watched his sister's face.

"Non?"

"If I knew for certain there was no hope to free Father."

"You'd be ready to buy passage?" Madeleine smiled wanly and turned and looked through the lace curtains out upon the busy city street. "I haven't yet grown used to the dampness, the narrowness, the nearness of political intrigue. I'm ready to build a new life, I believe."

"What about Major de Gandon?" Alexandre asked.

Madeleine's shoulders sagged, and the ruff of her white cap dropped forward, showing her equally white neck. Then, with what he perceived to be false conviction, she said, "I'm ready for a new life in America. Major de Gandon has ever been our friend, and I owe him your life and mine—and Louis' life too. But he's a soldier. He's a titled gentleman. His life will always be in France, and I can never go back."

"But you love him."

"Dear brother, marriages are rarely made on a foundation of affection. Beautiful tales of romance entertain young ladies, but since Abraham contracted a wife for Isaac, men and women have best established homes and founded families on the sounder foundation of financial and social advantages—and religious compatibility, of course."

"Like your contract with Mathieu?" Alexandre cut in. "I suppose you can set more value on promises from a man who thinks he'll gain a rich father-in-law whose influence will help him become a great theologian. Look what saintly Mathieu did when Father lost his money and position. Look how much he cared what became of you. I ask you, *mon chère sœur*, who was willing to lay down his life to save you?"

"Enough!" Madeleine cried. "I can't argue for Mathieu's virtue. But that was five years ago. A heroic act by a gallant gentleman doesn't constitute a lifelong commitment to the girl he saved." She turned swiftly to scan his face with tearful eyes and then dashed through the door and up the stairs.

"So she loves him!" Alexandre muttered. He grinned. "Mademoiselle Madeleine is almost as much a blockhead as Armand."

* * * * *

The summer was far advanced when Armand de Gandon arrived in the city. Though Madeleine wanted to run to him with the same frank affection with which Judith had greeted Alexandre, she was cool and self-conscious. And during their brief conversation, he was as formal as she, and when he left, she thought she would choke, her heart so filled her throat. He was intent, he said, upon contacting Pastor Merson, who, he had heard, was planning a pastoral journey into Huguenot territory in southern France. "Who is as qualified as I to guide and protect your old pastor?" Armand asked. He included Alexandre in this questioning look. "If such is the elderly clergyman's intention, I freely offer myself."

"Then you have cast your lot completely with the people of God?"

Just then, Judith stepped out of the washhouse and across the flagstone paving. When she saw Armand, she set her basket down and ran to him. It was clear she had transferred to him the love she might have borne her own long-absent father.

"Yes, Mademoiselle Cortot," Armand said formally after Judith released him. "I have committed myself irrevocably to the service of God. I am a Frenchman, and France is my *patrie*, most dearly loved. But I cannot serve God and serve its king. And I find I cannot sell my services to the enemies of Louis XIV."

Madeleine grasped her two hands behind her prim white apron. "Then you will dedicate your body as well as your soul to this dangerous mission?"

"It seems God has called me, *n'est-ce pas?* At least at this juncture."

"It would seem so," Madeleine agreed, bidding him good health as he left them.

"That sounds like my line of work," Alexandre told his sister when the soldier had gone.

"And passage to America?"

"You and Judith could sail ahead, get settled in with Cousin Daniel's household, and—"

"Do you think Judith will put the Atlantic Ocean between the two of you?"

Alexandre's right arm went around his sister's shoulders. He lifted her chin with his left hand. "Do you want the Atlantic between yourself and Captain de Gandon? *Je pense que non!*"

Madeleine dropped to the bench beside the kitchen door. Then Judith stepped between brother and sister, reaching one hand toward each. "Captain de Gandon, I think he is a wonderful man . . . very nice, very kind—but probably a little stupid."

Madeleine sat for a moment. "You know, *ma chere*, you are absolutely right. But he's not the only one." And she pulled Judith down to the seat beside her, laughing and crying and wiping her eyes on the edge of her immaculate apron.

CHAPTER 10

Betrayal in Saint-Martin

"Ah, then," said Armand de Gandon, gripping the hand of Alexandre Cortot and looking the young man almost fiercely in the eyes. "You must be their protector. I count on you for that."

The boy grinned his gape-toothed grin. "I'm learning to take orders."

Not entirely convinced, Armand nevertheless took his farewells of these who were the only family he might ever have: Madeleine in a gray gown with a rose underskirt, tall but somehow almost slight in the damp chill of the harbor. Alexandre, only a little taller than his sister but broad of chest and showing the faint dark beginnings of a beard on his lower jaw. Judith, resolute and eager in a dark green woolen skirt and bodice, but rather than slippers, wearing boots that matched Alexandre's. And Louis, still looking young, but now manifesting the confidence he had gathered from his work in the print shop.

Armand, cut by the stiffness in Madeleine's manner, took the hand of each as the departing ones stepped into the ship's boat. When she finally smiled at him, an unsteady sort of smile just as they pushed off from the jetty, he came near throwing himself into the dirty water and swimming out to her. Instead, he watched dismally as the squat sailors in their greasy, striped breeches and stocking caps rowed her out to the ship.

One permitted oneself some dreams that were perhaps not entirely reasonable. But it was over now—no more Cortots. He wished them success and happiness. They deserved it, but he must occupy himself hereafter without them. Was that possible? How should his plans go now? He must transfer all his energies to further the work of Madeleine's beloved pastor and to the work of God in France for as long as he could. He looked apprehensively at the sky, hoping that tomorrow would bring them fair weather to begin their journey.

But Armand's good wishes didn't result in fair weather. Indeed, day after day his friends remained in the *West Indiaman* in harbor at Amsterdam. They waited so long, in fact, that the always provident Madeleine sent Alexandre to shore in the ship's boat for additional food, uncertain whether the ship's supplies would be sufficient after this delay.

Returning from his welcome errand, Alexandre Cortot stepped off the rope ladder onto the deck and spoke to Madeleine, who sat wrapped in her blue cloak on a pile of rigging on the deck. "Isn't it rather cold and damp here? If you're going to sit up here till the fog lifts and we sail, you may have a long wait. It's been a week already, and I still can't see fifty feet here in the harbor."

"I know," Madeleine sighed miserably. "But I'd rather sit here in the cold where I can breathe. It's going to be dreadful below if the weather won't let us on deck."

Alexandre squatted on his heels beside her. "Here's the cheese and the other things you sent me for. It ought to last most of the way across. I expect we'll all turn green and stop eating as soon as we weigh anchor."

Madeleine shivered and doubled her cloak across her chest.

"Armand and Pastor Merson have left," Alexandre said. "God speed!"

Madeleine murmured something too low to hear. Then she lifted her head. "The bounties of our friends have made our passage possible, and I am grateful. But I'm still not resigned to abandoning Father to his fate. After all, it was I who . . . How can I ever forget?"

"Mais non, mon chère sœur!" Alexandre said as he laid his hand on her knee. "Half the refugees in Holland were taken in by that viper Tillieres. Don't berate yourself. If you want me to, I'll go back and find Father."

His sister immediately assumed her usual commanding posture. "You will not. *Non!*"

"Then let's be cheerful," returned Alexandre. "The sky can't remain foggy forever, and even the Atlantic Ocean can be crossed in a matter of weeks."

* * * * *

Armand de Gandon sat opposite his host, Pastor Merson, in the pastor's book-lined study in Rotterdam. As always, the pastor was clad in clerical black with a spotless white collar. "I am resolute, Armand," he said in his quiet way. "I *must* go back. The wolves were indeed clever to expel the shepherds that they might tear the flocks at their leisure— these wolves that wear brown and black robes! It was so sudden. The Revocation gave us but a fortnight to be gone or to convert. It is understandable, but all these leaderless flocks! I fear the shepherds were neither very brave nor very intelligent.

"I dream of these poor sheep at night; and they haunt my waking hours too. What paths may they be straying into without their pastors? But this doesn't involve you, and while I would feel a selfish—yes, a guilty pleasure in your company, I don't wish to see you risk your life in this way. This is a responsibility for pastors to meet."

"I too am resolute," said Armand. "I'm not of any use here, and if I can assist you in your journey, your good works, in any way, then I think I see my duty clearly enough."

"I would think there might be other places than France where you could be of use."

Armand's brow darkened, and he shook his head glumly. "I suppose you refer to my accompanying the Cortots to America. Believe me, Pastor, I have examined that from every direction, and while I regret that Mademoiselle has felt so hurt by my attitude that she could barely bring herself to bid me goodbye, still I cannot see how, in honor, I could have done other than I did."

He hesitated, hoping the pastor might agree. But the older man made no sign. Armand tried to further clarify his thoughts.

"You know I can't go back to France and the duke, to compromise with Babylon. Nor would it be right to presume on the support of a young woman who has others who depend on her, for I would have nothing certain to go to overseas. And your nephew? What would I do should the absent Mathieu turn up later to demand his rights? Invite him outside and run him through? No, I feel that if I am permitted to go with you, it will be for a purpose—to advance your work or to protect you."

The pastor started to say something but then sighed helplessly. Then he asked resignedly, "Must we always return to Mathieu?"

"I believe in promises, and I am convinced that whatever her feelings, Mademoiselle Madeleine is as steadfast on that point as I am. Perhaps the difficulty is all in my pride, but I would like to think it integrity." With that, Armand folded his arms, hoping the pastor would see that the topic was closed.

Merson's thin face brightened. "I have the word of the Estates-General that they will provide for the support of my family while we are gone. This is their regular policy now, and our passports with the assumed names should be ready any day now. I've been compiling lists of trustworthy brethren throughout France by consulting with many of the brethren exiled here. However," he said hesitantly, "if I should be captured with lists of new converts on me, it would go hard for us but perhaps even worse for those we go to relieve."

"Let us take no lists," said Armand, "but only commit to memory one or two householders in each city and trust the people we visit to provide us names and routes as we travel."

"Of course, you are right, *mon ami*, having been there so recently yourself. I should like to begin in Saint-Martin, for that was my parish, and those believers were my own flock for so long."

"Then let us outfit ourselves for our part. Let us look like gentlemen of modest means on a journey related to commerce." Armand took courage in at last seeing clearly what remained to be done. "Let us arrange passage to Bordeaux. And then we proceed on foot to Saintonge."

* * * * *

"I would never have guessed there were this many closets and wine cellars and haystacks in all of France," commented Armand de Gandon as he and Pastor Merson emerged from the cellar in the house of the former elder Henri Dufour of Saint-Martin.

"But we are still alive and free after nearly six weeks," replied the pastor with his customary good humor. In the gloom he felt cautiously for the top of the narrow stairway. "We have escaped every snare set for us, for which I praise the Lord. Our lives have been in the hands of servant girls, children, and poor folk who could indeed make good use of the reward if they wished to betray us. You remember that Catholic gentleman in Normandy? He certainly penetrated our disguise but held his peace. The Lord must still have service that we can render."

They could dimly discern the form of Monsieur Dufour, the only surviving elder of what had once been a flourishing church of several hundred in Saint-Martin. "In here, please, brethren," he said in a low voice.

They emerged into a small sitting room lit by a single candle set on a table. A large Bible lay on the table also.

"Pastor, please seat yourself by the candle."

Massed in the shadows, filling all available space, were about twenty-five believers. Each came forward to shake hands and embrace the pastor and to express their appreciation to the man who hadn't forgotten them, who had run such risks to visit them. All had been nominally converted from the PRR,* but their presence in the room demonstrated how little their beliefs had changed.

The pastor seated himself and began his discourse. His voice never rose above a murmur. The listeners hung avidly on every word, eager for promise and encouragement for those who must endure yet a little longer for the Lord's sake and seek comfort for their weakness in leading a double life.

There was no chanting or singing. Once in a while there would be a fervent but low-pitched "amen" or a groan of agreement as the speaker made a telling point. Those near the window listened with one ear for any strange noises from the unpaved street outside, and two young men were posted in nearby alleys to give warning if meddlesome neighbors showed any signs of life or if the watch approached. The moon was a mere sliver in the sky, and Saint-Martin slept, serenely unaware of the heresy in its very midst.

---

* Pretended Reformed Religion.

Armand sat squashed against a wall. By now he was used to meetings held in unorthodox and crowded places. The two men had worked their way south from one secret congregation to another disguised as traveling gentlemen. They spent two or three days in each place to exhort and console, always warmly received and carefully concealed. Then they moved on down the dusty yellow roads, hoping that the unusual activity among the new converts hadn't stirred any suspicions.

To perfect the disguise, the pair had to carry swords and pistols, but the pastor wouldn't charge the latter nor ever draw the former. The two argued about this as they traveled, for, as the pastor now sadly realized, even though Armand would agree that only the Lord could preserve them from their enemies, the soldier had much of Peter in him and was inclined to feel that it would be an educational experience for any Malchus they might encounter to lose an ear at least. However, while it was hard doctrine for a former major to agree to, he had to admit that it was not in the example of Christ to shoot persecutors, so, perforce, he too traveled with pistols unloaded.

Dawn meant danger for illegal worshipers. So, at four o'clock, Elder Dufour signaled that the meeting must end. The farewells had to be brief, though they all knew their chances of ever seeing the pastor again were slight. Then by ones and twos they slipped out into the dark street. When the last person had gone and the door was barred, their host handed the candle to Armand, and the visitors climbed upstairs to the little back chamber where they were to sleep. The old man remained in the dark for a few moments, peeking through the shutters, trying to see if there were curious eyes across the street.

Armand and the pastor didn't speak. It was frequently thus after these meetings. The joy of these simple people, the obvious comfort the visits brought them, the love that shone from their eyes as they worshiped together or partook of the Communion made the harrowing journey worthwhile. Armand put the candle on the nightstand and began to undress. The pastor sat distracted on the edge of the bed, toying with his neck cloth. Then there was a faint scratching at the door. Armand, in his shirt, stepped across and opened it. Dufour's white cap and nightgown loomed palely in the black hall.

"Brother de Gandon," he whispered in a shaking voice, "Mathieu Bertrand is here and insists that he knows the pastor is here. There is something not right about him, and I fear for you and the pastor, but I dared not argue with him at the street door."

"Is it Mathieu?" Merson inquired.

Armand nodded unhappily.

"I've been expecting him. Please show him up, Brother."

"Pray be careful," urged Dufour. "This could ruin us all."

On Dufour's return, he carried a light, and Armand, standing at the head of the stairs, saw the blond head and handsome features of Mathieu Bertrand for the first time since the rainy night nearly six years before when they had rescued Madeleine from the House of New Catholics just outside this very town. It might have been the imperfect light of the guttering candle or perhaps his own overactive imagination, but it seemed to Armand that Mathieu's face was drawn, his eyes sunken.

When the former schoolmaster raised his head and saw Armand looking down on him, he started visibly and paused on the stairs. On the landing, nevertheless, the two bowed formally, and Armand offered his hand, which Mathieu took after a slight hesitation. As the uncle and nephew embraced, Armand closed the door to the bedroom.

"Do you actually know that anything's amiss?" he whispered to Dufour.

"I wish I could say," said the other. "But don't stand there shivering. Come to the kitchen, and I'll tell you what I can."

As they sat together and the first streaks of dawn appeared through the eastern windows, Brother Dufour tried to explain his misgivings. "You must know, Brother de Gandon, that many folk hereabouts denied their Lord to save their families and possessions, and one often sees in them a sort of sickness, a guilt they bear. They are worried and unhappy people.

"The pastor's nephew has an ill look about him. He holds aloof from us and acts as though he fears us. He got his uncle's property back and works in the Hotel de Ville. I ask you, how often do you see that happen? The story is that he turned informer. If he is an informer, we are as good as dead. I straitly charged the brethren not to tell him that his uncle was coming here; I thought it safer so. Yet here he is." Dufour shivered.

Armand fought a sick, salty taste in his mouth. "But, Elder, would he come here if he planned mischief? Tongues always wag, you know that."

The elder didn't reply, but in the dim light he did not look convinced.

It was dawn when Mathieu reappeared. With only a slight bow to the two watchers, he slipped out the door and disappeared. Armand climbed up to bed again. He decided to say nothing of what he'd been told.

The pastor joined him in the bed and pulled the curtains but didn't turn over for sleep. "No doubt," he began matter-of-factly, "you have learned that the brethren here don't trust Mathieu. That your thoughts may not be troubled as we journey, let me give you some assurance. Mathieu knew where to find us because I wrote to him before we left Amsterdam. I had heard he was back here again."

"You *wrote* him!" said Armand despairingly. "Don't you know that mail from abroad is censored?"

"I sent the letter in care of a third party to forward," the pastor said quickly.

Armand relaxed slightly.

"I'm not at liberty to tell all just now, but I can say that five years ago Mathieu was caught trying to leave the country and was put to the question. Under this torture he did injury to one—to her—to friends. He is sorely distressed for this weakness, and of course when the authorities insisted that he return here, it made the brethren distrust him as well. He knows what they suspect, and it isn't true. He has told me that he wishes to make amends and to be of service to the Lord by joining us. So I have invited him to meet us at an appropriate time."

"Join us?" Armand's exclamation was louder than he had intended. He half sat up in bed. "You didn't tell him where we were going, did you?"

" 'Quench not the smoking flax,' " quoted the pastor, laying a calming hand on Armand's shoulder. "Let's be charitable. He will give his tormentors the slip and join us at the house of Brother Dulac in Montpellier next month."

"But, but—" Armand stammered helplessly.

"Must we not forgive if we hope to be forgiven? Was not John Mark given a second chance?"

"You are always right," agreed Armand unhappily. "I am flattered to be put in company with the apostle Paul, but from a purely human, unregenerate standpoint, I would say that we are likely to have our necks wrung like pigeons when we present ourselves in Montpellier!"

" 'Let him that standeth beware lest he fall,' " said the pastor, drawing the coverlet up under his chin.

"Of course," muttered Armand, "but if he fell once, they can help him fall again."

"I don't think Mathieu will fail twice." The pastor spoke as if reasoning with a petulant child. "I've looked into his eyes, and I've seen his soul's anguish. If you understood all that he has lost, you would be more merciful. Let *us* do the right thing, and the Lord's will be done!"

The pastor settled down and was asleep almost immediately. Armand lay awake for some time in spite of his fatigue. He envied the simple certainty of the pastor's thinking. If only he could sleep tranquilly like that on such a question! The daylight coming through the curtain also bothered him, and he tossed restlessly.

Armand tried to reason out his duty under the circumstances. *As the pastor says, I must be charitable. How do I know how I would behave under torture? I must admit I've had little use for the fellow and have been jealous of him. I certainly can no longer imagine Madeleine is still fond of him. But, indeed, if he weren't in the background, things would have been different in Holland. Her conscience is probably more tender than mine anyway. Well, as an apprentice Christian, I suppose my duty is to help get him safely out of the country so he can fly to her over the sea.*

He sighed. The sleeper was snoring gently.

I wonder what would have happened had I gone to America. No, I was right to refuse. The fellow probably still considers her his fiancée. It would only have made matters harder for her if he had come later.

Another thought occurred to him.

I wonder if it could have been he who informed the authorities we were leaving France through Sedan that long-ago winter? No, Mathieu Bertrand

201

was down south here, and I don't see how he could have known what was going on so far north. Unless her father had known. Unless he had followed her. Or she had spurned him. . . .

* * * * *

Midday after the night meeting, Alexandre Cortot showed up at the Dufour home. He had changed his mind about America, he said. He would try to find his father before crossing the Atlantic. He was holed up in the ruins of a *mas* that had belonged to his father. Madame Dufour pressed a long loaf of bread upon him, which, he assured her, would be enough. She added some apples and a few grapes.

The second morning after the night meeting, Pastor Merson left early for a visit to an elderly sister on the other side of town. Armand breakfasted in leisurely fashion and sat in the kitchen in his shirt-sleeves waiting for the pastor's return so they could resume their journey. The Dufours were sitting with him and discussing the changes the Revocation had brought to the Huguenots of Saint-Martin when Alexandre opened the door and stood breathless on the threshold. "Down the street," he puffed, "and coming on fast—a dozen dragoons. They may be out for exercise, but you know these yellow-coat devils aren't often in the streets this early for social calls."

"I don't wish to seem conceited," agreed Armand, rising, "but I suppose they are after us. Someone has talked."

"Not a doubt of it," said Dufour, heaving himself to his feet. "You mustn't be found here. Alexandre, if you can, go down the street the other way and head off the pastor if he should return. He's the one they really want. And Brother de Gandon, please step next door—they are our people—this very minute. The street is too dangerous, and you might be recognized as a stranger. I think Alexandre is safe there, for one boy looks much like another. They'll turn every inch of this place inside out."

He finished without an audience. Both Armand and Alexandre had plunged out the back door as he directed, and Madame Dufour had run upstairs to cover traces of visitors and hang their coats among her own clothes.

In a few moments, heavy footsteps and vigorous pounding on the Dufour door showed that their fears were correct. Armand, sitting ill at ease in the kitchen next door with a white-faced young woman and her two small children, could hear the tumult as the troopers ransacked the Dufour house. After a time, they spread out to neighboring houses somewhat halfheartedly, poking about and asking questions, knowing they would get little help for the neighborhood was mostly new converts.

Presently, there was a knock on the door of Armand's refuge. The housewife opened it a crack. A sergeant of dragoons in yellow coat and tasseled cap stood there with two troopers.

"I must search your house, Madame," he said as politely as a dragoon could be expected to manage. He pushed in past her, and the three men looked in every room, chest, and cupboard and under all the beds. They seemed a little perfunctory, as if they didn't expect to find much.

Then the sergeant turned to the silent quartet in the kitchen. As the troopers waited for him in the doorway, one of them muttered something about the accursed informers who wasted people's time with bad guesses. "Always hoping for a reward."

"Who lives here?" demanded the sergeant.

The woman told him truthfully, and if the soldier mistook Armand for the husband absent in the vineyards, was it her duty to explain?

The sergeant sighed, taking in the domestic scene: Armand in his shirtsleeves sitting at table with an empty plate before him and the two little children clinging to their mother's hands as she stood by the fire. The sergeant's face brightened. Children were sometimes readier talkers than their elders. "What a pretty child," he said, trying to sound ingratiating. He bent over to put his face on a level with that of the larger child. "My name is Dupin. What's yours?"

There was no answer.

"Would you like this new penny?" He held out a copper coin between thumb and forefinger. "Have you seen any strange people around—people who don't live here?"

The sergeant's unshaven chin, the white scar over his right eye, the bobbing tassel, and the wine-cum-garlic breath were too much for the child. He retreated bug-eyed behind his mother without a sound. The watching trooper said something under his breath that no nice child should have heard, and the sergeant straightened, glanced at the stony-faced mother, and turned to go.

The littlest child had stood his ground, but he seemed too small to be talking. Suddenly, he began babbling something and pointed at Armand. Though Armand's heart skipped a beat, he forced himself to remain seated and smiled what he hoped was an indulgent smile. The sergeant turned back, listened for a moment with a puzzled frown, shrugged, patted the child on the head, and gave him the *denier*. A moment later the soldiers were gone, and the housewife sank to the bench, her face as white as skim milk.

When certain that the neighborhood was free of unwelcome visitors, Armand thanked the woman for running such a risk for him and breathed a thankful prayer that the smaller child's enunciation was as poor as his judgment. He then slipped back to the Dufour house to resume preparations for the journey.

CHAPTER 11

Massacre in the Mountains

Pastor Merson and Armand de Gandon rested on a wooden bench by a smoky fire in a peasant hut set among the pines west of Nîmes in the high Cévennes. Alexandre squatted on the corner of the raised stone hearth, observing intently. Four small children could be heard at play outside. The woman stirring the iron pot was as meager and sun-scorched as the poor land she lived on. Alexandre was hungry but felt a little guilty when he realized that their hostess had nothing but chestnuts and herbs to set before them. But her welcome had been warm and genuine, and she seemed happy to share the little she had.

The woman didn't look convinced by Pastor Merson's admonition to be patient. She stirred the sooty pot and swung it back over the flames again. "How long then do we turn the other cheek?" she said. "It's all very well to argue about, but you haven't lived here like we have. It was two years ago come All Saints. A dragoon of Saint Ruth came on me and my husband on the path up from Anduze, and he cut my husband down with his saber—not a word of warning. When I screamed and ran to my man, who was bleeding on the ground, his fellow asked him why he did it. He laughed and said, 'I can see on their faces they are Calvinists.' Just like that. So they rode away. Some people coming behind me helped me carry my poor husband up here, but he died before we arrived."

Alexandre studied the faces of his companions.

"Last night," the young woman resumed, "some Judas got blood money. All good and well for you gentlemen to say 'Leave vengeance to the Lord.' But there has been too much innocent blood spilled in these mountains. If Monsieur Vivens feels the Holy Spirit tells him to kill an apostate, who is to say it is not the Lord's vengeance by the hand of His servant?"

The pastor looked pained but said nothing.

Alexandre thought about the summer's mission when he and Armand had counted by the hundreds those Cévennois stirred by the preaching of Vivens and ready to take up arms to regain their freedom. Indeed, after the campaign into the Vaudois valleys of the previous two years, Armand de Gandon had given up on armed resistance. Even when Catholic militia fired into the gathering the previous night, de Gandon had not drawn his pistol. Such a change in his hero was hard for Alexandre to follow.

Finally, he broke the silence. "I suppose, Madame, that it is only what apostates deserve, but it does bring more violence on the poor people when such accounts are settled. However, while the wicked will get their reward in the judgment, I'd like to pay a little on account while we're waiting. I suppose that's why I—we—are fighting in Piedmont and in Ireland for the Good Cause. I agree that the sword goes oddly with preaching the Word, but to say that suffering meekly will some day bring the wicked to repentance—I don't see that they're impressed by it yet." He stopped abruptly, meeting the pastor's eye.

"The young man is partly right, at least," said the pastor mildly. "If we resist, then they are justified in their violence, for they can say we are rebels. But even an apostate may repent, and they too have souls to save for which Christ died. I don't blame you, Madame, nor you, Alexandre, with your noble father in the galleys. It may be according to God's purpose that so much blood must be spilled in these great commotions of our day, but as I read Scripture, I see our Lord Himself, who 'answered them not again' and was as the sheep before the slaughterer. 'Put up your sword' he told Peter in the garden at Gethsemane."

Alexandre went down on one knee and thrust a half-burned stick back into the fire. "You may not have heard, Madame," he said, "that our Huguenots in Ireland have just lately defeated this same Saint Ruth at Aghrim, and he and much of his army are now in hell, where they have been so long overdue."

The pastor looked pained again and silently shook his head. "Alexandre, even now you don't understand. The firm determination of the Lord's people to witness publicly by worshiping as He commands should be the best witness to the purity of our doctrines. We ought to most scrupulously avoid bearing arms or inciting rebellion toward authorities ordained by God. Only in our assemblies do we obey God rather than men."

Alexandre shrugged. Pastor Merson's own authority was tarnished more than a little in the young man's eyes because he shared a blood relationship with the detestable Mathieu Bertrand, and all the more so since their encounter in Saint-Martin.

For three weeks since leaving Saint-Martin, Alexandre had been traveling with Armand de Gandon and Pastor Merson through the rugged *Massif Central* of southern France. When fortunate, they enjoyed the hospitality of peasant cottages. At other times, they slept under trees, behind rocks, or in caves. They had journeyed mostly south and east, avoiding the larger towns and the main highways.

After leaving Saint-Martin, they had cut east to avoid country that was largely Catholic and had eventually come to the upper reaches of the river Tarn. They spent days scrambling up and down stony banks, wading translucent green pools, trudging along white, sandy beaches, and, as gorges narrowed, climbing over boulders wet from the spray of rapids. There were a few little stone villages huddled along the steep banks where the gorge widened a little, and there were feudal watchtowers, often set on rocks commanding the stream. Some of these towers were long since in ruins.

The travelers tried to avoid habitations, for passersby in this remote country would be few and conspicuous. Climbing higher to avoid the little settlements, they walked at times near the edge of the precipice and saw breathtaking views far below; the green river winding along the floor of the gorge. In general, they met far more sheep and goats than people.

They left the Tarn at Le Rozier and, joined by a guide, climbed straight up from the floor of the gorge to high rolling uplands covered with scrub and pines. These highlands were almost deserted, which was why the guide chose such difficult paths. They were led through a country of bizarre rock formations and caverns avoided by the peasants, who said the original pagan demons still lived there among the dense thickets and the huge rocky outcroppings. With a little imagination, Alexandre could see in some of these rocks the forms of ruined buildings and castles eminently suited to be "full of doleful creatures." They reminded him of the scriptural description of a Judean wilderness: "Owls shall dwell there, and satyrs dance there."

But Pastor Merson and Armand de Gandon had their contacts even here: this desperate widow, and those who had gathered the previous night an hour's walk to the southwest. The young man was learning to bite his tongue and hold his peace, but the inner change of heart was slow in coming.

Alexandre was surprised only two days later when they came into a village of ardent Huguenots but hardly less surprised that the men of Intendant de Bâville had been there repeatedly. He stared at the disfigured forms gathered around Pastor Merson.

"This scar I had of a dragoon in the trouble of '83," said a gaunt peasant woman, pushing up her sleeve to show an arm from which most of the flesh had been torn before being patched together. "I didn't step off the high road fast enough for their pleasure, and I had raised my arm to save my face. Two days later, a party of them shot two men of this village at almost the same place on the road. One of those killed was my husband. No one ever knew why it happened; we feared to inquire. The Count de Tesse—may God smite him!—and his men did this sort of thing all through these hills. There wasn't much for them to steal, but they were wonderfully free with every kind of violence."

Others echoed her claims and recited in gruesome detail their wounds and their grievances. Pastor Merson spent several days soothing them, admonishing them to patience, and preaching the Word.

This ominous area ended abruptly on a high bluff, from which they descended almost straight down to the outskirts of Millau. The guide contacted the secret Huguenots of that town, and the pastor held a meeting for them in an abandoned shed south of town on the banks of the now wide and beautiful Tarn. The next day, bidding the guide farewell, the trio journeyed up the spectacular canyon of the River Dourbie into a more heavily Protestant region. Autumn had come to the high country. Alexandre admitted to himself, if not to Armand or the pastor, that he didn't relish the thought of the weeks they were likely to spend at these high elevations. All too well he remembered the winter of the Vaudois return in the Alps.

Coming up out of the gorge to the northeast, they found themselves in as poor a Protestant land as Alexandre had seen anywhere in France—a land of rough hillsides terraced with innumerable stone walls to husband the remaining soil and cultivated with infinite labor. Villages were small and scattered, some consisting of only a half dozen cottages. From the higher elevations, he tried to guess the distance to the blue mountains in ranges repeated off into the distance. For two days, battered by freezing gales that always seemed to strike them head on, they trekked across a high, bare plateau of grasslands with grotesque rocky outcroppings.

"And this is the south of France?" he muttered to de Gandon when they rested in the lee of a giant boulder. "It's as cold as ever I was in the north-most coast of Ireland."

"Present discomfort always seems the worst," Armand replied without pity. "Rejoice. Here you only march; you have no officers admonishing you to bold and bloody courage."

"The army traveled by roads in Ireland," Alexandre remembered. "Here we travel either straight up the cliffs or in the rocky creek bottoms, hemmed in by impenetrable thickets."

Alexandre didn't need de Gandon to remind him that militiamen prowled the main paths, armed by the government to keep an eye on the restless Huguenots and to note any strangers, who would presumably be on errands troubling to the public repose. "What keeps the brethren alive?" he asked himself repeatedly. About the only possession these people had was a burning loyalty to the Religion and a fearsome determination to keep it.

"The province is a powder keg," Armand told Pastor Merson. "Certainly that's no secret to Intendant de Bâville down at Montpellier. He must assume that any pastor who visits the area comes for just one reason—to preach rebellion against the king and resistance to the 'lawful church.' For their part, these people have been hounded, brutalized, spied on by minions of church and state, shot down at worship services, and packed off to the galleys and convents since long before you and the other pastors left."

"*Mais oui,*" the pastor sighed. "And thus the Cévennois are indeed in a highly suggestible state, particularly those who have succumbed momentarily to force and now long for forgiveness and an opportunity to redeem themselves."

During the following days, Alexandre witnessed a kind of fortitude that he hadn't seen during his summer travels with de Gandon. The Cévennois thought nothing of braving the elements or spies to walk for miles to hear any visiting preacher of the Word. They even risked death to hear one of their own neighbors if he could recite by heart or read from the Scriptures or pray "beautiful" prayers.

"The fault is with our Protestant leaders," Pastor Merson mourned. "We have neglected this poor country for generations—since long before the Revocation—and the sheep have starved for lack of a well-schooled preacher."

"Fortunately, they have also been neglected by the authorities through those generations," de Gandon pointed out. "But since the Revocation, spies and talebearers have been prodded into reporting secret meetings. Then regular troops and militia sweep in, and suspects are hauled off by the hundreds to prison or the galleys. The activities of the Huguenot Cévennois have drawn plenty of attention in recent years. This Alexandre and I have seen for ourselves during the early summer."

"They still have a few Roman priests," Alexandre ventured. "These cannot help but know their parishioners abhor them. They have to know the sullen people in their churches haven't been 'converted' at all. They're scared. Why else would they be so violent?"

"Ah, you begin to comprehend." Pastor Merson's face lit up. "But, Alexandre, we must not resort to becoming like them in that respect."

The Sons of the Prophets had told Alexandre all about what had happened during the military incursions of 1683 and 1685. New converts had reverted to Protestantism as soon as the troops retired, and they not only boycotted Catholic services but also were not above taking shots at priests who roamed about the countryside too freely and might be suspected of betraying neighbors to the prisons of Intendant de Bâville.

Now, Alexandre knew, the network of message bearers had spread the invitation. He wondered if the crowd the pastor expected would brave the dangers to come.

"I look with hope to our meeting tonight," Pastor Merson confided as they resumed their march.

Before dusk they arrived at the appointed place, a *mas* that looked more like a giant mushroom than a dwelling. After their meager supper, the three visitors were waited on by a wiry little old man with a towering shock of white hair, toothless gums, and a huge beak of a nose. His *patois* was so strong and his teeth so few that Alexandre could hardly understand him. As he trotted ahead down a narrow path in the moonlight, only snatches of his remarks reached them—that he himself had heard voices singing heavenly music over the site of the Huguenot temple, that Intendant de Bâville was a servant of the demon, and other items the boy failed to catch. Though their guide was an old man, Alexandre had to run to keep up with him. In the descending gloom, his white hair bobbed ahead of them like an apparition.

After ten minutes on a path overgrown with brambles, they emerged in a small clearing where stood four stone houses much like the hovel they had left behind. Their guide escorted them into one, a two-room cabin. A bed, a chest, some benches, a crude table, and the fireplace furnished its only equipment. Jammed inside must have been thirty people. A smoky fire burned in the grate, and Alexandre thought he would smother for want of fresh air.

The assembly was listening intently to a boy about two years younger than himself who was reciting psalms from memory. Alexandre caught two minor errors in the recital and wondered if the speaker had sat in some mountain classroom under a catechist as vigilant as Mathieu Bertrand. When the boy finished, a little girl of eight or nine cried out loudly, and, gazing upward, began to speak with vigorous gestures. Her audience squeezed back to give her room. Most of what she said consisted of bits and pieces from the Old Testament delivered in a sort of chant, accompanied by groans, cries, and sobs from her hearers.

" 'The LORD shall roar from on high, and utter his voice from his holy habitation. . . . He shall give a shout . . . against all the inhabitants of the earth. . . . This is a rebellious people; . . . children that will not hear the law of the Lord!' "

"Mercy!" cried several of her hearers.

" 'Turn ye again now every one from his evil way . . . and provoke me not to anger. . . . Yet ye have not hearkened unto me, saith the LORD.' "

"Mercy!"

" 'O Ephraim, what shall I do unto thee? O Judah, what shall I do unto thee? for your goodness is as a morning cloud, and as the early dew it goeth away. Therefore have I hewed them by the prophets; I have slain thee by the word of my mouth. . . . I have seen an horrible thing in the house of Israel. . . . The LORD also shall roar out of Zion and utter his voice from Jerusalem; and the heavens and the earth shall shake: but the LORD will be the hope of his people.' "

"Amen."

" 'Egypt shall be a desolation . . . for the violence against the children of Judah, because they have shed innocent blood. . . . Hide thyself . . . for a little moment, until the indignation be overpast. . . . Hold that fast which thou hast, that no man take thy crown.' "

"Amen! Amen!"

" 'Surely thou wilt slay the wicked, O God. . . . Do not I hate them . . . that hate thee? And am I not grieved with these that rise up against thee? I hate them with a perfect hatred: I count them mine enemies.' "

"Amen!"

" 'Strengthen ye the weak hands, and confirm the feeble knees. Say to them that are of a fearful heart, Be strong, fear not: behold, your God will come with vengeance.' "

"Amen!"

" 'Even God will come . . . with a recompense; he will come and save you.' Repent! Repent the abominations done in the land! 'If ye be willing and obedient, ye shall eat the good of the land. . . . If ye refuse and rebel, ye shall be devoured with the sword.' "

"Mercy! Amen!"

Like Alexandre, Armand had been listening to the girl with amazement. One peculiarity struck him during the child's performance: She used very good French and spoke with a distinctly educated accent, though most folks in these hills had such a thick local dialect that it was difficult for an outsider to understand them.

When the girl stopped, the pastor and Armand spoke to her. She seemed rather diffident and moderately shy, but brighter than the exhorter who had so effectively aroused the emotions of the little congregation. While she readily gave her name and conversed with the visitors about her family, her explanations of how or why she had made the public appeal and warning were vague.

The group begged Pastor Merson to address them also, and he did so for the next three hours, skillfully enlarging on certain of the girl's texts but explaining them in terms of patient endurance and of leaving vengeance to God rather than sallying forth to slay the Philistines themselves.

That evening when they had returned to the hut where they were to spend the night, the pastor expressed concern over the performances of the young people. Rumors of these strange occurrences had reached Holland, as did stories of heavenly voices chanting or singing. Ministers in exile disagreed vigorously regarding the origin of such performances. Some saw them, Merson said, as heavenly signs to encourage the faithful. Others were equally certain they came from evil angels to mislead the ignorant. After hearing the two types of speech used by the girl, Armand could only ask himself whether she had so thoroughly absorbed the preaching of her former pastor, whom she couldn't have heard more recently than three years before, that in a state of exaltation she could reproduce the upper-class French the minister had probably used.

In the wavering light of the wick-and-tallow lamp, Armand could judge how troubled Pastor Merson was by both performances. The pastor said, "I fear for the future of the church in such remote parts as these. It is not that there is less demand for the services of an ordained minister. The people are hungry for the Word. What I dread is that inexperienced child preachers might increase the dangers these believers already face. They're delivering fanatical, suicidal exhortations to revolt against the beast and ringing verses of Scripture presented without understanding of their proper significance or the effect they might have on the excited imagination of these suffering people."

"It could lead to a bloodbath," Armand said.

Merson leaned closer to the small fire in the hearth, his hands near the flames. "Furthermore," he said, "cut off from their regular pastors, what strange doctrines might emerge here in the Wilderness?" He recalled with alarm that some of his hearers had come to the meetings armed.

Alexandre turned on the older man suddenly. "Certainly you can't blame people for trying to protect themselves. Any assembly might be surprised by the authorities, and the troops mow down men, women, and children indiscriminately—'to make an example.' "

"Yet the king's men claim armed assemblies constitute proof that these meetings are seditious and rebellious and not the purely religious assemblies the people claim," Merson countered.

When Armand and Alexandre pressed him, Merson confessed himself unready to say that celestial choirs and child preachers were of the evil one, but he obviously feared that more evil than good might come of them. The only answer he could see was for the regular ministers to forsake their comfortable exile and risk their lives for these restless flocks left behind in France. Yet of the eight or nine hundred pastors in exile at the moment, how many were prepared to return to the vineyard? Most of them preferred to trust in the Protestant princes such as William of Orange to restore their religious freedom by defeating France, or they would wait until Louis XIV became "enlightened" and, conscience-stricken, invited them to return.

Though they had seen and heard many terrible things on this journey, Armand hadn't seen the pastor as upset as he appeared to be over the evening's events. However, before they blew out the greasy wick, Merson read a text from Jeremiah 23 that comforted him: " 'I will gather the remnant of my flock out of all countries whither I have driven them, and will bring them again to their folds; and they shall be fruitful and increase. And I will set up shepherds over them which shall feed them: and they shall fear no more, nor be dismayed, neither shall they be lacking, saith the LORD.'

"I feel," he concluded, "that the second promise must be fulfilled before the first, and if the ministers do their duty, then we may wait in all confidence and good conscience however long it shall be for the Lord to bring home the remnant."

* * * * *

About midnight on a warm September evening, Armand de Gandon lay on his back on the grass of a rugged hillside in the Cévennes looking into a purple sky, and Alexandre Cortot lay on his stomach beside the soldier. A few feet below them, in a natural amphitheatre and with a large rock as his pulpit, Pastor Merson was feeding those who were "famished for the bread of the Word." A single bonfire blazed beside him, giving him a little light in case he needed to refer to his notes. Mostly invisible on the surrounding slopes were more than a thousand devout Cévennois, some coming as far as twenty leagues for the rare opportunity of hearing a minister again. The pastor had just begun his discourse. The congregation was very quiet and attentive.

Here in the southern hills, where villages were usually small but congregations large, most meetings were held outdoors in a clearing or a cavern. It was obvious, as the *prédicants* moved from place to place, that the authorities were aware of their presence. The *curés* were alerted, and new converts were straitly questioned. But so far, the loyalty of the persecuted was proof against bribes or threats, and the roving PRR ministers' whereabouts never seemed to be reported to church or royal officials until they had traveled far enough to make their escape.

Tonight, the crowd was the largest yet. Sentries had been scattered for at least a league in each direction, and it seemed so safe that a number of psalms had been sung. The pines echoed with the triumphant chant, "I shall never cease to magnify the Lord."

The Communion service had taken a long time. Elders from many former churches had assisted, and the celebrants came forward uncovered, two by two. There had been confessions of apostasy, solemn protestations of repentance, and pleas for pardon and the sending of the Holy Spirit. Now the sermon was under way.

Armand had helped to build up the fire and then had settled to rest while Pastor Merson spoke. They had traveled far that day, and on light fare. It was good to relax in safety and to enjoy the fragrance of the warm night. The constellations overhead seemed quite near.

As Armand watched the fainter stars, they seemed to wink out if he looked at them too long. His mind wandered easily to his favorite subject, and he wondered if Madeleine had yet reached New York or what constellations she might see on shipboard—if she was looking at them also. It was not a very original thought perhaps, and it was just as well that Madeleine's disrespectful younger brother couldn't read minds. Alexandre's breathing suggested that he was asleep anyway.

Several of the listeners cried fervent "amens" at this point, and Armand's attention swung reluctantly back across the Atlantic. These Cévennois were simple, enthusiastic folk—untutored zealots offering impromptu testimonials, frequently flaming with the Spirit. As usual, Pastor Merson preached encouragement and endurance under persecution, but in this province the contest between the Huguenots and royal authority had been grimmer and bloodier than anywhere else in the kingdom. Armand had come to see that with patience wearing thin, enthusiasm could easily become fanaticism.

Sermons here must focus on fundamentals, Pastor Merson kept asserting. Here there was no place for the trivia of smug and sophisticated churches—the minutiae of Sunday observance, of whether theology students might properly wear ribbons, swords, or fringed gloves. There was no leaping from book to book in the modernist vogue, seeking for scattered texts. In the sound fashion of old, Merson developed his sermon from a single book of the Bible. It was Isaiah this evening.

" 'The people that walked in darkness have seen a great light: they that dwell in the land of the shadow of death, upon them the light shined. . . . Behold, the Lord God will come with a strong hand. . . . Behold, his reward is with him. . . . Arise, shine; for thy light is come, and the glory of the LORD is risen upon thee.' "

Suddenly, from up the slope behind the pastor a shot rang out, and then the scream of someone in mortal agony. Instantly, pandemonium broke loose. Everyone jumped up amid cries of "The dragoons!" and "We are betrayed!" In a moment the assembly had dissolved—men, women, and children running pell-mell over bushes and rocks, stumbling over each other in the dark.

Armand scanned the dark hillsides, noting the direction from which the shot had come and the directions in which the listeners fled. Had they been betrayed, he wondered, or had some sharp-eyed official noticed unusual traffic on the roads that day and made a lucky guess?

Leaping to his feet, he ran toward the bonfire, where the pastor had been preaching. He collided with Alexandre, who had also jumped up and crossed in front of Armand, headed for a group of women and girls who had been sitting on the grass just beyond the preacher.

Almost at once a ragged line of flickering lights materialized on the lower slope and began moving upward. It was a trap. Armand realized that the enemy was coming at them from both below and above. He kicked the fire apart. The blazing logs rolled and smoked, leaving only a bed of glowing coals.

In the instant darkness, he spoke in a low voice. "Pastor?"

The first worshipers had almost reached the line of torches but re-coiled. Cries, oaths, and more musket shots added to the din. The little flock now stampeded back upon itself and tried to escape before the cordon could be closed around them. Safety lay in climbing obliquely and getting around the end of the cursing line of infantry crashing up-hill through the rocky thickets. Armand wished he knew this slope as well as the Cévennois did.

"Pastor?"

After the second low call, Merson responded, and they began to climb rapidly, hoping to pass around their assailants. Shots and cries continued above and below them. Armand wished his pistols were loaded. What he wouldn't give for a company of his good musketeers from the Maine Regiment! He would like to try the mettle of the intendant's brave hunters, who were attacking unarmed civilians.

Coming abruptly around the shoulder of the hill, they almost fell into the arms of a party of dismounted dragoons clambering up to close that avenue of escape. One of the soldiers clutched a guttering torch, and by its light Armand saw a dreadful tableau. A young boy who had been running just ahead of them had run full tilt into the armed men. He now lay writhing at their feet, his life bubbling away while one of the dragoons stood with sword dripping crimson in the torchlight. Even as he grasped a fist-sized rock at his feet, Armand saw with relief that the dying *garcon* was not Alexandre.

The dragoon stared at him for a frozen instant. Armand flung the rock with all his might into the face of the man with the light, who went down with a yell. The light was dashed out in a flurry of sparks. A musket discharged with a yellow flash, and there was a groan and the clatter of a heavily laden body falling to the ground. *Good!* thought Armand, as he sneezed in the cloud of smoke. *He's shot one of his own.* He grabbed Merson's arm, and they plunged through the line, tripping and stumbling blindly over rocks, the briars ripping at their clothes.

Below them, unlucky believers had run into troopers or were seen in torchlight by the pursuers, who broke their line to run them down. The lucky and the cool heads who knew the paths had made for their villages or would lie quietly until the first gray of dawn to see their directions. There were pickets on the trails, Armand was certain, and many Cévennois would be arrested—principally women and girls. Those still hiding would hear an outburst of yells and screaming and then silence while two or three soldiers drove off the pitiful little processions of a half dozen captives.

Armand couldn't shake the images from his mind as he ran ahead of Pastor Merson. He had witnessed battle scenes often enough to face them without dismay. But such an attack on unarmed people at worship made his bones tremble. He guessed that since the vast majority of the listeners had by one way or another gotten away, and since no "important" prisoners had been taken, the authorities would feel compelled to make a show of vengeance on those they had collected. He shuddered.

They ran till they could run no more, and then they threw themselves on the grass, gasping with aching lungs, far enough away now that they could no longer see lights nor hear screams. They lay there for a time, but no one came near. Finally, they rose and began to climb another slope, but the pastor was staggering from exhaustion. "*Les pauvre gens!* The poor people!" he murmured repeatedly. "I must go back. I must encourage the bereaved and help the wounded."

Armand drew a quick breath. "Not at all! Your mission would end here. Even the dead died well-fed spiritually this once—and blessed."

The next afternoon, the fugitives lay in the underbrush on a steep mountainside above a rushing stream while a troop of dragoons combed the lower elevations under the brilliant autumn sun. Alexandre had rejoined his friends about midday, and he and the pastor were now dozing. Armand chewed a blade of grass and swatted at gnats. He watched the ineffectual efforts of the distant officers below with a degree of amused contempt. They sat their horses at the mouth of the gorge, glints of gold or bronze occasionally catching the sun as they squirmed in the heat. It was a sweaty and ungrateful task, and the troops keeping at it only under the curses of the noncommissioned officers. He remembered such afternoons when he too had been as tired and disgusted as these officers, and as uncertain that the task at hand was as important as some distant colonel claimed it was.

Armand himself nodded the afternoon away while the crickets chirped and the other insects buzzed a continuous refrain. Gradually, the sun sank toward the western mountain rim, and the shadows became increasingly purple and the breeze cooler. Armand jerked awake as the thin, clear notes of a trumpet sounded the recall. In a short time, the dragoons had mounted their waiting horses and, leaving a picket at the mouth of the little valley, rode off to impose themselves for the night upon some unfortunate mountain village.

Pastor Merson and Alexandre sat up and stretched.

"We'll wait until dark to slip around the picket," Armand said.

"I wonder how many poor souls were caught last night?" the pastor brooded.

"No one knows the exact number yet," said Alexandre sleepily. "Most of our people knew the country better than the soldiers and ran through their lines, but some say almost a hundred were taken."

"We were much concerned about you, young man," said the pastor with a smile. He patted Alexandre's rumpled, dusty locks.

"Don't give him any more of an exaggerated opinion of himself than he already has," grunted Armand. "One born to be hanged will never be shot. I knew he'd turn up."

Alexandre looked flattered.

"Well, now that he has," said the pastor, "I am most grateful for the mutton he brought. It would have been a long, hungry day without it."

"Agreed, I suppose," said Armand rising to his feet. "Truth be told, I'm a little tired of the delicacies of this region—the sheep and the chestnuts too. But I imagine it's better eating than in the jails of Monsieur l'Intendant." He pulled two pieces of dried meat out of his knapsack and handed them to his companions.

Alexandre asked, "Now, after last night, won't you agree with me, pastor, that meekness is useless? It's like throwing away one's weapon and trusting to the gentility of a brigand in the forest. Anyway, the king and the church will always mistrust those who want to worship differently, and no matter how abjectly or patiently we suffer these outrages, they'll go on mistrusting us. We *are* heretics, after all."

The pastor shook his head but waited until he had finished chewing before he answered. Then he said, "I don't agree, *mon ami*. The blood boils at the suffering of these innocents, but to take up the sword, even against an oppressor—that is the sin of rebellion. How could we then ask God's blessing on our cause? Calvin truly observed that 'it will often happen that a good cause goes badly because one adds to that which is worthy of praise too great a confidence in one's own counsels.' Was this not true in the old days when the nobility were wont to mix politics with their religion?"

Conversation ceased while they worked their way down to the floor of the narrow ravine. They knelt and drank, then set off again. The pastor resumed his argument where he had left off a quarter hour before.

"For fifty years now we have tried to demonstrate to our monarch our absolute loyalty and our love—"

"Ah, yes," said Alexandre, shying a flat stone into the stream. "And what has it done for us?"

Pastor Merson ignored the interruption. "Kings are ordained of God. Peter admonished us to honor the king. Paul declared we must be subject not only for wrath but also for conscience's sake. Calvin went so far as to say that he who resists the magistrate resists God Himself. Unjust rulers are raised up to punish the iniquity of a people, and if a ruler does none of his duties, we still may not rebel but only implore the merciful intervention of the Lord. We must obey and suffer except where the ruler actually commands disobedience to the law of God. Then we must be ready to renounce life itself, if need be, rather than crucify Christ afresh."

"This is all very well," said Armand, "and you can always out-quote me with your texts, but I like the view of the tract *Vindiciae contra tyrannos* better, for the author says we have a *duty* to resist evil rulers—not as capricious individuals, of course, but in lawful fashion, through magistrates or estates, as they do in England. The ruler is under contract with the people, and he is bound as well as they and must respect their rights and liberties. It seems to me that we made a beginning in governing ourselves through our synods and consistories and assemblies and that we were in error to let the king shut them off. Some of our people in Holland talk of this contract idea, and it sounds reasonable to me."

"Even Jesuits don't scruple to withhold obedience from a ruler they think is bad," commented Alexandre.

Armand persisted. "The patience of these Cévennois is not inexhaustible, and the day will come when it will take more than a theory of Calvin to hold them back."

"I know this well," agreed the minister sadly. "If this harrying of simple folk continues, in time the hotheads will meet violence with violence and murder with murder, and then what of the truth of the gospel? No, I cannot accept these English ideas. Resistance avails nothing. Rebellion will only convince the king that what he has been told all along is true—that we are a stiff-necked and rebellious people. Rebellion will be drowned in blood."

"Perhaps," shrugged Armand. "I suppose if the king would rather rule over a desert than over heretics, then a desert he can have. But," and his arms described a wide circle, "not easily! What a country for ambushes and surprises! Chasms, gorges, caves, dark forests, and shadowy defiles. With leadership, a few could hold off an army indefinitely. If one *must* die—what a setting!"

"It may come to that," said the pastor, rising to stand beside his companion, "but, as I said, what would that gain for the church of God? If only the king could be made to see that when he cuts the people off from their pastors, he nourishes violent resistance—that with the ministry exterminated, the people will listen to their own prophets and seers. And desperation breeds fanaticism. The people cannot be blamed, but the truth will be perverted by the ignorant enthusiast if sound preaching and doctrine are lacking. Some dream dreams and see visions."

Armand considered the pastor's claims for some time. Finally he spoke. "It would seem that there ought to be many men of moderation and good sense in France who could see that persecution is not Christ's way of seeking lost sheep."

"I think there are, Armand, but they fear to speak. Men of sensibility are revolted by the brutality and hypocrisy of the persecution, and I agree with them that the next generation of Frenchmen may be so disgusted with what passes for religion in this unhappy *patrie* that France will become a nation of skeptics. If forms of religion are what the king wants, he can compel them, but he cannot prevent doubt when the fruits of persecution will be revealed."

"*Tiens*, I wish we could fight them anyway," said Alexandre.

Unruffled by the youth's impatience, the pastor responded with a half smile. "To God alone belongs reward and punishment. You yourself, Armand, when I first met you long ago in the Cortot parlor, told us that resistance would be useless. These experiences are for our good if they lead us to put our trust in the Lord. If it falls out in God's providence that it be martyrdom, then God is good to permit us to follow in the footsteps of our Savior. It may be our portion, on the other hand, to live a faithful life in difficult times, and we should thank Him that we are accounted worthy to witness for His truth. In either case, it is our call to glory!"

"It would seem that last night it would have been no great matter for the Lord to protect us from that surprise," said Alexandre swinging his stick. "I heard this morning that some dog of a turncoat got five hundred *livres* for betraying us."

"You feel, my son, that God has not taken good care of His own? You should remember that we cannot measure our closeness to God or His regard for us by miraculous interventions in our behalf. Do you think that because the apostle Paul suffered sore trials and prison, shipwreck, and finally, martyrdom, he was less regarded by the Lord? No, the closer we walk with the Lord, the less we need to depend on miracles to convince ourselves of His regard. Miraculous occurrences are for the encouragement of babes in the faith."

Crouching low, they topped another ridge. Armand scanned the slope until he spotted the horseman left to guard the trail. He was maintaining a position along the stream where it left the gorge, blending into the landscape except for the glint of the setting sun on the polished barrel of his pistol and an occasional daub of the red of his cap.

"We'd best be on our way," Armand said. "We have to find that shepherd on the other side of this mount. He can guide us into the next valley without using the road. And let's have more silence now. If that picket hears our voices, we'll continue our discussion in a dungeon."

With infinite caution they made their way past the mounted sentry. The moon had not yet risen, and the lonely watcher appeared to be preoccupied and didn't hear them as they slipped past him over mossy rocks along the stream, hardly breathing. The sentry's horse was restless too, and Armand blessed the animal for its stamping.

They climbed up the hill back of the little gap. That was no easy task, but it was the most direct route to the place they sought. They worked their way up the slope in single file, Armand leading. No word was spoken.

The grade eased somewhat after a time, and it occurred to Armand that they must be close to the site of the ill-fated meeting of the night before. It was still too dark to see anything but shades of blackness. He guessed they were about halfway to the crest, for they were passing through the orchard he remembered from the previous day. The breeze was stronger now, and a little chilly.

As Armand passed beneath a tree, his cheek brushed against cloth. Instinctively, he reached out his hand and, to his astonishment, grasped an icy human foot at the level of his face. Too shocked to cry out, he halted in his tracks. The pastor blundered into his back.

At that moment, the moon came out from behind low clouds, illuminating the valley with a pale, diffused glow. They were in the orchard all right. All around were old trees with warped and twisted branches, and suspended from many of these branches, swaying gently in the night air, were more than a score of corpses in both men's and women's clothes, hanged by the soldiers the night before.

"There's no use picking the fruit of these trees till resurrection day," said Armand grimly. The pastor sank to one knee and prayed silently with bowed head. Alexandre, dumb-struck, just stared at the grisly scene. They resumed their climb, moving a little faster, anxious to leave the accursed place behind them.

* * * * *

At daybreak, enshrouded by a heavy mist, they found themselves at a crossroad. There was the usual gibbet with its load of decaying bodies. Cautiously, they reconnoitered, reassuring themselves that no one was near before stepping onto the roadway to read the notices posted there. A post indicated the road to Nîmes was to the left and another pointed toward Sommières.

The posts bore several proclamations. In the predawn light, Alexandre put his face close to a circular and read a description of Pastor Merson. "Fifty-five hundred *livres* they'll give for you now, pastor!" he cried in delight. "You're coming up in the world!"

Armand read his own description appended to the bottom of the pastor's notice, but he was worth only fifty *louis d'or*, dead or alive. "Well, at least they know whom they're looking for," he said.

"Am I to take offense that they don't mention me?" inquired Alexandre.

Armand reread his own description. "I am not much flattered. They are rather abusive, don't you think—'murderous assassin' and 'perturbator of the public repose' seem a little strong." The thought struck him, however, that the words sounded very much like the rhetoric of Mathieu Bertrand.

As if reading his mind and wishing to allay such suspicions, the pastor mildly observed, "I note that our descriptions mention the clothes we wore when we left the Netherlands."

"Yes," agreed Armand, embarrassed. "There must be treachery up that way. They didn't miss many details." He didn't say so, but all three of them still wore those same not-so distinctive garments.

Alexandre cleared his throat and spat. "I don't know about you, but I feel very conspicuous out here in the light of day, and there's still room on that gibbet too. If I had the price on my head that you do, I'd keep more to the shadows."

After several minutes of rapid walking southward, the pastor spoke. "The reward offered for me amounts to more than ten times my salary the last year before my exile. That much money will tempt poor folk!"

"Might it not be discreet to leave the country for a season," asked Armand, "at least until the pursuit dies down a little?"

"If there remain but the seven thousand who have not bowed the knee to Baal, I must remain and succor them," replied Merson.

Has the pastor decided on martyrdom? Armand wondered. It could only be a question of time until the men of the intendant caught them. Then he spoke aloud. "That could very likely prove fatal."

"It is as God ordains," said Merson, unmoved. "He'll decide how long I may be of service. In the meantime, I must occupy myself in His vineyard."

"We'll be even easier to track when Mathieu joins us," observed Armand after some minutes.

"This may be true, Armand, but there is no reason for you and Alexandre to risk yourselves. You have served well—beyond the praise of men. It would be entirely honorable for you to retire now to Switzerland or Holland. Indeed, it might be an advantage for me to change companions for a time. Might it not even confuse the informers and pursuers? I've come to love you both, but I wouldn't wish to lead you to your deaths from a selfish desire for your company."

Armand felt a flicker of jealousy. *He wonders if he might do better with Mathieu,* he thought. *He wishes to give Mathieu a chance to redeem himself.* Then he chided himself sternly. Such thoughts were unworthy. A gentleman didn't grow jealous of a schoolmaster!

"Remember, Armand," the pastor was saying with a hint of his seldom-indulged humor, "those who wait for you have admonished me for your safety."

Armand shrugged. "But what about you?"

"My calling before the Lord is different. My wife and I have enjoyed a good life together, and if, because of my obligation to the flock here, we don't meet again on this earth, then we should have no complaint. But this is not your case. You mustn't let either your noble instincts or your aristocratic pride overcome your judgment. Does your heart yet return to Versailles—or does it follow its beloved over the waters?"

"Wherever it may be," Armand responded, "it will wait until I can get you out of this country."

Armand's mind began a rapid journey over the past few weeks. What did Pastor Merson mean? The older man had never said anything either for or against Mathieu before, but these comments could mean only that he wished his nephew to be supplanted.

He fell into a brown study, his legs carrying him on without his volition. Was the Madeleine Cortot in his mind a real woman who might love him, or was she a dream fabricated from a few sweet memories? Try as he might, he couldn't focus on one Madeleine, neither the

well-groomed beauty in her father's parlor at Saint-Martin, nor the di-
sheveled but desirable fugitive of the northern woods, nor even the unhappy, almost angry face of the exile in Holland. The pastor was right:
His trouble was pride, false pride. *Eh bien*, it was probably too late now.
The net was closing about them here, but one couldn't desert in the face
of danger.

For hours they walked along the high road, meeting no one in the
dense fog. The country was now mostly orchards and vineyards, and
one could dimly see on the rises around them villages with red roofs and
church towers. Near dusk they left the road and made themselves comfortable among the stones in a gully.

"Pastor," said Armand as he sought for a smoother rock to use for a
pillow, "I'm going to stay with you and see you out of this. I'm almost
glad the royal crew knows I am here, for too long they have seen me
halting between two opinions. I want them to know I am finished with
this indecision—that I couldn't be content to live the empty life of a
courtier. I think the Lord's hand is in the matter, and I thank Him for
it."

Merson smiled, obviously delighted and proud. "Your soul they shall
not have for a prey, and they need not have the body either. You must
go, Armand, and take Alexandre with you. Soon after we begin our
journey tonight, we will come to a fork in the road. You two must go
toward Lunel and east. You should seek word of Brother Cortot, and if
you journeyed toward Marseilles and Toulon, it might throw our pursuers off their track. I will be in Montpellier tomorrow, and, with Mathieu, will still have a companion on my travels. You must go, for others
besides myself have claims upon your duty!"

Exasperated, Armand sat up abruptly. "I respect your sanctity and
your erudition, pastor, but not your judgment. You weigh too heavily
on my heart. Alexandre must go, yes. But even if Mathieu joins us, my
place is with you until you are out of danger for good. As for these
other matters, I see now that I had my chance, but I lost it. It is too late
now."

Later, Alexandre took Armand by the sleeve and whispered, "Then
what you are really saying is that this mission is a lost cause?"

"I'm sorry. Yes. Hopeless." Armand rested his hand on the boy's
shoulder as an older brother might have done.

Alexandre's lips sagged where his front teeth were missing, but his shoulders stiffened.

"In any case," Armand continued, "there is no reason for you to go with Pastor Merson and Mathieu. If the outcome is bad, you wouldn't be able to change it, and there would be one victim the more."

"*Bien.* What about yourself? If the pastor is determined to go to Montpellier to meet Mathieu in spite of all warnings, how would your being there change it?"

"My death wouldn't directly affect others. . . . *Je sais!* I know!" he added hastily, raising his hand to silence the objection he knew was coming from the boy. "There is Madeleine. But I have no claim on her, and she has no claim on me, whatever might have been. Please understand. Our chances may be poor, but I'm not throwing my life away in some suicidal gesture. Something must be done: It has fallen my lot as I see it to save the pastor. Yours is to get yourself to your sister and Judith in America."

Alexandre cast him a fierce look. "I see your point—I do indeed. But I don't like it at all. You think you can perhaps change his mind about this rendezvous in Montpellier and somehow extricate him if it is a trap." He shrugged. "I suppose I would argue more with you were it not for Judith. And I'd like to get some word about my father."

Armand waited while Alexandre hesitated.

The boy straightened his shoulders. Their eyes met, and Armand recognized in Alexandre the strength of purpose one would expect in a man ten years older.

"I'll do as you say."

CHAPTER 12

The Execution

Alexandre Cortot, although adept at living off the country, grew more cautious as he approached his goal. Even with young vagabonds numerous in France, it was dangerous to make inquiries about convicts. He was what was called a "sturdy vagabond." He might be seen as a deserter and find himself arrested and drafted for service in one of His Majesty's regiments.

Soon after leaving Armand and the pastor, Alexandre had his narrowest escape at the malarial village of Marsillargues, where, as he sweet-talked a housewife for his breakfast, he was noticed by the local constable. Whether the man was suspicious or merely wanted to bully someone smaller than himself, Alexandre didn't wait to find out.

For a hot and difficult week, Alexandre trudged through the delta lands of the Rhône, along canal banks and through swamp country, heading by a roundabout route for the great port of Marseilles, where rumors in Saint-Martin claimed his father had been seen on a galley. Now many of the king's galleys would be careened on the beaches there for winter repairs. These cranky craft were not good sailors in bad weather, and most of them would be on the beach for several months, a fellow vagabond told him, the crews living ashore in prison stockades.

As he traveled the marsh country, the settlements were scattered and poor. It was a region of reeds and brackish water where dry land seemed ready to sink from sight. Alexandre arrived in Marseilles damp and hungry. He avoided the massive Fort Saint-Jean, which probably contained many of his fellow Protestants. It wouldn't be healthy to show curiosity around such a place.

There were no galleys along the quays, so Alexandre wandered out of town along the beaches. His conversations with seafaring men had so far brought him nothing more than the names of the galleys wintering there—little that helped in his search for news of his father. But now he found a dozen naval vessels 20 feet wide and 150 feet long on the sand above the tide line, with only a few galley slaves aboard.

Alexandre fell into talk with an old man sitting on a plank between two tar barrels and taking some afternoon sun. The man looked him up and down twice and then shrugged. "You're not from the seacoast."

"There's not much promise for someone such as me," Alexandre said. "My sister thinks I should learn a trade, but for myself, I would just as soon be a soldier or join the king's navy." He nodded toward the vessels beached nearby. "Not on a galley, however."

The old man leaned forward and spat into the sand. "Your sister, she's a wise woman. She's right. There's no end of war as long as there's kings and bankers. But war's a bloody business, just in case you hadn't thought of that fact."

"I'm off for a bit of adventure myself," Alexandre said.

"Now these galleys—" the old man seemed not to have heard him, "they're hell for the very young and the old. Strictly speaking, they're projectiles to be rammed into enemy craft, particularly useful in shallow seas and when there's no wind for maneuvering the big sailing ships. Of course, they also smash up and sink quite readily if rammed in their turn or if hit by gunfire. Rowers chained to the benches are doomed with the ship."

Alexandre picked up a short length of frayed rope. The old man spat again.

"Still, the human animal can become accustomed to almost everything, and *débrouiller*, to muddle through is the watchword aboard the galleys as well as in all other branches of His Majesty's fighting service."

"Ah, but if I joined the navy, I'd become an officer," Alexandre ventured, hoping brashness would prolong the conversation.

The old man guffawed. "The likes of you? You must be almost twenty. Officers come with recommendations from a gentleman and start training at half your age. It's too late for you if you want to be an officer."

His expression took on a benign flatness. "But not even the officers enjoy a comfortable life on a galley. There's not much deck to sleep on. Officers and one or two of their favorites might have room to sling a hammock in the soapbox of a cabin in the stern. But galleys, with their shallow draft, feel every motion of the sea."

Alexandre hadn't seen his father since he was twelve years old—since he had been spirited off to a House of New Catholics. In what condition his father might be now, after years of confinement, he hardly wanted to guess.

Farther down the beach, cautious never to seem too curious about Huguenot galley slaves, Alexandre gathered bits of information. Discipline among the seamen was, Alexandre soon discovered, slack in the fall; the officers entertained themselves in taverns up the shore. He learned that some "difficult" cases among the galley slaves might be confined in dungeon cells during the fall and winter, and even now, a large number languished in prison hospitals ashore.

One evening he was pleased to find a group of men in light leg irons sitting around a fire, cooking beans in a pot. They wore floppy red caps and coarse, loose red shirts cut halfway to their belts. They were a villainous-looking lot, but water and shaves might have done much for some of them. An armed guard dozing some distance away didn't seem to care when the hungry boy edged closer to the group.

The galley slaves made Alexandre welcome, and he wolfed down more than his share of the beans and oil. With his stomach appeased, he began asking questions.

The good-humored convicts were eager to impress an admiring young fellow. It turned out that they were the ordinary, or original, type of galley slaves, sent there for every conceivable crime and breach of decorum. The prisoners "for the sake of religion" were also ashore but under tighter guard.

"They're a different sort from us," said a convict, whose nose had been cut off for bad behavior. "They're all a little crazy, for when the missionary priests come on board of a Sunday in port, the heretics won't doff their caps at the elevation of the Host. There are enough common causes for a *galérien* to get flogged for; why sweat blood when a cap comes off easy enough? Yet, they're fine men, those heretics."

Other criminals spoke highly of their Huguenot comrades too, expressing sympathy for them. It was true, they added, that the Huguenots were odd.

To man the oars, the French government also brought in large numbers of Turkish Muslims. "They don't complain, these unfortunate aliens," said the man without a nose in a wheezy voice. "If these Turks weren't here, they'd be rowing galleys for some Barbary potentate at home."

The criminals and particularly the Turkish slaves claimed they had tried to help the Huguenots. When the Huguenots' quarters were searched, the Turks hid their Bibles and other forbidden books, for they, being Muslims, weren't suspected of having Christian books.

Any convict with a trade was allowed to practice it during the winter layover, and though the Huguenots weren't permitted to go into town, the regular criminals and the Turks were, and they would peddle the handicrafts of the Huguenots for them. With the extra money, one could arrange for more and better food to be brought on board.

Prisoners with special abilities might be released from the oars and become servants to the officers. These days it seemed most of these servants were Huguenots. It was true that new arrivals often died quickly if unable to endure the toughening, but once a *galérien* was hardened, he got along reasonably well on most galleys. Not all the *comites*, or petty officers, were cruel just for the fun of it.

Huguenots were sentenced to the galleys for life. Few of the regular criminals expected release for themselves either, they said—especially in wartime, and when was France not at war? It was hard to keep the benches filled, and the officers could use any misconduct to prolong one's sentence.

After befriending several of the convicts, Alexandre asked about his father. The men were off the *Indomptable* and were positive no one named Cortot was aboard her. However, prisoners were occasionally transferred from one galley to another, and some men had seen service on three or four. They volunteered to question the Huguenots of their own crew, whom Alexandre might not safely approach, and see what they might know.

From these men and other galley slaves to whom he talked along the beaches, Alexandre became fairly certain his father wasn't in Marseilles. His informants suggested that perhaps his galley was stationed at Toulon, a couple of days' walk farther east along the coast.

In Toulon, Alexandre quickly made himself acquainted with the convicts on shore. After a week of questioning, he learned that his father was on the *Fière*, which they supposed was wintering in Monaco, still farther east, beyond the French border.

Since the post roads ended at Aix, Alexandre took rugged goat paths over the Maritime Alps to the little principality allied to France. Some of the trails were in sight of the incredibly blue sea, but the harsh and rocky route, while picturesque, left his feet bruised by the time he limped into his destination a week later.

Monaco was simply an old castle and a tiny village set on a striking rocky promontory with a fine little harbor below. The "hinterland" was a few acres of olive trees and vineyards that were mostly set on edge as they climbed up the steep heights behind the settlement.

The harbor sheltered several galleys, and he found the *Hardi*, the *Gloire*, and the *Audacioux* careened there. However, unlike in Marseilles or Toulon, Alexandre saw immediately that he was conspicuous in the narrow alleys of this small, remote place. The *gendarmes* of the prince, recognizing him as a stranger and a vagabond, gave him a routine beating and, with harsh words, urged him on his way.

Discouraged, Alexandre returned to the beaches at Toulon. There he encountered some of his previous informants. They had news. "While you were away these three weeks, they made up a squadron for winter service off the kingdom of Naples. One of the galleys was the *Fière*, which came in from somewhere down the line. This Isaac Cortot you are seeking is indeed on board—he is storekeeper and valet to the commander. So you see, he is doing all right. He sent a letter ashore by one of the Turks in case you came back this way. One of our Huguenots has it hidden in the stockade, but we'll get it for you. Too bad you played the mountain goat, but you never would have been able to get near a galley on active service anyway."

Alexandre had mixed feelings of disappointment and relief. He thanked the convict for the news and promised to return the next day for the letter. At least his search hadn't been entirely without result—

there would be something to report to Madeleine if he ever had the opportunity. Tonight he would compose a short message to be smuggled to his father, and tomorrow he would begin the long march back to Languedoc. He hoped to find Pastor Merson and Armand again. He would have plenty of time as he walked westward toward Montpellier to wonder if they had survived the nearly two months he was gone.

*   *   *   *   *

Through the kindness of a reluctant new Catholic, Armand and the pastor approached Montpellier on horseback. Something like constraint had fallen on them. The pastor, Armand felt, was a little vexed with him—not angry but sorrowful perhaps that Armand couldn't hide his pessimism about the plan to meet Mathieu. The soldier hadn't aired his misgivings for some time, but each knew what the other was thinking.

They climbed the hill and entered the inner city without difficulty, for it was a busy commercial center with many visitors. Armand noted the citadel dominating everything, its numerous garrisons, and the headquarters of the fearsome Intendant de Bâville, the king's deputy in the province. "We had best not go directly to the home of Brother Dulac," he warned, considering the risk of calling attention to that house—which too many visitors would certainly do.

Most of the citizens had once been Huguenots, and as rather sullen new converts, they weren't trusted by the king's people. However, the travelers were disappointed in the attitude of the new converts who had been recommended to them as trustworthy individuals with whom one might find refuge. Some were regretful, but all remained firm: harboring a pastor was too dangerous to risk. As one merchant said as he shut the door in their faces, "I've already lost my soul to save my business and my property. You can't expect me to lose *them* now just to help you—they're all I have left."

Armand said, "Alexandre would have laughed at these former brethren's 'silly reluctance to be hanged by the neck and have their houses pulled down' if they sheltered Protestant visitors. The rural believers up there in the Cévennes are either braver or more reckless. Maybe these city merchandisers feel they have more to lose."

After a half-dozen rebuffs the pastor felt that they had no other choice than to go to Brother Dulac's house. Armand disagreed, thinking of King David fleeing time after time from Saul. "Let's lodge with one of the Philistines," he said.

The pastor demurred. It didn't seem fitting somehow.

Armand insisted.

They continued their argument in low tones as they passed some beautiful formal gardens—the Peyrou, where local lickspittles promenaded by the grand triumphal arch commemorating the great victories of le Grande Monarque in the Low Countries, and most especially his Revocation of the Edict of Nantes. Descending the hill, they eventually found themselves in the shabby suburb of Devillier on the west side of the city.

"Well, we have to do something," said Armand. "Mathieu isn't due until the day after tomorrow, and it's getting dark. If we don't roost somewhere, we'll be picked up by the watch."

Observing a newly painted sign trumpeting the "Arms of Flanders" over a ramshackle inn, Armand entered and the pastor followed somewhat helplessly behind him. The innkeeper rose respectfully to meet the two men. He had close-set eyes, bad teeth, and a mop of tangled hair over his forehead—not a face that inspired trust. And though the host's own clothes were dirty and his apron greasy, he turned a cold eye when he saw the travelers' stained and tattered garments. However, as soon as they assured him that he would be paid in good coin, he seemed to lose interest in his guests' appearance. This reassured Armand, if not the pastor, and they engaged a moldy chamber with a lumpy, husk-filled mattress. The ceiling sagged and mice could be heard scurrying about their business under the eaves, but at least it was an out-of-the-way place.

The next day Armand arranged pasturage for their horses just outside the city and made discreet contacts around the town, confirming that the Dulacs were still undetected. Then he said they must purchase new clothes of markedly different style than what they had arrived in, something more appropriate for men riding from town to town on well-bred horses.

As they shopped, Armand argued for a delay of several more days in contacting Dulac. But the pastor wouldn't hear of it. What would Mathieu think if the rendezvous were not kept?

"And if it is a trap?" asked Armand. He didn't get an answer.

"It's quite understandable that you should feel as you do about my nephew," said Merson as they closed the door of their gloomy chamber at the inn. "I've tried to arbitrate. It is a pastor's office, you understand—a lifetime habit as natural as preaching and praying. You know, my son, that I wish most heartily for your best joy."

Armand was startled by the last word. "*Joie?* You might wish for my salvation or even my survival, but joy?"

"I speak of your relationship with Mademoiselle Madeleine Cortot, of course."

"Yes, joy would then be a matter to—"

"She has for four years now felt a deep attachment for you, Armand. Of that I am most certain."

"And yet, I could not . . ."

"And, of course, *she* could not."

"I should have pressed the matter in Holland," Armand admitted. "But I didn't want to take unfair advantage of feelings of gratitude she may have had then. This she understood—I suppose very naturally—as a lack of interest. I also was troubled that we hardly had a *sou* between us, and a penniless soldier is a very poor choice for a lady who should be able to do much better. Besides, I wasn't aware that her commitment to Mathieu had ever been broken. As you see," the soldier ended wryly, "I have worked out many excuses, some better than others."

"But I insist!" said Merson. "Do you not love her? Do you not wish to marry her?"

Faced with so direct a confrontation, Armand was forced to admit what he had suppressed for so long. "Yes, I do," he said, "with all my heart."

"It's a pity you never told her so. You should have realized that she, too, didn't want to presume on the feelings you shared in your escape, and, being a lady, she wouldn't take the initiative to tell you her feelings for you or even that her feelings for Mathieu had changed long ago. She was waiting for you to reveal your feelings before she dared to express hers."

"It seems Alexandre was right—bothersome cupid though he was— that I should have carried her off and matters would have arranged themselves. Delicacy and good manners appear to have been a handicap."

Loaded with their parcels, the two men walked slowly down the narrow street between buildings four or five stories tall. Armand hardly knew what more to say.

Pastor Merson finally broke the silence. "I've spoken my mind, and I think I have represented hers accurately. You've been frank with me. May I ask then what you are of a mind to do about it?"

"I don't know," said Armand. "Perhaps when our mission here is accomplished, I should present myself to her in America and confess what I should have long ago—and hope that she'll still have me."

"I doubt there would be any question about that," the pastor said, smiling. "Mademoiselle Cortot is doubtless already comfortably settled in New York, employed, and saving as frugally as if she were Dutch to set up her own household." He paused, and Armand stopped in his tracks while that comment soaked in.

"But then," continued Pastor Merson, "my mission here has no necessary termination. I'm here to console the people as the Lord gives me opportunity. While I most certainly do enjoy your company, yet it would seem that when we are positively certain Mathieu joins me, you could return to Rotterdam to learn if the young lady has sent word of her arrival. Your duty is clearly to dedicate yourself to Mademoiselle Madeleine. *Vraiment,* I would like to have both of you young men with me for companionship, but my safety doesn't depend on your capable arms but upon the Lord's will, *n'est-ce pas*? Mathieu can help me in some ways, even though he doesn't have your soldierly background."

"I wish I weren't so suspicious, pastor, and that I could leave you with peaceful enough heart to travel with Mathieu. Yet, I don't know . . ." Armand bit his lip. "Perhaps when Alexandre returns."

The pastor remained patient. "I know your feelings in this matter, Armand, but I will hope to see a new Mathieu who has regained his courage again. In his cowardice during the flight, he forfeited any right to claim that he truly cared for Mademoiselle Madeleine. And he knows her judgment is just. You will see, Armand, that you have distressed yourself for nothing."

Armand held his tongue.

The Execution

* * * * *

On the morning of October 19, Pastor Merson was to meet his nephew Mathieu Bertrand at the fountain on rue de Saint-Jacques. "We shall need the horses, for it would be better to leave yet today," Armand told the pastor a full two hours before the scheduled rendezvous. "I'll bring them in from their pasturage before we go to the fountain. That way we can leave at any moment we desire. I'll be but a half hour."

Armand left the inn by a narrow lane that led to a stone-fenced meadow, glad that he had found a third horse the day before. With all of them mounted, they could take up their journey south to Cette with greater dispatch. If they were to travel with Mathieu, they must be mounted.

When Armand returned to the inn, he tied the three horses in the stable and went to the room. It was empty.

In the common room, several drunken travelers, too poor to pay for a room, sprawled between table and wall, still half asleep. In a whisper, Armand asked his host if he had seen his companion.

"Why, yes," he answered. "He left a few minutes ago and said to tell you not to worry about him for he would take care of the business himself. He said he wouldn't be gone long."

Armand's heart stopped. "Did he say where he was going?"

"No, but he did ask the way to the rue de Saint-Jacques," the innkeeper said. Then he stared. "Are you ill, monsieur?"

"Yes," said Armand, "but if we don't see you again, just forget you ever saw us. I pray I'm not too late." And he spun on his heel and shot out the door at a dead run.

* * * * *

Mathieu Bertrand, dressed in his usual brown fullcloth with a white neck cloth, stepped out of the Hotel de Ville in Montpellier with a single companion, a rubicund man of sixty with a jet-black beard and a graying fringe around a bald head. They walked perhaps a hundred yards from the fountain and dropped into the shadow beneath a shopkeeper's balcony to wait.

"Is that Monsieur Merson across the street approaching the corner where you were to meet him?" the older man asked in a restrained whisper.

Bertrand nodded stiffly.

Suddenly, from an arched alleyway to the right, a cluster of soldiers fired a ragged volley. Confused, the startled pastor halted and then turned.

An officer galloped out into the street waving his sword. He shouted at his men, "Cease, *fous!* We have him!" Then the soldiers swarmed out and pinned the pastor's arms.

Mathieu Bertrand bolted. He would have shouted, but no sound came from his open mouth. At that moment a second officer, coming from the direction toward which Mathieu had just turned, caught him across his throat with the tip of his sword, and the white neckcloth was flooded with scarlet.

Another fusillade erupted, and bullets ricocheted down the street. A soldier standing in a doorway was shot in the calf and fell to the pavement with a surprised yelp, his musket clattering to the ground. Other soldiers threw themselves flat as musket balls shattered street-side windows and buried themselves in heavy wooden doors.

The mounted officer noted Mathieu's yellow hair and realized his mistake. He shrugged. "There were supposed to be two of them," he shouted at his men as he waved his blood-stained sword. "Spread out! Search the quarter!"

He turned on the sheepish sergeant coming from another house. "Don't you dragoons have any better control of your men than that? It was your clever *feu de joie* that must have scared off the other one."

The streets filled with people, some curious but more looking downright unpleasant. The soldiers felt this, and after poking about half-heartedly, they soon fell back to where the captain and their fellows were holding Pastor Merson prisoner.

"Maybe there wasn't another one," offered one searcher hopefully.

The man on horseback had better control of himself now. "I didn't expect you dolts to find anything." He wiped his sword on a wooden doorpost, cleaning off the blood, and then returned it to its scabbard. The crowd moved back as he maneuvered his mount toward Pastor Merson.

"Well, Monsieur, I suppose you're the preacher. At least we have *you*—that's the important thing. The Intendant de Bâville will be delighted to make your acquaintance. He's been waiting for this for some time!"

The officer assessed the size and mood of the mob that blocked the street in both directions. Then he addressed his men. "If we can't cut our way back to the citadel, we may all be in hell together tonight. I hope you *fous* are satisfied!"

* * * * *

Armand, running as fast as he could, heard the sound of musket fire reverberating down the narrow street ahead of him. The streets filled with the curious and excited, impeding his progress. He knew it was now too late, that the pastor was either dead or captured, but he slowed himself to a walk and forced his way through the thickening press, earning angry looks and retaliatory shoves. When he reached the street where the ambush had occurred, he found it packed solid with humanity in near riot mood.

"A pastor has been taken!" several voices affirmed. Hundreds of townspeople, most of them former Huguenots, passed the word.

Winded and almost in a frenzy, Armand looked around, uncertain what to do next. The mob in front of him began to press backward, and in a few moments, he could see why. An escort of soldiers, some mounted, some on foot, was pushing its way down the alley. The captured pastor was tied to the saddle of one of the horses, and Armand caught a glimpse of his pale but composed face. Bracing against a wall, Armand held his own as the growling press of citizenry were pushed past him. Suddenly, he realized that the soldiers, who were elbowing their way along and striking out with the flats of their swords or pushing with musket butts, were upon him; the people in front of him had retreated, and he was now on the front row.

A soldier kicked a crumpled body in brown broadcloth lying in the middle of the street. Armand shuddered. In a few moments he might himself be lying in the street lifeless, his clothing soaked with his blood. The body rolled, and Armand recognized the pastor's nephew. But there was no time to wonder why or how Mathieu had died.

Armand knew the soldiers were nervous and that they had reason to be. That realization gave Armand some hope—perhaps the pastor could yet be freed. A riot could erupt at any moment, and in these narrow alleys, with houses overhanging the street, it would go very badly for the military. However, though hatred could be read on almost every face, still the citizens hesitated, for the first ones to act against the soldiers would almost inevitably be shot down whatever happened afterwards.

Still with no coherent idea of what he could do to help the pastor, Armand found himself locking eyes with a mounted, sweaty-faced sergeant. Instantly, recognition flashed in the soldier's black eyes. "*Sacre bleu!* I've seen that fellow before! He's the other one!"

In what was almost a reflex action, he dug his spurs into his horse and tried to pin Armand against the stone wall of a shop. But Armand was quicker. Bending low, he leaped for the nearby corner of a side alley, bowling over citizens who happened to be in his way. In the shouting, screaming, and scrambling that ensued, the dragoon whipped out his heavy pistol and fired at the fugitive without the time to take proper aim. Armand spun and started to fall but was dragged around the corner by those near him. He disappeared from the soldier's sight in an instant. Furious, the latter urged his horse into the throng at the intersection, but his animal, more fastidious or frightened by the racket, reared instead.

"No more shooting!" screamed the captain. "Do you want to get us all massacred?" However, the shot proved useful, for those in front of the mob scrambled back to get out of the way, and the ones behind who had bent to grasp loose cobbles were forced back also.

It took another quarter of an hour of slow progress in an explosive atmosphere before the party got close enough to the gate of the citadel for the captain to relax. "Do you think you hit him?" he asked the sergeant in a low voice.

"Maybe," grunted the sergeant, his eyes restlessly searching the bobbing faces around them, "but who could know?"

* * * * *

Intendant de Bâville leaned back in his huge chair and stared across the table at the prisoner. His full brown wig cascaded down his heavy shoulders and nicely accented the pale blue of his suit and the silver work of his undervest. He clasped his ringed fingers across his extensive stomach and studied the pastor with frank interest.

Pastor Merson stood before him in a shaft of yellow light that shone down from a high, narrow window near the roof of the judicial chamber in the citadel. Ranged beside the official in comparative gloom stood the bishop, the subdelegate, and several missionary monks.

The little Reformed minister, pale and composed, was dressed in the brown suit that he had purchased just the day before. His shirt was slightly torn and his hair was somewhat disordered after the buffeting he had suffered during the arrest and his journey to the citadel. His right wrist was chained to the left wrist of a trooper, and two musketeers stood behind him. The arresting officer and a noncommissioned officer with a halfpike stood stiffly behind them. The slight figure of the pastor made this show of force seem a little ridiculous.

"So this is the wolf that has been tearing the sheep!" said Intendant de Bâville almost to himself. "An unlikely looking villain, I would say, but I suppose we mustn't judge by appearances." His manner was polite, and he didn't use his customary hectoring tone. "Monsieur, you have put us to great trouble to arrange this meeting."

"I regret the inconvenience, Monsieur, but you understand my reluctance."

"No doubt you are aware of the published penalties for one of your sort taken in France?"

"I am, Monsieur."

"This doesn't disturb you?"

"No, Monsieur. If it is the Lord's will that my work close in this manner, I am content."

Bâville glanced at the priests. "Such an ending is not altogether necessary."

A twitch of surprise crossed Merson's white face, but he said nothing.

"I feel certain that His Majesty would regret the loss of such a courageous and ingenious subject. It is possible that one might arrive at an accommodation."

"I appreciate His Majesty's gracious interest, but I must decline any accommodation if it assumes I will give information about my brethren."

"We have ways of gaining such information, even from the most stubborn."

The prisoner didn't flinch. "That I know," he said tranquilly. "I only hope that the Lord in His mercy might permit my soul to leave this weak habitation before I prove unworthy."

The intendant stared at the calm face for a moment. "Perhaps that won't be required. There are other ways in which you might atone for the trouble you have caused the servants of His Majesty."

"I thank you for this consideration, but I am not at liberty to abandon my trust."

The bishop broke in with a voice of liquid silver. "Surely you have heard of the affair of Fulcran Rey not long ago. A most deplorable business. Most unpleasant for us too. You may believe that we take no joy in punishment."

The bishop smiled a gentle smile of pity and condescension that he knew wonderfully became his ascetic but handsome face, which was set off by dark brows and silver hair. In his robes and skull cap, he felt as if he had just stepped out of a devotional painting.

"I've heard of Fulcran Rey," replied Pastor Merson. "I hope that I might meet God as worthily as he, if it comes to that."

"It was a most distasteful business," said the intendant, "yet I hope it may have proved instructive. Then we need never have another such denouement."

The Huguenot said nothing but raised his brows as if in question.

"I believe I am privy to the thought of His Majesty in this matter and can promise the utmost consideration for one who would assist in allaying the fanaticism of these poor deluded folk among whom you have labored," said the intendant smoothly. "A word from you urging them to accept things as they are, to abandon rebellious plotting and convocations, would go far to restore tranquility to this province."

The pastor shook his head.

"*Certainment* the sufferings of these dear people would make one with a heart of stone weep," interjected the bishop. "The laws must be carried out for the preservation of the kingdom itself. Think of the bloodshed you might prevent, the lives saved, the souls won to eternal life if these ignorant and uneasy peasants could be persuaded to abandon their resistance to their sovereign and the true church!"

"Your concern for the welfare of these people is most gratifying, Messieurs," replied Merson softly. "You do them an injustice, however, if you think any word of mine could cause them to give up the faith of their fathers. And though my life depended on it, I wouldn't undertake to weaken their faith if I could. It wouldn't change them, but it would cost me my soul."

"The saving of lives and the prevention of needless misery to many men, women, and children might better save your soul," urged the bishop, still urbane.

"You wouldn't be sent away empty," added the intendant. "You would be allowed to depart from the country if you wished, and the expression of His Majesty's appreciation would be large enough to enable you to settle wherever you might wish." He paused. "You have a family, *n'est-ce pas?*"

"I do, Monsieur, and I fain would see them again. But I couldn't look them in the face if I had denied my Lord." He shook his head. "I thank you both, but this reminds me too much of the thirty pieces of silver of Judas."

The monks stirred impatiently and looked at the bishop. He kept his composure.

"We had expected your firmness, and it does you credit, but *c'est possible* that you haven't sufficiently thought of the good you could do by taking our suggestion? The apostles counsel obedience to the authorities ordained by God. The responsibility for deciding what is error doesn't lie with these poor people but rests with the church and the king, who represent God on earth. The people can't set themselves up to decide what they will or will not obey. It would lead to anarchy in both church and state."

"I see you would reopen the debate between Bishop Bossuet and Pastor Claude," said Merson with a fleeting smile. "I must agree with Pastor Claude that ultimately, each human being is responsible for his own choice, and if enlightened by God's Holy Word through the Spirit, though he differ from kings and prelates, there he must stand. The apostle Peter says that we ought to obey God rather than men. What, may I ask, if our Lord Jesus Christ had accepted the authority of the synagogue? *Non*, my lords, not one of us lightly refuses obedience to the king. In fact, we have been the most devoted of his subjects throughout his reign. But our consciences we cannot yield to him."

The bishop and the intendant exchanged glances, and the bishop's carefully composed face relaxed.

"We do not fear to die," continued Merson, "because we have a sure passage to a better life, and we know that our blood will be as seed to propagate the divine truth that some men now despise. When God permits pastors to be put to death, they preach more loudly and effectually than they did in their lifetime, and meanwhile, God raises up other laborers for His harvest."

"*Eh bien*, Monsieur," said Intendant de Bâville, "I believe His Grandeur the bishop may be correct and you should take time to think more deeply on these questions—especially in the light of your duty to the people of this province, whose future you hold in your hands. Let us not be hasty. The king and the church will prevail. We are many and you are few. In time, this heresy will be extinguished no matter what you do, but you have it in your power to advance the peace of the realm. I pray you, think on these things for several days, and we will talk again soon. In the meantime, we will see that you are comfortable."

Bâville nodded to the subdelegate. Merson bowed politely, and the intendant and the bishop inclined their heads. The subdelegate took the Huguenot by his free arm and led him from the room.

When the prisoner and his retinue had left the room, the bishop turned to Bâville. "I'll wager a hundred *louis d'or* you'll not get him to crack. And you'd best not drag this out, or the whole countryside will be in a broil! Teach the lesson and get it over with quickly. God knows what schemes may soon be afoot or already are. Remember, you failed to get his companion."

The intendant got to his feet with a grunt, scattering papers on the table.

"It's a nasty business. I'd postpone the hanging a long time if I thought we could win over such a one. And don't fret about the people. I've been able to handle them well enough for fifteen years now. There won't be any rescue, if that's what is troubling you."

"Just as you say," shrugged the bishop. "But for a heresy that has been extinct by law for over five years, there seems to be a marvelous number of secret meetings being held in this province!"

The intendant's face flamed a bright red. "When you offer His Majesty's servants advice, don't forget that the present trouble comes from having to clean up after the clergy! The people were docile enough before I had to wash your dirty linen for you."

The bishop smiled his superior smile and swept from the room, followed by the brown-robed monks, who cast shocked and indignant glances over their shoulders at the intendant. Bâville ignored them and was scowling out a window when the subdelegate reentered the room.

"You've seen him to his cell already?"

"Yes, Your Grace. He's going no place."

"I'm in a filthy mood, Charles. His Grandeur often has that effect on me."

"Yes, Monsieur." The subdelegate stood sympathetically as the older man sat again and began to toy moodily with the curls of his wig.

"You know I have no great concern for religion. My responsibility is to govern this province for His Majesty. It's hard indeed to have these clerical pantywaists adding to our troubles by inflaming all the fanaticisms of years ago. I was on the staff of the ambassador in Rome when we forced His Holiness to beg His Majesty's pardon and to disband the papal guards. Times have changed," he added wistfully.

"Yes, Monsieur. The Revocation has complicated matters not a little."

"I've always condemned that confounded Revocation. It was a gross blunder, and the only one who doesn't know we have a crisis on our hands is His Majesty. That triumphal arch! Can you imagine a grosser manner of establishing a new order among subjects whose city has been razed, whose living has been destroyed, whose religion has been wiped out? To memorialize their subjugation seemed to the king a lasting evidence of his divinely appointed majesty. To the people, it is a constant reminder of what they have suffered at his hand."

"I suppose the king is well-protected from disturbing word of that nature, Monsieur. And we should not disabuse him."

"We can't retrace our steps. That would be to plunge still lower into the abyss. We have no choice now—we must finish the conversions even if we have to break every man, woman, and child in the province on the wheel. There can be no pity when it is a question of saving the state." The expression on the face of the intendant belied the words he had just uttered. He turned his hands over and examined the jeweled rings adorning his fingers. Then he continued. "I always said it was a mistake to press the heretics on the sacraments. Such a matter was unnecessary."

"Ah, yes," agreed the subdelegate. "They need preachers, not masses and ceremonies—their former worship was sermons, hymns, and prayers. We would do better to approach their hearts, for that is where religion dwells. There's no other way to reach them. And what we are doing infinitely profanes our own faith."

"Rather than troops and books, we should use more Jesuits," Bâville said. "The people despise these Jesuits, and I can't say I blame them. But even the Jesuits jaw too much of fines, prisons, and the devil. And the *curés* are simply worthless."

"I doubt we persuade many, Monsieur," said the subdelegate, losing something of his earlier confidence. "If we round them up, they listen to our preachers as to enchanters, and all they do is undone at night in their secret assemblies." He studied his slim white fingers. "How soon do you wish to see this heretic pastor again?"

"What difference? He knows his own mind. We'll have to hang him, without a doubt. The one that got away, the major—there's a dangerous one. If we wait too long, who knows what he can stir up."

"I hear this major stood well at court."

Intendant de Bâville bristled. "Not as well as Madame de Maintenon and Louvois, of that you may be sure! Let me disabuse you, my dear fellow. As long as I rule this province, it makes no difference who some rebel may know at court. We have a rope ready for that one too!"

* * * * *

To a connoisseur of executions, the breezy October day was a perfect one for a public hanging. And only the most critical victim could have asked for a more striking setting for his departure. From the high ground of the esplanade of Montpellier one could see the distant peaks of the Pyrenees on the west and the Cévennes on the north, and the thin blue line of the Mediterranean was visible a few miles to the east.

Hanging, brandings, whippings, and burnings would draw a certain number of the curious to what were intended as edifying spectacles, but this affair was different—and well Intendant de Bâville knew it. To execute a Reformed minister in a town still secretly more Reformed than Catholic was to invite trouble, and the authorities were taking no chances. Instead of the usual ragtag of halberdiers and local militia, regular troops had been brought in from other garrisons, and the town had been swarming with these visitors for several days. Numerous country people with Reformed sympathies had also come in for the occasion. Bâville's spies circulated through the crowds, but he didn't need them to tell him the temper of the people. It was evident on their faces. The mixture in town was approaching the explosive. But the swift hanging of the Dulacs had been an object lesson, and by proceeding quickly to dispose of Pastor Merson, the authorities hoped to dampen any disorder before it got started.

As the morning dawned, the intendant felt reasonably certain no *coup de main* would be attempted. The major was still missing but apparently hadn't been able to accomplish anything yet, and informers brought in rumors that he might be wounded or dead. Today's performance, Bâville grimly purposed, would be a salutary lesson to secret rebels in Montpellier and would give pause to other Huguenot pastors who might be thinking of slipping back into France.

In the center of the open area, a platform surmounted by a gibbet had been erected. It was surrounded by a hollow square of infantry. Flanking them on each side sat squadrons of cavalry, their horses stamping and whisking their tails, their riders sitting impassively and staring at the growing crowd. The early morning chill was lifting, and the breath of horses and men was no longer steamy.

A double line of infantry maintained an open path through the intensely hostile crowd along the avenue back to the citadel. This appeared to be a danger point to the officers who sat their horses nearby, and they occasionally ordered the spectators to move back to a safer distance. The officers looked over their shoulders frequently, seeking reassurance from the sight of reserves lined up under the wall of the citadel—as if they regarded the angry stares of citizens as grenades with crackling fuses.

At about nine o'clock, a little party left the gate of the citadel to cross the short distance to the gallows. A score of musketeers marched with them between the stationary double line of foot soldiers up the avenue. At their center walked the diminutive figure of Pastor Merson. His was perhaps the only serene countenance in town that morning. He walked without limp or stagger, for they hadn't tortured him much, the intendant convinced that in view of the firmness of the prisoner, it would serve no useful purpose and would only inspire pity among on-lookers. He had also ordered that the prescribed breaking of the prisoner's bones by the heavy hammer on the wheel should follow rather than precede the execution. These proceedings must be shortened as much as possible.

Two men walked with the prisoner. One was an exceedingly nervous priest, who was sweating though the day was not yet warm. The other attendant was the subdelegate, also uneasy, but for a different reason. He had once served in the Regiment of Maine. If Armand de Gandon had escaped, the people had a formidable leader. His eyes darted continually over the scene, trying to gauge the size and temper of the crowd. The hangman, in black, followed them, also looking this way and that, uneasy that only a row of soldiers stood between them and the mob.

When they reached the steps of the scaffold, the subdelegate and an officer of infantry assisted the prisoner, whose hands were tied behind him. The priest, visibly unsteady, also had to be helped up. As they stood together on the platform, the crowd grew silent, and thousands of eyes stared intently at the scene etched so sharply under the brilliant sunshine.

The prisoner exchanged civilities with his escort. He appeared to ask a question, but the subdelegate shook his head. It was the moment for the condemned man to address his last words to the audience, and the crowd strained forward expectantly. Five hundred pairs of hands grasped musket barrels more tightly, and two hundred hands grasped saber hilts. The pastor opened his mouth, but the officer immediately made a sign, and twenty drummers ranged along the base of the platform began a furious tattoo that completely drowned out his words. It continued while the final preparations were being made.

Suddenly there was a unanimous intake of breath by the crowd. In a moment, it was followed by a general sigh. The drumming ceased, and thousands gazed bleakly at the black figure dangling between heaven and earth.

CHAPTER 13

Three Letters

When Armand and Alexandre finally met again, late in November, both appeared worse for wear. Alexandre had inquired carefully in Montpellier about Armand, and after being passed from person to person among the new converts, had finally located the convalescent soldier at the Arms of Flanders in the suburb of Devillier, where the pastor and Armand had originally stayed. A cautious host went to the door of Armand's room with the visitor. Armand sat on the edge of his bed, pale and drawn. He reached out his left arm in greeting, favoring his right.

Alexandre was thinner, he noticed, sunburned to a deep russet—and barefoot. "Sit down," Armand said, indicating a three-legged stool.

Laying the Cortot letter beside him on the bed for reading later, Armand listened to Alexandre's account of his adventures. Then he told the boy of his own experiences. He concluded, "I fear I have been a burden to the brethren, but without them I would have been on the gallows very shortly myself. They pulled me from the street when that accursed dragoon shot me, but my wound wasn't serious. The ball went through my shoulder without striking bone. But by the time our poor pastor came to his martyrdom, the wound fever had me, and I was out of my head and my life despaired of. The hunters sniffed after me for days, but I was moved from cellar to cellar by night and nursed by faithful souls who surely would have forfeited their lives also had we been betrayed."

De Gandon touched his right shoulder gingerly.

"They called no physician, for which I am grateful, for I did want to see all of you again, and I have seen enough of these learned men at work to know that theirs is a more murderous profession than we soldiers can claim. When I was able to discuss my situation with our friends, I insisted on being brought here. Our host has taken good care of me. I know he does it for money, but though I have never told him who I was, he is no fool, and I suspect he knows well enough. I think it might not go as hard with him as with a new convert if I were discovered. I would be only a guest at an inn about whom the host could say he knew nothing."

"This has been a slow affair," commented Alexandre.

Armand nodded. "I'm still as weak as a child compared to what I think I should be. There were enough gloomy matters to ponder while waiting for you to come again, and though I'm glad you are returned thus far safely, I must say I can see nothing very hopeful in the future. I understand now how the pastor could contemplate his approaching martyrdom so calmly. To drop to earth this mantle, this body, he said, would be a joyful thing, and I can see now why this earth might no longer seem very attractive."

"*Qu'est-que possible,*" mused Alexandre, "that you have been nursing these thoughts too long? I suppose you and Pastor Merson really didn't expect me to find my father but wanted me out of the way when the calamities happened. Well, I thank you for the thought, but having this letter from my father rewards me for the journey, and I suppose even if I had stayed by you, I couldn't have stopped any of the calamities. But all that is behind us. Now what do we do?"

Armand shrugged listlessly. He studied the symphony of rags and tatters that covered the boy. "I might better ask you the same question, Alexandre. All I know for certain is that I cannot accept the offer of the duke even if he would still have me—not after all I've seen and learned these past few months. But then what? I don't know.

"I would that I could continue the pastor's work, but I'm not qualified. What else is there but soldiering? This wound will weaken my sword arm for a long time, perhaps permanently, but I might be an instructor for some prince forming companies in the German principalities—perhaps in Brandenburg. There are rumors of movements there that may mean a new war one of these days, and this time it may be all the Protestant states together against France.

"I hear, too, that some of our men have been welcomed in Muscovy, where the new emperor wishes to teach his army the European drills. Of course, the war with the Turks drags on, and there are some Protestants in Hungary serving with the imperial forces. In one way, I would rather go there if I could than along the Rhine or in the Lowlands—I should less likely have to fight against my old comrades in the armies of the king. So it seems that if I don't starve in the meantime, there should be plenty of employment in a little while."

Neither said anything for a time. Armand sensed the deep sympathy that inspired Alexandre's uncharacteristic silence. Strange that this boy, barely sprouting a beard, should best appreciate what in joining the Huguenots he had given up in France. With a sudden pang he knew this feeling for what it was. He had come to look upon the young Cortot as his younger brother.

"And what about you, Alexandre?"

"Oh, I plan to go where you go," he said matter-of-factly.

"That can't be," Armand objected. "I have no prospects. You know that well enough. I'm like hundreds of other exiles for the Religion. Barring miracles, the king and the church will never give way here in France, and we shall be wanderers very likely all of our days. There is nothing in that life for a bright young fellow. As a major of the Regiment of Maine or colonel of my own regiment, I would have been happy to help you put your foot on the ladder. Now, I appreciate your loyalty, Alexandre, but I must insist that you say nothing further about this. You have been a witness this past year of what future a man of my talents may expect, and you are young enough to avoid walking in my footsteps. If you love and respect me, I want your promise that you will obey the order I am going to give you."

"And what is that?" Alexandre smiled as if he knew what was coming.

"The place for you is America. I wish you might have spoken to your father, for I know he would have said the same thing. This is not just to be with your sister, though I confess I would feel more at ease if I knew you were together again. But America offers the prospect of freedom— if such a place may exist anywhere. You could find a profitable trade and also be able to worship freely without the oppression and persecution we find here in Europe. There would be no advantage to you to tag along with me. There's too much chance of dying of fever in some Polish

swamp or being spitted by the lance of some *pandour* in a quarrel between barbarian princes you never heard of before. It is a hard life to
carry a pike, as they say, 'for a crust of bread and a truss of straw.' "

He hesitated, but again Alexandre said nothing.

"So, for all of us who are concerned for you, you must obey like a
good soldier and report to your sister in America and crave her pardon
for deserting her. If it will make it easier for you, tell her I sent you as a
last token of my love for her. Tell her also that I shall never forget her
and that I wish her happiness. You must be her protector; I had once
dreamed of doing it myself."

He stared sadly at the floor and then up at his companion's face.

Alexandre didn't look much impressed. "Let's forget Brandenburg
and Russia," he burst out. "My sister told me while I yet worked at the
docks in Rotterdam last spring that if you wanted her over on those
shores, she would go. On the other hand, she confessed that she would
follow anywhere you might wish her to go, whether you had any 'prospects' or not."

"But, Mathieu? Had she then given up her betrothal to him?" Armand was surprised at his own outburst.

Alexandre hooted. "When you swept in on us the first time, the
damage was done, no doubt. But Madeleine is as pig-headed—or honorable, if you prefer— as you, and since she was affianced to Mathieu,
that was that in spite of your undeniable charm. What a lot of trouble
you would have saved everyone if you had just carried her off like your
ancestors used to handle such situations! Even the pastor knew what
was happening, and he told me early in our journey that from what he
knew, Mathieu was out of it and it was better so."

Armand sat for a long moment. "*Mais oui, il le dit.* He said it." His
miserable pride had nearly ruined him time after time.

Finally he assayed a smile. "*Eh bien,* it would have been pleasant to
have been assured of some of this sooner—before I left Holland that is.
But I can see that the way I was behaving might have raised some doubts
about me."

"Judith is with Madeleine," Alexandre reminded him. "If you command me to New York, I am not terribly aggrieved."

Armand's throat tightened with emotion, always dangerously near
the surface since his fever. If Madeleine would have him or not after all

this misunderstanding, he'd still be a stable boy or a peddler if need be to be near her.

"I think I can travel now, so permit me, Monsieur, to assure you that after I deliver a certain letter to Paris—"

Alexandre quickly disagreed again. "You don't look to me like a man fit to travel. Let me deliver your letter. It's not as risky for me as for you. Your description is placarded all over the province, believe me! You should guard your strength and head for the Atlantic, not for the Mediterranean, though it is near. It's the cheapest way out and probably safer than trying to go by way of Geneva—only seven *livres* a head, they say, on some English boats. The brethren here know the regular routes to the coast, and they'll help you so that you needn't travel farther or faster than your strength allows. We can meet beyond the waters."

Armand smiled wryly. The boy had become a man—rational, decisive.

"You are right, Alexandre." Armand agreed after brief thought. "I'll write the letter now, and while it's here, I'll copy your father's also. If we go by different routes, the letter will have a better chance of being delivered. Now if our good host can find a chicken ready to give her life in a good cause, you shall have supper and a rest while I am busy."

* * * * *

It was dark outside now. The stubby candle sent flickering shadows about the walls of the dismal chamber. Alexandre slept on the bed in the corner, covered by Armand's cloak. Laying down his quill, Armand folded the sheet of paper on which he had been writing. On the outside face of the folded letter he wrote carefully, "To Monseigneur, *le duc de Lauzières, a son hotel*, Versailles." He slipped off his ring and found the piece of wax, but before sealing the letter, he unfolded it for a quick rereading.

Montpellier
November 17, 1691

Honored Sir,

Once more I wish to thank you for your kind interest in me, calling me "son." I have not taken that appellation lightly, but I have a Father whose authority I must place before yours and beyond the king's. I can choose only to serve Him. Except for the pain I have caused you, sir, I have had undeserved good fortune in that I have discovered in time that *patria cair, carior libertas.** I will likely never see you again. I would, therefore, my lord, bid you a respectful and affectionate farewell.

Armand sealed the letter carefully. He glanced at the sleeping Alexandre and then turned to the letter written by Isaac Cortot. The sheet was not addressed to anyone, nor, as Armand noted when he unfolded it, was there any signature at the end. People who smuggled letters from galley slaves were wise to be circumspect. The letter was on paper of poor quality and the ink was worse, beginning to turn brown already. A miserable pen had also helped to make the missive difficult to read.

As Armand prepared to copy the letter, he glanced through it. He could almost hear the fine old fellow speaking the words. He remembered how more than six years before, he had sat at the table of Isaac Cortot in his comfortable house, surrounded by his wife and family. In renewing his boyhood acquaintance with this old comrade of his father, he had involved himself with his family. How differently had their fortunes gone since that evening! Picking up his pen sadly, Armand copied what Isaac had written.

It is my hope, my dear children, that these words may cheer you with evidence of God's mercies, to the strengthening of your faith in the tribulations that surely await you in these perilous times. When I was stopped just before the bridge at Geneva, there were those who wished to dissemble the purpose of our journey, but I felt it would dishonor the Lord to do so and plainly stated that I had hoped to flee from the kingdom. For some days I was well-treated and frequently visited by those who hoped to instruct me. For civility's sake, I consented to their visits though assuring them that I was well persuaded that my religion was the good and true one. If I was in error, and it should please God to convince me of it by giving me new light, I should not fail to follow them with zeal and joy for the glory of God. When I made it plain that I could not force myself to a worship that I esteemed disagreeable to God nor join in communion with those who would oblige me to such worship, they went away and I saw them no more.

---

* "The fatherland is dear, but liberty is dearer."

I was sent to a dungeon, only leaving it once to hear my sentence to the galleys pronounced and then waited until a chain could be made up. God having put it into my heart to remain faithful to Him even unto death if need required, I made what face I could to cheerfully endure hardness for the Lord's sake. I lay in that dungeon the better part of a month and was there given reason to hope that He will continue His favor to me to the end, and that He will always proportion His gifts and grace to the trials to which it shall please Him to expose me.

When the chain was made up, we suffered some little inconvenience from the irons placed on us and from the cold, wet weather as we journeyed south. Our collars and chains weighed about one hundred and fifty pounds. Many of us were sick, and I also had a bout of the fever. But neither crowding, nor blasphemies, nor poor fare, nor the thieving of our effects by the guards could separate us from the love God has shown us in His Son Jesus Christ.

The trip was long, and we tarried at one place a week while some of the brethren from Paris were added to the chain. There were times when I thought I would soon be released from the fatigues of this life, but it pleased the master of the chain to be moved by compassion, and I rode in one of the carts for most of the journey, though there was no straw for a bed and I used my hat for a pillow. I arrived in Marseilles somewhat lean and weak from fever, but, I thank God, on the mend.

There was talk of sending me with the other invalids as a slave to the American plantations. Though it be no matter whether I die on land or sea, in Europe or America, the Lord judged I might better glorify Him in the galley to which I was allotted. For a time I was on the *Grande Reale*, which was the depot vessel, and then was put on the *Hardi*.

I was chained at first to a bench with four others and thought I would scarce survive the rods of the *comites*. We were eaten alive by creeping things and slept one upon another as hogs in a sty. We were to have a pound of flesh and a pound of bread each day, but most was stolen by the stewards. On Sundays, the Host was elevated in the stern, and if we did not raise our caps in respect, we were bastinadoed with good will by the *comites*. They call this in their pleasant fashion "painting Calvin's back," while rowing they call "writing in the water with Calvin's pen."

After a short time, I was moved to the *Fière* and released from the bench. I have become a servant to the steward and have obtained credit with one of the officers, to whom I teach algebra. He has offered me money as I need it and sends me delicacies from his table.

The captain of our galley has used me with great civility and respect and has permitted me in cold weather to put my hammock in his cabin. We rejoice in good air, and none of us is sick. Let all these succors that God affords me give you comfort and joy. I am already as used to the place as if I had been here all my life. The iron I wear on my foot at night weighs but three pounds, and I have liberty to walk to and fro in the daytime. I assure you I have not so much reason to complain as you might imagine.

Only when missionaries come on board are we abused or put in chains or beaten. Our comrades then tell us to take off our caps by way of civility—not to indicate a change in our religion—and afterwards pray to God, Calvin, or to whom we will; but it does not seem convenient to us to act in this fashion. It is only in port that we are vexed in this way.

I doubt not, my children, that God will continue His favor to us and will bring you to a safe place. I am certain that the affliction He is pleased to visit upon us will not compare with the future glory that is to be revealed in us, and I put my trust in the saying of James, "Blessed is the man who endures temptation; for when he shall have been tried, he shall receive the crown of incorruptible glory and immortality which God reserves for His elect." Blessed, says the Savior, are those who suffer for righteousness' sake.

I desire, my dear children, that you afford me always the assistance of your prayers, for I of myself am nothing but weakness and infirmity. We should be burning lamps, but in our own strength are but smoking matches.

For some time after he finished, Armand sat in thought. Finally, he roused himself, rose, and went to the bed to shake the sleeping Alexandre. "Time to be on your way, old boy, if you want to make a good start tonight."

"Very well, major. I'm ready. Take care of yourself, and we'll meet along the line somewhere—perhaps in New York."

"Have you the money you need?"

"A few *livres* would be helpful if you can spare them, but I don't need much. I appeal to the motherly housewives, so I eat pretty well considering. I suppose you'd do better with a slightly younger type?"

Armand smiled. "God go with you, Brother—I may as well call you so. And if you reach New York before I do, you know what message to deliver."

Alexandre would have none of it. "Madeleine has a low opinion of my honesty as a messenger. Write!" He picked up the pen and handed it to Armand.

Feeling foolish but at the same time pleased to create a document expressing his great longing, Armand obeyed. "I am coming to you, Madeleine, and if you love me, all will be well." He suspected that Alexandre had cast a curious eye over his shoulder but paid no heed. This letter too he carefully sealed and committed to his longtime companion.

* * * * *

"We trust that Your Grace will soon be restored to health," said the king in his usual courteous manner. "Undoubtedly, repose on your estates will again hasten this happy condition, and we will again be able to enjoy your loyal attendance on our person in the spring."

The news passed through the massed courtiers like an electric current. The Duc de Lauzières, so long an unassailable favorite, was under a cloud. How delicious!

The duke bowed silently, and the royal progress continued. He stood impassive until the double door at the end of the hall closed behind the royal party. Then he turned and shuffled off. Men of less importance would have been sent with a *lettre de cachet* to one of the elegantly furnished prison apartments at the Bastille, there to regain proper respect for the king's authority. Ah, well, he did suffer still from the malady that had taken him to Dauphiné a few months past. The respite would indeed be medicinal. In a few months he would be welcome at court again and could resume his purposeless existence. Who holds the candle at the *coucher* tonight? Will *he* smile tomorrow as he passes by? "Will Your Majesty provide the dowry for my niece? She has thirty-two quarterings of nobility but little cash."

What to do but gibe at one's rivals, crack yawns, and see who stays ahead in the endless wrangles for precedence—the "shelling of the shrimps." Maybe the boy had been right. Maybe he understood better than the duke himself what there was to live for—or risk dying for. How had he put it in the letter? "Time is nothing, and eternity is all." *"Patria cara, carior libertas,"* he had said. The duke could still handle his Latin—"The fatherland is dear, but liberty is dearer."

How different it might have been! Assuredly, there would be no one to replace him. Well, the duke was too old and tired to change his own way of life even if he wanted to. One carried on as befitted one's station—as befitted the last of a great line. Then one day, the doctor would make certain discreet suggestions, and he would hie himself to a monastery, one of the more comfortable sort. There would be instruction, a making up of some neglected devotional formulae, and then—well, who really knew what then?

When that pert young ragamuffin had badgered his doormen and the butler until they had let him in with Armand's letter the other evening, he had started to reward him with a gold piece. But then, for reasons he didn't care to examine too closely, he had given the young rascal a draft on his Dutch banker for one thousand *louis d'or* to take to Armand. A senseless thing to do? *Certainment,* but he had always believed in the grand gesture. *Noblesse oblige!* Even so, he could hardly match Armand's deed of renunciation for sheer indifference to the practical consequences. It was a farewell gesture anyway, and he hoped his act would be understood by the son he almost had. He couldn't hate Armand for the hurt he had caused him, but it wasn't given to many men to lose an only son twice.

As the duke made for the door, he noticed that he could move for the first time in years as if he were invisible. His usual trail of sycophants was strangely missing. It was rather amusing. They would be back in full strength, ready to fawn over him again the moment it was known he was restored to favor. His lips twisted in a wry grin. These were the "friends" one had at Versailles! At the door of the chateau, he climbed into his sedan chair and was carried out into the night.

CHAPTER 14

Escape by Sea

A week after Alexandre's departure, Armand was dressing slowly for his journey in his dim, cramped attic room at the Arms of Flanders. He would leave in a half hour, when it became dark. Armand still felt weak and tired, but his courage had greatly improved during the past week. A borrowed horse was waiting for him at the door. The brethren had given him meticulous instructions that would take him across France, right through the hostile center of Toulouse and then northeast to the Rochelle area. At each stage of the journey he would, hopefully, find a secret sympathizer with whom to lodge.

Armand had just pulled on his gloves and was reaching for his hat when he heard voices in the common room below. His door was slightly ajar, and he stepped closer and listened, leaning against the doorjamb and peering sidewise.

Seated at the table in front of the fire was a yellow-coated dragoon. He was alone in the room except for the landlord, who was standing by to refill the soldier's tankard. The dragoon, who had just wiped his mouth on his sleeve, was asking questions. ". . . Perhaps you have seen this fellow. He's tall, well-made, bears himself like a soldier, and he probably favors his right arm, which may be broken or wounded. There is a big reward for this wretch, and as one of the ladies down at the well thought she had seen such a one at your inn, I thought you might have some idea where he could be found. It would be greatly to your advantage if you could help. The king doesn't stint when it is a question of catching traitors."

The dragoon glanced around the room and so missed the wary look on the host's face. He continued, "You have a guest at the moment? I noticed a saddled horse outside."

The innkeeper answered in such a loud voice that the dragoon looked up startled and puzzled. "That old woman is quite a gossip, isn't she? Now I don't make everybody's business mine, the way some do. Any number of tall men with bad arms could come through here, and I'd not give them a second look. My memory is so poor that by tomorrow I'll have forgotten already that today a nosy dragoon tried to pump me!"

"Are you deaf, man?" asked the dragoon. He evidently decided in the negative and rose to his feet. "Some civilians have an insolent way of answering an amiable question. Sometimes a bit of a kicking helps their defective memories."

"You don't scare me," shouted the innkeeper in the same unnatural voice. "I served my time in the Vermandois, and I know all about the likes of you. Dragoons are simply infantrymen who are too lazy to walk!"

"An innkeeper who thinks himself a wit!" said the soldier. "Unless you take back those words, as sure as my name is Dupin, I'm coming over this table to push your teeth down your throat. I'll . . ."

Suddenly, a great light dawned on the dragoon. His eyes narrowed, and he started to draw his saber—but it was too late. A quiet voice behind him said, "Keep your hands away from your weapons and stand right where you are."

The dragoon did as he was bid, cursing himself aloud for his stupidity. The search had dragged on so long that he hadn't really expected any leads now. He'd wandered into this inn more or less aimlessly. If any other troopers were in the neighborhood, they were probably drunk in another cabaret. He shouldn't have come in alone when heretics were so thick in the province, but one didn't expect to find Huguenots in low inns. He cautiously turned his head.

In the doorway stood a tall, handsome man in traveling dress. The light wasn't very good, but the man's face seemed pallid, yet there was something familiar about him. What was most interesting to the dragoon, however, was the cavalry pistol in the man's left hand and pointed at the dragoon's stomach. Then, even worse, came recognition: He had indeed found his quarry—Major Armand de Gandon, the hero of the

Regiment of Maine. But de Gandon held the gun. The dragoon's eyes darted around the room. There were a few benches and some heavy tables but nothing within reach that he could throw.

"Nothing heroic just now," said the major levelly. "You might bring someone, but it would be too late to help you any."

A look at the tall man's eyes convinced the dragoon that he meant what he said. The pistol seemed very steady for the left hand, but perhaps the fellow was left-handed. A slight noise behind him, and he saw the host was holding a poker.

"I'm convinced," he said quickly.

"Stand still, hero," said the innkeeper unpleasantly. "I want your sword and pistol."

"Careful, Monsieur," said the man in the doorway. "No abuse. He was but doing his duty, but I regret for all our sakes that he should come here just now. I didn't want to involve you in this business."

"I was trying to warn you to take English leave, major. They'd have gotten nothing from me, and a beating wouldn't have mattered."

"I know," said de Gandon, "but I thought perhaps there might have been others outside, and since he had noticed the horse, he might have stopped me when I tried to mount. So now I think this trooper—sergeant, *n'est-ce pas?*—and I had better go for a journey together. We may not get far, but I can't have you rewarded with evil for all the kindness you have shown me in my time of need."

The dragoon's skin crawled, and his mouth went dry. "You'll never make it out of town," he croaked.

"If you are right, my friend, it will avail *you* little. I'll ride just behind you, and in case we meet any of your friends and you fail to lend me your most convincing collaboration, I shall have no choice but to empty this pistol into your kidneys. This would distress your friends, but at least your troubles wouldn't be prolonged."

The soldier gulped. There seemed no appropriate rejoinder. De Gandon spoke to the innkeeper though his eyes remained fixed on the dragoon. "*Mon ami*, take the man's gun. And do bring my horse to the door and cover us while we mount. We'd best hasten before any more company comes. Our visitor and I will then ride out into the country in a friendly fashion, and I hope he will keep his predicament clearly in mind, for if we are stopped! . . ."

The dragoon grew increasingly overwrought, his earlier rudeness fresh in his memory.

"What would Your Eminence like this chitchat to be about?" he said. "I am subject to fits of nervousness when someone holds a gun on me, and the springs of my invention might not flow freely."

"Oh, there are any number of things agitating the kingdom these days," said de Gandon casually. "Who, for example, has the better of it in precedence—barber-surgeons or surgeon-barbers? Is it certain His Majesty has married Madame de Maintenon? Is it healthy to eat fish? Is there a notable case of poisoning current in the realm? I will lead, and you may gloss my remarks."

The innkeeper reappeared in the door. Armand de Gandon politely indicated that his prisoner should precede him, and they passed out into the January night. The stars shone frostily above, and the moon was just beginning to emerge from behind the hill on which Montpellier was built. The acrid fumes of the dung heap in the yard smote the nostrils. The dragoon mounted in silence. The street was deserted. Hope, which to this moment had persisted in the sergeant, died. He had a fresh rush of saliva and swallowed hard.

The major mounted with difficulty. The dragoon noticed this with interest, but the innkeeper kept the captured pistol trained on him. De Gandon turned in his saddle. "I am most grateful to you, Monsieur. You have been most kind to one not of your religion. I regret that you have been placed in danger, but I shall do what I can to keep it from reaching you. God bless you and this poor country. I doubt we shall meet again."

"Godspeed, Major, and a safe journey. Don't worry. If this horseman here doesn't talk, nothing will happen to me. I'm glad to see the prey escape the great ones, and it was a pleasure to help. Some day, I hope we can turn about with them for a change, and then we will let intendants and bishops and all the other *monseigneurs* find out what prisons are like, and we'll cut off some heads too. You Huguenots may not preach this, but some of the rest of us are tired of being robbed and walked on." He laughed nastily. "And good night to you too, dragoon! Do not shiver so. You'll soon be warm enough, for hell is well-fueled."

De Gandon and his host exchanged salutes, and the sergeant led the way out of town. He saluted the sentry at the edge of the city, and the sentry waved them on without comment. They rode through bare-boughed orchards and began to climb through the scrub of the foot-hills, heading west on the road to Grabels if his sense of direction was right. The moon shed enough light for the horsemen to see distinctly. A breeze rattled the few remaining leaves; the only other sound was the melancholy clopping of the horses' hooves in the dirt and the occasional tremulous cry of a night bird.

"Turn to the right here," said de Gandon, breaking an hour's silence. The dragoon rode into a grove of pines. When passing through the shadows he was tempted several times to chance bolting. But with the gun's barrel pointed at his back, any discharge would explode in his vitals. If he'd been wearing armor, it might have been worth chancing.

"We might as well halt here," said de Gandon finally when they were miles from anything human. He reined in his horse in a little clearing. Now there were some indistinct ruins between them and the edge of a scrubby grove. The rows of gravestones beyond the crumbling chapel gave the dragoon no reassurance. Although his religious education had been sparse, the innkeeper's reference to the horrors of hell had stirred his imagination.

The major drew abreast of the prisoner, who regarded him in the moonlight. "I regret this, you understand," said de Gandon civilly. "You must agree that in the circumstances, I have little choice."

The dragoon stared at the pistol and said nothing. The moonlight was so bright that he could see the ornamental engraving on the barrel. He was facing no common gentleman with a jeweled sidearm but a military leader whose valor was a legend.

"Even if my own escape were sure," continued Armand, "I couldn't have my host punished for taking pity on me. If you hadn't come in when you did, I would have been gone soon and no one the wiser."

"You'll not allow me to say my prayers, to confess my sins?" asked the dragoon, his throat dry, his voice hoarse.

"I really wouldn't have time for such a catalogue as that might prove to be," de Gandon replied.

"Your opinion of dragoons seems a little jaundiced. Do you think shooting me will even the score?"

"I'm not trying to even a score. That would be an ambitious scheme, to say the least! Don't feel distressed. If dragonnades and hangings continue, men like you will drive these people frantic, and in spite of all the efforts of their brave pastors to prevent it, yours won't be the last blood of the king's minions to be shed."

"I thank you for the consolation," said the dragoon, this time his courtesy sincere. "Would it help if I told you I am no hanger of pastors or anyone else and that I have a very defective memory, one that by morning would be unable to recall where I had spent the previous evening or anyone I had conversed with? Overindulgence in the cheap wine of the region has this effect, I'm told."

His body stiffened as de Gandon stared at him thoughtfully.

"God knows I don't like this business, but it seems to me that you are most bold to ask mercy after what you and your cohorts have done to the south of France. I have friends who went through some of this. One is in the galleys now, and another is in America—penniless probably. And then there was Pastor Merson, who is now in a lime pit back in Montpellier."

"You may believe me, Monsieur," said the trooper earnestly. "I have no joy in pursuing pastors. I follow orders as a soldier must. You are an officer yourself and might have said the same. I think Huguenots are foolish folk to make such a to-do about the forms of religion, but they are French, and I am ashamed for what has been done to them.

"I met your pastor once at Saint-Martin when he was told his church must come down. He took it like a gentleman, I must say. I know they were your friends up there, and I have no excuse for what was done to them. Since at our last meeting it was my bad fortune to wing you but not capture you, I can understand that you can't have any goodwill toward me. I can't blame you if you don't believe me, but I'll make this offer: Let us part here without further ado, and I engage my word of honor—and I still have some left—that I will say nothing of you or that nervy innkeeper—in view of your intention of leaving the kingdom. If you can't take my word, my luck is out and the next move is up to you."

He hoped desperately that this lengthy outpouring might inspire a certain fellowship with de Gandon, who had himself spent years committed to settling matters in the name of his king regardless of his own humanity, doubtless trying to keep a sense of his own integrity while carrying out business offensive to his own better nature. Had de Gandon too felt degraded further with each assignment, his sensibilities growing more gross after each violent deed?

De Gandon gazed thoughtfully at the dragoon, who kept his eyes level. "What's your name, soldier?"

"Dupin, sir. Etienne Dupin. Sergeant in the Queen's regiment of dragoons."

The silence that followed seemed like a lifetime. De Gandon finally drew a long breath. "I don't really have the right to risk the life of my friend back there, but, as God is my witness, I'm sick of bloodshed and would like to take your word. If it's false, I'll return from wherever I may go and spend the rest of my life, if I have to, to find you.

"My best judgment tells me to shoot you where you sit, but you may thank Pastor Merson, whom I loved above all men, for he thought it displeasing to God for me to carry a loaded pistol, deeming it better that the Lord's people should suffer as sheep among wolves than that we should resist injustice or shed blood in our own defense. Since he is dead, he couldn't prevent me from charging this piece. But I was with him too long, I think, and you are fortunate that I met that godly man. A year ago I would not have hesitated to do what seemed necessary."

"You have my word," exclaimed the soldier, giddy with relief, "and though I'm not much of a churchgoer, I'll have a prayer said for his soul. Doubtless a man of his parts would consider the source and not be offended."

"Thank you for the thought. While you're at it, say prayers for the thousands of French citizens still in this land or escaped abroad who eat the bread of affliction, whose only offense was that they wished to worship God as they believed He wished to be worshiped. I'll pray for the king that he may have better counsel and that his army may have more honorable employment. Now, farewell!"

"Farewell," replied the dragoon, suddenly uncomfortable with something almost spiritual stirring in his breast. He spontaneously reached out to shake hands, and then the Protestant rode off through the trees and vanished. The dragoon sat on his horse for some time, lost in thought, his animal grazing contentedly while night creatures whirred by softly in the moonlight.

"What a crazy business!" he muttered to himself. "What have we done? What couldn't we do if we hadn't driven out the ones like him and filled the armies of our enemies with them? And now, Dupin, you'd better think of a story to concoct about your sword and pistol. This life is getting too much for me. I'd better look up a likely wench and retire from the army while I'm still inside a whole skin. This one was entirely too close!"

He turned his horse and started back for the road.

"I could always claim I got drunk in a tavern and was robbed, but that shows such a poverty of invention. Still, being clever can be dangerous, as I found out this evening." He shivered. "I wonder if his pistol *was* actually loaded."

* * * * *

There was a nervous stir around the table. Madame de Maintenon sat up straight in her chair, and she and Louvois exchanged glances. Then the Secretaire d'Etat took his signal. "What Your Majesty sees in these . . . trifling manifestations—the return of a stray minister, the desertion of a few ill-affected officers, this riot—these are the death agonies of the monster. Such abominations never go down without that last desperate gasp."

Under the table, Louvois tapped the toe of his suede slipper on the shin of the king's confessor. Pere de la Chaise, ever the smoother of troubled waters, moved in gracefully.

"France *has* been saved and purified! Your Majesty should be reassured that the country as a whole is well content. Millions of souls have been saved by the revocation of that pernicious edict. The altars of the true faith are reestablished, and Your Majesty is acclaimed by the pious as the new Charlemagne, the new Theodosius, the new Constantine. As the fathers said of the Council of Chalcedon: 'You have strengthened the faith; you have exterminated heresy.' Truly, sire, it is the great work of the reign—the one deed for which the world will remember you."

Madame de Maintenon composed herself after a tense moment, noticing her husband's changing expression, for secure as she felt in his devotion, she didn't welcome an outburst of the rage of which he was capable in such private settings—and he had all but charged her with duplicity, "a conspiracy against his integrity" as he had phrased it. Now, in response to his confessor's quiet assurances, Louis XIV almost smiled, his noble face reflecting the piety for which she so loved him.

Pere de la Chaise resumed his homily, his face a picture of saintly grace. "We all know that Holland and the German princes encourage fanaticism, for they are our enemies. We have won great victories over them in the past, and if need be, we shall again. The accession of William of Orange in England may seem an unhappy augury, but when has not England been our enemy, and most profoundly so? How shall the righteous stand except when they stand against such foreign evil? But within the kingdom, in France herself, is the happiest encouragement. The destruction of ancient heresy, the purification of a nation, all accomplished without violence, not a drop of blood spilled—"

Louvois cut in abruptly. "I can report that the number of fugitives who return has greatly increased."

Louis looked pleased. The confessor beamed benevolently on the assemblage, turning most conspicuously to address Madame de Maintenon. "The future of the church being especially on your heart, Madame, I know this must give you most holy joy."

Her heart swelling with satisfaction, she allowed herself to speak with more than her usual animation, her eyes fixed upon the king. "The good father is right, Your Majesty. Your foreign enemies may claim that it is religious feeling that at times disturbs your domain. But it is the spirit of insubordination, of disobedience, even as in that young man who was the protégé of the Duc de Lauzières. Nothing is actually as cruel as laxity. Heresy cuts itself off from God and man; the church doesn't cut it off. No constraint need be used, only gentle, wise, efficacious firmness. Nothing has been so effective in converting the deluded people of your realm as the example of Your Majesty's own exemplary piety."

"You are without doubt correct in your assessment, Madame," the king said.

Thus encouraged, Maintenon glanced about the table before proceeding. "Gradually, the few who are ungrateful to Your Majesty for the pacification and salvation of the realm will pass on. The flesh and this world are nothing, and it needs be that when dealing with these unregenerate ones we should remember the truest charity is the capture of the soul. If some of the fathers remain hypocrites, at least all the children will be Catholics."

With that, she smiled proudly at the Grande Monarque. He relaxed; his conscience was reassured, his anxiety assuaged. As a good wife should, she had brought him through this dark uncertainty to spiritual peace.

And then this new affliction. She saw the brief twitch of the muscle in his jaw. The chest pain had hit him once more. But ever faithful to his duties of state, he reached wearily for the next pile of papers. He would, she knew, ignore whatever personal suffering he must for the sake of France, the nation that owed its very being to his powers of dedication, the focus of all his energies and the energies of all his subjects on common values, common dogma, common purpose. This Grande Monarque, this man she loved so deeply, was in a sense the embodiment of France.

Though he had reached for a new set of documents requiring his attention, she sensed that his mind still lingered upon the matter they had just discussed. That was his nature. She must be patient with his minor hesitations.

"Well, gentlemen, see that the disorders are sternly suppressed," the king sighed. "What is next for our consideration? The control of the price of wheat?"

* * * * *

Armand de Gandon stood on a windswept Atlantic beach. It was past midnight, and the air was charged with an approaching winter storm. Somewhere off in the blackness lay an English schooner, lightless and nervous, waiting to pick up the Huguenots shivering at the edge of the waves.

Nerves were taut, almost at the snapping point. Three times the ship's boat had come in, guided by a darkened lantern, had been overloaded with men, women, and children, and had pushed out into the void again. Each time an age had passed before it returned. Anxious watchers, their ears straining for the sound of oars, were rewarded by sand blown in their eyes. To those waiting on the beach, each rustling tuft of long grass was a dragoon advancing stealthily, and in every shift of the moaning wind they heard an approaching patrol.

There had been more people on the beach than the English captain had expected. His sailors were just as afraid of being caught as were the fugitives. They objected in their barbarous tongue when the guide told them they must come back once more. Few on the beach understood what was said, but the import was plain enough.

Armand remained calm. After so much, one couldn't become discouraged now. He helped a distraught widow locate her five children and tried to reassure an elderly couple who had been elbowed aside during the last embarkation.

Then there was the welcome grating of wood on the sand, and the bow of the longboat could be dimly made out, the timbers creaking as the boat rolled with the waves. The English were still grumbling to themselves.

The remaining fugitives rushed to the boat, heedless of the hip-deep, icy water; anxious only for the precarious safety of the sea. The guide snatched up his lantern, and Armand watched it flash and then vanish among the dunes. The man's job was done once more.

The widow clucked frantically for her brood. Except for an aristocratic old gentleman whose hat had just blown away in the darkness, they were all that remained on shore. The woman had three of her little ones in the water, and the coxswain was hauling them aboard. Armand picked up the smallest child, hoisted him to his shoulders, and stepped aside to let the other precede him. Now the trembling old man was being helped over the side and enfolded in a blanket. Armand handed the child to a sailor.

The icy water lapped around Armand's body as he paused to look for the last time at his native land, invisible now as streamers of mist floated across the blackness. He grasped the coxswain's hand. Out beyond the dark, heaving waters was England, and beyond England lay America. There he would face a thousand uncertainties; there he must find a new profession, must learn a new language. But of some things he was certain: He could never again take up the sword for pay; he could never accept wealth or power at the price of conscience; he could never surrender his soul to a king's domination.

He came up over the side of the ship's boat, water sluicing from his clothing and sloshing about his ankles as he struggled to keep his balance while the boat rode the waves out from shore.

"Madeleine," he whispered. And though she was three thousand miles away, he felt in his heart that she answered.

Epilogue

Throughout the rest of the war pictured in Part I, the Vaudois served their duke loyally. An Allied army formed in Italy in the summer of 1692 made a halfhearted attempt to invade Dauphiné, but little was accomplished. The local Huguenots prudently laid low and didn't join the invaders, and the Swiss continued their neutrality. In 1693, Catinat severely defeated the allies at Marsiglia, near Pignerol, ending any further chance of invading France. Huguenot regiments fought so stubbornly in this battle that they were almost wiped out. Among the dead was Captain Huc.

Almost as soon as the duke of Savoy joined the allies, he resumed secret negotiations with the French, and in 1696, he joined them, changing sides again. His price was the cession of Pignerol fortress and the valleys leading to it, thus eliminating the "finger" of French territory and moving the frontier back to Mont Genèvre, where it is today. Also, his twelve-year-old daughter was promised to the grandson of Louis XIV. She later became the mother of Louis XV. (During the next war, in 1703, the duke switched back to the allies again!)

In the general peace treaty signed at Ryswick in 1697, the Protestant rulers "forgot" the Huguenot hopes for a return to France and the restoration of freedom of worship. The war had been essentially a stalemate, and the main concern of the great powers at that moment was the forthcoming division of the Spanish empire. The disappointed Huguenots had to wait ninety more years for the reestablishment of toleration in 1787 by Louis XVI, just two years before the French Revolution. François Vivens and Claude Brousson were early leaders in the "Church in the Wilderness." Vivens was hunted down and killed in 1692. Brousson was ordained to the ministry and, after three long and dangerous missionary sojourns in France, was captured and executed by Bâville at Montpellier in 1698.

Though again an ally of Louis XIV after 1696, the duke of Savoy *did* permit his Vaudois subjects to remain in the valleys, but in 1698, he decreed the expulsion of any Protestants of foreign birth. Consequently, Pastor Arnaud had to leave. He spent his last years in the Vaudois settlements in southern Germany and died near Stuttgart in 1721. Continued foreign Protestant concern for the Vaudois helped prevent any more violent persecutions. Civil rights were at last granted the Vaudois when constitutional reforms came to Piedmont after 1848.

Don't miss the beginning of this exciting story!

No Peace for a Soldier—Part One of the Cortot family's gripping tale of courage and commitment to Christ.
Walter C. Utt and Helen Godfrey Pyke.

Follow the adventures of Monsieur and Madame Cortot and their four children as they and family friend, Armand de Gandon, are forced to choose between loyalty to their king or to their God. The French Reformation comes alive in this historically accurate story of seventeenth-century French Huguenots and the dangers they face to remain true to their Lord.

During severe persecutions, devout French Protestants combined faith and works in heroic proportions. Some abandoned their faith; some were martyred. Some, like the Cortot family, struggled to follow their conscience—and survive.

No Peace for a Soldier begins the exciting and inspiring story that is concluded in *Any Sacrifice but Conscience.*

No Peace for a Soldier
Paperback, 256 pages.
ISBN 13: 978-0-8163-2172-8
ISBN 10: 0-8163-2172-8

Order from your ABC by calling 1-800-765-6955, or shop online at our virtual store—www.adventist bookcenter.com—where you can:
- Read a chapter from your favorite book.
- Order online.
- Sign up for e-mail notices on new products.

Price subject to change without notice.